The Road to Noviel

The Road to Noviel

TRICKSTER'S SONG ❧ BOOK 1

Tom O'Bedlam

Podium

Published in 2023 by Podium Publishing, ULC
www.podiumaudio.com

The Road to Noviel

Unexpected Depths

Chapter 1

*T*here was a deep chill running through the stone beneath him. Robin groaned. That bootleg mead he'd whipped up carried a *kick*. Maybe he should have taken it easier on the psilocybin? Never get simultaneously drunk and high off your own bathtub brew while practicing ritual magic naked—naked? Yup, still naked—on the quad.

Robin opened his eyes. Everything was still black.

Well, that was less than ideal.

He felt the stone in front of him. Shouldn't there be grass? He slowly edged his fingers out; there should still be an athame nearby, and the last thing he needed was to cut himself.

All his fingers found was stone, stone, and more stone. Wait, there was something carved here—

Congratulations! You have found a shrine to the Lost God Rhyth!

The words appeared in the blackness before him, floating in a bright blue box. It didn't do a lick of good for lighting the darkness around him, but he could at least see something.

Do you accept the Blessing of the God? Y/N?

Well, this was a trip, and not the one he'd expected to be on. *Of course* he'd end up on a vision quest where he wasn't able to see a goddess-damned thing. Par for the frelling course.

Sure, Robin thought. He could use a blessing right about now. He waved his hand somewhat ineffectually through the apparition. Something worked, and the pitch-black darkness began to fade into gradients of shadow.

He was in a small cave. Well, small in diameter. The space above his head rose quite far, and a small forest of stalactites hung overhead, draped in shadows. Most of his surroundings looked entirely natural, the stone unworked. The exception was in front of him: the small shrine his questing fingers had found.

Seeing it was harder than feeling it; the graven image danced in and out of focus. If he looked too closely, the features all faded into just another expanse of stone, but if he sort of unfocused his eyes, a figure slowly came into view. Humanoid, with just the hint of a face. The lips were turned up in an unmistakable smirk, and the suggestion of hands cupped in front of the figure were filled with a bit of water.

Not how he'd imagined Plato's cave would look, really. But he also hadn't imagined his ritual attempt to translocate himself to a different reality would come with hallucinatory gaming prompts, so . . . yeah. Party. Should he drink the water? Odin would drink the water. Fionn would . . . well, not drink the water, but if there was a tiny minnow in there, that might work as well.

The rest of the cave came into focus as Robin's eyes fully acclimated to their new sight. There was *not* a minnow swimming in the water. Before Robin could take a drink, however, another message appeared.

Blessing Bestowed!
Your Heritage has been changed to Shadeling.
All Finesse Properties have increased by 1.
Proficiencies Unlocked: Stealth, Deception, and Insight.
You have learned the [Lesser Phantasm] cantrip!
Peculiarities Unlocked (1 slot available): Tongue of the Fallen Tower;
Mask of Myriad Faces; Chronicle of Infinite Visions.

This . . . was not at all what Robin had expected. Enlightenment, even the kind temporarily bestowed by indulging in psychoactive substances of questionable provenance, wouldn't look like this. Would it?

No. This was some kind of weird trip, though he was only feeling mildly buzzed at best. Hardly even that, in fact, since the latest message had popped up. Had his body actually changed? That would probably clear out some of the more exotic substances floating about in his blood.

Cantrips? Proficiencies? Sure, he'd played as much D&D as the average PhD student—no, probably a bit more—but this system didn't track with that one. There were other odd elements. That being said, it had been described as a blessing, and in the interest of engaging with the wisdom that comes unexpectedly . . . yes, he felt like he knew something he hadn't known before.

Robin's fingers flexed through a quick series of positions, the ones his instincts told him were necessary to invoke [Lesser Phantasm]. A small ball of blue flame appeared, flickering, above his upturned palm. It rippled and snapped, surreal in its silence. Robin repeated the gestures. The flame winked out, and this time, the crackle and pop of a small campfire flared up. So he could conjure sight and sound, but only one at a time?

He was unable to ponder the issue further, however, as the sound sparked a disturbance among the stalactites above. Shadows flitted and chittered above him before a horde of small, winged forms descended. Robin only had time for a brief glimpse before the things were upon him.

Like the unholy offspring of a squid and a flying squirrel, they had dropped down around him, spinning as tiny tentacles lashed out and drew small lines of blood across his naked and entirely vulnerable body. Robin yelled, flailing his arms wildly in the air around him. The things spun around, neatly evading his blows while lashing out with more of their own.

There was nowhere to run. He was trapped in this cave with no visible exit. Naked. No weapons. All he had was a cantrip, the same thing that had called these creatures down upon him in the first place.

Robin seized at the idea. If the cantrip had gotten him into this mess, maybe it could get him out. These things clearly reacted to sound, so maybe a sound could drive them off? He went through the gestures again, focusing on the first annoying sound he could think of: that of his morning alarm.

A blaring, repeating shriek, like a cyborg climaxing after electronically edging for a full power cycle, echoed throughout the cave. The little beasties staggered a bit midair but didn't retreat. Still, Robin was encouraged. These things weren't bats, but they lived in caves and responded to sound, so maybe if he amped up the frequency? Was there a volume limit? He felt like there was, but also that he wasn't anywhere near it yet.

With his skin stinging from the myriad cuts and blood running into his eyes, Robin tried again. [Lesser Phantasm]. This time, he summoned the voice of an opera diva, hitting a perfect C above high C. Not enough. He added a second voice, and then a third. He wasn't this good with music; the magic was compensating to a degree.

The little monstrosities flitting around him grew visibly more agitated, and several missed their attacks on his person. Didn't like high-pitched noises, eh? Well, then maybe . . .

Robin cast his cantrip once more, and this time, he imagined turning up the frequency to the top of his audible range and beyond. The sound vanished from his hearing, but clearly not from that of his assailants.

They went berserk, exploding away from him and flapping in ungainly and staggering trajectories until they disappeared once more among the stalactites.

**Congratulations! You have defeated a Swarm
of Juvenile Shadowmantles! Experience awarded!**

Robin collapsed back against the cave wall, wincing as the cold bit into the bloody scratches all over his body. This did not feel like a hallucination. This did not feel like a vision quest. This felt real. This hurt.

He was bleeding, for fuck's sake!

At least he could do something about that.

With a mental prayer for forgiveness sent winging toward wherever Rhyth might be, Robin dipped his bloody, bleeding fingers into the water of the shrine. It wasn't much, but it would clean some of the blood off his face and ease the tight, parched feeling of his throat.

Do you wish to make a small sacrifice to the memory of Rhyth? Y/N?

Robin froze, fingertips in the water. Sacrifice? Sacrifice wasn't generally something he engaged in. He was more of a freewheeling, free love kinda guy. Not so much with the letting of blood and offering smoke to powers unknown.

Still, Rhyth's blessing was what had allowed him to fend off those little beasties. And there was more where that had come from; things he hadn't yet explored. Maybe not pissing off the mysterious power whose shrine he was a guest in wasn't the worst idea?

Robin suddenly and with stark clarity understood a bit better what it must have been like being at the dawn of human civilization calling out to an unknown and mysterious sky. And he didn't care for it.

No, not at all.

"Yes," he said after a long moment. "I do willingly and respectfully offer sacrifice to Rhyth."

New Quest: [Gone, But Not Yet Forgotten]
The God Rhyth has been lost from the memory of most of Mayaser. Recover

knowledge of his worship and uncover the mystery of his disappearance before
all memory of him has faded.
Reward: *Unspecified.*

Oh joy. A quest.

Well, at least the sacrifice was free time instead of blood?

Robin blinked and looked at his arm. His scratches were gone. Huh. Looked like the quest came with a fringe benefit. Not that he was going to complain.

Of course, before he could embark on a quest, he'd first have to figure a way out of here.

Between the attack and the touch of a lost god, Robin had shifted his perspective. Whatever was going on, this was his reality now, so he might as well embrace it. If he woke up in a hospital in a few weeks having fallen into a coma after imbibing experimental psychoactive mead, well, so be it. He'd deal with it as it happened—or not.

There had to be a way out farther up the cavern wall. Those things clearly ate, and the lack of bones and droppings suggested this was not where they usually did that, ergo, there was an exit up there somewhere.

However, there was also a shrine right here, and he doubted anyone would build such a thing without an easier way to access it than rappelling thirty feet every Sunday. Rhythsday? Whatever.

Well, he wasn't climbing out of here; not with anything he had on him. Clearly. But he wasn't totally without resources. He had the Blessing of Rhyth, and at least one—what was it? Peculiarity?—to choose. Though how he did that was anyone's guess. Maybe something to do with the screens he'd been seeing. There had to be a command they responded to.

"Peculiarity selection?"

The screen blazed across his vision. He'd guessed correctly, then.

After some experimentation, Robin discovered the information responded to his thoughts, and he could often garner some additional insight by focusing on the names of things, not unlike a more traditional tooltip interface.

Tongue of the Fallen Tower
Grants the bearer the ability to speak, read, and write all languages.

Mask of Myriad Faces
Grants the bearer limited shapeshifting ability.
Bearer is limited to shapes of the same general form (bipedal life-forms cannot

shift to quadrupeds, hexapeds, etc.), but can freely shift particulars of appearance (hair, skin, etc.) and biology (sex, internal organs, etc.). Physical abilities of the target form may be used, but exceptional or supernatural abilities may not. This ability has no effect on clothing or equipment carried.

Chronicle of Infinite Visions
Grants the bearer the ability to use [Visual Phantasm] *at will without the need for any invocation costs or components.*

Robin considered his options. **[Tongue of the Fallen Tower]** was amazing, and it would clearly be useful in the future, but it offered little in the way of an immediate solution to his predicament. The same was true of **[Chronicle of Infinite Visions]**.

His final choice, on the other hand, had some definite possibilities. A lot would depend on whether or not he could assume a humanoid form with wings and master learning to fly with **[Mask of Myriad Faces]**, but it was the only way out of this cave he could see using any of these abilities. Or peculiarities, as they were called.

Before Robin could make a final decision, however, his circumstances changed. Or at least, something new entered his cave. He cocked his head to one side and closed his eyes, straining to chase down the new sounds.

There were voices drifting into the cave.

Chapter 2

Robin padded softly around the space, trying to get closer to the voices. At least here, being naked was a bit of an advantage, though he would have totally traded that advantage for some shoes. Fortunately, the floor was relatively smooth, though the chill soaking up through his feet left a lot to be desired.

He could only make out snatches of conversation, but nothing he heard sounded like any language he knew. If he was truly in another world—or on another plane—that would make sense. It sucked, but it'd make sense. **[Tongue of the Fallen Tower]** suddenly seemed a lot more appealing.

The voices were too quiet to be drifting down from above, so there had to be something he was missing. The voices got louder the farther he got from the shrine. Robin couldn't see any door or air vent they might be coming through, but, as he'd only recently established, his new world was one of illusion.

He put his hands out and began to carefully feel along the wall. It all felt like stone; the same cold, clammy stone he'd felt throughout the whole cave. Of course, if an illusion could fool the eyes and ears, it might also fool any attempts to touch it.

Maybe if he used a little more pressure?

Robin deliberately pressed firmly into the stone, turning his mind to seek any flaw, any hint that there might be an illusory entrance nearby. Solid stone . . . solid stone . . . soli—*whumpf!* Not solid stone!

Robin's arm shot through the seemingly solid wall, unbalancing him; he pitched forward and fell. That was a failed dex save if he'd ever seen one. Did he have stats here? Was dexterity one of them?

The thought brought up an increasingly familiar blue screen. *Not now!* He didn't have time now! Robin mentally flailed at the screen, dismissing it. The voices—the voices were slightly louder to the left? They were high-pitched and very animated. He could hear more clearly now, but he still had no idea what was being said.

Well, he'd found the way out. Now he needed information; information was always key. In every game he'd played, the more information, the better options, the greater chance of success.

Knowledge was power.

With that thought, he opened the screen in front of him and selected **[Tongue of the Fallen Tower]**. Languages poured into his mind like honey wine. Oh *frell*, did that feel good. He felt full and warm and positively pulsing with pleasure.

Thank you, Rhyth! No need to buy a guy a drink first. Just lead with that next time!

Robin carefully lifted himself up. The voices were drifting away. If he wanted to follow them, he'd have to move quickly, which was not going to be easy. The stone here in this tunnel was rougher than on the cave of the shrine, which meant it was harder on his feet. He'd have to watch his step.

He pressed forward anyway, a bit heedless of the sharp bursts of pain that spiked up through the soles of his feet as he followed the voices. His ex, Dan, had been big into barefoot running, and Robin briefly regretted not letting himself be dragooned into making it a habit. That would have helped here. *Never mind that now! Focus!* He needed to get close enough to hear clearly. Fortunately, he swiftly gained on them.

"—why searching tunnels? Nothing new in tunnels! We live in tunnels! Why think we not know tunnels?"

Robin could understand the words now! He ran his tongue over his teeth. He got the feeling that his tongue wasn't quite properly suited to this speech, but also that it wouldn't matter if he tried to speak it himself. He crept forward cautiously so as not to overtake the speakers.

"—because chief tell us search! We search. We no find, so what? We search. Time to hunt crunchies-munchies in tunnels. Time away from smelly fire. So what we no find stupid shrine? No one else find either."

Robin's heart sped up. They were looking for the shrine? That was something he could use! He knew how to find it, even how to get to it. From here, at least. He could trade that knowledge for food or directions out of this cave system or—

He froze.

He'd been edging closer and closer as the two voices spoke. The thought of food, clothes, a way out—it had been too tempting. He'd drawn too close, and now he'd caught sight of whom he'd been following.

There were two of them, each standing about three feet tall. They were humanoid but reptilian, covered in scales with protruding snouts and brow ridges and—*oh sweet fuck*, those were kobolds. They were armed with short spears and daggers, and those mouths full of razor-sharp teeth were at the same height as Robin's very exposed soft bits.

Robin jerked back and wrapped a **[Lesser Phantasm]** around him to blend into the stone. He almost had a heart attack when nothing in his view changed. Had the cantrip failed? No, the nearest kobold whipped its head around but didn't react. It was looking right at him, yet gave no signs of seeing him.

Then it flicked its forked tongue out, testing the air. It gave a faint hiss. Robin flinched. *Please don't find me. Please don't find me—*

Would you like to raise Stealth to 1 with experience? Y/N?

Yes! Frell yes! Robin mentally bashed at the prompt. There was a flash of something like enervation shooting through his limbs, and then an influx of a different sort of energy. Robin felt his muscles shift and grow still.

The kobolds were gesturing to one another with hand signs. Robin couldn't interpret those; his gift must not extend to codes or nonverbal languages. *Dammit.*

Not knowing what the kobolds intended, Robin held still and watched them. The two prowled through the cave, tongues questing through the air.

After several agonizing moments of searching, the larger of the two jabbed a curt gesture at the smaller, and the two of them moved off along the tunnel, continuing the way they had been headed. Robin almost didn't follow, but what else would he do? He could be miles away from an exit from this cave system. The shrine had water but no food, no clothing. The kobolds clearly had access to both. Though how he was going to get it . . .

Robin slowly detached himself from the wall and cautiously followed after the kobolds. Tunnels branched and wound, widened and narrowed as he went. Stress mounting, Robin made a concerted effort to pick out landmarks and commit them to memory so he could return to the shrine if needed. If nothing else, it should be a fairly safe hiding place.

**Proficiency Unlocked: Survival. Increase Survival to 1 with experience?
Y/N?**

Robin mentally assented. Once again, he felt a curious energy drain, followed by an influx of vitality and knowledge. He felt more assured about not only finding his way back to the shrine but also about trailing the kobolds ahead without losing them.

And trail them he did, all the way to a large cavern.

His first hint that something was about to change was the presence of light—*light!*—flickering and firelike. It had to be the fire the kobolds had mentioned earlier, so this should be their main home cavern.

Robin crept forward slowly. His ears brought him the sounds of many voices and various hints of industry. The smell of roasting meat came to his nostrils, and his mouth suddenly watered. Thank Rhyth his stomach didn't growl.

Thank Rhyth? Robin mentally shrugged. Why not? The god had been decent to him so far, and it wasn't like any other deity had stepped forward to help. Not that he'd seen evidence of any other deities, but if Rhyth had been lost and this was any kind of standard fantasy world, there had to be others. That was the safe assumption, anyway.

Robin put the issue out of his mind as he drew close enough to get a full view of the cavern. The ceiling rose several dozen feet after the tunnel opened up into the wider space ahead. He couldn't see precisely from his angle, and he didn't want to risk getting too much closer yet, but it was a big space.

Several kobolds swarmed around the floor, bickering and going about small tasks. Three tended to a large firepit in the center of the cavern, turning something on a crude spit. Others slept in piles of rags or came and went from other tunnels.

Robin moved as close as he dared and hid among a patch of stalagmites. He wrapped a [**Lesser Phantasm**] around himself. Being able to see through his own illusions was turning out to be incredibly useful.

Eyes scanning over the cavern from his new vantage point, two oddities leapt out at him. The first was a large figure lounging on a massive wooden chair, almost a throne. She was definitely not a kobold. Green skin, black hair, a pair of small ivory tusks jutting from her lower jaw—unless Robin missed his guess, that was probably an orc of some sort.

The kobolds gave her a wide berth. She, for her part, mostly ignored them; though, as Robin watched, she barked out an order and a kobold scurried off to carve off a hunk of meat from the spit and brought it to her.

The other oddity was a group of people up against one wall. They were practically crammed into a natural niche formed by the stone and were bound with greasy-looking ropes. Adventuring party, maybe? There was a pile of equipment not far from them, which two kobolds were digging through.

New Quest: [You Gotta Have Friends]
You have discovered a group of adventurers being held prisoner. Free them.
Reward: *Basic clothing; possible allies.*

Well, that answered that, though Robin was still very much outnumbered and underarmed. He resisted the urge to move to find a better vantage point; he was safe here for the moment. Maybe when the kobolds fell asleep—

Robin's planning session was derailed by the arrival of a new figure to the cavern. *Human!* An older man, his left eye was covered with a black patch and the armor he wore was dark metal embossed with a curious red sigil.

"Bula!" the man snapped. "You promised me results! Where is that shrine?"

"Not here." Bula, the orc on the throne, shrugged. "Maybe you were wrong."

"Have you even looked?"

"Kobolds looked." Bula took a bite of meat, and bloody juices ran down her chin.

"Right." The old man sneered, looking at the kobolds scurrying around. "Because you have such a firm hand on the situation here."

"Don't preach at me, priest," Bula said. "They do as I say."

"They don't fear you. They're running about, likely lying to you about even searching." The priest glared about him.

Several of the kobolds made themselves scarce. Robin doubted this was the first time the priest had visited.

"You're running out of time, Bula," the priest continued. "My Lord has commanded this shrine be found and destroyed."

"Then maybe Urkhan should come down and do it himself."

"Don't play at blasphemy and think you'll get a rise out of me," the priest sneered. "Just do the job I hired you for. Or I'll have you replaced with someone who can do it."

"I'm doing the job!"

"It doesn't look like it! I'm warning you, Bula. Consolidate your hold over these vermin, find that shrine, and do it swiftly, or I will send you to the Hell of Chains myself."

New Quest: [Just a Spark of Rebellion]
Incite a rebellion among the kobold servants of Bula Bloodfist and disrupt the plans of Urkhan, God of Tyranny. Bonus points if you can kill the bastard's lapdog priest in the process.
Reward: *Enmity of Urkhan, Increased Favor of Rhyth. And the fun of pulling it all off, of course.*

Robin thought quickly. Maybe there was a way to kill two birds with one stone. Or to complete two quests with one trick.

Chapter 3

Robin watched the activity in the cave, moving his hands through the gestures needed to regularly renew his [Lesser Phantasm]-generated hiding place. The illusion didn't last long, but thankfully, he had yet to hit a limit on casting it.

With an eye out for danger, Robin opened the status page he'd found earlier but hadn't had time to examine in detail. He was far from safe here, but he needed to know more about what he was working with if he was going to incite a rebellion and rescue the captured adventuring party.

Robin Parker

Heritage: Shadeling, Juvenile
Profession: None
Tier: 0
Progress to Tier 1: 36%

Properties

Physical
   -Strength: 11
   -Dexterity: 14
   -Fortitude: 11
Mental
   -Intelligence: 17

-Cunning: 18
-Resilience: 14
Social
-Charisma: 15
-Manipulation: 13
-Poise: 15

Proficiencies

Physical (2/9)
-???
-???
-???
-???
-???
-???
-???
-Stealth: 1
-Survival: 1
Mental (1/9)
-???
-???
-???
-???
-???
-Insight: 0
-???
-???
-???
Social (1/9)
-???
-Deception: 0
-???
-???
-???
-???
-???
-???
-???

Peculiarities

Blessing of Rhyth
Tongue of the Fallen Tower

A couple of things stood out immediately. First, nowhere on his sheet did it say human, and the closest thing he could see to some kind of species designation was the *Heritage* line.

Yeah, no. Worrying about the implications of that later.

Second, that whatever this system was, it liked the number three and multiples of the number three. Third, it also liked alliteration.

From a D&D perspective, his stats would be good, but this clearly wasn't D&D, so a comparison with those stats might get him nowhere. Without knowing standard averages in these "properties," or if there was a soft or hard cap on them, Robin couldn't say how good or not they were.

He also didn't like that his *Deception* was ranked at zero, in light of the plan he was forming. It'd be nice if he could get it higher.

Well, maybe he could.

He focused his intent, and luckily, the desired prompt appeared.

Would you like to raise Deception to 1 with experience? Y/N?

Yes, please and thank you!
But could he get it to two?

You do not have the required experience to raise Deception to 2.
Continue adventuring, complete quests, or otherwise engage in shenanigans to amuse the gods to continue increasing your proficiencies!

Shiz. Not enough experience. Robin reopened the status page. *Huh.* His percentage progression to Tier One had gone down to 34 percent. So the system didn't outright tell him how much experience he had? Or he hadn't found a way to make it show him.

Frell. There was no way he could do the necessary math to break this all down.

The *Heritage* line caught his eye again. *Shadeling, Juvenile.* What the heck did that even mean?

The screen blipped as his focused attention activated the more-info-sorta-tooltip function and rewarded him with a few paragraphs with some basic information on the subject.

Well. Robin was now either more or less human than he'd been before. A shadeling was a being with an inherent connection to the powers of Shadow, whatever that meant, which granted him several abilities that he'd already seen and a couple more that were hidden in the descriptive text he was reading.

Shadelings receive triple experience when they use illusion or trickery instead of brute force to solve a problem.

Well, if that wasn't a sign that he was on the right track with this plan, he didn't know what was! Not that he had any idea how experience worked or how much of it he'd accumulated. Problem for another time.

The problem at hand was the kobolds, their orc chief, and the mysterious priest hunting the shrine of Rhyth. Hopefully the priest would move on. He didn't seem the sort to hang around, but he was definitely the sort that could put a crimp in Robin's plans.

Robin dismissed his status to examine the cavern more closely. The priest was gone, sending a chill down Robin's spine. He hadn't noticed the man leave, hadn't heard if he was coming back soon. He might have just stepped out to use the latrine.

Robin gnawed at his lower lip. Nothing to do about it now. He needed a bit of time to listen to the kobolds anyway, so he'd keep an eye out in case the priest returned.

He set to it, picking threads out of the conversations nearby. There was a lot of boasting, a lot of complaining. These kobolds were not happy with their lot in life.

Good. Robin could use that.

His hand was starting to ache from the constant casting of [**Lesser Phantasm**]. It only required one, so Robin eased the discomfort a bit by alternating hands. Still, there was going to come a time when his muscles rebelled, and he wouldn't be able to maintain his cover.

The cold from the stone around him seeped into his flesh. He shifted as quietly as he could, stretching his muscles; he'd need to move quickly when his opportunity came. He mentally plotted a course along the outer rim of the cavern. His route was thick with dancing shadows thanks to the massive cook fire.

Time for a test. Robin rehearsed the words and phrasing he wanted to use in his mind, made sure he was as well hidden as he could be, and let his illusory hiding place drop so he could cast some phantasmal words among a nearby group of kobolds, their heads down as they scraped some hides with sharp stones.

"Work, work, work. All Ratscale does is work!" one of them complained. "I's tired of it."

"All any of us does is work, stupid!" another replied. "Is always same."

This was his chance! Robin slipped his conjured words into the conversation.

"Is not always same." The words came out sounding much more kobold-y than if he'd tried to speak them himself, thankfully. "Was better with old chief."

"Old chief gone," Ratscale said morosely. "Bula chief now."

They didn't seem to notice that none of them had said the words. Each probably assumed one of the others had spoken. *So far, so good!* Robin waited to see how the conversation would turn before adding anything else.

The conversation continued in a grumbling vein. These kobolds seemed predisposed to it, though Robin wouldn't assume this was true of all kobolds. That was the sort of lazy thinking that got adventurers in his old D&D group killed.

"Maybe we need new chief," he conjured when the conversation sounded like it was starting to die out.

For once, this didn't evoke a reply. A few heads nodded, then several pairs of reptilian eyes shot nervously about the room. One or two even eyed their compatriots, as if trying to figure out who had said those words.

There was fear there, along with the resentment. Robin wasn't exactly working with a tinderbox here, but there was some fuel to set fire to. For now, though, he let the embers just burn and turned his attention to another group.

Robin repeated the process twice more, sounding out the small groups of kobolds gathered near enough to his hiding spot that he could hear them. He'd had to shift his position a few times to listen clearly, and his heart had hammered in his chest each time he'd done so. He was just one naked guy against a small horde of fanged, scaly monsters.

With some experimentation, Robin found he could overlap invocations of [**Lesser Phantasm**]. The duration wasn't great, maybe ten to fifteen seconds, but he could switch between his camouflage and his ventriloquist act, refreshing his hiding place before adding a sentence or two to the conversation, then refreshing the image of stone around him again to keep himself hidden. It made him feel a bit more secure.

He'd even figured out how to program a small delay in the audible version of his cantrip, which allowed him to follow up one of his statements with general sounds of agreement a few moments later without having to recast. Once he hit upon that refinement to his technique, he noticed his conjured words carried a great deal more weight. From that point on, he started upping the ante a bit.

"Bula bad chief."

"Bula not care about kobolds."

"When last time we got shinies not Bula?"

"We need new chief."

"Bula gots to sleep sometime."

"Big and strong still bleed when you cut they's throat."

The general noise level of the cavern increased as Robin fanned the flames of the kobolds' discontent. He needed to speed this up. He was getting tired, and his hands were starting to cramp.

He spared a glance for the prisoners. They didn't seem to have noticed the mood in the camp shift. Maybe they couldn't speak kobold. Maybe they were too preoccupied with being stripped nearly naked (*Oh, to be so lucky!*) and tied up.

If he'd known the language they spoke, he might have risked trying to send them a message with **[Lesser Phantasm]**, but being uncertain, he didn't want to tempt fate. He'd just have to hope they moved quickly when presented with an opportunity.

Robin chanced moving once more before executing his plan. He wanted the best angle to dash along the edges of the cavern. There was no path that would keep him completely hidden, unfortunately, and his camouflage wouldn't work while he was moving, so he'd just have to hope he got lucky. Or pray to Rhyth for aid.

He crossed his fingers and did both. For better or for worse, he needed to move now. He was nearing the end of his endurance.

Taking a deep breath, he ran through the three things he could fit in his next casting of **[Lesser Phantasm]** and went for it.

"This stupid! Bula should scrape own hides!"

The words rang out, clear and loud and predictably disruptive. Rather than stunned, terrified silence, however, Robin had made sure to add in a few barks of laughter and a couple indistinct murmurs of agreement.

"Bula bad chief! Kobolds want kobold chief!"

This time, there were several real voices intermixed with the fake shouts of agreement Robin had woven into his **[Lesser Phantasm]**.

Bula was turning red, her temper clearly rising. The unexpected outpour of discontent stymied her, however, and she was slow to react.

"New chief! New chief! Down with Bula!"

The third and final illusory statement elicited a roar of approval from the assembled kobolds. There was a lot of jumping and clashing, but no outright violence yet. Robin had planned for this, however.

Quickly, he flung a rock he'd gathered during one of his tactical relocations. It flew over the heads of the assembled kobolds right at Bula's face. It came in at a bit of an angle, so it caught her by surprise, thunking against the back of her throne.

Robin wasn't so great a shot he'd expected to hit her, but his aim was good enough for his purposes. As soon as the kobolds saw *someone* attack Bula, their fear vanished. They were, to some degree, packlike animals, and they smelled blood in the water.

Bula bellowed a war cry as a horde of the small reptilian monsters swarmed her. Robin didn't bother to watch. He dashed along the edge of the cavern, trying to keep to the shadows and draw as little attention to himself as possible. Thankfully, the other residents of the cavern were otherwise occupied.

The party he was trying to rescue had been taken completely by surprise as well. Only one of the four had the presence of mind to take advantage of the distraction to try and escape. She was wrestling with the ropes around her wrists when Robin appeared out of the shadows. She jerked back, but he held a finger up in front of his lips.

The woman, an elf if he had to guess (ethereal beauty, pointed ears; this would be so cool if he wasn't naked and under threat of messy, painful death, ahhh!), eyed him only for a moment before thrusting her wrists at him. Robin went to work on the knots. They were fiendishly tight, but nothing like the Gordian knot his nephews turned their shoelaces into, so he managed it.

Hands free, the woman undid the ropes on her legs and slunk over to their packs, rummaging around until she came up with a knife. Robin had moved on to help the next woman, but before he could even get started, a great shout echoed across the cavern.

"Bow before the might of Urkhan, vermin!"

Frell. The priest was back.

Chapter 4

Robin swore as he bent a fingernail back trying to undo the knot and free another one of the adventurers. The priest's reappearance threatened to put a damper on his revolution as the magical force Urkhan provided the priest's words forced one of the kobolds to bow to him. Without time to think, Robin threw out another **[Lesser Phantasm]**.

"Urkhan stupid god! False god! Will bow before true god of kobolds!" Robin punctuated the words with a couple kobold battle roars (or his best guess what they would sound like).

"How dare you!" the priest roared, swinging around him with his mace. "I will—" He cut off midsentence and cocked his head to one side.

Robin, glancing over as he finally undid the knot he was working on, locked eyes with the priest. The man had seen them! They needed to get out of here *now*.

All four women were now free and scrambling for their equipment. The elf was furthest along and the only one to notice the priest's attention aside from Robin. She grabbed her closest companion and pulled her toward the nearest exit.

"The pris—" the priest began to shout.

Robin couldn't let him do that. He twisted his aching hand through another casting of **[Lesser Phantasm]**, and this time, Bula's voice rang out.

"Fuck this! I'll make any kobold who kills that priest the new chief of this tribe!"

Chaos erupted anew as the battle shifted and several kobolds charged the priest in a mad fury of bloodlust and ambition. The smarter ones paused. Bula was still laying about with her weapon, foaming at the mouth in the grips of an insensate rage.

The adventuring party Robin had rescued were running away down a tunnel, so Robin followed. It was easy; the elf in the lead had conjured a small magelight, and it danced in the shadows ahead of them.

The women were a few lengths ahead of Robin and moving quickly. He tried to catch up but caught his foot on something in his haste. There was a *thwang*, and his shoulder erupted in bloody fire. He'd tripped a trap and been skewered by a crude crossbow bolt.

Forcing himself to ignore the pain as best he could, he continued on. This time, he paid more attention to where he was going. The women ahead seemed to have no trouble avoiding the traps, and he followed their lead.

The yipping and sounds of battle behind them swiftly faded. Robin bent one ear behind him, trying to catch any signs of pursuit, but he came up empty. They might have successfully gotten away in the confusion! A moment later, his quest prompt confirmed it.

Quest Complete! [You Gotta Have Friends]

Congratulations! You have liberated the **Sisters Sharp** *adventuring party! Due to your use of illusions and trickery in doing so, you have been awarded triple experience!*
Reward: *They might not be allies yet, but they aren't dead, so you're moving in the right direction! Trousers . . . well, you'll have to wait and see. Who knows? You might still get lucky!*

Robin felt an influx of energy. It did nothing to ease the ache in his hands or feet, nothing to salve his tired muscles, but it made him feel a bit better nonetheless. He quashed the urge to open his character sheet, though. Time enough for that when he wasn't surrounded by traps. He dismissed the notification, only for it to be replaced by another.

Quest Complete! [Just a Spark of Rebellion]

Congratulations! You have successfully sparked a rebellion amid the **Bentscale** *tribe of kobolds, inciting them to revolt against Bula Bloodfist. Due to your use of illusions and trickery in doing so, you have been awarded triple experience!*
Reward: [Mark of the Trickster] *Rhyth may be lost, but even the memory of a deity can hold power, and some of that power has been used to mark you. Kindred spirits are more likely to take a liking to you, while humorless stuffed shirts are more likely to hate you on sight. Have fun with that!*

Bonus Reward!

Congratulations! Your exploits in fomenting a kobold rebellion have drawn the attention of Nevarre, Elvish God of Mischief. Because you used words to such lethal effect, he has granted you new arcane knowledge!

You have learned the [Cutting Words] cantrip!

Elvish God of Mischief? Because there's no way that could go wrong. Robin wasn't sure how common it was to attract this much divine attention in one's first day in a new reality, but he suspected it was not ideal. New cantrip, though? That was a welcome reward.

Your actions during the recent conflict have unlocked the following proficiencies: Ranged Combat; Sleight of Hand.

Ranged Combat must have been the rock he threw, but what had unlocked Sleight of Hand? Untying the ropes under pressure? Picking up the rock while sneaking? He really wished he had a copy of whatever *Player's Handbook* worked with this system.

"Fiamah," the elf said to the human woman next to her. "He's bleeding. Can you heal him? Else he'll leave a blood trail behind us that even a kobold hatchling could follow."

Robin blinked. He hadn't realized any of them had noticed. The human woman, Fiamah, stepped up to him, and before he knew what was happening, she ripped the bolt out of his shoulder and set it alight with divine fire. Robin screamed.

"Sorry," she spoke. "This is going to hurt." She dug her fingers into the wound. "Try not to scream. You'll bring the kobolds down on us."

And then the fire was in Robin's veins, burning away both any potential infection and the wound itself. As it passed, it left euphoria in place of the pain, and his extremities began to *tingle*. He managed not to scream, but he started to giggle through his teeth. A song about hurting So Good started playing through his head.

"Thanks," he managed through both giggles and pain.

"Do you know any safe places nearby?" the elvish woman asked him.

"Yes, but we'd have to go back through the cavern to get there, so I'm going to say no?" Robin replied as he gently prodded his now intact shoulder.

"Don't poke at it," Fiamah ordered.

"Yes, ma'am." Robin immediately removed his hand.

"Lantha!" the dwarven woman said urgently to the elf. "We need to move. We can't wait here."

"We can't rush off half-cocked, either," Lantha replied. "Unless you can lead us to a safe cavern somewhere in these tunnels?"

"Not my thing. Ask Ora-Jean. Maybe that badger spirit that follows her about can sniff something out. They like tunnels." The dwarf crossed her arms.

Robin got the sense that this was either an argument that happened often or a super tense version of the regular banter a tight-knit group like this usually developed. Ora-Jean, whom Robin identified by process of elimination, was a diminutive woman (halfling?) who was nonetheless built like a brick shizhouse.

"Taterpicker says we should go this way." Ora-Jean pointed down the tunnel to her right. "Says the air smells fresher."

Robin had neither seen nor heard any badgers, spirit or otherwise, but as the highly competent women (including the one who had just burned the hurt right out of him) seemed inclined to trust this development, who was he to object?

"Right. Move out. We go until we find daylight or a safe-looking place to rest. None of us are at peak, and I'd rather face whatever is down here closer to full strength."

"We don't even have all of our packs," the dwarf protested.

"Grathilde, so help me, I will gut you if you say one more thing about the packs. We've got what we've got, including our lives, so let's focus on holding on to that, shall we?" The elf glared at the dwarf. "There was a priest of Urkhan back there, and I don't fancy facing him and that orc and all her kobolds. Not down here in the dark where they can see without torches or light spells. Unlike *some* of us."

Lantha looked pointedly at Grathilde.

"Fine," the dwarf grumbled. "But I don't know what supplies survived, so I make no promises in the magic department. There's only so much I can do without all of my ritual components."

"Understood. Now, can we please move out?" Lantha began walking after Ora-Jean, not waiting for an answer.

Ora-Jean, for her part, was already several lengths ahead of the party, moving down the tunnel she had indicated moments ago. Fiamah and Grathilde followed, and Robin trailed along.

The women ahead of him were whispering to one another, and after a moment, Robin realized they were using a different language to the one they had spoken when they were talking to him.

"Can we trust him?" Grathilde was asking.

"We don't have to trust him; we just have to keep an eye on him," Lantha replied. "He helped us once; he might be useful in the future. If he gets out of line, I can carve him a second smile or Fiamah can turn him to ash."

That was less than comforting.

Robin kept his face neutral. Right now, [Tongue of the Fallen Tower] was a bit of an ace in the hole, and he wanted to keep it that way. Knowledge was power, and he needed every scrap of it he could get.

"Wait." Ora-Jean paused at the fork in the tunnel "Taterpicker says we have to choose here. There's fresh air to the left, but if we head to the right, we'll hit a section of switchbacks in the tunnel system and can find a safe place to hole up for a bit."

Lantha pursed her lips in thought.

"Taterpicker says he can't say how far it is to the surface. These tunnels are windy as all get out."

"But you can find a safe space to hole up?" Lantha looked to the halfling. "That I can do."

"Then we do that," Lantha decided. "We need to take stock of what we have in the packs we managed to recover, then rest and recuperate as much as we can. I don't want to run into those kobolds again like this."

Ora-Jean nodded and turned to the right, leading them through several increasingly narrow and jagged switchbacks. Robin made careful note of the landmarks in case he needed to flee. He almost missed it when Ora-Jean slipped back and wriggled through a diagonal gap in the wall.

The others followed, and Robin left behind a layer of skin from his chest as he squeezed through. In short order, they found themselves in a small, oblong cave. It was more a jagged niche than anything, but it was out of the way and had enough room to spread out and sleep if they needed to.

"Fiamah, take inventory. Grathilde, lay down whatever magical protections or alarms you can. Ora-Jean, slip out and see if you can forage some mushrooms. We've seen a few species while we've been down here. I want to pad out our supplies if we can. Don't take more than an hour."

"And Fiamah," Lantha added in that second language. "See if there's anything in there we can give our bard friend to clothe himself."

"Why would you think he's a bard?"

"He's naked. Of course he's a bard."

Fiamah shrugged and, after a few moments of rummaging, tossed a loose pair of trousers, some burlap, and a roll of cloth bandages to Robin. "Here. See what you can do to cover yourself with this. Don't have any shirts in here, unfortunately."

"Thank you." Robin quickly donned the trousers, and then, after considering the burlap and bandages for a couple minutes, ripped and folded and knotted himself a pair of rough cloth sandals. They wouldn't do much, but they'd protect his feet a little. Unfortunately, his torso would have to remain cold and at attention for a while longer.

Robin was just finishing the last knot when he found himself with a knife at his throat. The elvish woman—eyes bright, teeth white—smiled sweetly at him.

"Start singing, bard."

Chapter 5

Robin was so incredibly conscious of the cold, sharp line of the knife at his throat that when Lantha ordered him to sing, he did. The first thing that popped into his head.

And because Lantha so clearly wanted to have a pointed conversation, that song was . . .

> *Let's kiki*
>
> *Queen, kiki*
>
> *Sit down and dish the goss*

Lantha recoiled. She hadn't expected him to actually sing. Well, "sing."

"What?" She stared at him, all tension gone out of her knife hand.

> *All life is just a party*
>
> *Sit down and calm your nerves*
>
> *Until we spill the tea and dish the just desserts you just deserve!*

"What," Lantha repeated. "No. What? I didn't mean actually sing. What even is that? It's barely singing." She sighed. "Bards."

"I'm not a bard," Robin said, scraping together a scrap of presence of mind.

They looked at him. He looked back. He almost started to explain, but then, a notification popped up in his field of vision.

**Congratulations! You have unlocked the Bard class option.
Advance your Heritage to Paragon level to enable classes.**

"Or at least not yet," he amended.

"I want you to talk," Lantha said, pressing her knife against Robin's throat when he opened up his mouth to do so immediately. "And not just ramble. I want specific answers to specific questions. Can you do that? Blink twice if you understand me."

Robin carefully blinked twice.

"Good. I want to know who you are, what you are doing here—in this cave system, specifically—and what allegiances you have. Fiamah, do you think you can manage a truth spell?"

"No," the cleric shook her head. "Not until I've had a chance to rest. We're all exhausted, and I spent most of my energies on the fight that got us captured. After food and some sleep, sure. But not right now."

"That's fine." Lantha turned back to Robin. "I'm sure our apprentice bard here understands that if he lies to me today or I suspect it, I'll question him again tomorrow under a truth spell, and if it turns out he lied, he'll wish that I had cut his throat."

"Understood! Understood!" Robin's voice cracked.

He'd been attacked by flying Cuisinarts, gained mystical powers and the attention of two—no, *three*—beings of deific power, been exposed to a pitched battle he'd orchestrated, shot with a crossbow—all of it *naked*, by the way—and now he was being threatened by the people he'd risked his life to help? Too much.

Too fucking much.

Tears started streaming down his face, and Robin began to shudder. He suppressed the sobs as much as he could because he *still had a knife to his throat*, but this was it. He was at his limit. He was done.

"Here. You need to eat something." Grathilde pressed a flat ration bar of some sort into his hand. "What?" She matched Lantha's glare with one of her own. "He's clearly starving and having a breakdown. You're not going to get any answers out of him like that. Maybe rein in the whole specter-of-blood-and-vengeance act for ten minutes and see if he'll just answer your questions without the threat of imminent death? We've all had more than enough of that today, I would think," the dwarf huffed then turned away.

The unexpected kindness, combined with the relief of Lantha sheathing her knife and stepping away, was too much for Robin.

He let go and just sobbed it all out, biting his lip to keep as quiet as possible. The kobolds were still out there, and gods knew what else. So, he cried and ate and cried and ate, and eventually, he felt better.

"There was some sort of magical mishap," he said when he'd regained a bit of composure. "It was an experimental translocation spell. Magic herbs were involved. The guy orchestrating the ritual . . . I guess he lost control? Maybe the gods intervened. I don't know. All I know is I woke up here, in the dark, naked. I don't even know where *here* is. I have no idea which way my home is—" He swallowed.

Lantha and Fiamah were watching him closely. Grathilde was studiously not looking at him, but Robin could see her adjusting her posture to hear him better. What else had Lantha asked for?

"My name is Robin. Allegiances? I'm not entirely sure what you mean by that, but I suppose the university? None of the people I'd think of as friends or allies are here."

He measured his words as he spoke them. He made sure they were all heavy with truth, though he was careful not to let slip the *whole* truth. He didn't want to tell someone who'd put a knife to his throat that he was from another world. He had no way of knowing if that was a common occurrence here, or what the implications might be.

"I woke up in a shrine. I don't know if that means I'm considered to have an allegiance with the god. It was old; there was nothing in it that told me which god it had been dedicated to. So . . . yeah, I just don't know.

"I am not your enemy. I'm just scared, alone, and far from home. Please. Please believe me." Robin slumped, feeling the cold rock beneath him in every bone in his body.

Proficiencies Unlocked: Persuasion; Expression.

Lantha looked at him, calculation in her ageless eyes. Fiamah was clearly more sympathetic. Robin sat in the silence and rubbed his fingertips on the rough burlap of his makeshift sandals.

"That will do for now," Lantha said abruptly. "We can't trust him, not without further verification, but he seems safe enough."

"He's certainly proven himself to be useful," Fiamah spoke.

"He's not getting a share of the loot, though," Grathilde added. "If he's coming along, he gets paid in food." She paused. "I suppose he can have some scavenging rights if we find some more clothing. He still looks ridiculous."

"Fine." Lantha turned and began to rummage through the packs. "Rations and rest, in that order. We're going with a double watch tonight, so sort yourselves accordingly."

She didn't look at Robin, but he knew the double watch was at least partially because of his presence. And while he hadn't known Lantha long, he knew her well enough to realize that she'd made a specific point of saying what she said when she said it so he could hear it. He was in for a world of hurt if things continued in this vein.

New Quest: [Laughter is the Best Medicine]

Elicit a smile from each of your new companions and move yourself firmly from threat to tolerated ally.
Reward: *+1 rank in either Insight, Expression, or Socialize.*
Note: *Rewards tripled if you can get a laugh out of each of your companions as well as a smile.*

Proficiency Unlocked: Socialize.

Robin wasn't quite sure the quest system he was interacting with was completely sane. The rewards were wildly inconsistent, and it occasionally exhibited odd bursts of personality. This quest didn't seem too bad, though. Not easy, of course, but relatively straightforward.

It'd be nice if he could just ask any of these women about any of these things, but with the way he'd been treated so far . . . yeah, no. Not now. Maybe after he'd gotten a few smiles.

For now, he'd take the time he'd been given and sleep. He sighed and curled up on the cold stone, pillowing his head on his arms. In moments, he was out.

Robin awoke to darkness. He did not wake up naked on the quad, hungover from experimental mead. He did not wake up from this world as if from a dream.

He hadn't really expected to at this point, but it had been a nice thought while it lasted.

Seeing he was awake, Grathilde presented him with several mushrooms. Fiamah and Lantha were talking quietly on the other side of the niche, and Ora-Jean was nowhere to be seen.

She was probably off scouting again with her spirit badger—whatever that looked like. Could anyone see spirits, or just the one bound to them? Was it a cultural phenomenon or a class that anyone could take? All questions Robin would likely not get an answer to any time soon.

Since he had some free, not-about-to-be-murdered time, Robin busied himself exploring what he could of his system interface. Such as it was.

None of the others seemed able to see what he saw when he activated any of the prompts. That was both comforting and frustrating. Comforting, as it meant his secrets would stay his. Frustrating because it meant he likely wouldn't be able to see theirs either—if they even had interfaces.

It could all be a hallucination.

Whatever. Doesn't change anything substantial.

Oh, hello!

Robin had finally managed to find his [Spellbook] interface. There wasn't much there, but more information on the two options he did have was very welcome.

[Lesser Phantasm]
Tier: Cantrip
Circle: Illusion, Shadow
Range: Short
Duration: 9 seconds + 3 seconds/level
Effect(s): Create a simple illusion that can fool a single sense at a time.
Constraints: Sound generated by this cantrip is equivalent in volume to that made by three shadelings, plus an additional three shadelings per level. Images generated cannot exceed a space greater than that occupied by three average shadelings and must be simple objects or forces.

So [Lesser Phantasm] was a bit better at producing sound than images. Made sense. Visuals were a lot more complicated, with multiple dimensions and angles to consider, color, texture, shape size . . . or maybe it was just magic, and magic was weird like that.

Multiple voices, though, and extreme volume control. He'd have to experiment with that. At the very least, if he practiced, he should be able to sing in harmony with himself.

Rhyth, he was going to end up as a bard, wasn't he?

[Cutting Words]
Tier: Cantrip
Circle: Enchantment, Curse
Range: Audible (Special)
Duration: Instantaneous
Effect(s): Your insults or other cutting observations are infused with harmful psychic energy. This has two effects. The first: your target suffers a minor amount of psychic damage. The second: your target's next action suffers a moderate disadvantage.

Constraints: *Each utterance can only affect a single target. Repeated uses of the same insult on the same target produce diminishing returns. Conversely, particularly creative or effective insults have a small chance of intensifying the effect. Targets must be capable of hearing, but they do not need to understand the language of the insult in order to suffer the effects of* [**Cutting Words**].

Interesting. Nice to have a damage option, at least, with a minor debuff attached, too. Robin wondered how much impact the target not speaking the same language would have on the boost provided by particularly good insults. His instincts told him something was going on there.

Good thing he had [**Tongue of the Fallen Tower**]. The synergy there was pleasing. He'd have to try and get each of his companions to speak in their native tongues so he could add their languages to his mental file.

So far, both food and fashion in this new world left a lot to be desired, but the magic? That wasn't bad.

Robin's mind wandered to the other two peculiarities he'd unlocked but hadn't yet taken. Shapeshifting and more illusions. That was not going to be an easy choice.

Robin's musings on his future "build" were interrupted by the return of Ora-Jean. The diminutive fighter dropped a rough sack to the ground. It smelled strongly of mushrooms.

"I've got some additional provisions, good news, and bad news. Which do you want first?"

"Good news," Grathilde insisted.

Fiamah had picked up the bag and was inspecting the contents. Lantha just nodded in agreement with the dwarf.

Robin didn't say anything. He didn't feel like his opinion would be welcome just now.

"Well," Ora-Jean started. "The good news is that Taterpicker and I managed to find a path that should lead us out of these tunnels."

The look on Grathilde's face was like the sun rising after a dark, stormy night. Then she blinked, and that same sun vanished behind a cloud.

"And the bad news?" she asked.

"We found goblin sign on the path."

Chapter 6

Robin chewed on a mushroom—rubbery, earthy, absolutely vile, but technically food—as he listened to Lantha and Ora-Jean argue in hushed tones.

Ora-Jean was all for charging in swinging, decapitating goblins left and right, and winning their way to the exit that way. Lantha was a bit more reserved. The elf liked to have options and disliked—intensely, from the sound of it—how underequipped they currently were. She wanted Tater-picker to sniff out another way.

Eventually, Ora-Jean won out by the simple expedient of refusing to do any more scouting until this path was explored further. Robin stood up as the party gathered their gear, such as it was, and prepared to move out.

"We move smart," Lantha emphasized, shooting Ora-Jean a look. "We don't know how many goblins there are, how far it is to the exit, or what else might show up to ruin our day."

"This whole excursion has been a disaster," Grathilde grumbled sourly. "Bad enough you dragged me back underground, but—"

"We move *silent* and smart," Lantha interrupted. "You know the signals if we need them. Bard—"

"Not a bard," Robin quipped. *Not yet*, something whispered in the shadows of his mind.

"Fine, *baggage*, stay close, stay quiet, make yourself useful, don't stab us in the back, and you might have a shot at getting out of these tunnels alive."

Robin bit back the urge to respond. Lantha didn't seem to be in a joking mood; he'd probably have to save her for last. She was nearly as humorless as Mr. Elrond Smith.

Or Queen Victoria.

He simply nodded. For a moment, Lantha looked him over, weighing the pack in her hands. Then she grunted and passed it to Grathilde to shoulder.

Yeah, she still didn't trust him. That was going to be one tough nut to crack a smile from.

"Let's move." Lantha jerked her chin at Ora-Jean, and the halfling slipped into the tunnel.

The rest of them followed. Lantha went first, with her conjured mage-light bobbing ahead of her, then Grathilde and Robin, with Fiamah bringing up the rear. They moved fairly silently, which was a double-edged sword. While the party had had time to grab their weapons in their escape, armor was bulkier, harder to carry, and took too long to don, so there wasn't much of it around right now.

Robin was likely the only one wearing more today than yesterday.

He and Grathilde were the only ones not carrying weapons. Come to think of it, hadn't the dwarf said something about losing some of her magical equipment? Robin glanced over.

Grathilde was stomping down the tunnel, a sour look on her face. She looked insulted to be alive. Well, she was clearly unhappy about something, and unhappy people tended to love talking about whatever it was that was pissing them off, so . . .

"Yeah, I don't love being trapped underground either," Robin said softly to Grathilde, conscious of Lantha's insistence to "stay quiet."

"It's the absolute worst!" The words burst out of Grathilde in a fierce murmur. "I didn't leave Doran-Dorlin for the fresh air and ever-shifting skies of the surface—Goddess *above* do I miss the sky—only to end up down in yet another *bjurking* hole."

"It's definitely the pits," Robin deadpanned.

Grathilde shot him a startled look. A nervous laugh, the kind that bursts forth more out of confusion than any actual appreciation for humor, escaped her lips.

[Laughter is the Best Medicine] Progress: 1/4! Bonus: 1/4!

Robin smiled. He'd gotten lucky there, but still, it was a start.

"Sometimes it helps to laugh about it," he told Grathilde.

Proficiency Unlocked: Empathy!

"Quiet!" Lantha ordered.

Robin and Grathilde subsided, but Robin sent another smile Grathilde's way. This time, her answering smile was more genuine. He waited several more paces before speaking again.

"So why are you down here?"

He needed to know more. Humor was situational; if you wanted to make someone laugh, you needed to know what made them tick.

Grathilde shrugged. She shot a nervous glance toward Lantha's back.

Right. Why would it be that easy?

Robin mentally pulled up his interface, glancing at his progress bar. He had some experience to play with. As much as he'd like to rush to the next tier or level or whatever, he got the feeling that doing so without also levelling his skills—sorry, *proficiencies*—and investing in spells—peculiarities?—as he went along would be a mistake.

He mentally prodded at his proficiencies list. He could take any unlocked skill up to a maximum of four. He focused on various areas of the screen until he managed to find the desired information.

Proficiencies are capped at 3 + Level. To increase your proficiencies, further gain experience and progress toward higher tiers!

So tiers weren't quite levels. How many levels were there per tier? Robin looked at his character sheet. Probably either three or nine. He couldn't spend experience enough to lower him further than 33 percent on his progress bar . . .

He did some quick mental math.

He'd need to get past 45 percent or so and try to spend down below that level. That would tell him if he was functionally a level one or a level three right now. He assumed level one, but there was no way he'd found to tell for certain. Yet.

Well, he wasn't going to get anywhere like this. To paraphrase the maxim, ya gotta spend XPs to get XPs! Now, could he get some more information out of this interface on what each proficiency actually did?

Expression

The fine art of Expression governs all manner of communication, whether you intend to express yourself with words or actions. Useful for all manner of performances, making yourself understood, or otherwise making your point! Words can hurt, darling!

Well, that would certainly be useful. He had stubborn people to make smile, as well as insults to craft to fuel his **[Cutting Words]**. Hopefully there was some nice synergy there.

After a moment's consideration, he upped *Expression* to three. That should give him a feel for the skill and the chance to try it out in conjunction with **[Cutting Words]** at multiple skill levels, in case it made a noticeable difference.

Then he upped *Empathy* to one and *Deception* to three. He still felt *Deception* would play well with his **[Lesser Phantasm]**, even if it did not have a direct impact.

He rode out the strange sensation of growing weaker then growing back stronger, and then checked his character sheet.

Robin Parker

Heritage: Shadeling, Juvenile
Profession: None
Tier: 0
Progress to Tier 1: 34%

Properties

Physical
   -Strength: 11
   -Dexterity: 14
   -Fortitude: 11
Mental
   -Intelligence: 17
   -Cunning: 18
   -Resilience: 14
Social
   -Charisma: 15
   -Manipulation: 13
   -Poise: 15

Proficiencies

Physical (4/9)
   -???
   -???
   -???
   -???

-???
-Ranged Combat: 0
-Sleight of Hand: 0
-Stealth: 1
-Survival: 1
Mental (1/9)
-???
-???
-???
-???
-???
-Insight: 0
-???
-???
-???
Social (5/9)
-???
-Deception: 3
-Empathy: 1
-Expression: 3
-???
-???
-Persuasion: 0
-Socialize: 0
-???

Peculiarities

Blessing of Rhyth
Tongue of the Fallen Tower
Mark of the Trickster

Yup. He was farther away from Tier One now, but his skills had advanced. *Ugh*. This was going to be tough. He really wanted to unlock more peculiarities, but smart money was on the slower road to power. He needed to up some of his skills and master them first.

He reviewed his recent interaction with Grathilde, trying to *empathize* with her. There was a slight but noticeable difference. He could clearly see nonverbal cues, and his instincts prompted him with an educated guess as to what those cues meant for her emotional state.

The tightness of her lips when she talked about being underground, for example. She didn't like it, but not because she was afraid. There was some personal hurt or dislike there.

Robin was jarred out of his thoughts by an abrupt halt.

Lantha stood, one fist raised. Grathilde's hands came up, and she flexed her fingers. Robin couldn't see Ora-Jean, and Fiamah was behind him.

They held position for a long moment until Ora-Jean reappeared, looking grim.

"What?" Lantha asked, voice pitched low to keep from carrying.

"I think the kobolds sent out search parties that have ranged this far." The halfling grimaced. "With the way these tunnels all twist, I can't promise that we won't run into them or the goblins with little-to-no warning. As far as I can tell, both are nearby."

"*Foegathi*," Lantha said. It sounded like a curse.

Robin mentally filed it away with the rest of the language fragments that keyed him in to [Tongue of the Fallen Tower].

"Do we continue forward?" Grathilde asked, face twisted with indecision.

Ora-Jean's face was set; the halfling clearly wanted to carry on. Lantha looked sour. Fiamah was unreadable; serene.

The decision was made for them, however, by a volley of crude black arrows. The missiles shot out from the shadows, and Lantha was the only one to escape unscathed.

"Ambush! Defensive positions!" Lantha sent her magelight soaring up near the ceiling, and it disappeared into the shadows.

Robin didn't need to be told twice. He backed himself up against a wall and wrapped himself with a [Lesser Phantasm] of cave stone. His blood thundered in his veins, and his eyes darted through the shifting shadows, trying to pick out the enemy.

Fortunately, as a shadeling, he could see in the dark. Even with that boon, however, his first sight of a goblin came when one of the small, green humanoids tumbled out of the shadows to splat on the stone near his feet. A second smile grinned ruby at its throat. Lantha's work, no doubt.

The elf was hard to follow, even with his ability to see in the dark. Fiamah, on the other hand, was easy to pick out; she tended to gleam with a burning light as she laid about with a mace. Grathilde moved with extreme grace, almost dancing through the air, as blasts of air sent the few goblins that got too close to her tumbling.

They didn't look very robust, at least. Though there were probably a lot of them.

Robin flashed his hand through the motions of [Lesser Phantasm] again, renewing his camouflage.

Ora-Jean howled with fury as she swung around her a double-bladed axe. Goblin war cries answered her fury, echoing off the stone. [Tongue of the Fallen Tower] translated them all. "Blood," "kill," and "filthy elf" figured prominently, as did several anatomical impossibilities.

"Who are you calling filthy?" Robin seized on the idea and spun it into some [Cutting Words]. "You put the 'dirt' in *dirt cheap*."

The goblin who had been shouting about filthy elves staggered. Red eyes darted around the tunnel, seeking the source of the voice. Robin renewed his camouflage. Seconds passed, but the goblin didn't make any move toward him.

"Come to think of it, you look like you put the 'cheap' in it too," Robin added, taking another shot with his cantrip.

The goblin's green skin went an apoplectic gray. He howled in fury and began to foam at the mouth. Before Robin could say anything else, however, the little beastie dropped to the floor, dead.

Well, that's one way to do things. Robin blinked. He hadn't expected the cantrip to be that effective. These goblins must be similar to the ones he was familiar with in D&D: very low hit points—or whatever the equivalent was here.

Robin began calling out every schoolyard insult he could think of. He insulted the goblins' mothers, their personal hygiene, their sense of taste— anything he could think of. Noses were fair game, and a few seemed very sensitive about the size of their ears. It was hard to tell when an insult really landed, but Robin had a feeling those landed particularly hard.

Once or twice, he had to dash out of hiding as the battle spilled near him. Fortunately, the goblins were more concerned about the women with weapons cutting them down, and Robin managed to hide himself away again each time without getting caught.

In what seemed both a very long and very short time, the skirmish was over. Goblin bodies littered the floor of the tunnel, and the party stood— splattered and bleeding—victorious.

Ora-Jean was ruthlessly looting the bodies for what little there was to be found. Mostly a few coppers coins, though she also took a small spear.

"Do you want any of the bows or arrows?" Ora-Jean asked Lantha, who shook her head in the negative.

Fiamah moved from person to person, her hands bringing healing light and purifying fire. Curiously, after she finished, each member of the party was spotlessly clean as well.

"Your [**Hearth's Blessing**] is much better than my [**Cleanse**]," Grathilde complained. "Not that I'm complaining."

"Finish up," Lantha commanded. "We need to keep going. I don't want to be here when more goblins find this place."

"How many more do you think there are?" Robin made the mistake of asking.

Lantha's face was grim when she answered.

"Hundreds."

Chapter 7

$\mathcal{T}$hey moved through the tunnels, Robin glad to leave the coppery scent of blood behind.

Once or twice, he tried to again engage Grathilde in conversation, but the dwarf was intent on following the elusive breath of fresh air. Robin assumed Ora-Jean had led them close enough that Grathilde was able to forge some kind of mystic connection.

She stepped lightly and quickly, moving faster than she had before. Robin fell behind, bit by bit, until he was walking nearer to Fiamah than to the others.

The woman had a few pieces of armor strapped in place, and a large pendant engraved with a stylized sun hanging from a chain around her neck. The whole thing screamed "cleric" and "holy symbol" to Robin, but he couldn't say for sure, and he couldn't ask without prompting uncomfortable questions about why he didn't know.

As he was searching for a way to break the ice, he nearly broke his foot. The thin burlap protecting him was no match for the stone impacting against his appendage. He'd missed it in his surreptitious study of Fiamah.

"*Frelling thing,*" he bit out, remembering almost too late to keep his voice down.

He glared down at the rock, a strangely square bit of stone. "Huh. That's odd." It looked almost like a brick. Well, one end did. The other was ragged, broken stone.

"What is it?" Fiamah asked. Her voice was surprisingly smooth and cool for someone who tended to burn with her touch.

"Looks like worked stone." He glanced around their surroundings, seeing if there were any more.

Proficiency Unlocked: Perception.

That would have been more useful about forty-five seconds ago.

"Are you certain?" Fiamah's normally placid facade cracked a little. "Let me see."

Robin hefted up the stone and offered it to her. Fiamah took it; it sat much lighter in her grip than it had in Robin's.

He suddenly had even less desire to be on the business end of the mace she carried. The woman was *strong*.

"Lantha!" she called out, voice soft yet carrying.

The bobbing magelight up ahead paused, then reversed direction. Lantha appeared.

"What is it?"

"Look." Fiamah held out the stone. "I think we're closer than we thought."

So they had come here looking for something. Something or someplace made by human—humanoid? Sapient?—hands. Well, hands or agency. Even snakes could probably carve stone if they had the right magic.

"That was only ever the secondary mission," Lantha replied, though she did not take her eyes off the edges of the stone. Her whole body was tense, like she was standing too close to something venomous. "And neither matters if we don't get out of here and back to—" She cut herself off, shooting a glance at Robin. "If we don't get back."

Lantha gave the stone one more look and returned to trying to suss out the exit with Ora-Jean and Grathilde. Robin waited until she was safely gone and Fiamah had reluctantly returned the stone to the floor.

"I'll remember the way," he said. "I've been keeping a mental map in my head. I'm probably not as good at it as Ora-Jean, but . . ." He shrugged.

Fiamah simply nodded and resumed walking.

"What do you think it was from?" he asked after a moment.

The woman was quiet for a moment. Robin was wondering if he'd have to try another approach, but she spoke before he could formulate one.

"Historically, this region has always been contested. As far back as records go, various peoples have clashed over the wealth of riches in the mountains, the natural treasures that grow in the forests that blanket the slopes, and the pass that is the region's sole overland route across the mountains. That"—she jerked her head back in the direction of the mystery stone—"could be from any number of subterranean cultures that have settled in the area."

"Now you've done it," Grathilde called back over her shoulder. "You've gotten the scholar lecturing. I hope you didn't have anything else for your ears to do anytime soon."

Robin hadn't realized they'd drawn so close to the rest of the party. Fiamah ignored the dwarf and continued speaking.

"There are maps in the Athenaeum of Elaxendrie going back several millennia that show several kingdoms claiming these lands. The elves and dragonkin have oral histories that theoretically stretch back even farther and speak of ancient empires also battling over these very lands. Though it is unclear to modern scholars if those conflicts were specifically over these lands, or if they were merely the site of great conflicts." Fiamah was definitely in full-on lecture mode.

Proficiency Unlocked: Learning.

"I'm guessing those peoples don't include kobolds or goblins," Robin said, thinking back to the cave he'd found the kobolds and their prisoners in.

"That's debatable." Fiamah was the most animated he'd ever seen her. "Just as there are many nations at different stages of development, with the so-called "civilization" of cities and the so-called "primitives" of the wild tribes in the icy reaches of Tar'Kata or the Burning Lands of the Ever-Sun, there is a lot of evidence of what you could call civil actions of goblinoids in the past—"

"Unsubstantiated nonsense!" Grathilde took the time to shoot back over her shoulder. "Monsters, all of them."

"Don't be closed-minded," Fiamah chided gently. "Or do you want to try debating the status of the Dvimmerdveld with me again?"

"We're not here looking for mythical fallen dwarves," Grathilde grumbled. "We're here looking for evidence of the Ssathessti—"

"Grathilde," Lantha's voice drifted back, carrying a note of warning with it.

The dwarf shut her mouth with a snap.

Interesting. And he wasn't the only one that seemed to think so.

New Quest: [Below Ground and Between the Shadows]
Investigate the possible presence of the Ssathessti, ruins of their settlements, or artifacts of their civilization in the caverns beneath the Dragonspine Mountains.

***Reward:** +1 Arcane Lore; 1 undetermined minor magical item.*
***Bonus Objective:** Uncover what interest the **Sisters Sharp** adventuring party has in the matter.*
***Bonus Reward:** Power. In the sense that knowledge is power. Good luck!*

Proficiency Unlocked: Arcane Lore.

Robin filed the name away for later, along with the oddity of unlocking a proficiency merely from hearing about it from a quest prompt. Fiamah was still lecturing, though she'd pushed the conversation in another direction.

"As I was saying, there have been any number of civilizations throughout the world's history, and it would be foolish to discount a whole group on the evidence of a small fragment of the whole." She looked at the walls.

She had been studying the walls the whole time they'd been walking, Robin realized. Ever since he'd found that stone. And she'd peered closely at every adjoining tunnel they'd passed. That told Robin two things: there was more riding on finding evidence of these Ssathessti than the group was letting on, and Fiamah was at least partially distracted.

"Did these ancient peoples have magics that have been lost to time, or gods that have since been forgotten or fallen from active worship?" That should be oblique enough to get him some information, at least.

"Oh no," Grathilde groaned. "Stop encouraging her!"

Lantha must have been preoccupied because no rebuke came from the shadows ahead.

"Lost knowledge, almost certainly. We lose knowledge all the time. Well, we mortals do. There is debate as to whether the gods actually ever allow any knowledge to be lost."

"I don't imagine that's something easily proved, from a practical standpoint," Robin said drily, suspecting that was the humor Fiamah might respond best to.

He was rewarded with a tinkling laugh. *Yes! Empathy* and *Expression* were paying off!

[Laughter is the Best Medicine] Progress: 2/4! Bonus: 2/4!

"No," Fiamah replied. "Though many have claimed otherwise."

"Luminaries." Grathilde snorted. "Can't trust half of what they say. And you can trust even less of the tripe the bards sing of. No offense."

"None taken?" Robin said. "Still not a bard." He pushed away his annoyance at the interruption. "You were saying about lost gods?"

"Hmm?" Fiamah was eyeing a perpendicular tunnel that had a more-than-usual amount of regularity to its shape. "Oh yes. Lost gods. There are multiple schools of thought on the matter."

"There always are," Grathilde mumbled, but Fiamah didn't appear to notice.

Robin resisted the urge to ask her how tracking the airflow was going. There were already enough distractions coming from that direction, and he was on the verge of collecting some more information.

"One school of thought holds that the gods can never be lost, only the outward faces they present to certain peoples in certain times and places." A hand went to the symbol around her neck. "Those that hold that position would consider my goddess, Serenya, to be the same entity as the elvish god Úrin, who also holds dominion over the sun."

"Nonsense." This time, the exclamation came from Lantha. It seemed even their leader was getting bored with the winding tunnels if she was tolerating the discussion behind her.

"This position tends to ignore or minimize slight differences. For example, Serenya is also considered a goddess of healing, whereas Úrin does not concern himself much with that art." Fiamah didn't respond to Lantha's interruption.

"So in the first case, lost gods are similar to someone adopting a new name and persona. It's not that the god is gone, per se." Robin frowned. That did not sound like it fit with the quest he'd been given.

"Correct. Though many scholars do believe that gods are unique, and that they can and do move on, sometimes forcibly or against their will."

"Deicide?"

"There are plenty of stories in the oral traditions of the elves and dragonkin of gods slaying gods, and gods slaying even older primordial beings and being slain in return. So yes, some do believe that the gods can die."

"They say Mnimvor vanished after delving too deep into the void beneath the world," Grathilde offered. "And she is considered lost. Her son took up her mantle as the deity of the forge. At least that is how it is told in Dweomerdeep. The arcane and theological schools there agree on that much, and they agree on precious little else. It's supposedly the reason—well, one reason—a forge fire is never supposed to completely go out; to help her find her way back."

"Has a lost god ever returned?" Robin thought oh he might as well draw as much from the well as he could while the water was flowing.

"Debatable." Fiamah looked thoughtful. "There are many deities who have returned from death, if you would count that. It's a common feature of those who end up ruling over the dead."

"Makes sense," Robin said. "It always helps to have firsthand knowledge of a product."

Fiamah did *not* laugh at that. She frowned, but after a moment continued.

"There is some historical evidence—all circumstantial—that certain gods have been known to wax and wane in power. If that's true, it's possible that a deity might return from being lost, called back to the world by the tie of faith. But this is not really an area I've studied in depth. I wouldn't be able to tell you more without consulting—"

"Wait!" Grathilde interrupted. "The airflow is stronger coming from the right fork up ahead. I think we're nearly to the exit."

Ora-Jean appeared moments later, face grim.

"There's a big cavern up ahead, and I think I see the tunnel out, but you're not going to like it. The place is occupied." She shook her head. "And you're never going to believe what is roosting in there."

Roosting? To Robin, the word brought to mind chickens, but that was far from comforting. He'd grown up regularly visiting his grandmother's farm. Chickens were vicious, bloodthirsty creatures not to be underestimated.

"What's roosting up ahead?" Lantha's voice was grim.

"Goblins. With *wings*."

Chapter 8

Robin took a deep, quiet breath as they paced through the tunnels. The air was the same nearly temperate chill as far as he could tell, but Grathilde was charging forward full speed ahead. Lantha and Ora-Jean advanced, but more slowly, trying to rein in Grathilde as they went.

"I have been trapped down here for weeks. Weeks! I haven't gone this long without seeing the sky since I ran away from home. Because I wanted to see *what*? The sky. Do not get in my way."

"We won't, but you can't charge in half-cocked. We have to be smart about this. Unless you have some megaspell that can defeat several dozen winged goblins on their home turf you haven't told us about?" Ora-Jean hissed.

The halfling was a pretty sarcastic person. Robin filed that detail away for later. He still needed to get a smile and/or a laugh from her and Lantha.

Before anyone could say anything further, Ora-Jean's hand shot up. They were here. Slowly, they crept forward, the tunnel around them widening abruptly into a soaring cavern.

The ceiling looked to be at least a hundred feet up. Large stalactites and stalagmites were present around the edges of the cavern, with smaller—often broken—specimens in the center. There was also a distinct smell to the place, like moldy pillows and fermented locker-room jocks.

"I thought you said there was *fresh* air in here," Robin said in a low voice, trying not to choke on the scent.

"There is," Ora-Jean replied, holding her hand out. "You can feel the currents move. Look at Grathilde."

The dwarf, eyes shining, had a hand out in front of her. She wafted it gently to and fro in front of her. Whorls of pale blue light flickered at her fingertips.

"There's clear air here. High, fresh mountain air. We can't be more than a couple hundred feet from it."

"At least a hundred of those feet are straight up, though," Robin noted. "Or can you fly us there?"

"Not yet." Grathilde grimaced. "But we have rope."

"I don't know that we have enough to scale that, Grathilde," Fiamah said gently. "And we certainly can't make the ascent with all of those still roosting here." She pointed up.

Robin followed her pointing finger and bit back a curse. There were several dozen green forms hanging from the stalactites above. Winged goblins. They were green like the last band he'd seen, but they also had clawed feet and large wings, black as tar. As he watched, one or two shifted in their sleep, wings rustling gently.

"That's . . . that's one frelling high-ground advantage," he said. "But if we're careful, we might be able to kite them in small groups and handle them that way? It'd be risky, though."

"Kite them?" Ora-Jean looked to him. "I'm not familiar with this term."

"Ah, basically, it means to draw the attention of a small group and lure them away from the rest; you can defeat a few foes far more easily. Then you repeat as needed until you've defeated the whole group."

"We can do that! Let's do that! Then we can scale the cliff and get out of here," Grathilde agreed eagerly.

"It's dangerous, though," Robin replied gently. "Because if you make a single mistake, you can alert the whole group and bring them all down on you. I don't think we're capable of facing that."

"We're not," Lantha confirmed, voice like a tomb door slamming. "And we can't risk it."

"We have to!" Grathilde retorted. "We've been down here too long. We need fresh air; fresh supplies. We need to get back to civilization and reequip, we—"

"Quiet!" Fiamah whispered. "Look!"

Lantha immediately dimmed her magelight to next to nothing. A troop of two dozen or so goblins had started streaming in through a tunnel across the cavern. They carried torches and baskets.

"No wings on these," Ora-Jean murmured.

The goblins made their way toward the sheer side of the cavern that Ora-Jean and Grathilde thought led to the way out of these caverns. The baskets were settled, one in front of each goblin, and the torches thrust into crannies between the stalagmites. One goblin brought out a rough flute carved from bone and began to whistle on it.

The sound was high and screeching, with only the barest hints of a melody to it. The goblin played a few bars, waited, then repeated himself. Again he stopped and seemed to wait for a response.

These actions repeated themselves several times before there was an answering trill from farther up in the cavern. Robin focused on the top of the underground cliff. There was movement up there. More wings.

"Something's up there," he whispered.

"Something with wings," Lantha confirmed. "But I don't think it's more winged goblins."

Her words were confirmed moments later when winged figures began spiraling down through the air. They were like huge birds—condors, maybe—but with the heads and chests of women.

Harpies!

They landed near the baskets and began tearing into the food. They shrieked about food and laughed about sating their appetites. Their words were screeches and airy cries, and Robin marveled again at how easily he understood them. The goblins around them began murmuring excitedly and fidgeting with their loincloths. It was becoming increasingly clear just what was going on here.

"*Oh.* Oh no." Robin grimaced. "So *that's* where the winged goblins are coming from."

"We need to retreat out of hearing range," Ora-Jean said with a tightly controlled urgency. "We don't want them to spot us and start singing."

"What happens if they start singing?"

"Their song can ensnare the minds of creatures who hear them," the halfling explained. "Us, they'd eat. You?" She jerked a thumb toward the goblins. "They'd likely have another use for you."

"Right." Robin went green. "Let's get out of here."

"We can't! We're so close!" Grathilde was almost frantic. "I can't go back down into those cramped, choking tunnels! I just can't. We can take them. They're clearly distracted. We should strike now!"

"Can you silence their song?" Lantha asked harshly. "Do you have a store of beeswax you haven't shared? No? Then we skip this fight and try to find another way out."

"*Fine,*" Grathilde snapped. "But not before I gather some power. If we're this close, I want some air to carry me through the rest of this nightmare."

"Grathilde! No! It's too risky—" Fiamah whispered.

It was too late. Grathilde's hands flickered with pale blue light. Robin fancied he could see her gathering cloudlike wisps of power to herself. The air in the room suddenly shifted, a breeze blowing toward them instead of the cool stillness of cave air.

Robin wasn't the only one to notice, either. In the cave, a shriek went up from the harpies. They could feel the air currents shifting too.

"Uh, I think they noticed," Robin said. "Maybe we should get going."

"Just a few more seconds," Grathilde insisted. "I need more."

"We're going. Now." Lantha grabbed Grathilde by the arm and hauled on the dwarf.

Grathilde didn't budge. Her feet might as well have been part of the stone floor. Robin swore and tried to throw the illusion of rock over the tunnel mouth where they stood, but he failed. The illusion flickered out, stretched too thin. Wrapping himself in illusion was one thing, but his [Lesser Phantasm] couldn't stretch much beyond arm's length.

Fiamah and Ora-Jean joined Lantha on tugging at Grathilde. The dwarf's eyes, now glowing sky blue, were fixed on the wisps of power she gathered from the air. If he wanted to help, there wasn't any room for him to barrel in.

Robin fixed his attention back on the harpies and goblins. The harpies were fluttering their wings, trying to catch the shifting air currents. They hadn't spotted the group in the tunnel yet, but they would soon.

Unless he distracted them.

"Sisters!" he cast the words out in the tongue of the harpies using [Lesser Phantasm]. "We are betrayed! The goblins have stoppered their ears with wax! It's a trap!"

He tried to match the tone of one of the voices he'd heard earlier and prayed to Rhyth that his *Deception* skill was up to the job.

The harpies began to shriek madly. Three of them began to lash out at the goblins with their talons while the goblins howled back and tried to scramble away.

"No! Sisters! Deception! Someone has stolen my voice!"

It was the harpy he'd tried to impersonate. Frell.

Well, he'd cast the whole area into confusion for now.

Behind him, Lantha and the others had managed to pry Grathilde off the stone and were carrying her away, moving far too slowly.

"Sisters! There! Movement in the tunnel."

Too slow by half.

"Run! Run, run, run! They've spotted us," he yelled.

They dumped Grathilde on the ground. The blue light around her had completely faded, but she looked dreamy and a bit dazed. Robin grabbed her arm and urged her along.

Behind them, the harpies shrieked, commanding the goblins to follow, to kill, and to return with the heads as tribute.

"I think they're pissed at us," Robin yelled. "The goblins are coming after us."

"You see as well as an elf," Ora-Jean swore. "Here they come!"

"Go back to a fork in the tunnels. I'll try to throw them off our trail." The beginnings of an idea—two, really—leapt into Robin's mind, courtesy of the last time he'd played a low-level character with his D&D group.

They ran, pelting down the tunnel with the howls of the goblins nipping at their heels. Lantha darted ahead, her magelight shining, with Ora-Jean and Fiamah close behind. Robin attempted to shove Grathilde ahead of him to get her to run faster.

"I can't believe I have to waste my power already," she complained, but her feet lightened, and she began to dart gracefully over the stone.

Robin ran, his feet bruising against the uneven stone. What he wouldn't give for a solid pair of cross-trainers right now! Still, the bloodthirsty howls of the little green monsters behind him were more than enough motivation to keep moving.

Proficiency Unlocked: Athletics.

He dismissed the notification immediately. He needed to keep one eye fixed on Lantha's magelight dancing ahead, the glimmering white of starlight. The other he kept on the lookout for the upcoming fork in the tunnel. It shouldn't be too much furth—*there!*

Robin twisted his hand through two quick instances of [**Lesser Phantasm**] in a row. The first conjured a replica of Lantha's dancing magelight speeding down the tunnel he didn't plan to take. The second he set to a three-second delay and programmed with the sound of feet slapping wildly on stone.

If he was lucky, the goblins would be far enough behind that they'd fall for his diversion. He didn't dare stop running to check behind him and see. He threw up a prayer to Rhyth and hoped for the best.

He was a little early on the cast, done with both several seconds before he made it to the fork the others had taken. He put his head down and ran.

He needed to get out of sight as fast as he could.

Behind him, he heard a confused yowl go up. *Yes!*

Robin darted ahead, gaining on the magelight in front of him now that half his attention wasn't on spellcasting.

The noise behind him got quieter, but not by enough. There was still the sound of hoots and battle cries, and they didn't sound too much farther away.

Fuck. They must have split up at the fork!

At least half of the goblins were still hot on their heels.

Chapter 9

Robin wasn't sure which hurt more, the sharp stones jabbing at his feet or the harsh cries of the goblins shrilling in his ears. He ran, the little green beasts hot on his heels. He ran until he turned a sharp corner in the tunnel and Ora-Jean shouted at him.

"Here! We're making a stand." The halfling hefted her double-bladed axe. As the first goblin came charging around the corner, she let it fly and buried the blade deep in the goblin's neck.

Fiamah took the next one, her mace swinging at his head. The goblin threw up an arm and traded a crushed skull for a broken wrist. He howled and slashed at her with the dagger in his other hand.

Grathilde hung back and Lantha was, predictably, nowhere to be seen, though Robin expected her knives to dart out of the shadows at any moment and deprive some goblin of his last breath.

Robin put his back to the nearby tunnel wall and wrapped himself in a **[Lesser Phantasm]**. So far, the adage of his old gaming group still held out: the best armor is not getting hit in the first place.

Time to sharpen his wits and throw out some **[Cutting Words]**.

Ora-Jean's axe was stuck in the neck of the goblin she had nearly beheaded, and two more were sneaking up into a flanking position behind her. She swore and tugged harder at the haft of her axe.

"Hey, Snaggletooth!" Robin yelled at the one closer to him. "Did you murder a tooth fairy or are your teeth just naturally as crooked as your moral compass?"

The goblin spun around and glared at him.

"What? What that even mean?" it snarled.

So he didn't get it. At least he was offended. Robin's cantrip was still having *some* effect.

"Hey," he said as a follow up. "At least you're as bright as your smile!"

The goblin began foaming at the mouth and collapsed over, dead of a magical rage aneurysm. In the meantime, Ora-Jean had extricated her axe and was trading blows with the other goblin.

A blast of air sliced past Robin's ear and slammed another goblin up against the wall, the impact staggering the little monster. Before the goblin could so much as shake his head to clear it, one of Lantha's daggers flew out of a nearby shadow and lodged itself in his eye.

"Don't waste your energies!" Lantha shouted to Grathilde. "We're paying a high enough price for them as it is."

"Less talky-talky, more stabby-stabby," the dwarf yelled back.

Fiamah was holding off three goblins with wild swings of her mace. They danced around her, not giving her the chance to focus on any single one of them. The cleric was bleeding from a few shallow cuts, and each of the goblins' daggers had bloodied blades.

Robin flicked his hand through the gestures of **[Lesser Phantasm]** and conjured the sound of a harpy commanding the goblins to fall back and defend her. Two of the three paused, and Fiamah was quick to take advantage of the breather to cave in the head of the third. Lantha's dagger flashed out of the nearby shadows and got another one in the back. That one died with a look of surprise on his face as he slumped to the floor. He didn't even manage to cry out.

The final goblin didn't stand a chance. Fiamah's mace went for his head at the same time Ora-Jean's axe cut him off at the knees. The spray of blood that resulted painted the wall Robin had his back against green.

It also splattered him with more than his fair share of gore. In disgust, he dropped the illusion and stepped out into the tunnel.

"Well, that was bracing," Ora-Jean said drily, leaning on her axe.

"Are you serious?" Grathilde glared, clearly upset that she'd had to spend such a large portion of her elemental energies so soon after gathering them.

"Yeah, I just love being mobbed by a swarm of smelly, green murder puppets," Robin deadpanned. "NOT."

Ora-Jean snorted a laugh, startled.

Wicked! Finally, a use for the high art of '90s sarcasm. Party on, dude.

[Laughter is the Best Medicine] Progress: 3/4! Bonus: 3/4!

Grathilde glared at them both. Robin ignored the look, wondering what else he might be able to recycle from his home world.

Ugh. No more movies. Frell. And his choice of games and books was likely to be sharply limited.

He shoved the thought out of his mind. He had bigger problems right now. Like staying alive. Or finding a shirt he could actually wear. Or scavenging some food that didn't taste like dead, chewy dirt. If he got any hungrier, he might be tempted to try fried goblin.

The thought made him go green.

No, probably not. Not even mushrooms were *that* unappetizing.

Close, but not quite.

"Do you have enough energy left for a [**Hearth's Blessing**], Fiamah?" Grathilde asked hopefully.

"Loot first, cleanse later," the cleric replied. "I'm not going to waste the divine favor of my goddess just because you want to hoard your own energies."

The dwarf pouted. Robin was secretly disappointed as well. He didn't fancy wearing goblin blood any longer than necessary. In fact, his skin was crawling at the thought.

Which god did he have to talk dirty to to get a hookup like [**Hearth's Blessing**]? It didn't really seem like Rhyth's bag, but maybe it was a universal thing all gods could grant? Or a power he could learn. Maybe he could learn [**Cleanse**] from Grathilde. Though he'd probably have to unlock whatever class she had to do so.

If she even had a class.

That's it, focus on the unknowns. Ignore the greasy goblin blood going sticky and itching across your skin.

"Ora-Jean," Lantha said. "Do a quick scout of the tunnels. I don't want any more goblins following the sounds of battle to us. Or more kobolds, if those tracks we saw earlier were as fresh as you thought."

Ora-Jean nodded and slipped off down the tunnel, back the way they'd run. She'd shout a warning if there were more goblins approaching, and if not, slip out to see what else might be in the area.

Fiamah was healing the last of the small lacerations she had sustained during the battle. Grathilde was morosely looking at her fingertips as if she could spool back the power she had expended through the sheer force of her pout.

Robin took a deep breath and let it out. Still alive, and hopefully wiser for the experience.

And speaking of experience, he should check how much he'd gathered. If he was lucky, tricking the harpies would count as well.

He opened his interface and loaded up his status. Fifty-seven percent of the way to Tier One? He *had* to have gotten harpy experience. There was no way it had jumped that high just by fighting off a dozen goblins.

His progress was above 45 percent. Now was the time to invest a little more heavily in skills and see if his calculations about level markers and skill costs bore out.

He increased *Persuasion*, *Perception*, *Insight*, and *Learning* to one, and *Deception* and *Expression* to four. While *Ranged Combat* might be useful, he didn't have a reliable ranged weapon, so that option could wait. Besides, he was rather enjoying **[Cutting Words]**, and could otherwise rely on his wits and **[Lesser Phantasm]** to get him out of trouble.

Robin checked his percentage to Tier One. He was back down to 36 percent. *Yikes*. Skills must increase in cost as they ranked up. That, or his mental calculations were off, a distinct possibility. He shouldn't have spent that much experience.

He considered his character sheet.

Robin Parker

Heritage: Shadeling, Juvenile
Profession: None
Tier: 0
Progress to Tier 1: 36%

Properties

Physical
   -Strength: 11
   -Dexterity: 14
   -Fortitude: 11
Mental
   -Intelligence: 17
   -Cunning: 18
   -Resilience: 14
Social
   -Charisma: 15
   -Manipulation: 13
   -Poise: 15

Proficiencies

Physical (5/9)
-Athletics: 0
-???
-???
-???
-???
-Ranged Combat: 0
-Sleight of Hand: 0
-Stealth: 1
-Survival: 1
Mental (4/9)
-Arcane Lore: 0
-???
-???
-???
-???
-Insight: 1
-Learning: 1
-???
-Perception: 1
Social (5/9)
-???
-Deception: 4
-Empathy: 1
-Expression: 4
-???
-???
-Persuasion: 1
-Socialize: 0
-???

Peculiarities

Blessing of Rhyth
Tongue of the Fallen Tower
Mark of the Trickster

Still, it confirmed that his next milestone was likely 67 percent progress. It was annoying. His next level would give him access to another peculiarity; either shapeshifting or a bigger and better illusion spell if he didn't unlock any other choices.

Well, he was this low, he might as well spend a little more.

Robin paid to raise *Sleight of Hand* to 1. He'd done quite well so far with his other trickstery skills. He might as well make sure he was raising all of them.

"Oi, bard!" Grathilde called. "Help us search these bodies for loot."

"Am I getting a share now?" he shot back.

"No, but slackers never even get the chance at one, so chop-chop." Grathilde gestured at the bodies.

Robin grimaced. Killing charging monsters out for blood with magic from a distance was one thing, but digging through the pockets of the stinking and recently deceased was another. His mouth stung with pre-vomit acid.

Deep breaths. Pretend it's just a very immersive VR game.

Part of his childhood had been spent on a farm, so he was no stranger to death, disgusting body fluids, or cleaning up after such things. Didn't mean he had to like it, though.

At least there weren't a lot of pockets to go through. Most of the goblins just wore loincloths and kept their valuables in small pouches.

"I don't suppose I could get a dagger to cut these free?" he asked.

"Nope," Lantha said.

"Not until you earn it, greenbeard." Grathilde grinned.

He didn't even have a beard.

Robin sighed and fought with the hide straps used to tie the pouch to the bit of poorly tanned leather that served as a belt for the loincloth. His fingers would never feel clean again.

Finally, however, he managed to get it open. Inside were a few copper pieces, some shiny pieces of quartz, and a dirty rag. Robin almost threw the rag aside when he noticed it had markings on it. He spread it out and angled it toward Lantha's magelight to get a better view.

It was a map! Crude, to be sure, and it probably didn't trace all the tunnels, but it was more than they were working with.

There had to be another entrance on here. There was no way those goblins never left the caves; not with the food they'd had in those baskets. And they certainly couldn't rely on the harpies for transport up and down those cliffs.

He had to show this to the others!

"Hey! I think—"

Robin looked up and stopped in his tracks. "Uh . . . y'all, we've got company," he said slowly.

Ora-Jean stood a few meters away in the middle of the tunnel. Behind her, the one-eyed priest of Urkhan loomed, a wicked-looking dagger held tightly to her throat.

Ora-Jean twisted her lips bitterly.

"I found the kobolds."

Chapter 10

The air was suddenly heavy and still. The priest holding the knife to Ora-Jean's throat was not alone. Several kobolds, many showing evidence of freshly bandaged wounds, accompanied him. They looked like beaten dogs and flinched away from the priest whenever he spoke.

"By all means, make the attempt," the priest urged mockingly, his gaze fixed on Lantha.

The elf held a dagger in each hand, the one in her left drawn back and primed to throw. Her eyes glittered with frosty hate.

"You think I'll miss?" she asked.

"On the contrary, I am quite certain you won't." The priest's smile broadened. "But I am equally confident that it is of no consequence."

"Bladeward." Lantha lowered the dagger and spit. "*Boduimel.*"

"Good. You are capable of learning."

"Your foul god can't shield you forever." Lantha shifted her stance. "And he certainly won't bother to protect your underlings."

"I assure you that *My Most Noble and Exalted Lord* can and will protect me more than long enough for this current purpose." The smile dropped from the priest's face. "You and your companions will surrender yourselves. Again. Come now; we all know how this will play out. None of you has the power to challenge my will in this scenario."

Was this how they'd been captured before? Ora-Jean or one of the others captured in an ambush and the others forced to surrender to save her life?

Robin briefly considered trying to throw a **[Cutting Words]**. After all, it wasn't a blade as such and should be able to bypass something called "bladeward." He dismissed the idea as too dangerous. They were outnum-bered, and the priest was clearly capable of putting down a kobold insur-rection on his own.

No. They needed more information.

"And what's to keep them from escaping again?" Robin asked, drawling out the words as insultingly as he could. If the bastard was talking, he wasn't cutting throats or ordering his minions to attack.

"I assure you, they will not have that chance." The priest eyed him, his gaze wandering from Robin's blood-splattered torso down to his rag-wrapped feet. "Nor will you. And I warn you; My Lord takes a particular dislike to those who do not know their place."

"I'm getting a pretty good handle on my proper place, thanks," Robin shot back. "And I think it's entirely reasonable to ask what you intend to do. Let's face it, if you are just going to slit the throat of everyone here after you've had your beastly way with us, what's the point in coming quietly? At least if we fight, we've got a chance."

The priest considered that for a moment, staring at Robin with a look of intense distaste.

"Very well," he said finally. "I am not an unreasonable man. If you and your compatriots answer my questions to my satisfaction and submit your-selves to the rightful dominion of Urkhan, I have no objection in allowing you to go on your way."

Because *that* didn't sound ominous at all. Robin wasn't opposed to a bit of sub/dom play, but he certainly wasn't going to engage in it with this dude or his petty tyrant god.

"How about we just agree to answer your questions truthfully and hon-estly? To 'your satisfaction' is a bit too nebulous a condition to put on an agreement like this," Robin countered.

Lantha, Fiamah, and Grathilde were all staring at him, but he ignored them; he couldn't afford to break his focus away from the cadaverous priest. Ora-Jean was looking at him as well, eyes intense, but if she was trying to tell him something with her body language, he wasn't picking up the message.

"Not good enough," the priest declared. "I don't think you appreciate just which way the balance of power tilts." He pressed the knife ever so slightly into Ora-Jean's throat, drawing a small line of red. "I'm afraid I'm going to have to insist you lay down your weapons and submit to me."

Lantha shifted her weight and flicked her eyes from Robin to Ora-Jean.

Was that a signal? Should he try to keep the priest distracted?

Well, he had already opened his big mouth once.

"Yeah, no. I don't have any weapons, so can't comply with that, and I have no intention of ever submitting to you or Ur-can't-get-it-up, so I won't comply with *that* either." Robin shrugged. "So, sit and spin, asshole."

"You—" the priest choked, purple in his fury. "You *dare*—"

Robin regretted not packing those insults with the power of [**Cutting Words**]. From that reaction, it would definitely have done some extra damage. Ora-Jean flashed him a look, eyes intent. She definitely wanted him to do something.

Frak it.

He opened his mouth to let the priest have it, but before he could say a single word, the old man shrieked out a command at him.

"You will [**Bow**] before the might of Urkhan! I will have you on your knees!"

The words slammed into the roof of his mouth and were lost as Robin literally collapsed to the ground, prostrating himself against his will. He struggled against the impulse, but he felt his mind—his soul?—being crushed in the grip of a merciless fist and dragged downward.

Ora-Jean used the priest's distraction to lash out at the arm controlling the knife at her throat. In a moment she was free and dashing across the cavern to rejoin the rest of the party. The priest spat invective after her.

"You will all submit before me and the will of Urkhan!" he all but howled. "You, kobolds, attack! But I want them alive! I have questions and they will answer, and they will all submit before Urkhan!"

Robin struggled back to his feet. The crushing compulsion had only lasted long enough to force him to kneel; it did nothing to keep him prostrated. His knees screamed in agony, however, from the impact.

Lantha tossed a spare dagger to Ora-Jean. Grathilde's hands began to glow with sky-blue power. Fiamah's mace was the burning glory of the midday sun. And Robin . . . well, Robin was going to have *words* with that unholy wankstain.

If the priest wanted a fight, well, he was going to get one.

Robin awoke to find himself bound hand and foot. The spear of light that knifed into his brain forced him to shut his eyes immediately. The side of his head felt swollen and sticky, and he immediately regretted moving it enough to find out even that much.

Slowly and with great deliberation, he carefully opened his eyes in small increments, reaccustoming himself to the light.

It came from a leaping bonfire. Again.

He was in a cavern full of kobolds. Again.

But this time, he was tied up alongside the rest of the party.

He squinted through the dancing shadows. The other four were all here, and all seemed to be breathing, at least. His memories of the fight were fragmentary at best, but he did recall having his will crushed by the unholy fist of Urkhan multiple times.

He really needed to do something about that. If blanket immunity wasn't an option, there had to be something he could do to up his resistance. Increase his level, probably, and/or his properties. Though he still hadn't figured out how to increase his properties. Quests? A much larger chunk of experience than skills?

Well, not a now problem.

Now, he needed to figure out where he was and how to not be in that place. Preferably with everyone he liked in tow and everyone he didn't far away.

It didn't take long to realize that this was not the same cave the kobolds had occupied before. For one, it was much, much larger. For another, the walls were worked stone, not natural. Robin could even make out some remnants of decorative carving and statuary.

Oh, great. Creepy ruins filled with monsters. Because that will make every-thing better.

Robin shifted in place, trying not to draw attention to himself. From his vantage point, he couldn't see that damn priest anywhere. Not that it meant anything. This place was huge, with several entrances and exits, as well as niches and various other obstructions blocking his view.

He did find Chief Bula, however. What was left of her. Her head was sitting in front of a large wooden chair. It was currently being used as a footrest by the largest kobold Robin had ever seen. Not that he had the largest sample size, but still.

It even had wings! What was with these tunnels and monsters growing wings? Did the magic not realize everyone was underground?

Robin squinted, trying to get a better view. The kobold looked familiar, somehow.

Weird.

"Food!" the winged chief bellowed.

That voice sounded familiar too.

"Food!" another kobold yipped. "Food for Chief Ratscale!"

Ratscale? The grumbly kobold from before? *That* was Ratscale? *What?*

Magic was a trip. Just a frelling trip.

Robin took advantage of the noise and the distraction to flop himself onto his other side. He bit back a yelp of surprise as a pair of eyes met his.

Lantha stared at him.

"Fancy meeting you here." The words slipped out before he could think. The elf did not smile. She did not laugh. No quest points for Robin.

"Quiet," she murmured.

He nodded his head a fraction, indicating he heard and understood. Now that he'd turned over, he had a better sense of his surroundings. They were piled up together against one side of the room—and it was more room than cavern at this point. They occupied a large niche all to themselves.

The stone was wet with moisture, and the detritus piled on every corner had given rise to a surprisingly lush bed of moss and quite a few mushrooms. Robin repressed a shudder at the ones that looked like dead men's fingers clawing up through the soil.

There was no sign of their equipment nearby.

Of course. Even kobolds learned; especially when their zealot of a tutor would probably gut them for failing. Fear of death was a great motivator. The magical compulsion probably didn't hurt either.

Robin wiggled his fingers. He had some range of motion! They'd just lashed his wrists together behind his back, not bound his hands entirely. He flicked his fingers through a quick series of gestures, summoning a tiny [Lesser Phantasm] in front of Lantha's eyes.

Blink twice if you can read these words.

The elf started but then blinked twice, slowly. Was it Robin's imagination, or did he detect just a hint more respect in her gaze?

Do you know where they have brought us? Blink once for no, twice for yes.

Lantha blinked once.

Do you have a plan to get us out of here?

Lantha blinked once. Then she frowned and blinked twice.

Is that a maybe?

Lantha blinked twice.

Robin paused, considered what to ask next. They hadn't bothered to gag any of them. That meant he still had access to [Cutting Words], and while he wouldn't be able to maintain a chained casting of [Lesser Phantasm], he still had access to that as well.

Was Grathilde bound the same way he was? He couldn't see from here without moving his head; he could just make out Fiamah's torso. The holy symbol she usually wore around her neck was missing. Did that make it impossible for her to draw on her goddess-granted gifts? Or did it just make it harder? He couldn't see any other reason to deprive her of it.

No, wait. Being a dick. That would certainly fit with what they'd seen so far from the priest that had captured them.

If it did interfere with divine spellcasting in some way, however, it might be a weapon they could use. Robin tried to recall what, if anything, on the priest's person looked like a holy symbol. There were the markings on his armor.

Damn.

That was too much. Each piece had its own marking, and any of them might serve a purpose or be a decoy or something. So that wasn't immediately useful.

Before he could consider their predicament further, the priest reappeared. Robin couldn't see him, but the old man's voice carried well enough.

"Bring the elf to me. I will interrogate her in the North Chamber."

The kobolds started yipping, and Robin could hear the pitter-patter of their claws over the stone, rushing toward them.

"Pretend you're still out," Lantha whispered quickly, closing her own eyes.

Robin followed suit, not having any better options at hand. He forced himself not to move when he felt the cool pressure of their scales and the sharp prickling of their claws on his chest. They dragged Lantha off, right over him.

And then he was alone again, the sound of blood pounding in his ears.

Chapter 11

*R*obin's eyes stung. The fire was smoky, and for some reason, the size of the room didn't help. The smoke came right for his eyes. The ropes contorting him into unnatural shapes weren't helping either; he felt like his chest was two sizes too small.

He had no idea how long it had been when the kobolds finally dragged Lantha back. Dried blood clung to one corner of her mouth, and she hung limp as they dragged her back to the party. They dumped her unceremoniously next to Robin and departed.

There was no sign of the priest.

"Is she alright?" Fiamah called softly. "I can't reach her."

"Can you heal her if you do?" Robin asked.

"Not as much as I should be able to, but a bit." There was some serious leashed rage in Fiamah's voice. "Can you push her closer to me?"

"I'm fine," Lantha rasped.

Robin paused midwriggle.

"What happened?" Fiamah asked.

Good. Robin had been too afraid to ask. He was still a little afraid to hear.

"What's the priest after?" Ora-Jean asked from somewhere behind Fiamah.

"And why didn't you snap his neck with your feet or something when you had the chance?" Grathilde grumbled from behind Robin.

"Enough," Lantha said before a coughing fit stole the rest of her words. "He's after information. Who we are. Why we're here. I told him we're fortune hunters, in the mountains to hunt rare beasts and prospect for precious metals."

"You did *not* tell him I was a miner!" Grathilde sounded mortally offended.

Robin thought that was kind of missing the point.

More interesting was what Lantha was—and wasn't—saying. She was saying what she told the priest, and she wasn't saying what their actual purpose here was.

"And was he stupid enough to buy any of that?" Robin asked.

Lantha laughed, a creaking sound, dry and mirthless.

Quest Complete! [Laughter is the Best Medicine]

Congratulations! You have elicited not only a smile from each of your new companions but a laugh as well! Never mind some of them were won on technicalities. Winning is winning in this world, and don't you forget it! You have moved yourself firmly from threat to tolerated ally.
Reward: *3 ranks which you may assign in any configuration among Insight, Expression, or Socialize.*

Apparently, that counted. Huh. He hadn't even been trying.

Robin quickly dismissed the notification. Lantha was still talking.

"No, no, he was not." The elf swallowed a bit, trying to get some moisture to her parched throat. "But he couldn't catch me in a lie. Not today, anyway."

"Not enough divine favor remaining," Robin guessed.

"Probably." Lantha shifted, grimacing, until she found a less uncomfortable position. "Which just means he'll be back. After a night's sleep; in a day. Whenever it is, he'll be back, and he'll have a truth spell with him primed and ready to go." Her eyes flicked to Robin. "He also asked about you."

"Me?" A spike of fear stabbed through his heart. "Why me?"

"Because you clearly didn't show up here with us," Lantha said.

"Because you charged in, naked, and rescued us from a cavern full of kobolds and their orcish chieftain," Ora-Jean added.

"Because—" Grathilde started to say.

"I get it! I get the picture!" Robin's voice rose.

The others shushed him, and they all fell silent. When none of the kobolds came over to investigate, they slowly relaxed, and the conversation resumed.

"Does he suspect—" Fiamah started before glancing from Robin to Lantha and falling silent.

Lantha gave Robin a measuring glance. Then, surprisingly, she answered.

"I think he does suspect we were sent here to scout the area and report back, yes." She smiled through a split lip. "But he's not as smart as he thinks. The questions he asked told me more about him and what he wants than my answers told him about me."

Robin hiccupped out a laugh. Seemed like Lantha was finally trusting him. And she had more of a sense of mischief to her than he ever would have suspected. He suddenly wondered what her *Deception* score looked like.

Lantha was coughing. Robin felt a whisper of air flow over him and clear the air around them.

"Thank you, Grathilde," the elf said. "But you should conserve your energies."

The air stopped moving.

"So, who is he and what does he want?" Robin asked. He had the feeling that each of his companions knew a lot more about things than they had let on so far.

"His name is Gis. He may be a priest of Urkhan, but his earthly loyalties lie with a wannabe tyrant called Basgar the Blinder. Basgar has set himself up in a nearby keep that's the only safe way through this mountain range for leagues and leagues in any direction."

Robin was definitely being let in on things now.

"Our mission was to scout the extent of Basgar's forces in the area and the tightness of his grip on the keep, then report back. These mountains are riddled with caverns and tunnels. We were scouting several locations as potential supply drops for future conflict with Basgar when a cave-in dropped us farther down into the cave system and blocked our way out."

"We've wandered down here for ages," Grathilde added morosely.

"In any case," Lantha continued. "We need to find a way to escape as soon as possible. Once Gis has what he wants from us, he'll have no reason to keep us alive." She looked at Robin. "What he wants from you, though, I'm not sure. But whatever it is, he wants it badly. Or his god does. And that cannot be good."

"I think he's looking for the shrine I woke up in when the magical mishap brought me here," Robin admitted slowly. "His god wants to find it."

"Clashes between the gods are no small matter," Fiamah said grimly.

"In any case, if we don't find a way out of here—and soon—none of us will ever see the sky again."

They all fell silent after that. Sleep followed soon after.

* * *

Before falling asleep, Robin had pulled up his interface and invested his quest reward ranks, two in *Insight* and one in *Socialize*. He'd already maxed out *Expression* in the hopes that it would aid with his **[Cutting Words]**, and *Insight* might come in handy trying to suss out Gis's motivations.

Socialize . . . well, he just hated the idea of having a zero in anything. He liked playing skill monkeys, jack-of-all-trades. And the ranks were placement limited anyway.

The kobolds brought them scraps of rancid meat, clearly resenting giving them even that. Robin guessed Gis had left them with orders. However, between the quality of the meat, the whole being-held-prisoners thing, and the likely threat of imminent death, Robin had trouble giving the priest any credit for that bare minimum of effort.

"Tell me about truth spells," he asked when the kobolds had vanished from hearing range once again. "It's not a magic I've encountered in person before. How do they know someone is lying? And can they be fooled? Truth can be a pretty subjective thing, after all."

Fiamah paused to consider. If she had any reservations about telling him how the things worked and potentially undercutting her own spell's usefulness to her in the future, she didn't show it.

"There are almost as many truth spells as there are gods," the cleric spoke, "though most of them follow a similar structure. Usually, there is some kind of outward manifestation when the spell is invoked. Mine, for example, causes the subject to glow. If they speak true, the glow becomes gold; if they lie, it turns red."

"But does it read intent? Or the truth of the words themselves?" Robin was angling, trying to find any useful loopholes or boundaries.

"I am not sure." Fiamah thought. "Possibly both. I was warned at the temple that it is not foolproof, and that half-truths or evasions could, if delivered skillfully enough, slip past the spell. Well, past the cleric invoking it." She slipped him a stern glare. "I was trained extensively in ferreting out such prevarications."

"Well, hopefully whatever priest school Gis went to wasn't as rigorous." That won him a wry laugh.

Robin grinned, in spite of their circumstances. He finally felt like he had allies in this world, beyond a Lost God who barely said anything to him. Honestly, a guy's feelings could get hurt.

The rise in his mood dropped sharply as a group of kobolds appeared, hissing to one another in their reptilian language.

"Priest wants the man one now!"

"Grab ropes! Hold tight!"

"Drag him! Drag him! Is too heavy to carry!"

The kobolds seized Robin in their sharp little claws and dragged him roughly across the ground. He put up just enough struggle to save face; he needed to conserve his energy for Gis.

They dragged him out of the main cavern and into a smaller room, presumably the North Chamber, whatever that was. There was little sign of the room's original purpose left. Trash clogged the corners—mostly dust and fragments of stone.

A low stone bench, crudely assembled out of three rough blocks of unshaped rock, sat on one side of the room. A fine wooden chair with a dusty velvet cushion was placed on the opposite side.

The kobolds muscled Robin into a sitting position on the bench and lashed him into place with more ropes.

"Tight! Tighter! He must not escape!"

There were red stains dotted on the floor beneath his feet. Robin's heart kicked into a higher gear. He was not at all temperamentally suited to withstand torture. Magic, he might be able to trick. But if Gis started cutting into him . . .

Robin shuddered.

That earned him a blow from the nearest kobold.

"No. Move." This time the words were in what Robin was beginning to think of as the common tongue. "No. Move."

"Hit me again, and I'll drop you with three words about your scale maintenance," Robin said politely in German. He held as still as he could. *Larger battles, Robin. Larger battles.*

Once he was trussed up to their satisfaction, the kobolds left him alone in the chamber. Little brats didn't even ask him his safe word before they left.

"It's *shawarmageddon!*" he yelled after them.

He was left alone in the dark with naught but his thoughts for company. It would probably have worked better as a preinterrogation tactic if he wasn't able to see in the dark.

Robin relaxed his arms. He had flexed them as he was being bound to the stone bench, so he had a bit of wriggle room. Not enough to slip out, but he didn't have a plan for escape even if he did. He tried for a small firefly with [Lesser Phantasm] to see if he could cast.

He managed it, but it was painful, and he failed two tries out of three. Before he could make another attempt, he caught the sound of approaching footsteps. Leather on stone, not claws.

Robin slumped into the picture of despondency right before Gis entered the room. He didn't have to fake blinking in the sudden brightness when Gis summoned an aggressively red magelight.

"The mysterious vagabond," Gis said.

His voice slithered up Robin's spine and into his ears. Robin tried to remain sitting stoically, but his heart leapt up another gear.

"My Lord is very interested in you and in what you might know," the priest continued. "Travelers come across so many unexpected places in their journeys, I find."

Oh yeah. He definitely wanted that shrine. Well, Robin wouldn't give it to him.

Probably.

The priest pulled out a dagger and began cleaning his nails with it.

Ok. Maybe. Maybe Robin wouldn't tell him.

Robin was suddenly sweating in the cool underground air.

"Well, let's get started, shall we?"

The priest reached up and lifted the patch covering his left eye.

Robin flinched back from the ragged hollow. He expected only shadows, but two pinpoints of amber light flared in the socket. *Something* moved in the pooled darkness.

What the . . . ?

Robin froze in horrified fascination. The flicker of movement came again. He leaned forward in spite of himself, compelled by some unseen force . . .

. . . and a snake slithered out of the priest's skull, its tongue flashing out of its mouth.

Flick. Flick. Flick.

"It fearsss, massster," the snake hissed. "I can tassste it."

The harp strings that were Robin's nerves snapped, and he began screaming.

Gis laughed.

Chapter 12

*G*is's laughter cut through Robin's horror more surely than the ropes binding him cut into his wrists. It was sharper, for one thing. Though both being laughed at and being bound against his will kindled a spark of anger in Robin.

He seized that spark and fanned it into a small flame, trying to drown out the fear with fury. It sort of worked.

He was still scared as fuck, but he could think through his fear now, at least.

"What do you even want?" he screamed at the priest.

Robin wasn't proud of his delivery, but at least he'd managed to take control of the situation.

"From you? Only one thing. The location of a certain shrine. I'm sure you've seen it, *illusionist*." Gis's smile was running a close second to the snake undulating *in his fucking eye socket* for the most disturbing thing Robin had ever seen.

"I've been in a lot of new places recently, but I don't know if any of them is definitely the shrine you're after," Robin babbled. He was very nearly losing it, but it was a controlled chaos. For now, at least.

The snake flicked out its tongue and tested the air.

"He doesss not lie," it informed reluctantly.

"He has been there!" Gis said intently. "I am certain of it. Our Lord directed me here to find the shrine of that forgotten troublemaker, and now there is a strange traveler stinking of illusion magics? Possibly even touched by the shadow of Rhyth's lost power? No. It's too much to be a coincidence."

You can smell *magic?* That was a new one for Robin. But then again—he glanced at the snake before quickly averting his eyes—that thing seemed to be able to smell or taste lies. So who knew? Brand new world. Brand new rules.

"Quessstion him quickly! Before My Lordsss's grace passsesss from me."

Ah. So it's not an inherent talent. It is some kind of spell, just channeled through the snake? Robin fixated on the details. Anything to keep him from thinking about his position or how utterly frakked this whole situation was.

"Have you been in any place within the last three days that you have reasonable cause to believe might have at one point been a shrine to the Lost God Rhyth, master of illusions and primordial power of shadows?"

"Um. . ." Robin stalled for time to formulate a response. That was a very specific question with looseness in all the wrong places. Fuck! He was going to have to say yes. Or at least, ". . . probably?"

"Truth," the snake whispered.

"Describe the place you are thinking of."

"It was a small cave," Robin began, talking slowly as his brain scrambled for a way to control this situation. "There wasn't much there, except for what might have once been a statue. It was hard to see among the rest of the rock."

So far, so true, though Robin suspected the hard-to-see statue was the result of illusion rather than natural erosion. His brain throbbed with the effort of trying to split focus like this.

Proficiency Unlocked: Concentration.

Of course. Well. That might be useful if he could steal a moment to increase it.

Gis was looking at him. He hurried to continue speaking before the priest got impatient.

"I thought I was trapped there at first, until I discovered an entrance that was covered by some sort of illusion spell. It was strong. I could feel it as well as see it."

"He ssspeaksss true!"

The snake seemed excited.

"Yes! Yes! This must be the place!" Gis crowed.

Did they share moods? They shared a body, so that might be possible. Disturbing AF, but possible.

"Where is it?" Gis demanded.

"I . . ." Robin's jaw worked. He couldn't say! They'd knocked him out before bringing him here. He'd need to be taken back to familiar tunnels to even have a chance. And that gave him an idea.

"I don't know how to get there from here," he said, following quickly with, "but I could probably find my way back from the place you captured us. Or I could try to describe it to you, if you know the area well," he fished for a bit of information.

"No." Gis flicked his fingers. "You will lead us, little shadow. I don't trust the kobolds to know tail from elbow. And the filth has rebelled against their rightful master once already."

The snake coiled around to hiss discreetly in Gis's ear. Robin hadn't thought his hair could stand any more on end, but that took things to new heights.

"Yes, good point, Gehn."

The priest eyed Robin.

"Tell me, did anything happen to you in this shrine that would fit the description of magical or miraculous? Then, after you have answered that question, tell me anything else strange that occurred while you were in that place."

"I was attacked by a swarm of creatures that lived in the stalactites above," Robin replied. "And after I drove them off, the water from the shrine healed me. There were only scratches and a few cuts, but that's definitely magical."

That didn't seem too much to give away. Healing magic was common here. Healing waters couldn't be rare, right?

"Is that why My Lord is so interested in this shrine? It holds another fragment of Rhyth's lost power?" the priest mused to himself.

Robin seized on that. A fragment of lost power? That sounded familiar. He thought of the changes he had been put through upon arrival to this world. And Gis had said *another*, implying there were more.

Was Urkhan trying to seize the power for himself?

Robin felt queasy at the thought. If that was true, it did not bode well for his odds of survival. Hardly the most comforting of insights.

Speaking of insight and other proficiencies, Gis seemed distracted. This might be Robin's only chance to see if he could wring any other advantages out of his recent experiences.

He pulled up his character interface.

Robin Parker

Heritage: Shadeling, Juvenile
Profession: None
Tier: 0
Progress to Tier 1: 38%

Properties

Physical
- -Strength: 11
- -Dexterity: 14
- -Fortitude: 11

Mental
- -Intelligence: 17
- -Cunning: 18
- -Resilience: 14

Social
- -Charisma: 15
- -Manipulation: 13
- -Poise: 15

Proficiencies

Physical (5/9)
- -Athletics: 0
- -???
- -???
- -???
- -???
- -Ranged Combat: 0
- -Sleight of Hand: 1
- -Stealth: 1
- -Survival: 1

Mental (5/9)
- -Arcane Lore: 0
- -???
- -Concentration: 0
- -???
- -???

-Insight: 3
-Learning: 1
-???
-Perception: 1
Social (5/9)
  -???
  -Deception: 4
  -Empathy: 1
  -Expression: 4
  -???
  -???
  -Persuasion: 1
  -Socialize: 1
  -???

Peculiarities

Blessing of Rhyth
Tongue of the Fallen Tower
Mark of the Trickster

There wasn't much he could do. He hadn't garnered enough experience since being captured to alter any of his stats significantly. He could probably raise one of his proficiencies to one, but nothing beyond that.

Not knowing how much longer this interrogation might go, Robin slammed a point into *Concentration*. The quickly becoming familiar feeling of weakness and then power filled his frame.

"Where did you go, little shadow?"

Robin blinked the screen away only to find Gis's face thrust right up in front of his. The snake could have flicked out its tongue and licked Robin's left eyeball.

He jerked back. Gis laughed, and the snake hissed an echo of that amusement.

"Your attention went elsewhere. I'm not used to such distractions when I'm interrogating someone. You seemed to be reading something in the air. What did you see?"

Gis's eyes glittered in the sanguine light. Robin's heart hammered in his chest. The priest had noticed him checking his status screen!

Then something else occurred to him.

Yes, Gis had noticed, but he hadn't seemed to recognize the action. If a character interface like Robin's were common in this world, surely a person of Gis's station would be familiar with it.

"What visions are you seeing? You cannot trust them, you know. Rhyth was driven out and destroyed for a very good reason. Illusions," Gis spat, "Trickery. Lies. You cannot trust what you see, little shadow."

Robin needed a plausible lie, and fast.

Deception, *don't fail me now!*

"It's just"—he swallowed for dramatic effect—"I don't know what I'm seeing; not really. Sometimes I see shadows"—*shadows* being a completely acceptable Shakespearean turn of phrase for illusions—"and they move in ways I don't understand." He certainly didn't understand his interface or how the numbers "moved" up. "I wish I understood, I really do, but I don't, so I can't tell you exactly what you want to know."

The snake flicked its tongue out. There was a long pause while Robin's heart nearly stuttered out of his chest.

"Truth," the snake said finally, but it didn't look happy about it. "Thisss one is near the breaking point. We will get nothing more of ussse out of him."

"That's quite alright, Gehn. We have what we need. Soon, our little shadow here will lead us to the shrine, and we can dispense with this tedious pilgrimage beneath the ground."

The priest rose.

The snake withdrew back into his eye socket, and Gis affixed his eye patch once more in place. Then he called for the kobolds, and Robin was returned to the main cavern and the rest of the party.

They waited just long enough for the kobolds to depart before interrogating him in low tones.

"Anything useful?" Lantha asked.

"Did you manage to draw any blood?" Ora-Jean demanded.

"Never mind that, just tell us what happened." Grathilde was trussed up behind him, but she slammed her shoulder into his back imperiously.

"I saw what was behind his eye patch."

Robin shuddered.

"What was it?" the dwarf asked in horrified fascination.

"You do not want to know," Lantha said firmly.

"But—"

"You really don't," Robin agreed. Then, to cut off further conversation: "I have a plan."

That quieted even Grathilde.

He explained his intent to the rest of the party, making use of [**Lesser Phantasm**] when possible to make sure they were not overheard. Naturally, there was some skepticism expressed.

"Do you have a better idea?" Robin asked. "Lay it on me, and I will happily cede the floor. *But*"—he stressed the syllable—"if you don't, I say we go all in. We're outnumbered, at a distinct disadvantage in terms of armament, and there is no way Gis or his pets have any intention of letting us live after that priest gets what he wants."

No one had an answer to that.

"Right. In that case." Robin gestured toward the nearby mushrooms with his chin. "Do any of you know which of those aren't poisonous?"

"Don't look at me," Grathilde said instantly. "Just because we both grew up underground doesn't mean we know one another."

Robin snorted. It wasn't the best joke, but he'd take it. He needed a laugh after his meeting with Gis.

Fiamah, for her part, fell into lecture mode. Robin was happy to listen, happier when her words triggered another notification.

Proficiency Unlocked: Natural Wisdom.

"None of them are terribly nutritious," Fiamah concluded. "Which I suspect is why they are still growing here. The kobolds would have snapped them up otherwise, for Gis if not for themselves."

"As long as they aren't toxic to the touch, I'm happy. I just hope I can work well enough with just my hands." He grimaced.

Proficiency Unlocked: Crafting.

Of course. And here he was with no experience points left to invest. Perfect.

Still, he had a plan. It might even work.

New Quest: [Grasp of the Tyrant Priest]

You have a plan to escape the grasp of Gis, Priest of Urkhan. Successfully execute this plan, save your newfound friends, and don't die in the inevitable chaos. Good luck!

Reward: *Isn't escaping with your life reward enough? Well, for those of you who are greedy enough that it isn't, successful completion of this quest will also award +3 proficiency ranks and +1 property rank.*

"Why are you smiling?" Grathilde asked.

"I've got a good feeling about this," he replied. "I feel like someone or something is watching out for us."

Now he'd best get to work before Gis got the kobolds to round them up and drag them back to the tunnels where they had been captured.

Chapter 13

Robin marched through the tunnels, Gis to one side of him, and an overly jabby kobold with a spear occasionally prodding him from behind.

That was decidedly not a privilege the little monster had earned.

"How much farther?" the priest demanded of the kobolds ranging ahead of them.

"Not far! Not far!" the lead scout called back.

"That's what you said ten minutes ago! Lie again, and I will feed you feetfirst to your chieftain," Gis threatened.

The kobold behind Robin jabbed him in the ass again. Robin took advantage of Gis's distraction to glare over his shoulder and hiss at the scaly frakker in the kobold tongue.

"You jab me one more time with that little stick of yours, and I will jam it so far up your cloaca, you'll think you're being spit-roasted by trolls."

Proficiency Unlocked: Intimidation.

The kobold meeped and shouldered the spear immediately. Robin dismissed the prompt, squinted out one more glare, and returned his attention to the tunnel in front of him.

They were close; he recognized that bifurcated stalagmite. Robin shot a glance along the group. Several kobolds marched between each of Robin's allies, keeping them all separate. Robin would have to time things carefully if they were going to have a chance to break free again.

Lantha caught his gaze and nodded once, a quick, sharp gesture. They were ready.

Gis was muttering to himself, distracted. Robin took the opportunity to slip a pair of earplugs he'd made from scavenged moss and mushrooms into place. The cavern he needed was just ahead.

"There," Robin said, gesturing with his still-bound hands. "We need to go through that cavern there."

The words were distant, hollow, heard more through the vibrations in his chest than through his ears. The spongy mushrooms were surprisingly good at canceling noise.

Gis barked a command to the leading scouts, who scurried forward. The rest of the group followed, not even slowing their pace.

The smell of the cavern rose up around them: aged jockstraps and rotten food.

Robin suddenly wished his vision were slightly less excellent. Some of the trash scattered among the stalagmites around the edges of the cavern was alive with maggots. If these goblins were anything like the ones in D&D, they were probably an additional food source. Or maybe the harpies considered them a breakfast delicacy; early birds and worms and all that.

Never mind. Robin shook the thoughts from his head. It was time.

Robin twisted his hands through the gestures that would summon a [Lesser Phantasm]. He failed. The bindings around his wrists were still making things difficult.

He tried again, and this time, he managed it.

An eerie flute melody (if one was feeling generous enough to call it that) echoed out through the shadows. The kobolds froze while Gis shot glances around the cavern. Nothing moved, but the series of notes replayed themselves.

The priest must not spend a lot of time underground, or he had so much power that he could afford *not* to pay full attention to his surroundings. He didn't look up to see the rustling of the winged goblins among the stalactites above them.

Robin gestured, and the melody sounded again. This time, it was answered by the cries of the harpies from their roost near the ceiling of the cavern.

"What is that noise?" Gis demanded.

"Goblins!" Robin whispered, putting on a terrified face as he pulled out every trick his *Deception* skill had to offer and prayed to Rhyth for all he was worth. "We heard that noise just before they attacked us last time. We need to get across the cavern, and fast, before they come out of one of these tunnels!"

The priest, already primed to follow Robin's directions to the shrine, accepted the directive without question. He shouted the order to the kobolds, and the party began to dash across the cavern.

The harpies appeared before they were halfway across. Robin twisted his hands through the gestures for [Lesser Phantasm], and a disembodied male voice echoed throughout the cavern in the language of the harpies.

"Bow before the Chosen One of Urkhan, beasts!"

The harpies shrieked in rage. Robin twisted his fingers again, and the symbol on Gis's chest plate glowed, painting him a very obvious target.

"Sisters! Sing!" one of the harpies called. "Sons, wake and take the kobold scum!"

The harpies began to sing as the winged goblins roosting among the stalactites shouted and dropped from their perches. Most of the kobolds were immediately ensnared by the harpies' enthralling voices, their faces going slack and the spears in their hands clattering to the floor.

Robin and his allies, the Sisters Sharp, seized the opportunity and all darted toward the right-hand side of the cavern, protected by the earplugs Robin had made for each of them from mushrooms and moss.

The winged goblins were darting down and snatching up the mesmerized kobolds, carrying them dozens of feet into the air and dropping them as soon as they began to struggle, usually on other kobolds.

Gis shouted, and his gauntlets began to glow with an eye-searing red light. One of the harpies, frustrated her song was being so easily shrugged off by the priest, made the mistake of swooping down at him.

Gis lashed out with one hand, grabbing the harpy by the neck. Her song was choked out of existence as she struggled wildly, the priest just tightening his grip on her throat while the other harpies wailed in distress.

"Sons of ours! The priest! Attack the priest who dares lay hands on us!"

The goblins began swooping around the priest. However, there were too many of them to attack effectively, and the harpy in Gis's grip was an effective shield.

We need to get out of here. Now. Robin flashed the words in front of the party's eyes with [Lesser Phantasm].

Lantha nodded in agreement, and her hands flashed through several signs.

The others nodded, and Robin bit his cheek in frustration. He had no idea what she was saying.

Ora-Jean noticed. She caught Robin's gaze and pointed sharply toward a tunnel leading out of the cavern. It was several dozen paces away and partially shielded by some stalagmites.

Robin bobbed his head, his neck flaring with spikes of adrenaline. To get to that exit, they would have to pass dangerously close to the battle. Not much for it, though. There were only a few ways out of this place.

He shot a glance over at the chaos.

Half of the kobolds were either dead or lying on the floor suffering from broken bones and worse. A few had broken free of the mesmerizing harpy song and were attempting to stab the winged goblins with their spears with limited success.

Most of the harpies remained flying out of range.

"Enough of this!" Gis had clearly figured out which of the harpies was calling the shots. The one who had attacked him was crumpled in a heap at his feet, her neck twisted in an unnatural angle. The priest reached an open hand out toward the leader and then clenched it into a fist as he muttered dark and unholy syllables.

Spiked chains of glowing red light materialized around her. She shrieked in distress, and the sisters nearest to her immediately tried to pull the chains off.

The whole battle descended into further chaos. Without the harpies directing them, the winged goblins were noticeably less effective.

Lantha gestured frantically, and the party moved more quickly toward the exit among the stalagmites. Before they made it halfway, however, one of the kobolds spotted them and yipped out in alarm.

"No!" Gis shouted. "Stop them! I need that bard to lead the way to Rhyth's shrine!"

The kobolds attempted to comply with the order, but too few were left alive and too many were tangled up in holding off the winged goblins.

"Freeze!" Gis shouted.

Lantha stopped midstride and almost fell over while the others paused, confused. Lantha shook off the effect in a few seconds, but their momentum had been arrested.

The elf jerked her head toward the tunnel, and the group started moving again.

"Bow! Stop! Halt!" Gis called out spelled word after spelled word. Some of them worked; most did not. The earplugs were helping.

Some detached part of Robin's mind which occupied a space near that section of his brain which handled strategy gaming wondered if the spells got through because Gis was more powerful than the harpies, or if it was just bad luck. Not that he wanted to stick around long enough to test any theories.

"I said *halt!*" Gis's voice lashed out across the cavern and froze Robin in his tracks.

What was that? [Command]? [Inviolate Order]? Robin hissed in frustration. How many times could that farquad use whatever ability that was, anyway?

They were never going to make it out of here if the priest kept halting their movements like this. Either the harpies would notice them or the kobolds would organize enough to come after them. The party had managed to grasp some crude spears, but they were sized for kobolds and not the greatest of weapons at the best of times.

Robin needed to do something to distract the priest so they could get away. Illusions were probably out. That left trickery or magical rage-inducing insults. Robin knew which one he preferred to use right now.

Resolutely, he caught Gis's gaze and took a single mocking step. The priest really shouldn't be so focused on him. There were still harpies and winged goblins nearby, even if they were temporarily distracted.

Maybe Gis needed some extra distraction.

"Hey! You! Unholy lickspittle!" Robin shouted, putting the full force of his staggered wit into his [Cutting Words]. "Is failure one of the profane rites of Urkhan, or are you honestly just this useless?"

The priest wavered from the impact of the words. He turned his full attention to Robin, hatred vibrating in every muscle of his face. The harpies took advantage of the distraction to redouble their efforts to free their leader.

The chains of red light began to flicker but did not vanish.

Robin couldn't resist taking one more shot.

"You know, they say that priesthood is a divine calling, but I think in your case, Urkhan had the wrong person answer." He followed the words with an insulting gesture for good measure.

Gis's eyes bulged in fury, and he turned a shade of red that nearly matched the unholy light seeping from his gauntlets. Robin's insult had definitely hit with extra force; enough that Gis no longer cared about taking Robin alive to guide him to the shrine.

The priest of Urkhan spat out a spell, and a sharp sound cracked above the party's heads.

A massive stalactite, sundered at the base, plummeted down toward them. Robin and the Sisters Sharp dove out of the way, narrowly escaping impalement.

It slammed into the stone floor of the cavern instead, and there was another, louder *crack*.

Proficiency Unlocked: Dodge.

Robin willed the notification out of his view even as the floor crumbled beneath their feet, stone falling into empty darkness. Robin tried to jump, but the stone under his feet provided nothing to push off from. It was already plummeting into the depths below.

Screaming, Robin, the Sisters Sharp, and one or two kobolds tumbled down as the darkness swallowed them whole.

Chapter 14

Robin groaned as he awoke, something sharp and rough digging into his back. His skin felt gritty and chalky, and his nose was full of dust. Opening his eyes, he found himself atop a large pile of stone and rubble. There was also an update waiting for him.

Quest Complete! [Grasp of the Tyrant Priest]

Congratulations! Your plan to escape the grasp of Gis, Priest of Urkhan, has been successfully executed. Complications notwithstanding. Neither you nor your new friends died! Result!
Reward: *Not only are you breathing and unbroken, you have +3 proficiency ranks and +1 property rank to assign! Yay you!*

Robin blinked the message away. Right. Gis. The stalactite. The collapse. The *fall*. Wait.

How did he survive the fall?

He prodded himself gently, shifting atop the stones. He barely even felt bruised! He should have several broken bones at a minimum, and he had the sneaking suspicion that he should rightly be very, very dead.

This creeping certainty was only confirmed when he spotted a nearby kobold. It was quite dead, nearly pulped by its impact on the stones.

He blinked.

Right now, his ability to see in the dark was definitely hitting double-edged-sword territory.

"La-Lantha?" He coughed the dust out of his mouth and tried again, louder. "Lantha? Fiamah? Grathilde? Ora-Jean?"

"Here," a voice came groaning out of the shadows. Grathilde. "I'm over here. Ora-Jean's here as well, but she hasn't woken up yet."

"How are we even still alive to wake up?"

"You're welcome," Grathilde replied despondently. "I used the last of the power I had stored the last time we nearly got out of this *zanagorov* tunnel complex."

"Ah," Robin said, as if that made everything perfectly clear. Which it did not.

"Air magic," Grathilde clarified gruffly. "I made us all light as feathers, and we drifted down. I didn't have enough power to fly us all to safety, so this was the best I could do."

"And you did excellently," Lantha spoke, appearing from around a chunk of stone the size of a minivan. Fiamah was with her.

"Tater!" Ora-Jean awoke with a scream.

"It's all right; it's all right," Grathilde comforted her. "Taterpicker is fine. You're fine. We're all fine." Then her voice cracked. "We're trapped hundreds of feet deeper under the goddess-forsaken ground, but we're *fine*."

"Maybe we can climb out," Robin suggested hopefully.

"Unlikely," Grathilde said sourly. "Lantha? Magelight up there?"

The elf looked surprised at Grathilde's commanding tone, but she nonetheless cast a ball of glowing light up above their heads. It drifted up . . . and up . . . and up, until it came to a rest at what Robin guessed was the edge of Lantha's range. It was several hundred feet.

There was no sign of the ceiling. No sign even of the edges of the hole they'd fallen through. The ethereal light played across the walls, slick with damp and heart-stoppingly smooth.

"Ah. Not climbing out, then," Robin noted. He swallowed.

"We're stuck down here," Grathilde continued bitterly. "After everything I did to get out, now I'm going to die in a *zanagorov* cave."

"We don't know that." The words came, surprisingly, soft and firm from Lantha. "Come on, get up. You've saved us. Let's see where we are. We'll find a way out."

Grathilde grumbled but rose to her feet. Together, they began to search the area. They found a lot of stone, three dead kobolds, two intact spears, three small daggers, and a lot of blood and guts and viscera.

They also found tunnels leading out of the cavern. Six of them. Each led in a different direction, not that there was an easy way to tell which direction was which down here.

"Wait, look at this." Robin knelt at the entrance of one of the tunnels. "This stone, it's been squared off. It looks like the chunk of brick or whatever we found farther up in the caverns."

"Let me see." Fiamah knelt down next to him. She ran her fingers along the faint groove Robin had spotted. "He's right. It's definitely been worked. And it does feel similar to—" She broke off and glanced at Lantha.

"To Ssathessti work?" Robin finished for her, remembering the name both from something one of the others had said earlier and from the quest prompt he'd been given. "That's one of the things you were supposed to be scouting for, wasn't it?"

He crossed his arms and leveled a challenging stare at Lantha. He'd rescued them from captivity twice now. If he didn't get some trust out of that—

"It was. It is," Lantha said.

Robin blinked. That . . . that was not the answer he'd expected. He'd been expecting her to be cagey and evasive and—and she was saying more!

"We're part of the White Star Company, operating under the auspices of the Adventurer's Guild of Noviel," the elf was saying.

Noviel? Was that a city or a country? An empire? No. Surely, she'd have called it "the Empire" if it was an empire, right?

"You already know we're scouting the area. We're also looking for signs of Ssathessti ruins in these mountains. It has to do with a bunch of incredibly tedious elvish politics—"

"And theological and academic funding at the University," Fiamah added.

"—and the possibility of recovering useful magical artifacts vital to Noviel's defense efforts. Now that a petty tyrant has seized the keep—" Lantha outlined the politics of the situation.

Robin followed as best he could. There were a lot of names, but the upshot seemed to be that someone Lantha's country or city didn't like now controlled the main trade route through the mountains, and there was likely a small war on the horizon. Made sense, with what he'd seen of Gis and Urkhan.

"Let's see where this tunnel takes us then," he said when Lantha had finished. "We're here. Looks like Ssathessti ruins—who were they again?" He risked the question.

"Elves," Grathilde said at the same time Lantha spat out, "Serpents!"

"A lost people," Fiamah replied more diplomatically.

"Not so much lost," Ora-Jean muttered. "You can find them if you go deep enough."

"I was speaking theologically," Fiamah said.

"Aren't you always?" Grathilde teased.

"Right," Robin added, still lost.

"They were a group of elves that fell into the worship of a primordial serpent goddess near the dawn of time," Lantha explained flatly. "There was a war. Nations were torn apart. The Ssathessti fled or were forced underground. Some of them still look like elves, some look part serpent, part elf."

"There's still a bit of a grudge between the two peoples," Fiamah murmured to Robin.

"Ah. Gotcha." Robin cleared his throat. "Well, that tunnel isn't just going to explore itself. Let's go!" Hopefully, they wouldn't run into any living examples of Ssathessti culture. His nerves were *not* up to it.

The party geared up as best they could and proceeded down the tunnel. After all, they had limited options. Ora-Jean scouted ahead as Lantha and Fiamah examined the stonework. Grathilde stumbled along, muttering darkly. Robin followed the others' lead and left her to herself for a bit.

As they moved cautiously through the tunnels, more and more of the stonework revealed itself. It was fascinating. The cuts were made in a spade-like pattern reminiscent of scales and fitted together in sinuous curves and swerves. After Ora-Jean led them along several forks in the way, she called out from ahead.

"Found something!"

The halfling led them through an entrance shaped like the mouth of a massive serpent into the ruins of some kind of living complex. It was hard for Robin to get a sense of the size of it, but it felt like an outpost of some kind, maybe the size of a small keep? It was certainly bigger than a house, bigger than the English Department building at the university.

The flowing and curving nature of the architecture remained unchanged. It made exploring the hallways more stressful, as it cut down on sight lines.

"There aren't any torches or light sources in the walls," he observed.

"All elves are born with an innate connection to magic," Fiamah explained. "They likely could all see in the dark or conjure light like Lantha is doing."

"Those designs there would have been regularly enchanted with fairy fire," Lantha added sourly, pointing to a looping, interlaced serpentine design near the ceiling. "That would have provided what little light they needed."

"Why not a permanent enchantment?" Robin asked. Maybe he could get some more hints on how magic worked.

"Too expensive," Fiamah answered.

"They wouldn't use something like that here," Lantha agreed. "This is clearly an outpost. Permanent enchantments for light, movement between levels, and timekeeping would be reserved for larger settlements."

"Hey, Grathilde," Ora-Jean called. "I think I've found a kitchen or a mess hall." The halfling was clearly trying to nudge the dwarf out of her despondency. "Help me search. There might be some knives or bags or something useful left behind."

The room was a mess. There were signs of hasty departure, but they were covered by a thick layer of dust. A large crop of mushrooms sprouted from what Robin could only assume were the ruins of some sort of food storage cabinet or niche.

"Food," Ora-Jean noted. "And we're not the only ones who have been here recently. Look!" She pointed out scuffs in the dust and a few places where the small forest of mushrooms exploding out of the wall had been thinned out.

"How recent?" Lantha asked, suddenly tense.

"Several weeks, a few months," the halfling replied after a long moment. "Not dangerously recent."

Grathilde suddenly pounced on something, scrabbling in the shadows beneath a long shelf of stone. After a few moments, she hauled herself back up, covered in dust and clutching a carved wooden spoon.

"Magic," she said.

"Is that—" Fiamah stepped closer.

"Get me a bowl and let's find out," Grathilde replied.

Ora-Jean was already there, placing a small, cracked cauldron or kettle on the surface in front of the dwarf. Grathilde placed the spoon in the cauldron and waited. Almost immediately, the pot began to fill with a thick, hearty-looking porridge.

"Thank Wenser," Ora-Jean said fervently. "We've got food!"

"And several knives," Lantha added, adjusting her belt.

Robin deliberately didn't add that they also had mushrooms. Porridge—even sketchy, magical snake porridge—had to be better than mushrooms.

Grathilde stuck a finger into her meal and raised it to her lips.

"Well?" Ora-Jean asked.

"Bland. But it's hearty. It'll keep us going." The dwarf sighed, but there was relief in the sound.

Robin stepped in for a closer look at the spoon. It was carved wood with a design on the handle, somewhat like a figure eight and somewhat like a snake with its tail in its mouth. *Makes sense. Fits with the general aesthetics of the place.*

Quest Complete! [Below Ground and Between the Shadows]

Congratulations! You have confirmed the presence of the Ssathessti ruins and artifacts in the caverns beneath the Dragonspine Mountains. You have also uncovered why the **Sisters Sharp** *adventuring party are interested in them.* ***Reward:*** *+1 Arcane Lore; 1 undetermined minor magical item (No, it's not the spoon; keep your eyes open.).* ***Bonus Reward:*** *You got that knowledge I promised you, didn't you?*

The boost to his *Arcane Lore* flowed into Robin's mind. Huh. Magical objects suddenly made a modicum more sense.

"Robin, Fiamah, harvest as many mushrooms as you can fit in this sack." Lantha tossed a creaky leather satchel at them. Most of the dust had been wiped off. "Ora-Jean, see if you can follow those tracks. I want to make sure we're actually alone down here."

"Come on, Taterpicker," Ora-Jean said to the air as she headed back out into the tunnels.

Robin could make out a few hints of the tracks she had mentioned, but his proficiencies were nowhere near high enough to allow him to follow the faint traces as Ora-Jean was doing. Or as Taterpicker was doing—not sure who was the better tracker there.

He set to filling the bag with mushrooms. Lantha even provided him with one of the knives she'd scavenged. Robin almost didn't know how to react, having this much trust shown to him by the cagey elf.

He and Fiamah had already finished their harvest and were helping Grathilde check the large storage amphorae when Ora-Jean returned. Well, stuck her head through the entryway and called for their attention.

"What is it?" Lantha asked, her body suddenly tense.

"Just follow me. You're going to want to see this." Ora-Jean's head disappeared.

Lantha jerked her chin at the exit, and the group headed out after the halfling and her badger spirit. They trailed Ora-Jean through several corridors and three rooms before she slowed and pointed ahead.

"I found our mushroom picker. What's left of them is just in here."

Lantha stepped cautiously into the room, followed by the others. What its original purpose had been was obscured by time and the fact that someone had been using it as a campsite. There were old and dusty signs of a cook fire, a couple packs, a bedroll, and a tangle of bones that almost certainly had been the camper in question.

"Looks like an explorer, from those clothes," Fiamah observed.

Lantha grunted in agreement. She crouched down near the remains.

"Grathilde, check the packs for anything useful. Fiamah, can you sense any residual spirits nearby that might be hostile? Ora-Jean, check the perimeter for me. Robin, see if you can find anything else unusual."

Huh. Responsibility too! Will wonders never cease? He stepped out of the way of the others and began poking around the room. It wasn't large, but it wasn't terribly small, either. Still, most of it was dust, detritus, mushrooms, and . . . hang on!

Robin blinked. Were there small, blue sparkles coming from that scrap of shadow near the wall?

While the others were examining the bones, he stepped closer. There was something here! It looked like a domino mask, not dissimilar to those worn by superheroes.

The black leather was surprisingly supple and entirely clean and free of dust. Robin ran through the *Arcane Lore* in his mind. Masks were often enchanted with spells of concealment or illusion.

That was certainly a familiar theme.

No one else had seen the sparkles. Was this what the quest prompt had meant? Not that it could be bothered to give him confirmation if it was.

The paranoid tabletop role player in him screamed that he should drop it. It had to be cursed—or a face-eating mini mimic. But something else inside of him recognized a kindred spirit, almost. It felt similar to the feeling he'd gotten when the Elvish God of Mischief had marked him.

Fuck it. Sometimes you just have to trust your gut. Robin put on the mask.

The leather was cool on his face, and it adhered in place as if it had been made for him. Maybe it had. *The deities work in mysterious ways, right?*

A notification popped into Robin's view, but before he could read it, Ora-Jean called for everyone's attention.

"That's not the only thing, though. Lantha, can you bring your light closer to the wall?"

The elf did so, and the party went silent as they beheld what was scrawled across it in rough, red-brown letters.

WATCH THE SHADOWS

"Looks like whoever this was wrote that message with their own blood right before they died." Ora-Jean glanced around the party.

Well, that's *not ominous at all.*

Chapter 15

Robin stared at the bloody words written on the wall. The shadows? That wasn't ominous at all. But had he meant literal shadows or illusions?

"Wounds?" Lantha was asking Ora-Jean.

"None. I can't see what killed him. Might have been poison. Might have been magic. He certainly didn't starve to death." She nodded toward a satchel full of desiccated mushrooms.

"Fiamah, Grathilde, grab the packs. Robin, grab anything else you can find that looks useful. Ora-Jean and I will take a closer look at the body."

"And whatever loot those bones have left on 'em," Grathilde pointed out.

"You'll get your fair share, never you fear," Ora-Jean said with a little heat.

"Focus!" Lantha snapped. "I want this done and us out of here as soon as possible. We need to find a secure place to camp."

Robin noticed she hadn't said a *safe* place to camp. He shoved the thought aside and set to his job. The sooner they were done, the sooner they could hole up someplace to eat and rest. He found a moderate pile of dried mushrooms, possibly used to fuel a cook fire, but not much else.

He wished he had a jacket. It wasn't cold, per se, but the ever-present chill was wearing on him. A bit of protection for all his exposed skin wouldn't be unwelcome either.

No sooner had he had the thought than he felt a cool tingle around his eyes. The next thing he knew, he was wearing a full-length black trench coat. Full-on *Matrix* realness.

"Whoa."

"What's that, Robin?" Grathilde asked, glancing over. "Where did you find *that*?"

"You can see it too?" Robin twisted into a half spin, feeling the hem of the coat flare out around him. It was a lot lighter than he expected.

He shivered.

And not quite as warm.

"Of course we can see it," Grathilde said. "At least you've covered up." She was squinting at the coat with an appraising look in her eye.

"Robin found it, he should keep it," Fiamah said firmly. "He needs it more than any of us do."

"Agreed," Lantha replied absently.

Ora-Jean waved absent assent. She was carefully prodding a ring still resting around the skeleton's finger.

"Fine," Grathilde grumbled. "Fiamah and I have the packs; Robin found some fuel. Are you two ready? I want a hot meal and some sleep. I, like the sorcerous energies at my command, am exhausted."

"Got it!" Ora-Jean crowed triumphantly. "We're good to go. I think I've got everything of use that is smart to take with us."

Robin glanced over. They'd stripped the skeleton bare, leaving only the bones. He suddenly realized that if Ora-Jean had thought it safe, she would have looted those as well.

"Right. Let's move out. We still need to find a defensible position."

Lantha stood, gesturing for Grathilde and Fiamah to shoulder the packs they had scavenged. Robin was left to carry the mushrooms, fresh *and* dried. Deep joy.

After about an hour of searching, Lantha pronounced herself satisfied with a medium-size room they found. It was rounded, as most of the architecture here was, but it had two ways in and out, each with a door they could close for defense.

"No fire," the elf said. "The ventilation is too poor, and I don't want the smoke drawing something down on us."

Robin was suddenly very glad for his mystery coat. Hopefully it wasn't eating his soul in exchange for the small bit of insulation it provided. He carefully prodded the mask around his eyes with a cautious finger. No one had commented on it, but he could feel it was still there.

Odd.

"Ora-Jean, scout down the tunnel opposite the way we arrived," Lantha ordered. "Grathilde, get things ready for dinner. Fiamah and Robin are going to watch the doors. I'll start sharpening the knives."

Everyone got to work, though no one moved quickly. They needed a meal and some sleep. It had not been a restful few days for any of them.

Robin sat with his back to the door. He cocked his head in an attentive pose, as if he was listening, but instead, he brought up his interface. He had free ranks to assign, and he didn't want to put it off any longer.

Or did he?

It clearly cost more experience the higher he raised his proficiencies, and he'd bet the same held true for properties. These free ranks could save him a lot of experience if he banked them until he had bought the lower ranks.

He pulled up his current character sheet as he pondered.

Robin Parker

Heritage: Shadeling, Juvenile
Profession: None
Tier: 0
Progress to Tier 1: 64%

Properties

(Free Ranks Available: 1)

Physical
   -Strength: 11
   -Dexterity: 14
   -Fortitude: 11
Mental
   -Intelligence: 17
   -Cunning: 18
   -Resilience: 14
Social
   -Charisma: 15
   -Manipulation: 13
   -Poise: 15

Proficiencies

(Free Ranks Available: 3)

Physical (6/9)
   -Athletics: 0

-???
-Dodge: 0
-???
-???
-Ranged Combat: 0
-Sleight of Hand: 1
-Stealth: 1
-Survival: 1
Mental (7/9)
-Arcane Lore: 1
-???
-Concentration: 1
-Crafting: 0
-???
-Insight: 3
-Learning: 1
-Natural Wisdom: 0
-Perception: 1
Social (6/9)
-???
-Deception: 4
-Empathy: 1
-Expression: 4
-???
-Intimidation: 0
-Persuasion: 1
-Socialize: 1
-???

Peculiarities

Blessing of Rhyth
Tongue of the Fallen Tower
Mark of the Trickster

He was getting close to a new level, if his theory on how progression worked was correct. There were still eight proficiencies, at least, that he hadn't yet unlocked. Several that he did have still didn't have a single rank.

After a moment's thought, Robin raised *Athletics*, *Dodge*, and *Crafting* to one with experience. He'd used all of those recently; they would likely come in handy again before they made their way out of these caverns.

He left his free ranks alone for now.

Still well above fifty percent of the way to Tier One. Robin bit his lip in thought. He didn't want to put off the next level too long; he wanted another peculiarity. But leaving his skills—his proficiencies—low to get there didn't seem like the smartest idea. Especially if gaining a level left him with little experience to invest in improving himself. And he had to *survive* to that next level.

Split the difference? Yeah. That feels good.

Which skills were the most likely to help keep him alive? *Deception*, certainly, but it was already capped until he leveled up. Short list was probably *Dodge*, *Stealth*, and *Perception*. Ora-Jean was a better tracker, so he could probably leave *Survival* for the moment. And if worse came to worse, he did have those three free ranks in the bank.

Before he could change his mind, Robin raised *Dodge*, *Stealth*, and *Perception* each to four. That brought him down to the low-to-mid 40 percent range. Good enough for now.

Robin poked around his interface a bit more. He'd already found his spells, and while there wasn't an inventory which allowed him free storage, he was hoping somewhere—aha! A list of personal equipment. It was almost like it appeared once he needed it.

Robin stowed his suspicions as to why *that* was. There was a magical item to investigate first!

[Mask of Disguise]
Status: *Bound to Robin Parker*

This rare domino mask is enchanted with shadow and illusion magic, and it bears a whisper of the Lost God Rhyth's power. Anyone who wears this mask may use it to garb themselves in the illusory raiment of their choice. This ability may be used at will.

When bound to an individual bearing the **[Blessing of Rhyth]** *or the* **[Mark of the Trickster]***, the mask's abilities are enhanced in the following ways:*

-Illusory raiment conjured by the mask's power gains demireality, to a degree equivalent to the wearer's own power over shadow manifestations.

-The illusion may extend to the body and form of the wearer as well, allowing them to take on the appearance of others. This may be a specific individual or a generic example of a given people or species. This effect is limited to the same general size category as the wearer of the mask.

Huh. That explained a lot about his new coat; it was actually his new mask. Oh, he was going to have *fun* with this!

Robin bit back a smile. Just to test it out, he willed the accent threads on his coat to red, then green, then a rich, royal blue.

Out of curiosity, Robin poked at the entries for the other items in his possession, but nothing was available on them. Either the interface only worked on magical items, or it only worked because the mask was somehow bound to Robin.

The paranoid tabletopper in his head shrieked at him again.

"Robin," Lantha called. "Ora-Jean's back. Why don't you and Fiamah get some food with her while Grathilde and I take a turn watching the doors?"

Food? Yes, please and thank you! Robin rose to his feet and made his way toward the center of their little camp. As he went, he tried to conjure himself the illusion of rag-sandals, like he'd made himself, but with a proper sole. It helped a bit!

Fiamah handed him a bowl full of hearty porridge when he got close enough. He sat cross-legged around one of Lantha's magelights with Ora-Jean and the cleric. They didn't have utensils as such. Ora-Jean was using a dried mushroom to scoop her porridge into her mouth, while Robin opted to go with his fingers.

It was porridge. Thick and hearty and warm, but completely bland. No berries, no cream, no nuts, no nothing. But very easy to eat. Well, aside from the whole scooping-with-his-fingers thing.

Robin quickly licked them clean. He wanted to try something and didn't want porridge to fly everywhere when he flicked his fingers. He passed through the motions of [**Lesser Phantasm**] and focused on what he wanted the porridge to taste like.

Quickly, as the spell would only last about twelve seconds, he scooped up another bite. This time, the taste of strawberries and sweet cream filled his mouth. *Oh yeah.* That was the stuff.

Robin groaned in appreciation. Ora-Jean looked at him askance; Fiamah had the manners not to, but Robin could tell she was similarly curious.

"Magic," he said after swallowing. "How do you like your porridge?" He cleaned his fingers again.

"With crushed acorns and honey, why?" Ora-Jean had suspicion written all over her face.

"When I say, take a quick bite. Not too big. The spell won't last long." Robin moved his hand through a casting of [**Lesser Phantasm**] again.

Ora-Jean squinted at him but took a quick bite when he nodded at her. Her eyes went wide, and she chewed faster. She made appreciative sounds and actually smiled.

"Not bad!" she complimented when she could speak again.

"I haven't had acorns in a long time," Robin said by way of explanation and apology. In fact, it'd been so long he could barely remember the taste, but the magic seemed to fill in the blanks to some extent.

"Fresh cream and honey, if you would." Fiamah held out her bowl.

Robin complied, and Fiamah likewise smiled at the illusory taste.

The meal took a good deal longer than it had any right to, and by the end, Robin's hand was beginning to cramp, but it was worth it.

Shortly thereafter, Lantha returned and divided everyone up into watches. Even Robin. He wasn't sure how welcome the responsibility was, but it certainly beat taking one of Lantha's daggers to the throat.

"I'll take first and third watch," the elf said. "Robin, you'll be on third watch with me. Ora-Jean and Grathilde will take second watch, and Fiamah, you'll be with me for first watch. Grab some sleep while you can. We need to be rested if we're going to find our way out of here."

After that, there wasn't much else to do. Those assigned to watch began their vigil while the rest chased slumber.

Robin bedded down, the unyielding stone beneath him softened somewhat by his illusory clothing. He was bone-tired, but even so, sleep was elusive. His eyes kept flashing to the shadows cast by Lantha's magelight, his mind on those ominous words written in blood.

Watch the shadows . . .

Chapter 16

*R*obin woke up from the best night of sleep he had had since waking up naked in the shrine of a lost god. The smell of warm porridge wafted to his nostrils, and his stomach growled out a demand as his mouth watered, too. His brain seemed to have associated the smell of porridge with the delectable illusory tastes he had conjured up.

He was even less stiff as he rotated his arms. The coat wasn't fully real, but the benefits seemed to be, slight as they were.

After a quick breakfast with only a few delectable bites for each of them (Lantha wanted to get moving so there was no time to chain cast [**Lesser Phantasm**] for everyone), they headed out to explore the outpost some more.

It was hours of tense, dreary searching to little avail. Robin lost count of the rooms and corridors. They were all formed of the same, scalelike overlapping stonework, all dark, all deserted, but all brimming with the potential for sudden attack and/or death.

By dinner, they had crisscrossed the area enough times that Lantha and Ora-Jean felt confident they knew all the major tunnels leading away from the place. What everyone was less confident about was which way to go.

Robin's opinion was not sought. He was instead tasked with helping Grathilde set up for dinner.

At least it was an easy enough task. Sort out a few mushrooms, make sure the containers they ate out of were reasonably clean, wait to apply magic spoon. Plenty of time to sneak in a few glances at his interface, make minor alterations to his coat, and chat with Grathilde, not to mention religiously check the nearby shadows for any unnatural behavior.

Watch the Shadows . . . he couldn't get those words out of his head.

"What's the deal with Ora-Jean and Taterpicker?" he asked as he poked through the satchel full of mushrooms.

"What do you mean?" Grathilde asked. Most of her attention was caught up in glaring at a clump of dried porridge stuck to the cup she preferred using.

"I've never had a chance to spend time around someone with a . . . what is Taterpicker? A familiar spirit? A totem? Something like that?" Robin tried to dance around the edges of his ignorance as best he could.

"Oh. I'm not sure. Not really my area of specialty." Grathilde shrugged. "I think Taterpicker has some sort of link to Ora-Jean's family. She doesn't say much about them, though, so I dunno."

Proficiency Unlocked: Gossip.

Really? Gossip? Robin made noncommittal noises at Grathilde and dug into his interface to try and get some more information. Hmm. Looked like the proficiency covered all kinds of information gathering. *So, generally useful but oddly named!*

The sound of Ora-Jean and Lantha arguing brought him back to his surroundings. The two were kneeling over a roll of parchment. Fiamah stood over them, arms crossed, face the picture of exasperation. Grathilde was filling the bowls.

No one was on watch. Well, except possibly Taterpicker, but Robin couldn't see him, so that was anyone's guess.

Well, if Lantha wasn't insisting, it should be safe enough.

He hoped.

Robin poked his head over to see what they were looking at. It was a map. Either they had it hidden away *really* well, or they'd found it on the body they'd looted yesterday.

"I think we need to go farther down," Ora-Jean was saying. "I don't recognize any of these markings, and there's clearly a passage—"

"We're already right on top of the crypt," Lantha replied. "How much farther down do we need to look? At some point, we're going to need to go *up* to get *out*."

We're where *now?* Robin blinked. The big, round stone not far from where Grathilde was setting up dinner suddenly looked a lot more ominous.

He forced his attention back to the map. Best not to think about what was under that stone.

Huh. Actually, that scratching there looked familiar, somehow. Where had he seen something like that before . . . oh!

As Lantha and Ora-Jean argued, Robin rummaged about in his trousers, pulling out the scrap of a map he'd looted from the goblins.

"I think it's the same landmark!"

"What?"

Robin looked up. Everyone was staring at him. He blinked.

"That shape, the sort of half circle with three squiggly lines running through it, is on this map too." He gestured vaguely at the scrap of rancid leather in his hand.

"Map? What map?"

That Lantha didn't snatch it out of his hands was a testament to how far their relationship had come.

Or a testament to how much the scrap stank. Robin's fingers felt positively greasy.

"This map," he said. "I looted it from those goblins right before—" he trailed off. Not a great memory nor their finest hour, to be honest.

"Before Gis captured us," Grathilde finished the thought for him.

Ora-Jean looked sour. Lantha's attention was on Robin's map. Fiamah glanced between the two.

"It does seem to match," the cleric said slowly. "And I think where the explorer's map we found lacks any sign as to which way the exit might be, the goblin's map has what seem to be two possible exit markings. Look."

She pointed to two rough archways sketched in on the goblin's map; each was the end of a twisting line of tunnel.

The others leaned over, and Ora-Jean nodded, a bit reluctantly.

"I think you're right," the halfling agreed. "Much as I hate to take even this much aid from anyone who tried to kill me."

"Think of it as reparations for attempted harm," Robin said.

Ora-Jean snorted. The mood lightened just a touch, and Robin smiled. The whole being trapped miles beneath millions of tons of stone was depressing enough. No reason to let the mood sink low as well.

Grathilde passed out the porridge, and Lantha conjured another magelight for them to gather around after insisting Ora-Jean roll up the maps and entrust them to Fiamah.

That worked for Robin. The cleric was by far the most reliable of them all. Well, so long as she didn't wander off a cliff while distracted with lecturing.

The meal was welcome after the long day, and they all perked up a bit with the hearty meal in them. Robin glanced around the group, surprised once again Lantha hadn't set a watch. Nervously, he checked the room once more.

Robin froze. Something was off.

Slowly, he looked again. *Frak.* There it was. He glanced around to the other members of the party and adjusted his position before saying anything, just in case.

"Ora-Jean," Robin started, supremely casual. "Why do you have an extra shadow?"

Everyone froze. Ora-Jean slowly rotated her head, counting the shadows. "Shi—"

Before Ora-Jean could finish the word, the darkness near her feet exploded into motion.

It rose up, moving of its own volition, and began lashing about with its claws. The edges of the shadow were sharp and slid through clothing as if it did not exist.

Ora-Jean roared in fury while Lantha nimbly dodged out of the way, not letting the thing touch her. Robin was shocked into flailing ineffectually at it with his fists. Unfortunately, they passed right through the creature.

Proficiency Unlocked: Brawl.

Robin was all for learning from your failures, but this was ridiculous. He banished the notification, but not before he took a hit. A bone-deep chill bit deep into him as the shadow slashed at his flesh. He staggered, suddenly feeling weak.

"Get back," Fiamah shouted. "It steals the strength from your limbs and uses it to enhance its own power!"

Robin easily dodged the next attack, seeing it coming. Oh yeah, he could feel the benefit to those new *Dodge* ranks.

Ora-Jean was bellowing, slashing wildly at the thing with her scavenged spear. It had little to no effect.

Lantha circled the battle, occasionally darting in with a slash of her kitchen knives, but she had similarly little success. The shadow lashed out at her, but the elf nimbly dodged aside. So far, it had yet to land a hit on her.

Grathilde was not so fortunate. While Robin was distracted, the shadow had landed two hits on the aeromancer. She lay on the ground, weakly crawling away from the center of the conflict.

Fiamah was the only one who seemed to have had any luck so far. The cleric held a conjured handful of white-gold flames. As Robin watched, she hurled a small ball of holy fire at the shadow; it struck the thing center mass and exploded as the creature keened in pain, flickering and slipping down to mix with the dancing shadows formed by the melee.

"Robin! Help me," Fiamah shouted. "We need to take it down before it can heal itself in the darkness."

That was a thing? Frelling magic. Well, fight fire with fire, right?

Robin scrambled for an insult. What would offend a shadow?

"Oi! You call that an attack? Nah, mate, that performance is well flat! Practically two-dimensional!" Robin channeled a bit of Cockney attitude. He was going to need all the swagger he could muster on this one.

There was a hiss from the darkness around them.

"Again!" Fiamah commanded, her eyes searching. "I can't find it! Flush it out!"

Right. Operation Rage Bait. Party.

"I mean, I know you're a shadow, but is that any excuse to be more than a bit dim?"

An arm lashed out of the dark. Robin ducked.

Dodged again!

A ball of flame sailed past his ear, narrowly missing setting his hair on fire.

"Sorry!" Fiamah called.

"As long as you take it out in the process, you can set me on fire any-time," Robin shouted back.

Lantha conjured another magelight, attempting to catch the shadow unawares and reveal its location. Ora-Jean howled in frustration, her eyes searching for any hint as to the damn thing's location.

"Fiamah," Lantha shouted. "Stand over Grathilde! She's too tempting a target."

The cleric shifted position. The shadows danced all around them.

It was playing with them now or stalling for enough time to heal.

His eyes were well-accustomed to darkness, so Robin turned as much attention as he could spare to sifting the shadows around them for their foe. If he could narrow it down, maybe Fiamah could take some blind shots.

"Keep going!" Lantha snapped at Robin.

Right. He had to keep whittling its health down with [Cutting Words] so it didn't heal before they managed to flush it out.

Once more into the breach!

Robin called the thing dim, flat, and a pathetic imitation. He insulted its attacks, its general shape, and the way it stretched when the light hit it funny. Eventually, out of sheer frustration, the thing lunged into the light in an attempt to rip out his heart.

Fiamah hit it dead center with three balls of flame in quick succession. As each one detonated, the shadow lost more and more cohesion, its shape warping and thinning from the concentrated light and holy power.

It didn't last long after that. With a hiss and a wail, the shadow dissolved into wisps of darkness and was no more.

Of course, no sooner had it gone than it was replaced with something else. In this case, a quest prompt appeared before Robin's eyes.

New Quest: [A Shadow Awakens!]

Congratulations on defeating the lesser shadow. Really. Great work. However, your conflict has done more than save your hide. It's also awakened the **[Shadow of Yvon-Rael]**. *Defeat this foe and survive—if you can. Best of luck!*
Reward: *Your life, obviously. No promises whether or not your sanity will make it through unscathed, though. In addition, the answer to a question will become clear, and you will find your way to some monetary and magical compensation. Yes, better stuff than you've found so far. After all, you're going to have to work for it.*

"Oh, fuck me," Robin whispered.

"What?" Grathilde looked up at him, eyes still wide in the aftermath of the battle.

"I think we woke someone up."

The stone separating them from the crypts below cracked with a sharp retort.

Chapter 17

*T*he crack of the stone breaking echoed down to Robin's very bones. Reflexively, he drew back against the wall and covered himself with a [Lesser Phantasm] to keep himself hidden.

"Something big is coming!" he shouted.

"Fall back to the last campsite!" Lantha urged. "Fiamah—"

Before she could finish her sentence, a massive wave of darkness coiled up out of the crack in the floor. It coalesced into the outline of an exaggerated elvish woman, brawny and sharp, whose hips tapered off into a massive serpent's tail.

"Yvon-Rael," Robin breathed.

The shadow jerked at the sound of its name, whipping around and seeking the source of the sound. Robin bit his lip and renewed his [Lesser Phantasm]. He needed to get to the door.

Before he could make his move, however, the shadow struck out at Grathilde. The dwarf shouted weakly and shot small arcs of electricity from her fingers. The blue-white bolts danced through the shadow, and the monster keened in pain and fury.

In retaliation, the shadow raked Grathilde with its claws, yanking so much strength from the dwarf that she collapsed, unmoving.

"Grathilde!" Lantha screamed.

Fiamah hurled a ball of holy flame at the shadow, driving it away from their fallen comrade. Lantha charged forward, knives slashing uselessly through the incorporeal form of Yvon-Rael.

"Fall back!" Lantha screamed. "Ora-Jean! Grab Grathilde and carry her out of here. Fiamah! Robin! Cover her!"

A distraction? Robin's mind scrambled, then he threw out the first thing he could think of.

The illusion of a miniature sun blazed to life in front of the shadow. It didn't throw out the same light as the sun. It wasn't any brighter than one of Lantha's magelights. It didn't have much effect at all. If the shadow was surprised or scared, it showed no sign.

Of course! Why would a shadow fear light or the sun? Light *created* shadow. It must be the fire or the holy energies in Fiamah's spell that did the damage.

He needed to do something else—and quick. Ora-Jean had slung Grathilde over her shoulder (so strong for someone so short!), and the action had drawn the shadow's attention.

Robin cast **[Lesser Phantasm]** twice in quick succession, followed by **[Cutting Words]**.

A full-face mask, the kind you saw on theater programs, appeared floating in the darkness, a mocking smile on its face. Moments later, it began to move and speak, the words provided by Robin's second **[Lesser Phantasm]**. The words and the motion were horribly out of sync, but hopefully, the shadow wouldn't notice.

As a distraction, it worked. The shadow whirled on the apparition, shrieking and lashing out at the mocking face. The party took the opportunity to retreat, Grathilde flopping weakly over Ora-Jean's shoulder.

Behind them, a frustrated wailing went up.

"It's going to be hot on our heels," Lantha gasped between breaths. "I'm not sure if we can lose it in these tunnels."

"Less talking, more running," Ora-Jean panted. "I don't see any of you running for two."

"Drop the magelight," Robin said. "I can see in the dark. I'll guide us."

It was gratifying that Lantha didn't question him. Or question why he was, now of all times, revealing his ability to make do without light.

A branch in the corridor appeared ahead of them, and Robin quickly adjusted his plan.

"No, wait, send the light down that corridor. I'll set the illusion of us fleeing down that way as well. It's close; hopefully, it'll hear and take the wrong turn and buy us some time."

Lantha didn't hesitate. She just nodded sharply and sent her magelight singing down the other corridor while Robin flexed his fingers through the passes of **[Lesser Phantasm]**.

Deception, *don't fail me now!*

Robin linked hands with Lantha as the party formed a chain, and he led them forward as fast as he dared. Behind them, they heard the keening of the shadow as it pursued the phantasm and the dancing magelight down the other corridor.

They had their head start! Now not to waste it.

The party dashed through the tunnels until they made it to their former campsite. The room had two entrances; Ora-Jean carefully lowered Grathilde down in a corner and then dashed over to secure one of them. Lantha was already securing the one they'd just passed through—not that either would keep out a being that could slip through the smallest of cracks. The doors were hardly hermetically sealed.

"Robin, come help me, please," Fiamah called quietly from her position near Grathilde.

"What can I do?" he asked, kneeling next to her.

"There's not a lot I can do right now. She needs time to regain her strength or I need time to intercede with my goddess on her behalf, neither of which we're going to get, I suspect. Hold her head."

Robin gently braced a hand on each of Grathilde's temples. Fiamah murmured a brief prayer and began checking the dwarf over.

"What are you doing?" Robin asked. "Anything more I can do to help?"

"No, you're doing just fine." Fiamah checked different points on Grathilde's body. "I'm checking for damage. See? Here and here, where the skin is particularly pale? Those are the places where the shadow made contact. They are colder than the surrounding flesh, but I don't feel any damage, and the skin's not been frozen or ruptured. She should be fine, so long as she can regain a bit of her strength."

Proficiency Unlocked: Healing.

Well, that might certainly come in useful, if he ever got a chance to use it.

"I wish I still had my satchel!" Fiamah cursed. "I had some healing herbs in there which might have helped."

"I'd settle for a potion," Grathilde croaked, opening her eyes. "I feel weak as a newborn flywacket."

"I'm afraid we don't have any of those, either," Fiamah said. "Glad you're still with us."

"We need a plan," Lantha called softly from the door. Her head was cocked to one side, and she seemed to be listening to something. "It's getting closer. I don't think we can get out of this place before it finds us."

"And we don't know that there isn't something even worse lurking outside the walls," Ora-Jean added. "This place has too many defenses to make me think there isn't something out there to defend against."

"Well, what do we have that will hurt it? And what do we know about it?" Robin asked.

"My flame, your words, Grathilde's lightning," Fiamah listed off the obvious ones. "I can bless Lantha and Ora-Jean's weapons for a short time, but it will only be temporary, and I only have enough favor of the goddess left today to do so once."

"Can you call out to her and get a one-time exception?" Robin asked.

"If only." Fiamah smiled grimly. "And it's more my limitation than hers. My body can only withstand channeling so much holy energy in a given day. If I push too far . . ."

"She'll go up like a firework on the winter solstice," Grathilde finished. "Same as I would if I tried to channel much more aeromantic power."

"So we need to hit it—and hit it hard—in a short period of time," Ora-Jean said.

"Preferably somewhere it can't sneak into the shadows and heal back up," Lantha added grimly. "That last one was trouble enough, and this one is bigger; more dangerous."

Robin really wished he had access to something like *Bardic Knowledge*. He had the name of the thing! If only there were some legends, that might give them a clue as to how best to defeat it.

"Does it heal in the darkness or only in the shadows?" he asked instead. "Because that would be one way. We don't have enough light to get rid of all the shadows, so can we do the opposite?"

"I don't know," Fiamah answered after a long moment.

"And none of the rest of us can see in the dark," Lantha reminded him. "We each need at least *some* light." She looked at him. "You'll have to tell us where you gained such an ability. It's not something one commonly sees in humans. Or bards."

"Still not a bard," he replied. He dodged the human question for now. He still wasn't entirely certain what the "Shadeling" entry on his character sheet meant.

Lantha and Fiamah looked like they wanted to ask follow-up questions, but Ora-Jean cut in.

"We can discuss who is what and why later. We need to know what we're doing *now* to defeat that thing, or none of us will be around to ask questions ever again." The halfling cast a grim glance over her shoulder at the door.

"We need to hit it and not get hit ourselves, right?" Robin stood and paced around the room. "I can hide two of us with illusions. They won't last very long, but they should provide some cover. And we've got those dried mushrooms, so we can build a few small fires. Yeah, there will be a lot of shadows, but if we've got enough light in here, maybe they'll be too small to be of much use to that thing."

"And then we just hit it with everything we've got, as fast as we can?" Ora-Jean grinned. "That's about as complex as I like my plans to be anyway."

"I guess that leaves me to be bait," Robin concluded reluctantly. "So Fiamah can enchant Lantha and Ora-Jean's weapons, and Grathilde can build up a bit of a charge to hit the shadow with."

"I could hit it as soon as it appears," the dwarf said stoutly.

"And then it would go right for you," Lantha countered. "I'm not sure you can survive another hit. What if it sucks so much strength out of you that your heart can't muster up enough energy to beat?"

"I'll wait for Robin's signal, then," Grathilde conceded.

"Let's get ready." Lantha cocked her head to one side. "I don't think we have much more time."

The party sprang into action, setting up small fires and choosing initial attack positions. Lantha crept over to the door and opened it a crack, setting a magelight right above so they would see as soon as the shadows moved.

Robin took position in the center of the room. Standing there, waiting, he gently massaged his hands and tried to talk his heart out of beating its way directly out of his chest.

He only had limited success.

This was insane! What was he thinking? Bait for a living shadow? His best weapon some schoolyard insults? No. He'd felled plenty of enemies with those schoolyard insults, and he was standing here as living proof.

He could do this.

He would do this.

The shadows moved. Robin yelped. *It's here!*

"Now!" Lantha shouted.

The magelight above the door flared bright, driving the shadow away from the entryway and toward the center of the room. Toward Robin.

"Oi! You call yourself a shadow? I've seen scarier inkblots!"

The shadow hissed.

Fiamah muttered a blessing over Lantha and Ora-Jean's weapons while Grathilde ran around the room setting fire to small piles of dried mushrooms.

Light began to fill the room, and the shadows shrunk. All except the massive one bearing down on Robin. It lashed out at him while he dodged.

Well, he tried to dodge. A single claw snagged him, and a bone-deep chill that stank of despair washed through him. Robin staggered as he suddenly felt like he barely had the strength to stand.

"What are you all waiting for?" he shouted before diving right into an attack with **[Cutting Words]**. "This sundial reject isn't going to vanquish itself. Or will it? I mean, at best, it's a literal shadow of its former self."

The shadow hissed venomously at Robin after that last quip. That one had landed! Did it not like being reminded of its former life? Robin mentally grabbed at the noises it was making and pulled—what, the language of Shadow?—out of them.

"You're nothing like the true Yvon-Rael," he spat in words of darkness and shade. "You're a disgrace to even the memory of the person you used to be."

I will eat your strength and break your bones with the weight of despair! The Shadow of Yvon-Rael howled noiselessly at him.

It was so fixated on Robin it didn't notice the rest of the party attack. Lantha's daggers flew; Ora-Jean's spear struck true; lightning lanced from Grathilde's fingertips, and Fiamah flung ball after ball of holy flame at the center mass of the shadow.

The Shadow of Yvon-Rael ignored them all. Its attention was fixed entirely on Robin. Hatred and malice rolled off it in waves as it lunged at him, raking with the shadow of its claws and lashing out with the shadow of its tail.

Robin stumbled back, shouting the occasional insult. He dodged and squirmed, but the shadow was too focused on him. It was taking terrible damage in its single-mindedness, but that same focus made it impossible for Robin to dodge every blow.

And each one that landed made him feel weaker and weaker. The weaker he felt, the harder it was to dodge. Finally, he stumbled and fell hard on his back.

The Shadow of Yvon-Rael loomed over him, tattered and torn but terrifying nonetheless.

I will suck the last strength from your body, and your shadow shall rise in my service. You will howl out your misery until the end of time, and I—

What the Shadow of Yvon-Rael would do to him would have to remain a mystery for the ages, as before it could finish speaking, the rest of the party tore it to shreds with their concentrated attacks.

Congratulations! Threshold Achieved! Level Bonuses Awarded!

Well, that was something.
Robin's eyes rolled into the back of his head, and he passed out.

Chapter 18

When Robin woke up, he was warm. A small fire flickered cheerily nearby, fed with dried mushrooms. He attempted to prop himself up on his elbow, but his arms were too weak to support his weight. There were notifications flickering at the edges of his vision, but he mentally sidelined them for now.

"Ah, you're awake," Fiamah said. "Would you like some porridge?"

"Yes, please." Robin felt as if a bottomless pit had opened up in the center of his stomach and was gnawing at his other internal organs.

Lantha pulled out the spoon and began filling a small crock with porridge. Ora-Jean was standing watch by one of the doors. Grathilde, like him, was laid out next to the fire, moving weakly.

Fiamah reached out, murmuring a prayer, and touched Robin right over the heart. He felt the sunbright burn of her holy magic, but when the pain passed, he felt noticeably stronger.

"You'll probably need a few more days to recover," Fiamah told him apologetically. "I can't channel enough holy energy to restore both you and Grathilde in a single day."

"Thank you," Robin replied fervently. "I feel a lot better already."

"Can you sit up and hold this?" Lantha offered him some breakfast.

Robin accepted the offering and began to eat slowly. It took a lot of effort, lifting the food to his mouth. His arms trembled with the exertion, and small beads of sweat appeared at his temples. He had to take regular breaks between every few bites.

To fill the time, he pulled up his character sheet.

Ah! His strength score looked different. The regular number was still there—eleven—but next to it in parentheses was another, much lower number four. Some kind of temporary score reflecting the damage the shadow had done? Very probable.

They'd defeated the shadow, though! Which reminded him, he should have a quest completion notice to review. And possibly new level benefits!

Quest Complete! [A Shadow Awakens!]

You have returned the **[Shadow of Yvon-Rael]** *to slumber. Permanently. And you didn't even die and rise as its shadow thrall in the process! Good for you!*
Reward: *You were promised insight, and insight you shall have! Think about those maps while you finish your porridge. Oh, and when you're next walking through shadows, keep your eye out for the blue lights . . .*

Right. Insight. Blue lights. Apparently, it was too much to hope for conveniently appearing chests or random showers of gold coins. Oh well. One more burden he'd have to bear with great equanimity.

Robin adjusted his coat. Mask. Whatever. At least the rewards were nice when they did show up. Even if he did have to wait and work for them a little more.

The map could wait a bit. He still had breakfast to finish. And level benefits to look at!

Congratulations! Threshold Achieved! Level Bonuses Awarded!

Choose one Property to increase by one (1) rank!
Proficiency rank-cap raised by one (1)!
You have gained one (1) new Peculiarity slot!

Robin pulled up his character sheet. His *Heritage* now read *Shadeling, Mature* and *Progress to Tier One* now read 71 percent. So 67 percent must have been the threshold he'd passed. How dangerous had the Shadow of Yvon-Rael been?

He shuddered. It had clearly been above his weight class. Bait class? No, that's not funny enough.

Property increases . . . Robin was tempted to use the rank in *Strength*. He hated how weak he was feeling. That probably wasn't the smartest move, though. He wasn't really shaping up as a melee combatant, and it didn't suit his nature at all.

He'd been doing pretty well with trickery and insults, so *Cunning, Charisma*, and *Manipulation* were all good options. *Dexterity* would probably enhance his stealth.

After all, the best armor class is not getting hit in the first place!

Robin assigned the rank to *Cunning*, in the end. It was his highest stat, so the free rank saved him the most experience points to use it there. He didn't have the energy to ponder further.

Grathilde was awake and eating. Fiamah was kneeling down near to the both of them, eyes closed. Meditation? Prayer? Maybe just a cheeky bit of rest. They could all use it.

It didn't look like Lantha was going to insist that they move on anytime soon, so Robin went back to considering his new options.

The biggest question was which peculiarity did he want to choose next? Limited shape-shifting or more illusions? His new mask covered each one to a small extent. Robin poked through his interface, searching for more information.

Mask of Myriad Faces

Grants the bearer limited shapeshifting ability.
Bearer is limited to shapes of the same general form (bipedal life-forms cannot shift to quadrupeds, hexapeds, etc.), but can freely shift particulars of appearance (hair, skin, etc.) and biology (sex, internal organs, etc.). Physical abilities of the target form may be used, but exceptional or supernatural abilities may not. This ability has no effect on clothing or equipment carried.

Chronicle of Infinite Visions

Grants the bearer the ability to use [**Visual Phantasm**] *at will without the need for any invocation costs or components.*

Robin focused on the description of [**Visual Phantasm**]. No point making his choice without the full information if he could help it.

[Visual Phantasm]

Tier: 1
Circle: *Illusion, Shadow*
Range: *Long*
Duration: *Concentration + 9 seconds + 3 seconds/level*
Effect(s): *Create the illusion of an object, creature, or visible force.*
Constraints: *Images created by this spell are visual only and do not include sound, scent, thermal, or any sensory effects other than visual. Images generated*

cannot exceed a volume greater than three 3-yard cubes + an additional 3-yard cube/level. While maintaining concentration, you can cause the image to move within the bounds of its original manifestation volume and location.

Long range? That was nice. All his other options were more close-range stuff. And that was a big jump in size. The limitations were pretty harsh, but "at will" sounded good. From what he'd seen of Fiamah's and Grathilde's efforts, higher tiered magics took a lot of energy and couldn't be used nearly as often as cantrips.

"Grathilde," he asked, because Fiamah still had her eyes closed. "Does your School of Magic measure effects in tiers? I just realized I have no idea if that is a universal descriptor or something I've only seen more locally."

"Huh? Oh. Yes. Everyone I know uses a tier system to measure spell effectiveness, and by extension, general mastery level of an individual skilled in the mystic or clerical arts." Grathilde seemed pleased to have something to focus on other than feeling weak.

"Naming conventions differ," Fiamah added, opening her eyes, "but generally speaking, everything breaks down into nine levels. Ten, if you include non-tier people and effects."

"How common are at-will abilities of Tier One or higher?" The questions was out before Robin could stop himself.

"Rare but not unheard of," Fiamah answered. If she thought it an odd thing that he didn't already know, she gave no sign.

"Though you usually don't hear of them outside the mastery tiers," Grathilde added.

"There are exceptions," Fiamah corrected. "Though they are often limited by cultural secrecy or strange circumstances."

"True. Having **[Minor Levinbolt]** at will would have come in very handy in that last fight." Grathilde grimaced. "But I've heard you have to be struck by natural lightning and survive to have a chance at manifesting a peculiarity like that."

Robin started at the familiar term. So there was *some* link between what he was seeing and how they saw the world here. Even though it seemed no one else aside from him had an illusory interface.

Well, no one so far.

Before he could ask any more questions, however, Lantha interrupted. She motioned Ora-Jean over and asked Fiamah to pull out the maps. Robin's ears perked up at that.

"We need to find our way out of here," the rogue said. "We know where we are, and we think we have two possible exits, but we haven't found the passage we need to—"

"We're going to have to go through the crypts," Robin cut in. The flash of insight nearly blinded his mind's eye. He could see it all so clearly now. "Look, this symbol here? I think it's the same one on the stone the Shadow of Yvon-Rael rose out of."

"How do you know that?" Grathilde asked.

"How do you know that thing's name?" Ora-Jean demanded at the same time.

"Uh," Robin scrambled for a moment, then sighed. "Legends. Lore. General"—he was going to regret this—"*Bardic Knowledge?*"

He didn't know if he was more relieved or annoyed that the party accepted that at face value.

"It's worth a shot," Ora-Jean admitted, studying the map.

"I think he's probably right," Fiamah added. "Look, if that does connect, it should bring us up via a series of galleries that match this set of lines here, and connect to the goblin map at—"

Robin let them hash it out. He knew he was right, and he knew they'd find their way out eventually. It was a lot of faith to put in a possible hallucination, but so far, the quest system hadn't steered him wrong. Steered him snarkily, yes, but not wrong.

While they debated, he opened his interface and filled his open peculiarity slot with **[Chronicle of Infinite Visions]**. He'd have the chance to take the other one soon enough, he hoped, and for now, this just seemed to offer more versatility.

"We go through the crypts," Lantha said, decisively ending the debate. "We go quick and we go carefully and we go now. I think we've spent long enough down here, and if this turns out to be another dead end, I want to know sooner rather than later."

The conversation wrapped up quickly after that. The party gathered their supplies and headed back to the crypt entrance. When they arrived, Ora-Jean easily shifted the large pieces of cracked stone and cleared the way down.

Lantha sent a magelight drifting ahead of them, and it painted the walls in faded golden light. The stone here was less worked than in the outpost above, more natural, and the walls dripped with condensation.

Down and down, they went, following a spiral staircase. At the bottom, it branched off into several tunnels, but each was marked with some kind of script. Robin was able to read it with **[Tongue of the Fallen Tower]** and direct them along the path he and Fiamah thought most likely to lead them to their destination.

Along the way, they passed through what had clearly been the tomb turned lair of the Shadow of Yvon-Rael. Blue lights sparkled at the corner of Robin's vision, and he called out for the party to stop.

"You've got good eyes," Ora-Jean said approvingly, hauling out several pieces of equipment.

It looked like the shadow had been bringing back trophies of its conquests. Moreover, the catafalque was cracked, revealing yellowed bones and the glitter of gold inside.

"We don't touch the grave goods," Fiamah declared firmly.

Ora-Jean and Grathilde seemed like they might argue, but a look from Lantha silenced them. Robin was just glad he didn't have to weigh in on the moral ramifications of the whole situation. He had enough mental stress to deal with in this new world as it was.

There was still plenty of equipment scattered about the tomb. While it was not enough to completely outfit the party, they were in much better shape in terms of weapons and armor than they had been.

While the rest of his companions were searching the room for usable equipment, Robin followed the blue sparkles he had noticed to a simple silver ring inlaid with blue enamel in a knotwork pattern. When he slipped it onto his finger, it felt *right* and refreshing.

"Good find," Grathilde noted when he returned to the party. "Well-earned."

Robin had worried she'd insist he surrender it to the party, that he would still be denied a cut, but it looked like he was even more accepted than he thought.

Fortunately, encountering Yvon-Rael's lair was the last bit of excitement Robin and his companions faced beneath the mountains. They had a few close encounters with goblin sign, but of the kobolds there was nary a yip. They followed the map and eventually found their way out of the depths of the mountain.

Robin stepped out into the fresh air, blinking in the bright light. The *taste* of it. It was so clear, so pure. *Grathilde must be ecstatic.*

They were on a small outcrop overlooking a vast, deep forest, though across the valley, Robin could just make out the signs of some sort of fortification.

It was breathtaking.

"*T'ressha's tits!*" Lantha swore. "We're on the wrong side of the bloody mountain!"

* * *

Robin Parker

Heritage: Shadeling, Mature
Profession: None
Tier: 0
Progress to Tier 1: 86%

Properties

(Free Ranks Available: 1)

Physical
-Strength: 11
-Dexterity: 14
-Fortitude: 11
Mental
-Intelligence: 17
-Cunning: 19
-Resilience: 14
Social
-Charisma: 15
-Manipulation: 13
-Poise: 15

Proficiencies

(Free Ranks Available: 3)

Physical (7/9)
-Athletics: 1
-Brawl: 0
-Dodge: 4
-???
-???
-Ranged Combat: 0
-Sleight of Hand: 1
-Stealth: 4
-Survival: 1
Mental (8/9)
-Arcane Lore: 1
-???
-Concentration: 1

-Crafting: 1
-Healing: 0
-Insight: 3
-Learning: 1
-Natural Wisdom: 0
-Perception: 4
Social (7/9)
-???
-Deception: 4
-Empathy: 1
-Expression: 4
-Gossip: 0
-Intimidation: 0
-Persuasion: 1
-Socialize: 1
-???

Peculiarities

Blessing of Rhyth
Tongue of the Fallen Tower
Mark of the Trickster
Chronicle of Infinite Visions

Interlude

$G$is, Priest of Urkhan, Initiate of the Second Circle, and Right Hand of Basgar the Blinder was in a foul mood. He had just spent days crawling about underground like a worm, one of his more promising protégés had been done in by a kobold rebellion, of all things, and after all that, all he had to show for his efforts was a handful of cracked stone which, to all appearances, held not even a trace of the energies His Lord had commanded him to search for.

To make matters worse, Basgar had insisted the priest join him at the top of the highest tower of the keep. Worn stone steps led upward in a continuous spiral as Gis climbed. The priest did so carefully and cautiously. The place had not been subjugated so long as to surrender all of its secrets, and the last thing he wanted was to meet with the business end of some rebel's dagger.

Fortunately, Gis completed the climb unharmed, save for a slight shortness of breath and some muscle pain. The top of the tower was crenellated all around, which provided both exquisite views and a supreme tactical perspective of the surrounding terrain.

The keep was built on a small plateau formed where three mountain ranges met. It was an ancient structure, built of massive stones in a roughly nonagonal structure. Three wide roads led to and from the keep, one toward each of the three regions bordered by the mountains. The one who controlled the keep controlled the Borderlands and all the trade that flowed between the nations nestled among the stony peaks.

"Ah, good. You've finally made it."

The words came from the man who currently controlled the fortification: Basgar the Blinder. Tall and fair of skin and clear of eye, Basgar's armor was worked with a motif of eyes, some enameled, some not. Those that were bore the color of an eye Basgar had plucked from a living enemy. He was one to rule through fear and intimidation.

And Gis—and His Lord—heartily approved.

"My lord," the priest greeted with a small inclination of his head. Respect had been earned, but he was still a servant of the Most Mighty and Terrible Urkhan. There was only so far he would bow before another.

"We've nearly routed the rabble that resist my occupation," Basgar began, "and I would have Your Lord's wisdom on the best direction to next turn my efforts toward."

Nearly? The word left a sour taste in Gis's mouth. It seemed to echo with Bula's lackadaisical attitude and the empty promises of Chief Ratscale. Still, His Lord had directed him to render what aid he could to Basgar's efforts in this region. So he would, while watching for any hint that the petty tyrant might become unsuitable for Urkhan's work.

"You haven't the might to challenge any of the city-states of the Confederacy," the priest said slowly, looking roughly northward out over the trees. "Not yet." He turned to stride across the top of the tower and look to the southeast. "You could challenge one of the lesser marcher lords, however, if you are smart and ruthless."

"Not the foolish merchants to the west?" Basgar joined Gis in gazing out over the edge.

The wind up here was mercilessly cold. It snapped at Gis's nose as the priest considered the best way to word his reasoning to the power-hungry lordling.

"The merchants have a great deal of money. It's far better to meet them on their own field of battle." The priest grinned nastily. "What care has that lot for loss of blood when you can hurt them far more with loss of gold. You can raise the toll for passage through the keep. Make them pay more. Weaken them as you strengthen your own hand."

"Mmm, yes, I like the way you think," Basgar rumbled. "The merchants will fund my conquest of the nearby marcher lords, which will in turn provide soldiers for my eventual assault on the nearby city-states of the Confederacy."

"Fools," Gis spat over the rampart. "If they had a single powerful leader, no one would dare carve away at their edges. As it is, when the time is right, you can nip away at your foes on all three sides, stealing away enough land to forge the heart of a new empire from your position here. All they will do is squabble. Or worse, put the matter of action to a *vote* or before a committee."

"Yes!" Basgar slammed a fist down onto the stone in front of him. "Bleed the merchants, subjugate the nearby marcher lords, then mount an offensive against the Confederacy." Basgar smiled. "Your god counsels you well, Gis."

"I am at your service, Lord Basgar." Gis inclined his head once more.

"And your own quest on Urkhan's behalf? Did it bear fruit?"

"Yes, though not as I expected," Gis replied slowly, measuring his words to set himself at best advantage. "Though there was no sign of the magics I sought, I did discover a band of spies sent by the Confederacy to assess your position here."

"Oh?" Basgar's tone was dangerous. "And what became of these *spies?*"

"I dealt with them. It cost me two promising recruits to our cause here, but I dealt with them." Gis gave a version of the truth that made him look better for having vanquished his foes.

"You'll have to tell me the tale over dinner! It sounds like it might be entertaining."

"True enough. The spies are likely worm food at the bottom of a chasm beneath that mountain, at any rate." Gis gestured to the stony peak he himself had so recently returned from. "If they are not, well, the wilderness around the keep will consume them."

Basgar laughed, a rough, barking sound that was swiftly swept away by the wind.

"Yes," the petty tyrant agreed. "The wildwood around here is full of strange and hungry beasts. To say nothing of the *other* things that lurk in the shadows."

Gis's laugh joined Basgar's on the wind.

It was hard to say which was colder: the laugh of the tyrant, the laugh of the priest, or the frigid wind dancing around the two of them.

Secrets of Wyndham Wood

Chapter 1

*R*obin took a deep breath of the forest air; it was heavy with the scent of loam and decomposing leaves. The sun was warm on his face where it occasionally pierced the canopy, but there was a hint of chill in the air. If this was home, he'd say they were somewhere between the middle to the tail end of spring.

It had definitely been early autumn when he'd enacted his ritual at home. Another hint that *we're not in Kansas anymore, Toto!* Not that he'd ever been to Africa to miss the rains down there. He began to hum quietly to himself.

Ora-Jean was leading them through the woods. After coming out halfway up a mountain, they'd spotted the keep in the distance across a small valley full of trees. They were making their way toward it, as there was apparently no other way for the Sisters Sharp to get back to their home base and report.

No one had said anything about what would happen with Robin. The thought gnawed at him a bit, but he wasn't yet prepared to ask that question and get an answer he might not like. A spike of unease went through him. He shivered and looked at the woods around them.

Nothing. Just trees. A big rock. Small animals and underbrush.

"...as I understand it, the differences are often largely cultural." Fiamah was in lecture mode again.

Robin had managed to steer the conversation to classes—professions— as they existed in this world. It sounded like the system (if indeed there was a universal system everyone could access) was not a highly structured one. Classes—professions—were a matter of choice and training, not a strict system of benefits per level. Though it sounded like training in certain professions might unlock some special or exclusive spells or abilities. Abilities—peculiarities—could be chosen pretty much à la carte. There was nothing stopping someone who trained as a knight from picking up the odd fireball spell or a small facility to channel divine energies if they could meet the requirements to learn it.

That squared pretty well with his experience with raising his stats so far. He hadn't encountered any limitations on the skills he could learn or increase. Oh, they might be there, hidden, but Robin suspected that if there were limitations, he'd have smacked face-first into them already.

"Right," Grathilde added. "My school of aeromancy is unstructured, but I've met a sorceress of the Stone Winds School, up in the Hanging Peaks, and every single one of them uses the same suite of spells and abilities. It's just the way they're trained."

Grathilde was a part of the Azure Winds School. Robin had also managed to learn that Fiamah was a scholar-cleric of the Church of Seven Stars. It sounded like a cross between a specialist research group at a university and an ongoing interfaith conference. Seven different deities were worshipped by the church and its members, and it even seemed like they were from differing pantheons? Robin had a long way to go before his theological knowledge of this world was up to standard.

It was also a bit hard to follow the discussion. Robin kept getting distracted by his surroundings. The trees were massive and old. Small animals darted through the underbrush, producing unexpected sounds that pricked him with small spikes of adrenaline. The forest was breathtakingly beautiful, with crepuscular rays of light falling through the leaves in curtains of gold.

"What did you say your country was called again?" Fiamah looked to Robin.

"Prydain," he answered. It was one name, at least. Never mind it hadn't been the default in several hundred years. Albion, Britain, it was all pretty much the same, wasn't it? "It's an island nation. Well, two big islands, five or so actual nations that more or less agree to be under the rule of the most powerful monarch."

"I've not heard of it." Fiamah frowned. "You must be very far from home indeed."

"I can't even imagine," Robin agreed. "I mean, have you seen any islands that look like this?"

He used [**Visual Phantasm**] to create a small outline map of the British Isles beside them as they walked. He deliberately smudged the edges a bit in his mind. He still didn't feel entirely safe telling them he thought he was from another world entirely.

"Maybe you're from another world entirely," Grathilde said, squinting at the image.

"Is that something that happens here?" Robin asked. "It's not something I've heard of happening where I come from. Well, there are always stories, but no documented cases. That I know of." He was babbling a bit, dancing on the edge of nerves.

Another spike of unease flickered through him. Nerves. It was just nerves. He was in a strange forest in a strange world surrounded by strange women.

Robin let the illusion flicker out as they walked past. The movement limitation on the spell was frustrating. Hopefully, higher versions would be free of that particular annoyance.

"It happens. More frequently than one would think," Fiamah answered before Grathilde had the chance. "There are many recorded instances, and often, such strangers bring alien knowledge or magics with them. Not all of them work. Some might be merely unstable or deluded. But some do."

"There are ships that travel the aether seas between worlds," Lantha added. "The *Morimbelena* trade with my father's tree sometimes. If the ships can make the passage, I don't see why magic itself might not provide a bridge."

Magic spaceships. That is what Robin was hearing right now. Magic. Space. Ships. There was apparently even more to this world than he had expected. Did that have something to do with his interface?

"So they're not all immediately captured and torn apart by mad mages seeking to learn the secrets of their blood?" The question was flippant, but it hid a very real worry Robin had.

"Not all," Fiamah replied, far too slowly for Robin's liking.

"You hear stories," Grathilde added. "But they're probably just stories. Usually. Sometimes."

"How very reassuring," Robin said, not at all reassured.

The group passed a large white boulder. Ora-Jean paused, then led them off to the right. There was no path here; not even a game trail. They just had to tramp through the woods and hope for the best. At least, the insect life was minimal so far, and the biggest threat had been getting whacked in the face with a springy branch.

"I suppose it makes sense," Robin spoke cautiously. "After all, I've not heard of . . . where did you say you were from? Noviel?"

"That's where our guild headquarters is," Lantha said.

It was and was not an answer. Robin wasn't the only one playing some cards close to the vest. He prodded just a bit more. Any information would be helpful.

"Right. Noviel. City-state? Capital? Country in its own right?"

"Noviel is the leading city-state in the Amadanian Confederacy," Fiamah went into lecture mode. "It's located to the north. We're currently in an area most refer to as the Borderlands, as it's been claimed by different powers so many times over the years that none have a proper claim—"

"Plus, there's only one real pass through the mountains between the three countries whose edges meet around here," Grathilde interrupted. "And the keep occupies the whole damn plateau. Plugs it like a cork in an ale barrel."

"Which means we're—well, we're in the Borderlands, but which country are we closest to here?" Robin flicked his fingers, and a rough map appeared. In the center was the keep, and three mountain ranges all led away from the central plateau. To the north, he placed the word "Noviel."

"Ora-Jean," Grathilde called out. "Which way is south?"

The halfling growled out something and pointed.

"We're probably closest to the marcher lordships," Grathilde said.

Robin reconjured his illusory map with the new information.

"So what does that make this area?" He pointed to the blank space roughly southwest of the keep.

"The Most High and Worshipful Gilded Conglomerate," Grathilde replied.

"I'm sorry, the *what* now?"

"About a century ago, the Republic that occupied those lands was overthrown—" Fiamah began.

"Bought out. They prefer the term bought out," Grathilde offered, entirely unhelpfully.

"—by a group of merchant houses," Fiamah continued, ignoring the short sorceress. "A few families own everything, and gold rules rather than elected officials or hereditary nobility."

"Got it." Robin blinked.

"Most people just call it Glomland," Grathilde said.

"They do not!" Fiamah gave her the side-eye.

"*He* didn't know that," Grathilde protested.

"And which country has the best record of treating people well, the longest history of fostering knowledge, and the highest chance of me finding out more about what happened to me and how I can get home?"

Not that he was sure he really wanted to go home. He flexed his fingers through a pass of [**Lesser Phantasm**] and filled the air around him with the scent of baking bread. There were advantages to be had in staying here, after all.

"If you've got the gold, Glomland," Grathilde said.

"Don't listen to her!" Fiamah looked scandalized. "The University in Noviel—"

"She's biased," Grathilde talked over the cleric.

"I would also say your best chance would be Noviel, of these three choices," Lantha added. "But I am also biased."

"Same!" Ora-Jean called back over her shoulder.

Of those three choices? That implied there were more than three. Robin really needed a map or an atlas or a direct download of geographical knowledge to his brain.

Robin paused hopefully, but no new proficiencies unlocked at his wish. Ah, well. It was probably already covered by some combination of *Learning*, *Natural Wisdom*, and/or *Arcane Lore*.

He settled instead for committing the rough map to memory as best he could. The last thing he wanted was to end up lost in the wilderness with no idea which direction to head.

At least his new acquisition would help with that, should the unthinkable happen. Robin pulled up his interface to look at the description again.

[Sustaining Ring of ————]
Status: *Bound to Robin Parker*

This unusual ring was discovered in the Crypt of Yvon-Rael, though how it got there and who its original owner was remains a mystery. The magic of this unique item manifests in the following ways:

-Sustenance: The wearer of this ring no longer requires food or drink to survive. All of their basic nutritional needs are supplied by the ring.

-Storage: (Growth Quality) The wearer of the ring may access a small extradimensional space for purposes of storing food, useful items, or anything else they can lift, provided the item would fit in a standard-size pack. Retrieving items requires only an exercise of will. Current storage limit: One cubic stride.

-Slumber: The wearer of this ring benefits from the effects of nine (9) hours of sleep for every one (1) hour they slumber.

Very useful. Robin sent up thanks to Rhyth, just in case. He needed all the help he could get.

"You alright?" Fiamah was looking at him with concern in her eyes. "You seem unfocused."

"Yes, fine. Sorry. Just thinking," Robin all but stammered. "It's a lot of new information for me. Things are very different. And I can't imagine what it would be like if I didn't have a gift for languages—" *Frell!* He didn't want to draw attention to his abilities!

"It's a useful ability," Grathilde noted. "Sometimes, it seems like half the University faculty have some form or another." She shot a sly glance at Fiamah. "I even heard that the Chancellor herself has a version that allows her to read any script ever written, though she had to make a deal with—"

"That's entirely hearsay!" Fiamah snapped.

"Yes, I'm sure the Gilded Papess would agree that such things are heresy—" Grathilde continued to tease Fiamah.

That uneasy feeling spiked again. Robin looked around, but nothing immediately leapt out as a threat. He shook his head as if to clear it.

They were passing a large white boulder. It looked rather like an overstuffed armchair crossed with a roasted marshmallow. And Robin was certain they had already passed it at least once before.

"Ora-Jean," he called out carefully. "Not that I doubt your skill, but haven't we passed that boulder before?"

Ora-Jean just growled in frustration. Robin was going to take that as a yes. Before he could say anything else, however, a strange sound caught his ear. It was faint, like the far tinkling of a bell.

It sounded like . . . laughter?

"What—" Robin stopped in his tracks. "Did you all hear that?"

Tinkling laughter erupted all around them.

Everyone else stopped as well. Lantha whirled around, eyes searching. Sparks began to gather at Grathilde's fingertips.

A small chorus of voices chimed in unison:

> *You're not getting out that way!*   .

"Pixies?" Fiamah looked around, wide-eyed.

"Pixies," Ora-Jean echoed sourly.

"*Melcorín*," Lantha swore. "We're in an enchanted wood."

Chapter 2

*B*ursts of light like fireworks exploded around Robin's head as a swarm of pixies zipped out from behind the nearby leaves. Red and green and gold and blue, they zipped through the air. A notification flickered in and out of his vision as he quickly minimized it to focus on the imminent attack.

Ora-Jean yodeled a battle cry and whipped her spear through the air wildly. Lantha was shouting at the pixies in a language that was liquid, musical, and completely ineffectual. Robin stored it away nonetheless. It might come in handy in the future.

Grathilde sparked with warding magic, and Fiamah was reaching out and shouting for peace and understanding. Robin, for his part, used [**Visual Phantasm**] to wrap the illusion of a tree around himself.

Hey, if it wasn't broken, don't fix it!

There were dozens of the little dancing lights. Ora-Jean wound up her spear like a baseball bat, squinted, and swung. This time, she connected with her target. A streak of roseate light blazed like a meteor and vanished into the underbrush.

Robin had never before heard a hostile ringing of a bell, but he was hearing it now. Tiny voices chanted, and the grass around Ora-Jean suddenly grew and twisted into life, tentacles of greenery wrapping around the raging woman and binding her tightly enough that she could no longer swing her spear.

"Angering that woman is not a bright move," Robin called out, picking a turquoise mote of light to target with [**Cutting Words**]. "How dim are you?"

The turquoise mote of light staggered in midair. His words had clearly hit! But it didn't fall from the air, stunned or otherwise.

Robin's blood went cold. These little things couldn't be that much more resilient than goblins or kobolds, could they? *Yes*, his gaming experience whispered to him. *Yes, they very well could.* It made sense that some magical creatures might be somewhat resistant to magic. And here he was without an ion of cold iron.

Grathilde was now also struggling with tentacular greenery. Fiamah was still shouting out about peace, but at least she had drawn the war hammer she had scavenged from the crypt.

Lantha, oddly, was the only one not trying to attack the pixies. Robin could hear her calling out about treaties and agreements, trying to invoke various pacts. So far, she did not seem to be having much luck.

The conflict had shifted away from his illusory tree. Chaos wasn't much for stationary engagements. Robin eyed the distance between himself and the rest of the party. Should he try to get closer? Would that even make a difference with his limited spell selection?

Or was he better off staying put? If things got too much farther away, though, he'd lose sight of what was happening. Hard to target what you couldn't see.

Unfortunately, before he could decide, the choice was made for him.

"Ah, there you are!" a small, soft voice whispered in his ear.

"Wha—" Before he could get more than that single syllable out, he was hit with a full face of glittering chartreuse dust.

Robin sneezed. Then yawned—a vast, gaping yawn. Why was he so tired?

Oh, wait.

Dammit. Pixies meant—

Robin's eyes rolled up into the back of his head, and sleep claimed him.

Something rough was pressing into Robin's cheek. He groaned, opening his eyes. He was in a dim and shaded hollow of some sort.

Bark. It was bark. His face had been pressed up against a tree. The scent of earth filled his nostrils . . . possibly because his nose was literally stuffed with dirt.

His mouth felt gritty. Robin grimaced and spat out loam and decaying leaves. He twisted around and froze.

He was in a cage, if a cage could be made out of the twisted roots of a massive oak. Which it clearly could because he was in it. One. Whatever.

The pixies. The battle. He must have been hit with a [Sleep] spell of some sort. No wonder they called spells like that 'Save or Suck.' He'd gone out like a light.

It also felt as if he'd been dragged here with his face taking the brunt of the forest floor all the way.

"You alright?" someone asked him.

Robin jerked back into the tree with a start, scratching his face in the process. He hadn't noticed anyone else in the cage, and after a moment of wildly looking about, the reason became clear.

The other person in here with him was so filthy they blended almost entirely into the background. Robin squinted. He could just about make out the upswept curve of an ear amidst that thatchlike tangle of hair.

"Are you alright?" the figure asked again.

"I, ah, I'm as well as can be expected, considering I've been ambushed and enchanted by pixies, apparently dragged across several kilometers of forest on my face, and tossed in a cage made of living oak, yeah." Robin cleared his throat. "Hi. You can call me—" He paused, suddenly very conscious of everything he had ever heard about the fey and giving out one's name to strange figures in the forest. "—Red. Call me Red."

Robin dusted off his hands and then ruffled his hair, as if shaking the dust out. As he did so, he used the power of his [Mask of Disguise] to turn himself ginger.

"Eli, Priest of Vané, though I know I don't look it right now." The man smiled wryly. "I've been here quite a while now."

"Where is here, exactly?" Robin shifted, trying to get a better view through the roots.

He could see grass and flowers and trees, though the latter were a fair bit off. Possibly a forest clearing of some sort? With the oak in the center?

"Cherry's Glade," Eli replied morosely. "A dryad living in the oak tree above keeps us trapped here. I can't even say how many weeks she's held me prisoner." He shook his head. "She's a vision. I'd say don't look, but eventually, you will."

"Why—what . . . er, what is she keeping us for?" Robin was really hoping his guess was wrong.

"Sport. I'd say bed sport, but there's no bed." Eli scratched at his arm. "The loam is pretty soft, but it's got nothing on a nice bed."

Robin was not wrong. *Frakking frell.* Wait, was that why he was the only one who'd been taken? He frowned.

Something about that didn't feel quite right, but it did make sense.

New Quest: [Freedom, Freedom, Freedom!]
*If I didn't know better, I'd say you had a thing for bondage! You spend so much
time tied up and in cages. Secure your freedom, little bird, secure it thrice over.
Escape the cage of roots that binds you; escape the snares laid to entrap your
heart and will; escape the enchantment that traps you within Wyndham Wood.*
Reward: *A threefold task earns threefold experience. This multiplier stacks
with all other relevant experience multipliers. Additionally, success in the first
segment of your quest will Unlock a Random Proficiency. Success in the second
segment of your quest will Increase a Random Social Property. Success in the
third and final segment of your quest will Unlock the Lumberjack, Clothier,
and Spellbreaker Professions.*

In his experience so far, this world had a bit of a problem with consent
issues. It was an interesting spread of rewards, but Robin didn't relish how
complicated the quest itself was. That implied escaping this forest would
not be easy.

"It'll be alright," Eli was saying. "I know it's a bit overwhelming, but I'm
still alive, and where there's life, there's hope." He grimaced. "Though I'm
starting to doubt I'll regain Vané's favor at this point. The Font and Highest
Paramount of Beauty doesn't look kindly on those faithful who don't
manage to keep up appearances."

Robin filed that tidbit of information away. Vané was most likely an
elvish deity of beauty. He wondered if Nevarre, the Elvish God of Mischief,
was part of the same pantheon or not. A thought to explore later.

"You'd give just about anything for a bath, I'm guessing." Robin tried to
look sympathetic. "And I suppose you don't have [**Cleanse**] or some form
of [**Hearth's Blessing**]?"

"Not at the moment, no." Eli looked around guiltily. "Vané is perhaps a
bit upset with me at present for attempting to refuse the charms of so lovely
a creature as Cherry."

"That must be difficult," Robin said, deliberately sidestepping the more
blasphemous words that suggested themselves.

There were already enough divine beings interested in him as it was.

"It's not easy." Eli sighed. "I've been here so long, I'm practically on a
first-name basis with our erstwhile jailer." He tapped the trunk. "This is
called Neher's Oak. It's quite the story, actually—"

However, Eli would not get the chance to tell it. At that moment, the
atmosphere in the clearing changed.

The priest froze, falling silent.

A gentle breeze caressed the clearing, coaxing the grass and flowers into a whispering hymn of praise. The light around took on a soft, almost fuzzy quality. Robin pressed himself back against the trunk of the oak, his cage suddenly a comfort around him.

False comfort, no doubt, but he would take it.

"Just look and get it over with," Eli advised in a whisper. "I tried to keep my eyes closed. She had the tree pry them open."

The hair on the back of Robin's neck prickled to attention. Before he could say anything in response, he caught movement out of the corner of his eye. Reflexively he looked, and beheld *her*.

Cherry, dryad of Neher's Oak, approached with a rolling gait. Her skin—her flesh—was the rich red brown of antique furniture made from the wood that bore her name. The natural grain of the wood showed on her skin like beauty marks.

She wore nothing but the fall of her hair, if it could be called that. Her head was crowned, flamelike, with a cascade of autumn leaves, yellow, orange, and red pink bright. They rustled as she approached.

Robin found his gaze drawn to her fingers. They were long and supple as new branches. So very long. At least thrice as long as they should be, by human proportions anyway.

When she drew close, it became very clear she was thrice his height as well. Hers was the beauty of nature more than the beauty of mortality, and yet she stirred very mortal reactions in those who beheld her.

Robin fidgeted, adjusting how he sat. He almost started out of his skin when Eli shifted around and put his hand on his neck. The feel of the other man's fingers sent shivers down Robin's spine. It was electric and comforting, all at once.

It certainly gave him something else to focus on. Robin took a deep breath and leaned into the sensation. The relentless attack of Cherry's presence seemed to ease a little.

"Who have we here?" Cherry's voice was the rustle of leaves on the wind, as sweet as the full flowering of spring. "Eli, introduce me to your new friend."

"This is Red," Eli answered promptly.

"Yes, yes, he is," Cherry observed with a breathy giggle as Robin flushed as crimson as his pseudonym. "Not so pretty as you were, Eli, when first I found you, but he looks more robust." She leaned in close, her face nearly pressing through the roots that caged the two men. "I do like his leaves, however. They are pleasingly autumn colored. And he smells very well-fed."

"A side benefit of freedom," Robin managed, drawing a spark of courage from the warmth of Eli's fingers on his neck. "You should let both of us go before we start to stink of incarceration."

"I think not, little man." Cherry's eyes, petal pale at the rim and fruit dark in the center, flashed with amusement. "You're mine now, to serve me as I see fit."

"I don't belong to anyone at present, save myself," Robin snapped back. "Least of all a conceited weed with delusions of grandeur," he couldn't resist letting fly with some [**Cutting Words**], no matter how foolish.

His captor's eyes flashed fully red-black for a moment, and the leaves of her hair shivered, three of them falling gently from her head, cut free by his words. It wasn't nothing, but it wasn't as much as he'd hoped.

Robin's stomach sank. He really needed some more powerful spells.

"Oh, I think I'm going to have *fun* with you." Cherry smiled, revealing teeth of jagged bark that would do a shark proud.

Chapter 3

$\mathcal{R}$obin stared into the dryad's jagged maw. He wasn't sure what was more disturbing, the smile in front of him or the inevitable thought his mind presented him with when faced with the . . . ah, physical effects Cherry was having on him. Those *teeth*!

He winced.

"Holding people against their will is wrong," he said, trying to make his voice as firm as—

You know what? Stop it, brain!

He bit down on the inside of his cheek. "Let us go. Now."

"No, little man, I think not." Cherry swayed like a tree in a gentle breeze. "This is the forest, and here in my domain, might makes right."

He was going to need more skill if he wanted a chance of persuading her to let them go. Robin willed his interface open and with the speed of thought raised his *Persuasion* to three. He could bump it again if he had to, but he didn't want to overcommit the points right now.

"So if I got an axe and chopped down your tree while you were away, you wouldn't resent it?" Robin tried again with his newly buffed stats. "My might of arms killing Neher's Oak? Splitting it up for firewood? Kindling? You'd be all *right* with that?"

"As if a tiny thing like you could perform such a feat!" Cherry laughed, but Robin's *Insight* ensured he caught the flicker of unease that flashed through her eyes.

Robin forced a predatory smile across his face. He needed to convince her he was a threat and force her to leave. Making her mad was a dangerous ploy, but he didn't exactly have a ton of options in his back pocket right now. If it were as simple as sweet-talking the dryad, Eli would have done it already. He'd only just met the priest, but he could tell the man was very good with his tongue. So the stick rather than the carrot.

He quickly willed open his interface and raised *Intimidation* to three, erasing all his gains from battling the pixies and then some.

"I grew up splitting oak logs for firewood on my grandmother's farm," Robin shot back. "I know what it feels like for the steel edge of an axe to bite through the flaky bark of an oak into the pale beige wood beneath. I know what it smells like to be surrounded by sawdust, rich like whiskey and sweet as wine." Robin was laying it on a bit thick, but Cherry didn't seem to do subtle anyway. He widened his smile. "This oak . . . well, I think it'd make a nice table, and maybe a rocking chair for—"

Cherry's eyes went deepest red-black, and she shook with fury. "You would not dare!"

She reached out with her branches to grab at his arm and draw him nearer. In her fury, the end of her fingers pierced his skin and left splinters buried in his flesh.

"If I have the might, it is my right by your own logic," he shot back, ignoring the minor pain of her touch. "Can't object without giving the lie to your own law."

Eli huddled back, close to the trunk of the tree. His eyes were wide and kept shifting between Robin and the dryad.

"Your might is lesser than mine," Cherry hissed before flinging him away from her.

"Is it, though? You didn't capture me. A horde of pixies got lucky with a [Sleep] spell. That's nothing to do with your might."

"They serve me because I am mightier than they. It is the way of the forest—"

"You keep going on about the way of the forest, but that's just a convenient excuse for you to bully people," Robin pushed. "Rats show empathy to other rats. Apes in the great forests and jungles will help one another—even members of another species—when one falls into a pit or gets tangled in vegetation. The way of the forest, my ass. It's just a convenient excuse."

"What. Are. You. Doing?" Eli forced the words out one by one.

Robin flicked a reassuring hand his way but didn't allow his focus to slip from Cherry for an instant.

"You have quite a large mouth for so little a thing," the dryad rumbled menacingly. "I could close it for you. Would you like that? Eli there likes it when I bind his hands."

He was getting to her. Robin was definitely rubbing this dryad the wrong way. He just needed to push her a little more and hope she stormed off rather than decide to break his neck. He was counting rather heavily on the fact that she'd kept Eli alive so long, and that she seemed to have taken a liking to his red hair.

"Tch. Bri-yanch, don't test me. I will put an adze through your neck and plane your ass for an end table." Robin popped his tongue mockingly at the dryad. It had the desired effect.

"*You would not dare!*" Cherry shrieked.

"Try me! Keep this tree holding us prisoner and just try me! I'll strike a bloody match and light this old relic up."

To emphasize his words, Robin snapped through an invocation of [**Visual Phantasm**] and limned the whole tree in the illusion of flames, followed moments later with a [**Lesser Phantasm**] to supply a satisfying snap, crackle, and pop of burning wood.

"He'Neher'a!" Cherry called out in a language Robin had never heard before. "Speak to me!"

Another language. This one that trees—or at least some trees—could apparently understand. He filed it away with the rest of his swiftly growing library of [**Tongues of the Fallen Tower**]. An idea bubbled at the back of his mind.

Robin gestured again, cutting the fire and conjuring an illusory mirror standing Cherry's full height before her. The dryad recoiled in shock.

"Shadows," she hissed. "Tricks and deceit!"

"Mirrors show us as we are, Cherry," Robin shouted. "That's no lie! Look! Look at yourself! That's you, isn't it?"

The dryad held out one hesitant finger, and Robin concentrated furiously, willing the illusion to mimic her motions.

"The might of the tree cannot withstand the might of the fire, nor the might of the woodsman with his axe. Are they right to cut you down?" Robin went back on the offensive. "Here, in this place, with us bound to your will and by the roots of this tree, *we* are the forest, and you?" Robin willed the image in the mirror to change. "You are the fire."

Cheery wailed and fell back from the image of herself as an elemental of fire. Robin had kept her eyes the same exact shade of cherry red. He thought it a nice touch.

"Are you the fire, Cherry?" he yelled. "Are you the axe?"

He willed the image in the mirror to shift again, this time to a flaming axe with a handle the same color as Cherry's skin.

The dryad moved back, stumbling away from the picture before her. Robin willed the reflection to drift after her. It moved a few paces before being forced to stop by the spell's limitations. Robin hissed. He'd need to find a way to overcome that, somehow.

"Lies!" the dryad howled. "Lies and shadows and trickery! Your false words hold no power over me!"

"Then prove it!" Robin shouted. "Free us! Face me and my friends without your pixies, without *your* trickery! Because you did not overcome me by might of arm. You relied upon the magical power of a host of others."

Cherry screamed in frustration and turned, her roiling gait carrying her quickly to the edge of the clearing and into the trees.

"Get ready," Robin urged Eli. He willed his interface open and quickly upped his *Deception* to five, wincing at the experience cost.

"What?" The priest stared at him. "What do you mean? What did you do?"

"I think she's going to let us go," he said loudly, in case the tree could speak the common tongue as well as whatever language Cherry had used with it. "I think she's seen the truth in my words."

Robin twisted his hand through the figures of [**Lesser Phantasm**]. A moment later, Cherry's voice—and only her voice—seemed to echo back out of the woods to Neher's Oak, in the strange language Robin had heard her speak but once and now knew as if born to it by virtue of [**Tongue of the Fallen Tower**].

"Release them!" the dryad's voice seemed to say.

Robin held his breath, hoping against hope that his trick would work. For what seemed an eternity, nothing happened, but then, the roots around both him and Eli began to shift and draw apart until there was enough space between them for the pair to wriggle free.

"Come on." Robin pulled himself out before turning to help Eli.

The elf stood on shaky legs. He stretched, limbering a body that had spent far too much time cramped and bound by twisted roots.

"We should move quickly," Robin urged quietly.

"What?"

"Now. Come on." Robin grabbed Eli by the arm and all but dragged him in the opposite direction to where they had seen Cherry vanish into the woods. He waited until they were out of the clearing entirely before he spoke again.

"We need to put some distance between that place and us before she gets back and realizes I tricked that oak with an illusion." Robin glanced over his shoulder.

"Ah! Is *that* what you did?" Eli looked delighted. "An illusionist! How handy."

"I've only got so many tricks. We need to find the rest of my party and get out of this forest."

"Easier said than done," the priest answered. "But I know a place we can hide for a bit. Neither Cherry nor her pixies will go near the place. We can rest there and search for your friends from a relatively safe spot."

"Lead the way!" Robin gestured, more than ready to be on their way.

Eli glanced about as if getting his bearings, then began to lead them off into the forest. How he was navigating, Robin couldn't say, but he assumed there were some landmarks one could use to get around as long as you weren't being actively harassed by pixies and—the pixies! They must have been using illusions!

That must be why he'd had such an uneasy feeling. His instincts had been telling him something was off.

Robin gnawed on his lip as they walked. It wasn't a perfect defense and it would be prone to a lot of false positives, but he should try and figure out what little tells there might be in the illusions he encountered. If nothing else, it would probably help him improve his own magical arts.

Speaking of magical arts, Robin checked for any notifications. Nothing yet.

They clearly weren't far enough out of the woods. Ha.

"Maybe we should move a little faster," he suggested. Surely, he'd get a notification that the first part of his quest had been completed when they got far enough, right?

Eli simply nodded and picked up the pace. Robin followed, but his mind was on recent events more than the path before him. His investment in *Intimidation* seemed to have paid off. How much experience did he have to play with if he needed to boost another stat, though?

He pulled up his interface to check quickly.

Robin Parker

Heritage: Shadeling, Mature
Profession: None
Tier: 0
Progress to Tier 1: 74%

Properties
(Free Ranks Available: 1)

Physical
-Strength: 11
-Dexterity: 14
-Fortitude: 11
Mental
-Intelligence: 17
-Cunning: 19
-Resilience: 14
Social
-Charisma: 15
-Manipulation: 13
-Poise: 15

Proficiencies
(Free Ranks Available: 2)

Physical (7/9)
-Athletics: 1
-Brawl: 0
-Dodge: 4
-???
-???
-Ranged Combat: 0
-Sleight of Hand: 1
-Stealth: 4
-Survival: 1
Mental (8/9)
-Arcane Lore: 1
-???
-Concentration: 1
-Crafting: 1
-Healing: 0
-Insight: 3
-Learning: 1
-Natural Wisdom: 0
-Perception: 4
Social (7/9)
-???

-Deception: 5
-Empathy: 1
-Expression: 4
-Gossip: 0
-Intimidation: 3
-Persuasion: 3
-Socialize: 1
-???

Peculiarities

Blessing of Rhyth
Tongue of the Fallen Tower
Mark of the Trickster
Chronicle of Infinite Visions

Robin had about 7 percent to play with. It wasn't a lot; it would boost one of his lower proficiencies. Maybe one of his lower properties?

He concentrated, testing to see if it would let him.

Level insufficient to raise selected Property with experience. Please advance in power to enable this option.

Huh. He couldn't use experience to raise his core stats until his level was higher than the stat in question? Interesting. Why on Earth—or wherever he was—might that be?

He was distracted from further pondering the vagaries of the magio-physical laws he was now subject to by Eli. The elf had his hand extended, and a small squirrel was chittering at him and running along a branch slightly to the right of the direction they were headed.

"Are you talking to that squirrel?" Robin asked. Hey, Ora-Jean talked to an invisible badger. Who was he to judge?

"No." Eli smiled. "I'm trying to get a sense from his movements about which way Cherry might be headed. I'm not having much luck."

"How can you tell he's afraid of her and not of you?" Robin looked from the elf to the squirrel and back.

"It helps if you speak softly and don't make any sudden movements, to start," Eli answered.

Proficiency Unlocked: Animism.

Interesting naming convention. Still, Robin knew the proficiency covered interacting with animals and that it would likely come in useful sometime, if not very soon.

"Where did you learn—" Robin began, but the rest of his sentence was lost.

A scream of rage resounded through the forest, cutting off their conversation.

Birds took flight, the sounds of startled wings adding to the cacophony. The underbrush rustled as small animals dove for their burrows, and a stag went leaping past, eyes wide and bloodshot.

"I think she might be over in that direction," Robin said drily, even as his heart began to hammer in his chest.

"Let's put some more distance between where we are and where she is right now," Eli suggested.

"Good idea."

They turned and plunged deeper into the woods.

Chapter 4

A stray branch etched a line of fire across Robin's cheek as he ran, following close behind the fleeing figure of Eli. Around them, the woods rustled, trees and plants moving in unnatural ways, bending under the brunt of Cherry's fury. Fortunately, they weren't at full-on *Evil Dead* levels of movement.

Yet.

"This way," Eli called from up ahead. "We're not far now!"

Not far from what? Shelter of some kind, yeah, but what? Robin's mind was spinning with all manner of warding stones or circles of flame, but he didn't know what to look for.

Best not get separated, then.

Robin tried to put on a burst of speed, but Eli remained almost out of sight ahead of him. The cleric was just faster on his feet. Robin really shouldn't have given up running after this past Christmas.

He also wasn't used to running in a forest that was quite this thick with underbrush and fallen branches. Robin tripped over a concealed limb and nearly went sprawling. It was only through dumb luck and some serious windmill action with his arms that he didn't face-plant in the dirt in front of him.

When he righted himself, Eli was nowhere in sight. He'd saved himself a tumble but lost his guide!

"Eli!" he shouted, "Eli, can you hear me? Where are you?"

Come on! Focus! It's a world of skills, one of which is Survival.

Robin quirked an ear in case Eli shouted back at him, then turned his eye to the woods, looking for signs of passage.

It can't be that hard, right? They'd been running full tilt, not exactly trying to conceal their tracks. And this was a forest floor, not the stone of a mountain tunnel. It should hold tracks easily.

It did, quite clearly. Robin's own trail was painfully clear. Well, he knew where he'd seen Eli last. He just needed to continue carefully in that direction until he spotted the trail.

Robin moved forward as quickly as he dared, which was not that speedy a pace at all. Anxious whispers mocked him from the corners of his mind where they partied with his fears and got drunk on the adrenaline spiking at the base of his jaw. He had to hurry. Eli could easily outpace him, and if the cleric routed up a stream or hit a patch of rocky ground, Robin might lose the trail.

A few agonizing minutes later, Robin found the signs of Eli's passage. At least, he hoped they were Eli's, though any of his allies would do. There were definitely footprints here; too big to be Grathilde's or Ora-Jean's, but the right size for Lantha or Fiamah. They were probably Eli's. It made the most sense that they were Eli's.

Focus!

Robin shook his head to clear it and set off following the trail, speeding up now that he had it. He still couldn't move as fast as he had before, but the pace soothed his anxieties a bit.

Though why hadn't Eli stopped? Had he not noticed? Robin picked up the pace a bit more. Maybe something had happened; he had no idea how Cherry might move through the forest. Dryads in some literature could literally step into one tree and out of another—a perfect ambush power, if used correctly.

Dammit. He really did not know enough about this world he found himself in. And relying on superficial similarities between this place and the games and literature of his own world would probably get him killed sooner rather than later.

"Robin! Stop!"

Eli's voice slammed into his ears just as he was about to follow the cleric's tracks into a small clearing. Robin windmilled his arms again, this time to grab hold of a nearby trunk and arrest his momentum. The bark scraped his palm, but he managed to stop himself from tumbling headfirst out of the trees.

It was a small clearing, only a dozen or so strides across. It was dominated by the blasted trunk of what had once been a massive tree. An oak? Robin had no way to tell. Its death had left a huge gap in the woods. Now, that space was filled with lush green grass and some form of flowering vine.

Verdant tendrils studded with starlike yellow blossoms wrapped around the tree and snaked through the grass. Robin could just make out several similarly bright-colored gourds in various stages of growth peeking through the grass.

Eli was sprawled near the base of the dead tree's trunk, one leg and an arm partially elevated into the air and bound to the dead wood with the living vines. Robin involuntarily began to take a step forward before he saw the nearest vine slither toward him. He froze.

"What is that thing?" he called to Eli.

"Ghilded ghourd," came the reply. "It's a sentient plant, very dangerous. You're going to have to find something you can use to smash as many ghourds as you can. That should weaken the vine enough that you can tear me free."

"On it!" Robin began searching around for something he could use as a weapon.

"Quick as you can," Eli yelled. "This thing is already trying to invade my mind."

"It's *what?*" Robin whipped around to look at the tableau again. As he watched, the vines shifted again, and this time, he clearly saw the tendrils coiling their way into Eli's ears. "Right. Be with you in a sec!"

What was with this world and snaky things trying to get inside your head, literally?

Robin shuddered at the memory of the priest of Urkhan and the serpent that lived in his empty eye socket.

There! A seasoned branch, reasonably straight. That would do for a quarterstaff.

Robin snapped off a few twigs and gave it an experimental twirl. Had he trained in the use of the staff? No. Had he spent too much time as a child pretending to be Robin Hood, Bugs Bunny, and various Jedi? Oh, *frells* yeah.

Proficiency Unlocked: Melee Combat.

Oh yeah. That would do nicely.

Robin whipped open his interface and dumped what little experience he had gained from his recent, well, experiences into the stat. It was enough to bring it up to two.

His opponents were mostly gourds—err, ghourds—so how hard could they be to hit, even if the vine could move under its own power. Staff in hand, Robin prepared to enter the ring of cleared woodland.

"You call that a gourd?" he called out as he moved into position. "I've seen bigger bulges at a beesting convention!"

Might as well try [Cutting Words] to see if or how well it worked.

The grass rustled, and Eli keened in pain.

Robin froze. What had just happened?

"Smash the ghourds!" Eli yelled. "Distract it from taking over my mind!"

Fucking hell! The vine was linked to Eli; the magic had hit them both. He'd have to trust the cleric that smashing the wannabe pumpkins was safer.

Robin roared a battle cry, lifted his staff, and brought it down like a spear, thrusting into the gourd. Ghourd. The seasoned wood easily broke through the tough outer rind, puncturing it like a nail through an overfull tire.

He was not prepared for what happened after. A jet of fizzing golden liquid erupted from the thing, propelling a handful of pearl-white seeds across the clearing.

Robin took it full in the face. And in his still open mouth.

"Yes! Just like that!" Eli yelled. "Quick! Smash some more!"

Robin yanked his staff free and blinked his vision clear. He coughed and swallowed, spitting to clear his mouth. The stuff tasted oddly of pineapple. His face was sticky, but at least his eyes didn't sting.

He brought the staff down lengthwise across the next ghourd, however, rather than spearing it. The thing cracked, and half the ghourd went skidding across the clearing, propelled by the eruption of the juices inside.

"Watch out!" Eli's voice rang out.

Robin looked around wildly. The vines were sneaking their way toward him.

He jumped up and freed a hand to dance through the motions of [Lesser Phantasm]. Any extra confusion had to help, right? He conjured a boulder and darted around it.

The vines lashed through it like it wasn't even there. *Fuck!* Either the thing was immune or it was using some other sense to track him, something that didn't equate to sight. Smell would probably work better. Plants communicated with pheromones, didn't they? Though that was in his world; who knew how it worked in this one.

Robin spun his staff around and clipped another ghourd, hitting it right at the juncture where it joined the vine. It shot off into the woods like a rocket. He *Dodged* out of the way of the lashing vine coiling madly like a snake with its head cut off.

Hit. Run. Hit. Run. Jump. Dash.

Robin panted as he sprinted around the clearing. The grass around him almost sounded like it was hissing its fury.

"Robin!"

Eli's warning caused him to glance around the clearing. The vines had bunched up around the remaining ghourds, but that wasn't all. The rich loam of the clearing shifted in several spots around the corpse of the old tree.

That was not good. No way was that ever good.

Snarling and spitting black dirt, ragged forms clawed their way out of the ground. The rotted form of a massive stag stared at him, golden gaze unblinking, while a trio of wolves slobbered and snapped as they struggled free of the soil, and several hares and badgers easily popped free due to their yellowed claws being so suited for digging.

"They've each got a ghourd in their skull!" Eli yelled. "That's what's animating and controlling them, so it's the same game as before! Smash them!"

Robin whirled his staff and scored a lucky strike, the end of it clipping one of the wolves right in the eye. The resultant explosion was messy, but effective. The carcass went down and did not rise again.

The other animals began to circle around him, showing an unnatural level of coordination as the vine controlled them all. This could get bad, fast.

Robin whirled the staff like a baseball bat, smacking one of the bunnies out of the air as it lunged for his jugular. It went flying, but he could tell he'd missed the skull. It would be back.

He dashed across the clearing, hurdling a ghourd and its defending vines. He had to keep moving or he'd be surrounded. As an experiment, he tossed out three **[Lesser Phantasm]**s as he ran, conjuring up the thickest, most pungent smells he could remember.

Bleach. Aging cheese. Weed killer.

His targets were the deer and the two remaining wolves; they were the easiest to see. Robin turned quickly and brought his staff down on the badger shambling after him. It cracked like an overripe melon, which . . . well, it kinda was.

The deer and one of the wolves were headed in his direction. The other wolf was shaking its head and trying to snuff something out of its nose.

So he could interfere with their communication, at least a bit.

Robin crushed the ghourd skull of another badger and darted around the tree. The badgers were the easiest targets: small enough to be taken out in one hit, and much slower than the rabbits.

"Deer?" he shouted. "More like, oh dear, what the fuck happened to you?!"

These ghourds weren't connected to the vine, so he was hoping his [Cutting Words] wouldn't be carried through to Eli.

A scream from the cleric disabused him of that notion.

"Sorry!"

"No, that wasn't as bad," Eli yelled hoarsely. "If you need to, I can stand half a dozen or so hits like that. Just—make 'em count."

Robin stumbled into action. He was panting, the adrenaline spiking his energy levels up even as he felt his muscles begin to protest their continued abuse. He played a deadly game of tag, trying to keep the tree trunk between himself and as many of his foes as he could.

Staff twirling and mind whirling, he fought his way through the rest of the badgers and all but two of the rabbits, smashing the rest of the ghourds in the process. The remaining wolf he managed to fell with a distracting insult that left the creature wide open for Robin to slam his staff down upon the thing's skull. The twin plumes of golden juice that the action prompted drenched him from head to toe.

The stag remained, with the two hares harassing him from the sides, keeping him from focusing. The massive rack the stag boasted foiled his attacks too easily, and he could only risk one more use of [Cutting Words].

Robin spared a glance for Eli. The elvish cleric had stopped shouting. He was pale, bound to the tree, eyes rolled back in his head. The vines had stopped trying to trip him up as actively when the squash-zombie-animals had arisen. The plant clearly had its own limits.

Blood dripped from cuts all across his body. He could tell that when—possibly *if*—he woke up tomorrow, he would be feeling each and every one of the bruises already purpling his flesh.

The end of his staff drooped. The rabbits darted in, trying to flank him as the stag charged. Robin let the rabbits sink their incisors deep into his calves, keeping his focus on the stag.

It lunged. He shouted.

"Oi! Bambi! If I were your mother, I'd have *let* that hunter kill me in front of you!"

The deer staggered, hit side-on by the insult, arresting its momentum enough for Robin to slam the staff into the rack of antlers and *twist*, bearing down with his weight.

The staff turned. The antlers followed. The stag's neck twisted around after, and Robin drove the rack into a tangle of vines. He lost his grip on his weapon, but rather than go after it, he reached down to the rabbits trying to savage his legs even further and popped the ghourds in their skulls by squeezing his fingers through their gaping eye sockets.

The scent of pineapple rose to his nostrils, sharp and sweet. Robin flung the juice off his hands and turned his attention to the struggling stag, now tangled in the same vines that controlled it. Already they were wriggling around, trying to untangle themselves from their puppet.

Robin's staff was still caught up between the mess. Well, there was more dead wood around; the tree's fallen branches had not yet fully rotted away.

Robin grabbed a nearby stick, thick as an axe handle, and stabbed wildly at the struggling stag's head until a lucky blow punctured the ghourd inside and ended the whole performance.

The vine quivered and went slack. Robin let himself collapse to his knees, panting.

He'd free Eli in a minute. He just needed to catch his breath first.

That, and one more thing.

Robin caught himself on his blistered, bleeding palms as he fell forward and vomited his guts out.

Chapter 5

$\mathcal{E}$very step blazed agony up Robin's legs; those frelling rabbits had bit deep into his calves. He and Eli leaned against one another as they staggered through the forest. Every rustle of a leaf or snap of a twig was a new threat, but Robin was running so dry on adrenaline that his body barely reacted.

"Almost there," Eli promised for the third time in less than a minute.

Robin just grunted in response. Most of his focus was on moving forward and leaving Cherry as far behind him as he could. Not that the other plant life in this frak-hole was much better.

He spit, thinking of the ghilded ghourds and the demonic vine that had spawned them. Well, he'd wanted magic! And magic he had gotten.

He'd recovered enough to tear Eli free of the stunned vine, ripping as much of it up by the roots as he could manage in the process. There were seeds scattered all across the clearing, however. Robin was sure it would regrow even stronger than before.

Unfortunately.

"Almost there," Eli said again. It wasn't clear if he was trying to motivate Robin or himself at this point.

Robin winced as his wounds burned. Between himself and Eli, there weren't even enough rags to tear apart for decent bandages, but the cleric had scavenged enough moss to pack the worst of them, so at least he wasn't leaving a trail of blood for Cherry or her minions to follow. Or to use in dark magical rituals.

Oh god. Gods. He really needed to learn more about how this world worked.

"There it is!" Eli's voice perked up, a trickle of energy running through the words.

Robin looked up, blinking through the cascades of sunlight falling into the new clearing. *Another clearing? Already? Please no.*

But this one was different. Massive menhirs rose around the perimeter of the clearing. Robin couldn't tell if it was a perfect circle or a very regular polygon of some sort from where he stood, but the clearing was definitely not natural, even if it had clearly been here for a long time. The boundary stones each grew a healthy crop of moss.

In the center of the clearing, the stump of a tower squatted. Robin winced as he saw the vines that wound irregularly around it.

Too soon, world. Too soon.

"Come on," Eli said. "We'll be safe inside. Neither Cherry nor those that serve her will come here."

"What stops them?" Robin really wanted a bit of clarity on that right now. He was in no shape to run away again.

"Wards. The important ones are still intact." Eli started forward, all but dragging Robin along with him. "So far as I can tell, anyway."

After a moment's consideration, Robin decided he was too tired not to roll the dice. Wincing, he took more of his own weight back from Eli. If they were this close to safety, he could manage a bit of a brave face.

He hissed as the added weight set more of his wounds to throbbing.

For now. He could manage for now.

Hobbling closer, it became apparent that the vines weren't *completely* random. There were spaces on the tower they seemed to avoid. Eli led him to the largest of these, at ground level. It was roughly the size of a door.

Eli laid a hand on the stone and simply asked it to open. The stone vanished, and Eli pulled Robin into the shadows within.

It was certainly the least terrifying thing he'd seen all day, so Robin allowed himself to be pulled along with a minimum of trepidation. The door sealed itself behind them, but as it did so, runes flickered to light in long chains along either wall of the corridor, providing a soft blue-white luminescence to everything.

[Tongue of the Fallen Tower] allowed him to see that the runes he focused on almost all read as *The Light of Tel'Perion Evenstar*, with a few that were structured as conditionals for *passage* and *renewal*. He couldn't quite see the magical links between everything, but his gut told him that making the magic was a bit more involved than scrawling the symbols themselves on a surface.

Not something to worry about right now.

As soon as the door had sealed itself behind them, Robin had received a quest update notification. He'd scanned it quickly before dismissing it to focus on the lights, but it went a long way to reassuring him that this was truly a safe place.

Quest Progress Update: [Freedom, Freedom, Freedom!]
Congratulations! You have successfully escaped the cage of roots that bound you and extracted yourself from the magical roots Cherry wrapped around your being. Parts 2 and 3 of this quest still pending.
Reward: *Random proficiency unlocked!*

Proficiency Unlocked: Streetwise. All Social Proficiencies Unlocked!

"Through here; come on." Eli tugged him on.

The cleric led him to a long, narrow room. A series of bunk beds and chests lined either wall. The wood was solid, with no signs of rot, but also dry and cracked. It had been a long time since it had been polished or cared for.

Each bed still had a mattress and bedclothes on it. Robin reached out to one. The weave was finer than he expected, more like cotton than home-spun or burlap. The cloth was stiff from disuse, but otherwise remarkably intact.

"Wait here," Eli said. "I'll go get some water; there's a well that stays fresh in here. No food, though." The cleric grimaced. "We'll have to go out and forage later. That's how she captured me last time, so we'll need to be careful."

Robin just nodded. That was a problem for Future Robin, not Present Robin, who was about to pass out from exhaustion.

"I'll wash up after." Eli smiled. "Be right back."

Robin all but collapsed onto the bed. Huh. Not much dust for an abandoned ruin. Before he could ponder that curiosity further, sleep took him.

Robin awoke suddenly, coming to consciousness in a sudden burst. He felt fully and completely rested. The sheet was cool against his chest as he stared up at the wood above him. Bunk beds. The tower. He shifted, and his wounds groaned with pain. The battle. The clearing.

There was a stone cup and a clay jug on the floor next to his bed. Water.

Wait, why wasn't he thirsty? He should be dry as dust.

Right! The ring he'd found. It could sustain him without food or drink. Nonetheless, he still had a bit of a foul taste in his mouth.

Robin reached down and poured himself a cup of water. It was sweet and clear, albeit room temperature rather than refreshing and cool. He could make it feel cool with [**Lesser Phantasm**], but it didn't quite seem worth the effort.

Then and only then did he notice he was completely clean. Clean and naked. Again. And if he hadn't done it, that meant Eli had. Interesting . . . and entirely unfair. Why should he get to see everything Robin had, when Robin hadn't seen—

"Morning," Eli called from the doorway.

Robin glanced over and stiffened. The elvish cleric was clean, quite naked, and entirely . . . what's the technical term? Hot as frelling frak.

Damp hair the rich dark blue of morning glories fell to a ragged halt around his shoulders. His eyes matched, and his skin was a green so pale as to be nearly white. He was also much more muscular than Robin imagined elves to be, but hey, who was he to complain?

"I thought I'd wash the clothes. They were a bit worse for wear, considering. They should be dry in a few hours."

"Smart," Robin said, focusing his gaze quite firmly on Eli's face. "What do we do until then?"

His pulse leapt up a gear as Eli smiled. The elf was really too handsome to be allowed to do that. No wonder he was a cleric of the Deity of Beauty. Or was it the other way around? Did it matter that he'd lost her grace? Or did he have it back now that he was clean and looking like *that*?

"Sorry I haven't been able to heal your wounds," Eli spoke, crossing the room to sit on Robin's bed. "I'm afraid Vané will require an extreme act of penitence from me before she restores her favor and I'm able to channel enough divine energies to heal again." He ran a hand through his hair. "It's been a long time since I had to wash with water instead of simply using [**Vané's Blessing**] to look my best."

"No one would be able to tell," Robin said. "You look great." He shifted under the sheet so his body wouldn't give him away any more than it already was.

"You are very kind." Eli smiled. "Would you like to see the rest of the tower? There are some fascinating sights."

There were plenty of fascinating sights to look at right here, right now. Robin shifted again. He needed a minute. Clearly, the elves—or maybe the Church of Vané—had no nudity taboos. He deliberately pressed on his calf as he sat up. Pain spiked through him and yanked his mind onto a less potentially embarrassing track.

"Yes, I'd like very much to see your tower—the tower." Still, Robin couldn't resist a touch of innuendo, just in case.

"This way." Eli rose and walked toward the door.

Robin bit his cheek. It wasn't the cheek he wanted to bite, but it was the one he needed to bite. *Tour now. Then clothes.* He considered using his mask to cover himself; he could still feel it resting around his eyes. But no. That would put them on uneven footing and make things even more awkward.

Where had his illusory coat gone, though? Could it be separated from his person, and was it real enough to be washed? Had it vanished when he fell asleep? Eli hadn't said anything.

Too many questions, not enough answers.

The tower wasn't large. There were several small rooms around the perimeter, and stairs leading both up and down, but the bulk of the space was dedicated to a large central room. A massive pillar of what looked to be crystal thrust a few meters into the air, albeit the ceiling rose farther still above it. Around the pillar was wrapped a heptagonal table of stone with runes both large and small etched across the surface.

"Much of the magic still holds," Eli was saying. "I managed to locate the wards and activate the basic protection spells. There are others, but either they have faded or broken with the passage of time, or I do not know enough to activate them."

"Is this kind of setup common among your people?" Robin asked, slowly circling the table. [**Tongue of the Fallen Tower**] spilled the secrets of the control runes as he went. Greater and Lesser Arcana. Botany and Biology. Wards and Protections. Cartography. Records. Communications. Provisioning.

"No. I do not recognize this style of architecture, nor most of these rune formations. I was able to deduce the ward functions from my childhood instruction in magic, and lucky to manage even that. I was not the most apt of pupils when it came to the arcane arts." Eli smiled ruefully. "And I suspect this section has something to do with interacting with the natural world." He gestured to the section Robin had read as dealing with Botany and Biology.

It all looked far more technological than Robin had expected. And it was so old. But it didn't seem like this level of tech—magitech?—was common, or Eli would have a greater grasp on things here. What kind of world was this?

His eyes strayed to the Cartography panel.

"This looks like it should be some kind of map," he said, gingerly running his fingers over the central rune of that station.

As he said the word *map*, the rune flared to life. An illusion appeared before him. In the center was a small icon that looked like a tower, albeit a much taller one than the stump they currently occupied. Around it spread a cartographic representation of a surrounding valley and what Robin thought must be mountains.

"Looks like you were correct!" Eli moved to join him.

The cleric's shoulder brushed Robin's as he leaned closer to examine the map. The contact sent a jolt of electricity down Robin's spine.

Map. Focus on the map.

Robin coughed, then cleared his throat. "I wonder if I can get a wider view."

Instinctively, he reached out and placed his hands at the edges of the image, moving them toward the center like he was zooming out on a smartphone or tablet.

It worked. Maybe some things were universal. The illusion shimmered, and a chunk of the continent was now floating before him; a regional map. He could clearly see the pass currently occupied by the keep he and the Sisters Sharp had spotted when they'd emerged from beneath the mountain. It was occupied by a keep in this map as well. Was it the same one?

"How did you know to do that?" Eli was looking at him with unabashed interest.

"Just . . . instinct," Robin answered. "Does it still match what you'd expect of the region? Or is it out of date?"

"Can you get it to show a bit more?" Eli asked, transferring his gaze to the map. "I'm not sure from what we see here. The cities I'm familiar with are outside this range."

"Sure!" Robin reached out to zoom the map further out. Flustered from Eli's attention, however, he flicked his hands harder than he'd intended.

Much harder.

The illusion whirled in front of them, mountains and forests and seas flashing before their eyes. Light flickered and images zoomed past until the picture resolved itself into something new. A mote of light blazed in the center like a star, and several shapes drifted around that point in a spherical cloud.

"What?" Robin blinked.

"A full orrery!" Eli grabbed Robin's arm. "This is amazing! I've not seen one since I last visited the University of El Darond."

"What?" Robin repeated.

"This is the sun." Eli pointed to the mote of light. "And these are the lands that Úrin shines upon. I've never seen an orrery this extensive before; I only recognize a handful of these lands."

Robin's mind began to race. This is what the world looked like? Not quite a Dyson sphere nor a ringworld, but a . . . Dyson cloud?

If this was accurate, what did it mean for gravity? Night? Magnetism? Things clearly operated on vastly different laws here. He wasn't even standing on a planet!

Here, if dwarves delved too deep, did they fall out the bottom of the world? And if the sun was similar to Sol, and the lands an equivalent distance away, that would be like—even with the cloud effect—something like 250 million times the surface area of Earth in habitable lands floating around this sun? Maybe even twice that?

This . . . this would take some time to process.

Frak Kansas! He wasn't even in frelling Oz anymore!

Chapter 6

$\mathcal{R}$obin's fingertips tingled. Perhaps it was psychosomatic; perhaps it was some side effect of interacting with the illusion magic. Whatever it was, between the strange sensation and the excitement of exploring the orrery, he had almost—*almost*—forgotten he was naked.

Eli had used what he knew of the various lands to direct their efforts, and Robin now had a much more in-depth idea of what the continent he stood on was like, as well as a solid idea of the three others nearest them in orbit around the sun. There were ships and sailors that braved the aethers between lands, and, if Eli were to be believed, vast monsters that swam (flew?) through them as well.

Fortunately, the elvish cleric had been focused on the map when a notification sprang up before Robin's eyes, startling him.

Congratulations! Perk Awarded: [Wayfaring Stranger]
You have beheld the entirety of the world and seen more lands than most can dream of in their time. A bit of this wonder remains with you always to act as a guiding star.
Effect: *You have an unerring sense of direction, as you always know your place in relation to the sun at the center of Mayaser.*

Perk? Similar to a peculiarity, it sounded like, but not one he was able to choose. Maybe it was like a title or an achievement? The phrasing certainly squared with that idea.

Well, this one would certainly come in handy.

Robin dismissed the notification. There was so much to learn—to memorize, if he could—of the land he currently stood upon. And the wider world was apparently called Mayaser?

The map was old. Ancient, even. He'd asked Eli about the cities the Sisters Sharp had told him about, but even when they'd managed to pull up a political overlay for the map, the nations and city names hadn't matched. But he did manage to get a general idea of where Noviel was likely to be.

After all, the landscape hadn't shifted so drastically that the sorts of places cities often cropped up had changed as well. Sentient beings still liked to congregate near rivers, for example. Still, magic should probably shift a lot of his expectations and assumptions. If you could conjure fresh water or teleport, rivers might become less convenient, although that would depend on how common powerful magic was.

Robin's stomach cramped. He hissed in pain.

Wow. That was sharp.

"Hungry?" Eli asked, glancing at Robin and the hand he held over his stomach.

"I dunno," Robin answered. "Maybe I had too much water? Doesn't feel like hunger." Because this wasn't at all an embarrassing conversation to have, let alone while naked with a handsome stranger.

"The clothes should be dry by now. We should probably try to sneak out and forage as much food as we can." Eli frowned. "The more we can carry, the fewer trips we'll have to make outside, and the fewer chances Cherry will have to ambush us."

Right. The demented dryad. They also needed to figure a way out of this enchanted wood.

Something teased at the back of his mind. A hint of song? He could almost hear the lyrics, whispering at the back of his mind.

He frowned.

"What?" Eli asked. "You have an idea?"

"Maybe. Not sure. Let me think about it while you get the clothes?"

Eli nodded and slipped out the door. Robin quickly stepped around the pillar and activated the central rune in the Records array. He was sorely tempted by the one marked Greater and Lesser Arcana, but he didn't have much time, and he wasn't ready to reveal he could read the language. Hopefully, the Records would have some information about this place he could use, maybe an instruction manual to figure stuff out before *coincidentally stumbling* across it for Eli's benefit.

A web appeared before him. Some sort of organizational system? He flicked through it quickly. Checking a few, uh, files? Robin quickly determined that moving his hands in a clockwise motion spiraled things forward in time, while counterclockwise did the reverse.

Keeping one ear perked for Eli's return, he swiftly dialed back as far as he could go. The first few files should have the operations information; maybe a log of why this place was built. If he was lucky.

He was and he was not. He was not lucky enough to find a simple operations manual. There were too many files, and many systems seemed to have one or more technical manuals all their own. He could read the words, but he lacked most of the necessary knowledge to really *understand* what he was reading.

Luckier was finding the research log of the being that had headed this outpost. There was a succinct outlay of mission parameters right there at the front!

Whatever the people who'd built this place were like physically, their minds were very ordered.

As best Robin could decipher without full context, this place had been both a border outpost and something like a research station. It sounded like when these people had arrived, they'd had no idea if this was all just wilderness or if they'd encounter other sentient or sapient beings. That explained the other stations.

There had to be a search function, but for the life of him, Robin couldn't find it. The dates were also useless for figuring out how long ago everything had happened. He wasn't at all familiar with the system.

He scanned through several more entries. The captain, as he was calling the person in his mind, detailed the complex problems of supply lines and additional funding, the implications of their early findings for the City of Novarrion—related to Noviel?—and dozens of other smaller matters of rules and regulations and the like.

Proficiency Unlocked: Bureaucracy. All Mental Proficiencies Unlocked!

Right. That was definitely a useful skill to have in certain situations, but maybe not super useful right now.

Robin flicked the notification away, but not before he noticed the similarities between it and the illusory interface the tower used. Both were illusions that conveyed information. Were they related?

He considered it briefly. It didn't feel like they were the same, for all their similarities. His interface certainly acted like something that was using advanced readings or logistics to quantify something that was more naturally occurring. Like a river had power and force, but you could build a small waterwheel and output screen to display how quickly the water was running without taking all the measurements each time you wanted to know.

That would also sort of fit with the way the Sisters Sharp had talked about their abilities. None of them seemed to have an interface, though they, like him, had magic and peculiarities and proficiencies and the like.

For a quick comparison, Robin pulled up his character sheet.

Robin Parker

Heritage: Shadeling, Mature
Profession: None
Tier: 0
Progress to Tier 1: 88%

Properties

(Free Ranks Available: 1)

Physical
    -Strength: 11
    -Dexterity: 14
    -Fortitude: 11
Mental
    -Intelligence: 17
    -Cunning: 19
    -Resilience: 14
Social
    -Charisma: 15
    -Manipulation: 13
    -Poise: 15

Proficiencies

(Free Ranks Available: 3)

Physical (8/9)
    -Athletics: 1
    -Brawl: 0
    -Dodge: 4

-Melee Combat: 2
-???
-Ranged Combat: 0
-Sleight of Hand: 1
-Stealth: 4
-Survival: 1
Mental (9/9)
-Arcane Lore: 1
-Bureaucracy: 0
-Concentration: 1
-Crafting: 1
-Healing: 0
-Insight: 3
-Learning: 1
-Natural Wisdom: 0
-Perception: 4
Social (9/9)
-Animism: 0
-Deception: 5
-Empathy: 1
-Expression: 4
-Gossip: 0
-Intimidation: 3
-Persuasion: 3
-Socialize: 1
-Streetwise: 0

Peculiarities

Blessing of Rhyth
Tongue of the Fallen Tower
Mark of the Trickster
Chronicle of Infinite Visions

Perks

Wayfaring Stranger

Huh. His experience bar was a lot higher than it should be. There had been
the fight with the ghilded ghourds, sure, but even with the zombie animals
and all, it . . . seemed like a lot of experience.

Then Robin remembered the perk he had unlocked. Exploring taught a person a lot. Travel broadened one, as it were. Did you also get experience for new, well, experiences? Not just combat? If exploration and discovery also counted, that would explain a lot.

Robin felt a part of himself relax. It also meant he wouldn't have to rush around like a murderhobo in order to develop his magic. And speaking of magic . . .

Robin glanced over at the Greater and Lesser Arcana panel.

No. Not quite yet. He needed to check a few more of the records. There was a reason this place had been abandoned and not dismantled when the research team had left. He needed to see if the latest log entries said anything about that, especially if there was a mention of Cherry.

He'd give his left pinkie for a search function at this point!

Maybe. Probably not.

Still.

Robin gestured in a clockwise motion and spun the log all the way to its last entry. No mention of Cherry or anything resembling a dryad, but "strange occurrences in the surrounding woods" came up, as did "evidence of sorceries unknown." Then the log just stopped. No discussion of withdrawal, no mention of steadily increasing attacks, nothing. Just . . . done.

Ugh. Well, so much for that avenue. He wouldn't get much more out of this without a lot more time and research. So maybe he should look elsewhere.

Maybe somewhere that could teach him more about magic, for example?

He'd just closed the Records interface and taken a few steps over to assuage his curiosity when he heard Eli's footsteps returning. *Curses! Foiled again!*

Another time.

Robin quickly stepped back to the Cartography panel and pulled the map back up. He was, to all appearances, busily trying to memorize nearby terrain features when Eli stepped back in the room wearing his clothes and carrying Robin's pants.

"Clean and dry," he said, handing the clothes to Robin.

"Thank you." Robin took them and quickly dressed, hissing as the material tugged at some of his wounds.

There was no sign of his illusory coat, and his improvised sandals were tattered and worn through to near uselessness. Shoes. One more thing to try and find.

"I don't suppose there are any storage rooms in here? Or closets?" Robin asked. Maybe he could check some of those chests in the room with the bunk beds. This place had been abandoned with little notice. Surely there had to be supplies left behind, or something he could use to improvise some better footwear.

"Ah, yes, I suppose illusory boots wouldn't do terribly much for protecting your feet, would they?" Eli mused.

Robin had to force himself not to react. For some reason, Eli knowing he had been using illusion for part of his clothing made him anxious. Why keep so many secrets? He'd used **[Lesser Phantasm]** in front of the cleric before. It was hardly a secret that he knew a few illusion spells.

But knowledge was power, and Robin held precious few cards here in this strange world. His eyes flicked to the orrery floating over the Cartography panel.

This very, very strange world.

"No. No, they don't," he agreed.

"I do appreciate you were kind enough to join me in the nude," Eli said. "It always feels odd when only one party is clothed in a situation like this."

"You get into situations like this often?" Robin asked, mostly to cover the rising tide of crimson that threatened to overtake his cheeks.

"Trapped in a remote location with a stranger and neither of us wearing anything save what we were born with?" Eli shrugged. "Happens more than you'd think."

"Especially for a priest in the service of the Deity of Beauty," Robin hazarded. "I can see it coming up often as part of your devotions."

Eli laughed, a bright, joyful sound that cut off suddenly.

"I'm going to need to find materials for my absolution," he said. "As well as food for us to eat. I need Vané's favor back, to help heal your wounds as well as for myself. Infection is still a concern." He looked a bit conflicted as he spoke.

"Yeah, considering what bit me, I'm not surprised." Robin winced as his wounds throbbed again. "What does your absolution entail, if I may ask?"

"I need to create something of beauty. The bigger and more beautiful, the better." Eli looked pensive.

"I'd think you just walking around naked would count." The words were out before Robin even realized he'd thought the thought.

"Flattery." Eli's eyes sparkled as he caught Robin's gaze. "You're too kind."

"Truth is truth," Robin replied. He'd said it; might as well own it!

Eli laughed and held out a hand to Robin.

"Come on. Let's search the place and see what supplies we can find. You need something for your feet, and there's no point in searching around for wood or something like that if I can use what is already here."

Robin reached out and took Eli's hand. This was a very, very dangerous man. He was too handsome and too charming by half. Even in his ragged clothes, he looked good enough to eat out.

Eat!

Focus on something else, Robin. Survival first. Maybe do something so there isn't quite so much distracting skin involved.

Robin conjured his coat back around him. It settled comfortably on his shoulders, its weight still far lighter than he expected, even knowing it was an illusion and only slightly "real."

He left it open at the chest, though, and didn't bother conjuring a shirt underneath.

No reason to be *completely* puritanical.

Chapter 7

*R*obin woke up to the soft and rhythmic sound of Eli's breathing. He hadn't been asleep long; he didn't need to be, with his ring. A single hour charged him up as much as sleeping for nine hours regularly did.

He carefully slid out of bed as his wounds twinged. Three were inflamed and looked to be in danger of hosting an infection. Eli was still working on his atonement piece for Vané, some sort of large wooden sculpture. The cleric had only allowed him the smallest of glimpses while it was still "in progress." Robin was hoping he wouldn't have to wait until then.

He paused to make sure Eli was still deep in the meditative trance state he enjoyed instead of slumber. The elvish cleric didn't so much as twitch, and Robin slipped out of the room.

The stone beneath his bare feet was cool and smooth. Much smoother than the tunnels, actually. In searching the tower, he'd managed to find an old pair of shoes, cracked with age but solid enough to protect his feet and large enough not to pinch, but he had no need of them right now. Besides, he kind of liked the feel of the stone on his feet.

The gentle glow of the runes in the hall guided him to the main chamber—not that he needed it. With a smooth motion, Robin called up the Greater and Lesser Arcana interface. Though he'd not managed to find any mention of Rhyth nor managed to decipher any new spells to cast, it was still a treasure trove of knowledge.

He'd done this each of the last two nights. That first day, they'd slipped out and retrieved a large cache of food; mostly edible plants that Eli had been able to identify.

Robin touched the ring on his finger. Again, not that he needed it.

The touch of the engraved runes on his fingertips was like cold fire; Robin savored the sensation. He'd read up on a bit of the specialty knowledge needed to create these high-level effects. Currently, it was well beyond him, but if pressed, he might be able to produce a simple effect or two out of a hastily scrawled rune.

Maybe.

If it didn't explode in his face.

There was a wealth of knowledge here, and that was the problem. There was so much to sift through, and like any kind of advanced knowledge in his own world, a lot of it relied on a base of common knowledge which he currently lacked. Still, that didn't stop him from reading and learning. Especially once his interface had rewarded his self-edification with several notifications, all in a similar vein.

Congratulations! You have advanced your personal knowledge! The next time you increase Arcane Lore, your experience cost will be reduced by 1/3!

It seemed the way Robin had been advancing was the shortcut method provided by his interface. If he did things the old-fashioned way and learned them properly, he got experience discounts, maybe even free ranks if he learned enough. He'd have to test it out. In addition to *Arcane Lore*, his research had helped him unlock discounts on *Natural Wisdom*, *Learning*, and *Bureaucracy*.

Robin took up where he had left off last night: magical properties of plants native to this region. This world had a lot of what he thought of as canned or easy-use magic—spells with discrete effects that were accomplished through power of will or simple words and gestures—but it also had a lot of lore and charms and hexes that didn't seem to fit into what he would consider a streamlined class system.

It was another point in the argument that the magical laws of this place were one thing, and the messages and interfaces he was seeing were merely a way to interpret those underlying truths. A very convenient one, but not something that should be confused with the *source* of this world's power. Like a smartphone held a metric ton of information, but it was only an interface, not the data or code itself.

Rowan. Deciduous tree. This species . . .

There was a description, as well as multiple images to help identify the tree. Robin scanned through and dug down to the magical properties.

Something was tugging at his mind; something he half remembered from—

Rowan tree, red thread . . .

What was the rest of that song!? And why was he so certain it was the clue he was after?

Rowan . . . rowan . . . good for spells of protection, particularly those warding against or piercing enchantments or dark magics. That certainly sounded promising, and beating Cherry's wood-based magic with a forest charm of their own had an appealing poetic justice to it as well. Bardic justice? Either was good.

There was also an entry cross-referencing the older folk tradition of magic with the more hierarchical, analytic classifications Robin was familiar with from tabletopping and his own current interface.

Naturally, there were nine "circles" of magic, with various subclassifications and descriptors also coming into place—frustratingly, *also* filed under "circle" in his own interface descriptions.

Illusion he was very familiar with, and *Enchantment* to a slightly lesser degree. Both circles featured in the few spells he currently knew. There was also *Abjuration* for protection, which linked to the rowan's magical properties, and purification; *Invocation*—calling or conjuring things; *Evocation* for projection or manipulating energies; *Divination* for spying, seeing visions, etc.; *Vitomancy* was magic dealing with the forces of life and death; *Transmutation*—changing things from one form into another or altering their base nature; and *Wayfaring*, mostly dealing with portals and teleportation.

There was also a huge database of subclassifications, like curses and shadow magic and pyromancy. It was more than Robin could currently memorize, but he was working on it.

Robin froze. Was that the sound of a foot scuffing on stone? He glanced into the shadows filling the hall leading into the chamber but could make out nothing, even with his ability to see in the dark. His stomach twinged again, sharp.

There was nothing there. Not a thing. He needed to relax, or he'd give himself an ulcer—if he hadn't already.

Robin absently rubbed his stomach as he turned back to the font of information before him.

Rowan tree, red thread . . .

Fine. Robin finished reading the entry on rowan trees so he could laboriously page through the Greater and Lesser Arcana looking for an entry on red thread.

He looked for an hour and didn't find anything. What he did find, however, sent him scurrying around the central column to the Communications panel. He brought up the interface with a touch.

When he'd first investigated this panel, he'd not managed to get it to do much. There were several preset communications lines or signatures, but none of them did anything. Whatever receiver was supposed to be on the other end was either off or long destroyed.

There were, however, another set of commands linked to scrying magic. He'd not managed to figure them out before in spite of how easy this interface was to work, but now that he'd read more about the underlying principles of *Divination* and cross-referenced with the scrying subcategorization and some of the instruction manuals from the Records panel, he just might—yes!

A nonagonal mirror—or the illusion of one—appeared before him. He could use this to search the nearby woods, possibly even find a pathway out of the forest. He should also be able to use it to track down the Sisters Sharp. He had spent enough time with them to at least try, and technically, some of the rags he'd been wearing were once in their possession, which should strengthen the link.

He paused before issuing the commands that would seek them out. Maybe he should check the perimeter first, and then try to find where Cherry was in relation to them. Just to be safe. Then perhaps they could mount another expedition in the morning for supplies and craft materials for Eli.

Robin had something Cherry had given him too. Though the small pricks left by her grasp had healed over, Robin had saved the splinters.

Hey, he was in a world of magic now. You never knew when the wood of a dryad might come in handy.

He pulled one out of the storage his ring afforded him. A piece of his target; this would make things a lot easier. Focusing, Robin quietly whispered the necessary command words to the magitech interface before him.

The image shimmered and blurred. It looked similar to watching the landscape pass while on a fast passenger train. After but a moment, the image stilled and became clear.

It was Cherry. She was pacing around Neher's Oak and gesticulating wildly at a cloud of pixies trailing her.

The dryad did *not* look happy. From the way she pointed from the cage of roots at the base of the oak to the expanse of woods around the clearing, Robin suspected she was still upset about their escape and continued freedom from her clutches.

At least there wasn't anyone else in that cage. He relaxed a bit at that. No new prisoners meant the Sisters Sharp still eluded capture. That is, if Cherry even had any interest in them, which she may not.

Robin shuddered as the sound of the dryad's voice barely caressed his ear. He had willed the sound so quiet as to be nearly inaudible. He didn't want to risk waking Eli.

The dryad whirled, and her enraged visage filled the mirror. Robin flinched back before he realized what he was doing. His heart began to race, and his mind screamed at him to look away, to turn off the scrying interface lest she spot him and somehow reclaim him as her prisoner.

Fu—

No, actually. No.

Robin took a deep breath. That's what she wanted. Him afraid. Vulnerable. Well, she wasn't going to get it. She wasn't going to get him. Cherry could go frak herself.

In any case, she was nowhere near and had no idea where they were. Was that odd? Shouldn't she remember where she'd caught Eli before? Or did the tower's wards have something to do with that? He'd have to figure out how to get Eli to show him how they worked and compare that knowledge with what he could sneak out of the Records interface.

Congratulations! You have successfully integrated your own knowledge of magical practices to the workings of this world's scrying apparatus. Arcane Lore advanced to 2.

That settled that, then. Learn enough, and stats advance without having to spend experience. Interesting. Robin would have to figure out what to focus his training on later. For now, he had other things on his mind.

With the scrying functionality up and running, he might as well scry out the Sisters Sharp. Maybe he could find them on one of their supply runs and work together to find a way out of this forest. If they were still alive, that—

No, no time to think like that. It wasn't useful.

Robin stored the splinter in his ring and pulled out the rags he'd been wearing for trousers for the last several days. Weeks? How long had he been here now? Well, at least his search had turned up some better trousers, as well as new footwear. He even had two spare sets of clothing stashed away in his ring, in case these wore out or fell prey to zombie bunnies as well.

The image whirled again. It took slightly longer this time, but the delay was barely noticeable. The mirror showed a small hollow in the midst of a copse of trees. There were large stones, and the vegetation looked scrubbier than any he'd seen since they'd entered the woods.

Huh.

After listening for only a few minutes, Robin frowned. They weren't *in* the wood anymore. They'd broken free of the illusion on their own, somehow.

Without him.

"We've waited as long as we can," Lantha was saying. "We've still got a mission, and we need to get through that keep and back to the Guild with our report."

There was a bit of muttering, and Robin realized they had been waiting—possibly even looking—for him, but that they couldn't delay anymore. The Sisters Sharp were going to leave him behind.

He felt sick, then outraged. He didn't know what to feel. He'd been thrown into a new world, thrown into danger and adventure, and formed a bond with these women as part of that, but he also didn't really know them. They certainly didn't know the real him.

Eli had warned him that something like this might happen. That first day they'd gone for food, Robin had reluctantly told him most of his story. The bits since he'd arrived via a freak magical transportation accident, anyway, with select edits covering Rhyth and how exactly his abilities worked.

Robin hadn't wanted to believe the cleric then, but it looked like he had been right all along.

"It'll take us several days to scout," Ora-Jean was saying. "If he catches up before we make our way through the keep, fine. If not, we go through and go on. We've done as much as we can safely do as it is."

Funnily enough, out of all of them, Grathilde looked most like she might object. Robin found that a bit surprising and rather touching. A small spark of warmth kindled in his chest.

Fiamah put a hand on Grathilde's shoulder. She opened her mouth to say something, but Robin missed it as an entirely different noise grabbed his attention.

Someone else in the room cleared his throat. Robin froze, then slowly turned. Eli was standing in the archway leading into the main room.

"I see you've been busy," the cleric said, raising one elegant eyebrow.

Frell. Busted.

Chapter 8

*S*o," Eli drawled as he strolled over to look over Robin's shoulder at the illusory display of text. "You've been holding out on me. You can read this?"

Robin stood there, his hands suddenly clammy on the cool stone surrounding the control runes of the panel. His neck pricked with small droplets of sweat in spite of the chilly air of the tower. His mind fumbled for an answer, an explanation, a lie, *something*, but all that he came up with was a less full version of the truth.

"Somewhat," he said. "I can't understand it all, but some—"

"And you thought it was a good idea to keep it a secret, sneak behind my back—me, the person who showed you this place and has more claim to it than anyone else?" Eli's eyes flashed. "You thought it was worth lying to me?"

"I—no, that's not—" Robin stammered. Why was he so on the back foot here? "I don't know you, and—"

"No. You don't. And it's becoming increasingly clear that I do not know you, either." Eli's voice could have frosted a glass of lemonade.

Why was he thinking of lemonade? Robin did not handle confrontation well; his mind kept latching on to distractions so he wouldn't have to focus on the uncomfortable situation he was in.

"Well, do you have anything to say for yourself?" Eli demanded.

Robin flushed. He tried—and failed—to speak a number of times. Was it hot in here? Why was this bothering him so much? His mind swam, his stomach cramped, and the pressure only kept increasing.

And as quickly as it began, it was over.

"I'm just giving you a hard time," Eli said with a laugh, the fierce look melting away like snow in springtime. "I've known since you tricked Cherry that you had to have some sort of ability that gave you an affinity with unknown languages."

"I'll give you a hard time if you're not careful," Robin shot back, relaxing a bit with the realization that Eli was just teasing.

"Is that a promise?" Eli's gaze caught Robin's, suddenly intense.

Robin froze. The moment stretched out, seemingly to infinity, before Eli relaxed slightly and winked at him.

"I'll take that as a maybe." The cleric pointed at the illusory display. "But now that it's out in the open, want to tell me what you've found? I might be able to help contextualize it for you."

"I figured out how to make the scrying function work," Robin said. His emotions were in turmoil. First Eli's joke and then that flirtatious exchange, all on the heels of discovering that he'd been left behind by the people he knew best in this world, for whatever that was worth. It was a lot. Speaking of . . .

He quickly spun the illusory mirror away from the Sisters Sharp. "My friends made it out of the wood."

"That's great! They're free of Cherry's influence." Eli glanced at him and then moderated his tone. "I know it's not great that you're still stuck here, but at least they're alive and free."

"Yeah," Robin agreed grudgingly. "That's true."

"And we'll win our own freedom soon, too." Eli tapped a finger on the control panel. "Especially now you've figured out the scrying mirror on this thing. I had no idea there was so much powerful magic here! And that it still works? Astounding."

"What does the scrying mirror have to do with our freedom?" Robin had a couple of ideas, but he wanted to hear Eli's explanation.

"I need paints to complete my masterpiece." The cleric pointed to the misty mirror. "With that, we can scout out the ingredients I need to make them, make sure the way is reasonably safe, pop out, grab the things, and be back before Cherry can nab us again."

"And then you'll have the Grace of Vané back—"

"—along with all my magic, yes." Eli nodded. "Then I can deal with those infected wounds you have, and possibly find a way to break the spell on these woods that keeps us from finding our way out."

New Quest: [Paint the Forest Red]
Aid the priest, Eli, in gathering ingredients so he might complete his masterpiece, and incidentally, heal you before that infection really sets in! Do so

without being caught once again by Cherry or her pixies for a bonus reward!
Reward: *+1 Crafting rank (if you pay attention to how he creates his paints).*
Bonus Reward: *+1 rank in either Stealth or Survival.*

Well, that was as good a sign as any that this was the right path, even if something kept whispering at the back of his mind. He shook his head, but all that did was make the sounds skip a track.

Rowan tree, red thread . . .

There was that song again. And the color red. Robin hoped it wasn't an omen; he certainly didn't want to have to open a vein to paint the forest red. He had a much better use for his blood, and that involved it staying where it was.

"Right," Robin said instead of any of the myriad of other things whirling in his mind. "So what do we need to find, then?" He twisted his hands in the air, and the scrying mirror's perspective withdrew to an eagle's-eye view over the tower and its nearby surroundings.

Eli leaned over the panel, resting his hands lightly on the edges. He was careful not to disturb any of the glowing runes. "I'd say we start here, here, and here." He pointed specifically to three nearby clearings.

Robin couldn't tell what the priest was looking for, but he had to have something in mind. "Anything in particular we're aiming for?"

"Yes. We need to find a nest."

"A nest?"

"Yes, a nest. I need eggs."

"Eggs?"

"Is there an echo in here? Yes, eggs. What else do you think makes the pigment stick to the wood?"

"Alright." Robin reached out to spin the controls. "Eggs it is!"

Robin and Eli spent a couple of hours scouting likely areas of the forest with the scrying spell. It was a very handy piece of magic, and Robin was already resenting having to leave it behind when he left this place. *Divination* was certainly a circle of magic he would need to look further into. Something else to search the Greater and Lesser Arcana interface for while he still had time.

"There!" Eli's sudden exclamation pulled Robin out of his reverie.

"What? Where?" Robin's eyes danced across the mirror.

"The clearing with a small hill. I think I saw something around the edge. Can you move the viewpoint?" Eli was staring intently at the image.

Robin twirled the controls, rotating around the hill. It was too regular to be natural—well, if he were still on Earth, that is. But even here, he suspected it was some kind of burial mound. Or fairy mound, given the nature of the forest. Something else to worry about.

Of course, it all fell out of his mind when he caught sight of what was lurking on the other side of the hill.

There were two birds there, although calling these creatures *birds* was something akin to calling a dire lion a cute, widdle puddy tat. The species looked not dissimilar to an ostrich or shoebill on megasteroids, with plumage of mottled brown and green, plus a beak that wickedly hooked both up and down, as narrow and sharp as an axe blade.

"Bladebeaks?" Robin asked, the word popping into his mind and out of his mouth almost on its own.

"Yes. You've seen them before?" Eli glanced over at him.

"What? No. Never." Robin's stomach clenched. Why was he so alarmed at Eli's interest?

"Well, then you're very good at guessing." Eli looked back to the image. "Those are a mated pair of bladebeaks."

"How big *are* they?" Robin blinked. The smaller of the two specimens had just walked in front of a tree, and unless he missed his guess, that thing was at least—

"Several feet high. Taller than many men or women, that's for sure," Eli said cheerfully. "They probably weigh as much as two or three of you."

"And you want us to tangle with them?"

"Big birds, big eggs." Eli grinned, though his humor withered a moment later. "Think about it. The fewer trips we make, the safer it is overall. Every time we go out, it's a chance for Cherry or her pixies or her ensorcelled walking trees to find us and haul us back to her."

"Right. Good point."

Robin slowly cycled the view around the two large birds.

They did seem to be keeping close to a large pile of twigs and leaves that bordered a shallow pit. Inside, Robin could just make out several massive eggs.

That would make a lot of paint. Possibly with enough left over for a week's worth of omelets.

"We'll need something to carry the eggs in," Eli said. "It would be a pity if they cracked before we got them back. The shells are incredibly tough, as you can imagine, but even so—"

Robin considered offering to use his ring to store the eggs. They'd certainly fit, and that would remove any danger of the things breaking in transit. But that paranoid part of him left over from endless gaming sessions really didn't want him to reveal any more secrets than he already had.

"—it'll be difficult to take them down without proper weapons," Eli continued speaking, "or any access to my magic, but—"

"What if we don't have to?" Robin interrupted.

"Don't have to what?" Eli looked at him.

"Take them down."

Robin was watching the large birds stalk around the nest and dart their heads toward the nearby trees. "We don't need the birds. Sure, some meat might be nice, or the odd feather pillow, but what we really need is the eggs. We don't need to kill the birds to get them. We just need to draw them both away from the nest long enough to snatch the eggs and run."

"True." Eli tapped his chin thoughtfully. "And the less commotion we raise, the less chance of drawing attention."

"That too," Robin agreed. "So, what do you know about bladebeaks? Any natural predators? Preferred prey? There has to be a way to lure or scare them away long enough to grab a few eggs and run." Robin looked at the powerful legs on the birds. "We'll have to lose them quickly. They look . . . fast."

"They are." Eli smiled grimly. "Fast and *mean*. They tend to hold a grudge and are good trackers."

"Then we'll have to make sure they can't pick up our trail, won't we?" Robin countered.

The two put their heads together and began to plan in earnest.

Chapter 9

*T*he scent of sweat and sweet grass was sharp in Robin's nostrils as he slowly crept through the forest. Eli moved next to him on silent feet, rippling through the bracken as silent as light on water.

Robin really, *really* wanted to get his hands on some kind of cleansing spell. He'd hated the feel of deep, long-lasting grime growing up on the farm, and that fact hadn't changed, even if the world around him certainly had.

They weren't far from the bladebeaks' clearing. Robin could see the gentle swell of the hill through the trees around him. The day was clear and just growing past morning.

The two of them had spent some time watching the bladebeaks and consulting both Eli's spotty knowledge of the creatures and the records in the tower interface. Neither were extensive repositories of lore, but they had provided enough of a base to refine their plan.

Eli gestured to Robin before slinking off to circle around the hill. Robin headed in the opposite direction until the bladebeaks' nest was just in view. Then, he proceeded to haul himself up a convenient tree and wedge himself into a position with excellent line of sight but hopefully out of reach of the large and violent birds.

He had some time before Eli would be in position, but it was time to set the scene. Robin was of the opinion that illusions were like ghost stories—they worked best if the audience was in an appropriate frame of mind. And if they weren't already there, you needed to *create* that state.

Robin twisted his hand through the motions of [Lesser Phantasm], chaining several castings together in a row as he concentrated. This would be better if the cantrip had longer range, but he'd just have to make do with it as it was.

The sound of a hollow wind and the rustling of leaves rushed through the clearing. There was no motion of the grass or branches accompanying it, but Robin was banking on the bladebeaks being too animalistic to notice that little out-of-place detail. They did have bird brains, after all!

Faintly, the sound of wolves howling in the distance threaded through the wind. Robin could see the bladebeaks suddenly tense, their heads perking up. The sharp edges of their beaks turned this way and that as they moved their heads to follow the sound.

So far, so good.

Next step.

Robin conjured the illusion of a wolfish scent. Not too strong—not yet. Just enough to reinforce the illusion and the mindset he was creating in the birds. The smaller of the bladebeaks squawked a challenge as the larger drew back to hover over the nest.

Robin frowned. Something wasn't quite right. He wasn't sure how he knew, but those were the howls of arctic wolves rather than the forest variety, and the scent needed to be earthier, loamier, to really trigger the bladebeaks' instinctual responses. He passed his hands through several more castings of [Lesser Phantasm], correcting the sensory details.

There. Both bladebeaks were uneasy, their feathers ruffling out in an intimidation display. If they hadn't looked big enough before . . . Robin shoved the thought away. They were still birds.

A flash of blue caught his eye. Eli was in position.

Robin increased the volume of the wolf howls and the intensity of the scent. The bladebeaks made a chuffing sound deep in their throat, like the roar of a car, and slashed the air a bit with the blades on their faces.

Time to start in with [Chronicle of Infinite Visions]. The fact that he could cast it at will, with no need for words or gestures or anything else, was amazingly useful. It allowed him to both keep his grip on the tree and reinforce the overall illusion with regular [Lesser Phantasm]s.

Robin concentrated, and a shadow dashed through the underbrush near the bristling birds. Though the leaves didn't move, it *sounded* like they did.

It was enough. The bladebeaks went berserk, trilling out a great, honking battle cry and whipping their heads around to look for the enemy.

Robin sent another shadow dashing through the trees, farther away this time, nearer the larger of the two birds. He followed it quickly with some more howling and more dashing shadows. Slowly, the birds were drawn apart from one another and, more importantly, farther away from their nest.

Small flashes of color kept him appraised of Eli's progress. The cleric was as close as he could get without stepping out from his cover and into the clearing.

But he couldn't safely do so while the bladebeaks remained so close to the nest.

"Come on, birdbrain," Robin muttered. "Take the fight to the wolves."

Bladebeaks were territorial, especially around nesting time, and had a habit of attacking or rushing potential threats to their eggs or young. It was equal parts scare tactics and equal parts just pure, lethal aggression. After all, if the birds managed to catch the threat, that was dinner they didn't have to otherwise hunt or scavenge for.

He had to take a risk. Robin mentally mapped out the series of steps he'd need to take, estimated the timing, then put his plan into action.

A deep, guttural growl—almost a roar—came out of the wood, and a wolf dashed out to nip at the larger of the two bladebeaks. As the image snapped and snarled around the bird's legs, courtesy of [Lesser Phantasm], Robin shouted out an insult, reinforcing it with [Cutting Words].

"If your beak is as dull as your brain, I'd be surprised if you could even cut cheese with that thing!"

He wasn't expecting it to do much; after all, the bird couldn't understand him. But it should be able to understand *pain*, and the most obvious cause of that pain would be the illusory wolf nipping at it.

The bird squealed in fury and lashed out at the wolf. Robin sent a knife of pain through his left eye while focusing hard to make the wolf dodge that blow. His *Concentration* skill was getting a serious workout. He needed to invest more points in it the next chance he got.

The wolf darted away, back into the forest and behind a tree. Robin was already hitting the movement limitations on [Visual Phantasm], though he could get around them a bit by chain casting.

The bladebeak shrieked in fury and pursued, crashing through the bracken. Before it was too far out of Robin's range of sight (the trees were *not* his friends here), he conjured another illusory wolf just ahead of the bird, keeping it running away.

One down, one to go.

Robin refocused his attention to the clearing but didn't see the other bird. Eli was crouched by the nest, hefting the massive eggs into specially prepared bags padded with dried grass and strips torn from the leftover bedclothes in the tower. Robin trusted the priest to know it was safe to go after the eggs, but if he was there, where was the other bladebeak?

A screech of rage tipped him off.

There it was! Sprinting right toward him!

Somehow, it had scented or spotted him. The bladebeak charged through the edges of the forest encircling the hill, dodging around the trees. That thing was *fast*. It was at the base of Robin's tree before he could come up with a plan, and it ended its mad dash by slamming itself wildly into the trunk of the tree.

The whole thing shook. Robin felt his center of gravity shift, felt himself beginning to fall. He grabbed for the nearest branches to steady himself.

He missed.

Robin tumbled out of the tree, limbs flailing wildly. Fortunately, he managed *not* to land on the ground in a vulnerable position. Unfortunately, the place he *did* land was arguably more dangerous.

He landed right on the bladebeak's back. Habits honed over years of riding bareback on the farm kicked in, and he hooked his legs around the bird and clung to its back for dear life.

Literally. If he fell off this thing, it would kick him to death with its powerful legs, slash him to ribbons with its wicked beak, or worse. Of course, at that moment, a blue notification box chose to blaze across his vision.

Congratulations! Ride proficiency unlocked!
All Physical Proficiencies Unlocked!

The bladebeak froze for a moment, staggered by the unexpected weight on its back. It was still for only a moment, however, before its brain took over and its instincts screamed out against the alien sensation of a rider.

Robin was saved from immediately being flung from the bird only by virtue of the beast only having two legs; it was very hard to buck off a rider with only two legs. The bird would have to resort to other means of ridding itself of its unwelcome passenger.

Luck was with Robin, as the bladebeak wasn't so flexible it could turn to slash at him with its razor-sharp namesake. That didn't stop the bird from trying.

Its body lunged left and right as it tried to swing its neck around enough to slash at Robin. Robin's legs clamped down hard, keeping him in place even as his body swung from side to side. His arm flashed up, counterbalancing the movement and reminding him of the time he and his friends had gotten far too drunk and spent far too long riding the mechanical bull at Flamin' Saddles.

Congratulations! You have successfully integrated your own experience in riding horses and mechanical bulls, along with your experience in driving motor vehicles, into the Pilot proficiency! This will replace the Ride proficiency. Pilot proficiency advanced to 4!

Robin willed the notification screen away. He didn't have time for this! He had to survive this encounter!

Even as he had the thought, he settled more firmly onto the bladebeak's back, aided by the skill changes his interface had just informed him of.

His mount—if you could call it that—went berserk. The bladebeak began running madly through the trees. It didn't seem smart enough to try and sweep him off using low-hanging branches, but Robin had to do something before it flung itself into a tree to try and dislodge him. It had already rammed into one trying to knock him down.

Leaves whipped him across the face, drawing stinging lines of pain, and he ducked beneath a large branch that might have otherwise knocked him off.

It wasn't a smooth ride. The bird's loping, uneven gait tossed him up and down in spite of the grip his legs had on it. Worst of all, he was without briefs, and the smallclothes he had made himself weren't great in the support department.

Robin swore as his nuts were caught between his pelvis and the bladebeak's spine. He needed to get off this ride and fast, preferably in a way that left him intact and not bleeding from a fatal gash.

The bird suddenly lunged left, nearly dislodging him. Robin looked forward as his mount picked up speed. There was a massive oak looming closer and closer by the second. If he didn't do something now, he was going to become pulp.

Left or right? Right. More ferns, less trees, less chance of a concussion. Robin only had a split second to make his decision before the bladebeak flung itself at the tree.

Robin relaxed his legs and pushed himself off the back of the bird as it exploded into the oak with a battle cry. He hit the forest floor—the soft loam cushioning his fall to an extent—and rolled into the bracken.

As soon as he stopped, he cast [**Lesser Phantasm**] to hide himself in the illusion of a log, quickly followed by a [**Visual Phantasm**] of himself sprinting away at a ninety-degree angle.

The bladebeak let loose a furious screech and set off in pursuit. Robin cast [**Visual Phantasm**] after [**Visual Phantasm**] in a chain as long as he could maintain his line of sight, leading the bird away from him and deep into the trees where it would hopefully lose itself in its fury.

The bladebeak was quickly out of sight, and the sound of it crashing through the forest was swiftly lost. Robin stayed exactly where he was, renewing the illusion masking him. The bird hunted more by sight than anything else, so he should be safe here for a little bit, catching his breath.

Slowly, his breathing calmed down and the pounding blood in his ears quieted. The forest was calm once more.

Of course, no sooner had he gotten his mind settled, something else leapt to mind.

Rowan tree, red thread . . .

This time, the snippet of song came accompanied by flashes of insight, fragments of memory. Hadn't he read something about rowan being a wood that resisted or dispelled evil enchantments? Something about binding spells cast with red thread for protection?

He could almost see the pages in his mind's eye . . .

Before Robin could bring it into mental focus, it hit him. That was it! He could make a charm of rowan wood and red thread that would shield them from Cherry's and the pixies' enchantments! With that, they could scry out the best path and just *walk* out of the woods. He could see how to do it, clear as day in his mind.

Hopefully, his carving skills were up to the task. Not to mention applying what he remembered to this world's magical system.

Further thoughts were scattered as a blue box appeared before Robin's eyes.

Would you like to—

The message box fuzzed, blurred, and was immediately replaced by another.

Congratulations! Your insight has resulted in an advance! Arcane Lore and Learning increased to 4. Concentration and Crafting advanced to 5.

The message sent a spike of pain through his mind. His body, already trembling and bruised, felt like his life force was leaking out of his pores. That agony only lasted a moment, however, before it was replaced with a worse one. Knowledge and skill blazed into his mind, searing itself upon his soul in a mnemonic overload. Like a brain freeze, if the freeze was fire and lightning.

What was that? What happened? His stomach clenched, and he nearly threw up.

He'd have to be careful raising multiple stats in the future. If it was going to be like that every time . . .

Robin suppressed the urge to groan.

He willed his character sheet open to see what the effects of that strange little episode had been. There was no hope now of knowing how close he had been to leveling up, but he could at least see how much he had left to work with.

Robin Parker

Heritage: Shadeling, Mature
Profession: None
Tier: 0
Progress to Tier 1: 69%

Properties

(Free Ranks Available: 1)

Physical
- -Strength: 11
- -Dexterity: 14
- -Fortitude: 11

Mental
- -Intelligence: 17
- -Cunning: 19
- -Resilience: 14

Social
- -Charisma: 15
- -Manipulation: 13
- -Poise: 15

Proficiencies

(Free Ranks Available: 3)

Physical (9/9)
- -Athletics: 1
- -Brawl: 0
- -Dodge: 4

-Melee Combat: 2
-Pilot: 4
-Ranged Combat: 0
-Sleight of Hand: 1
-Stealth: 4
-Survival: 1

Mental (9/9)
-Arcane Lore: 4
-Bureaucracy: 0
-Concentration: 5
-Crafting: 5
-Healing: 0
-Insight: 3
-Learning: 4
-Natural Wisdom: 0
-Perception: 4

Social (9/9)
-Animism: 0
-Deception: 5
-Empathy: 1
-Expression: 4
-Gossip: 0
-Intimidation: 3
-Persuasion: 3
-Socialize: 1
-Streetwise: 0

Peculiarities

Blessing of Rhyth
Tongue of the Fallen Tower
Mark of the Trickster
Chronicle of Infinite Visions

Perks

Wayfaring Stranger

"Red? Are you all right?" Eli's voice disrupted Robin's contemplation.

He dismissed the interface and groaned. He was alright. Bruised and a bit lacerated, but all right.

"I'm fine," he called. "Over here."

Robin heard the sound of footsteps through the bracken. The cleric wasn't making much effort to hide his approach, so the bladebeaks must not be anywhere near now.

Eli looked down at him where he lay, sprawled on the soft moss and loam of the forest floor.

Robin looked up at him.

"I think I know how we can get out of this forest."

Chapter 10

Robin's stomach gurgled as he watched Eli carefully pry the top of the bladebeak egg off with a sharp shard of flint. They were in a small room of the tower that amounted to the kitchen or mess. That meant there were places to sit and tables to work at.

Eli's bag sat on the other side of the cleric from Robin. Packets and satchels and chunky minerals were heaped in it, some spilling out across the table. Those would provide the pigments. In fact, some already had. There were containers with various plants steeping to release the colors Eli was after.

Closer to Robin were two stones. One was smaller and rounded at the end; the other large with a shallow depression in it. It was a far cry from a proper mortar and pestle, but the arrangement would do for some basic grinding.

Eli had walked Robin through the process a couple of times, and now the cleric was dipping out egg white and mixing it with dried and powdered bedstraw root: a practical demonstration.

"If the root is fully dry, then the paint sticks better, but if it's still a bit wet, the color is richer," Eli explained as he worked. "Although if you do it that way, your paint will flake off faster."

The mixture in the small bowl Eli was working with definitely looked like paint to Robin, though perhaps not the glossy acrylic he was used to from art class.

"It's a nice red," he said, more to take part in the conversation than out of an inherent admiration for the shade.

"Can't have an offering to Beauty without something red," Eli replied. "Right, I need to apply this fast or it will clump, and that would definitely ruin my chances with Vané. I will be back in a few minutes."

The priest hopped to his feet and swept out of the room.

Robin didn't follow. Eli had forbidden him from seeing the masterpiece before it was finished. Something about not risking drawing the deity's attention to it too soon.

Fortunately, Robin had something else to busy himself with, now that Eli had finished his demonstration. His quest completion had finally pinged.

Quest Complete! [Painting the Forest Red]
You have successfully aided Eli in gathering the ingredients he needs to complete his artistic work—and learned a couple of things in the process!
***Reward(s):** +1 Crafting rank, +1 rank in Stealth or Survival*

Unable to apply reward. Processing. Awarding closest equivalent. Expression has been raised to 5!

Huh. Well, that was interesting. Something about the system or interface definitely worked off of his actual, lived experiences. What he did and what he learned factored into his gains. Experience points weren't completely divorced from his stats, though he could apply them that way.

It was almost less efficient to do it that way, for whatever reason. An argument in favor of the interface simply interpreting the world for him, rather than being a controlling force within it. But at the same time, he *could* force himself to increase skills—proficiencies—he hadn't learned properly. So something else was going on. The interface or system didn't *just* give him information about the world. It also had some influence on it.

But how much? That was the question. One of many that would be worth answering.

Questions that would have to wait.

Robin assigned his other reward to *Stealth*; it took the rank to five and was far more efficient in terms of experience points than the alternative. Plus, sneaking around was useful. He had violent dryads and mischievous pixies to evade.

Speaking of, as there was no knowing how long Eli was going to be, there was no point in wasting the time. Robin pushed himself to his feet and padded to the central chamber. He shivered as he went, the stone too cold now—or his skin too hot. Infection was definitely setting in; another reason to hope Eli would be finished with his project soon.

And that Vané approved.

Robin quickly pulled up the scrying interface and checked on Cherry and the pixies. When he established that they weren't any immediate threat, he checked in on the Sisters Sharp. They were still slowly scouting the perimeter of the keep, likely looking for a way to bypass it altogether. At least they were on this side of the mountains and hadn't yet moved on. He still had a chance to catch up to them and guilt them into taking him to Noviel.

Going to the city-state seemed like the smartest move. Most importantly, he had an in: a set of guides. It also seemed the most reasonable option to deal with. Although, let's be honest: they were likely to be a nightmare all the same, with Robin's luck.

It was too bad the interface didn't have more information, but between the age of this place and the lack of any kind of search function, it was hardly surprising it wasn't much help to Robin. No reason to focus on the flaws, however. It was still an amazing resource, and one he needed to capitalize on as much as he could, while he could.

Robin shifted over to the Greater and Lesser Arcana station. It just seemed to have the most potential. Even if he didn't rediscover mighty spells of vast and forgotten power, at least he could familiarize himself with options he might be able to take, and maybe even teach himself a new cantrip. After all, how hard could they be? Cantrips were meant to be minor magics; training exercises, even.

He'd already found several illusion spells that had his mouth watering. The Tier Three version of his illusion spell chain, [Major Phantasm], looked to solve several of the weaknesses of the illusions he'd already mastered, for example. And in studying the illusion materials so closely, he'd also uncovered several abilities that sounded suspiciously like peculiarities to him. There was one which increased the effectiveness of his illusion spells by a whole tier, and one which seemed to enhance the potency of illusions blended with shadow magic. The language was very similar to that of his mask, which sounded very promising. And there was still so much more to discover.

So Robin buckled down and got to it.

The first problem was that there wasn't any red cloth or thread in the outpost. Almost all of it was uncolored: brown, beige, pale green, off-white, but no red. Nor was there any wood Robin could confidently identify as rowan, and he knew no spell that would help him identify it. Not insurmountable problems, however.

Robin had already scried out a sky-rowan to harvest the wood from, and they had plenty of thread. A bit of dye, and it would be red as anything. Gathering the ingredients would be a bit dangerous because Cherry and her allies would be on the lookout for them, but collecting them wasn't inherently hazardous. Not like stealing eggs from a blade-beak had been.

There was also the infection. Robin felt hot constantly, his head swimming. It was difficult to concentrate. Hopefully, the problem would be solved soon.

That was why he was here, now, in the room Eli had been using as an art studio. The scent of wood shavings and paint was strong. It made Robin's nose itch, but it was also kind of nice. It was different and reminded him of home for some reason.

In the center of the room was a large . . . something . . . covered with several spare sheets roughly knotted together to make a shroud or drop cloth. Of course the masterpiece had to have a reveal. Robin suspected part of the effectiveness of the offering was going to be in the reception of the piece. He was mentally preparing himself to be as impressed as possible, and had mentally practiced several different ways of praising the beauty of whatever was under that sheet.

Deities of Beauty in myth and literature were almost always notoriously vain and often could be flattered into dispensing boons. Robin had no intention of leaving the reaction to chance. He needed some healing, and for that, Eli needed his powers back.

"Ready?" Eli asked, raising a hand to the sheet with a flourish.

"Ready," Robin confirmed. "Unveil away!"

Eli grabbed the edges of the sheeting and almost snapped it, sending a sharp wave flowing through the fabric so he could haul it off his creation without anything catching. The off-white fabric billowed in the air for a moment before cascading away to reveal a brightly painted wooden statue.

The statue depicted an androgynous but stunning figure in a wrap not unlike a toga. The figure was painted with somewhat lifelike colors, but the shades were unnaturally bright, like technicolor made flesh. They were sitting triumphantly on a prone, muscular male body. The prone figure wore something similar to a Greek helmet and had a spear cradled in lightly curled fingers but was otherwise entirely nude.

His toes were curling, Robin noted.

Eli took his silence as appreciation. The priest beamed, circling the work. It was a beautiful piece of art, certainly, but it seemed faintly disrespectful to Robin. Of course, who was he to say what would and would not appeal to Vané?

"It's good, right?" It was clear that Eli certainly thought so.

"What's it called?" Robin finally asked, not quite trusting himself to say anything else.

"*Beauty Triumphs Over War*," Eli answered with a smile.

"It's stunning," Robin declared. What he really wanted to know was whether or not it had worked, but he didn't want to say the words aloud in case they offended Vané in some unexpected way.

Eli could clearly see his curiosity, however. The priest smiled and reached out to place his hand on Robin's chest.

"**[Purge Impurities]**," he said.

Robin felt nothing at first, then it seemed as if his blood began to bubble. It felt like fizzing in his veins. The agitation spread to all of his limbs, like pins and needles in reverse. The sensation grew more and more intense until he couldn't help himself and he opened his mouth and began to laugh.

"Well, that's a beautiful sound," Eli said, smiling. "You should be free of infection and disease now, as well as any small muscle pains or indigestion or things of that nature."

"What tier was that?" Robin asked when the fit of laughter (and the impurities it carried away from him) had passed. They said laughter was the best medicine, but this was taking things a bit far.

"Tier Two," the priest replied dismissively. "It's a relatively simple blessing. Obviously, the Church of Vané is better about the more *elegant* expressions of magic, so it's more effective than many similar spells you might receive from more prosaic members of the various clergies that populate this land."

"I'll keep that in mind," Robin said, absently rubbing his chest where the healing magic had begun its work. "And since you clearly have your powers back, what do you say we work on getting out of this forest?"

"I'm all ears," Eli said, wiggling the pointed tips of the appendages in question.

Robin laughed.

Robin had scried out the safest pathways between the tower and the skyrowan he planned to harvest. They wouldn't need much; even a fallen branch would do.

How hard could it be?

He should have scried the area more carefully. Yes, the sky-rowan was present, growing out of the large outcropping of rock that rose up from the forest ground in a small clearing. However, there were no fallen branches to gather, and the outcropping of rock was mostly a sheer face with few ledges or handholds.

If anything, the several hours of hiking through the woods to get here had been easier. There had been no sign of Cherry, her pixies, or even any sentient trees.

Robin stared at the rock, silently cursing the fact that he didn't have access to [Mask of Myriad Faces] yet. Even if it didn't allow him to fly, he was sure it would have helped him climb up that rock with relative ease.

Eli looked from him, to the tree, and back.

"So, what's the plan for getting up there?"

Chapter 11

*T*he breeze ruffled Robin's hair. It was a spring zephyr, warm one moment and cool the next, fresh with promise and rich with the loamy scent of the forest. If he weren't trapped in this place by an insane dryad, he'd be loving it.

The sky-rowan grew out of the rock above his head, branches swaying in the light breeze. Too much to hope that the wind would pick up and tear a branch off for him.

"How are your rock-climbing skills?" he asked Eli.

"I've never been much for that kind of physical exertion," the cleric replied blandly.

Robin grunted in reply, eyes scanning the few ledges and handholds he could see. How did a rock like this end up in the forest anyway? Magic was as good an explanation as any, but it wasn't a terribly *satisfying* one. Even if it was the likeliest answer.

"At least the red thread will be easier," Robin grumbled. "We have the thread, and you have plenty of red pigments from making your paint."

"Actually, I don't." Eli had the grace to look sheepish. "I used them all up, and I chucked all the paint I didn't use into a bucket, so it's just a brown mess at this point."

Of course. Couldn't get away with only one fetch quest, could he?

Robin resisted the urge to sigh.

"We'll just have to go gather some dye ingredients from the forest, then," he said instead. "But after we get the rowan wood. We're here now; let's focus on that." One thing at a time.

"As you say, Red," Eli agreed easily.

Neither of them was going to climb up easily. Robin considered dumping his meager experience reserves into *Athletics*, as that would probably increase his chances at climbing, but not by much.

Rope would be nice, but they hadn't managed to find any in the tower, so an improvised grappling hook was out. Could he do anything with the power of his mask? Climbing gloves and boots of some form? The illusions had at least a smidgeon of reality to them.

Robin willed the change in his apparel. Yeah, there was some added grip there, but not enough to make up for his inexperience with climbing. Not on a rock face this sheer.

What else could he do?

He flicked open his character sheet, hoping for inspiration.

Huh. His *Crafting* was currently maxed out. They were in a forest; there was plenty of wood around, some tough ivy . . .

Maybe he could fashion a crude ladder? That would be much easier to climb.

"Eli," he called. "We need to head into the forest and find some things."

He explained his plan—if it was complex enough to be called that—to the cleric, and they set out.

It took a couple of hours to gather enough suitable materials. Fortunately, there was a mix of new and old growth throughout the forest. Robin uprooted saplings with some effort, gathered larger fallen branches, and yanked up several lengths of tough, woody ivy.

It took a further three hours to assemble the ladder, matching the lengths of wood into two long poles, lashing them tightly together with the ivy, then adding crosspieces in the same manner to make crude steps. In the end, they had a very tall, incredibly rickety ladder, but hopefully it would do the trick.

"We should move quickly," Eli said. "We've been in one place a long time."

The unspoken worry was that Cherry or one of her minions would stumble across them soon. Robin didn't need to be told twice. He jerked his chin toward the ladder, and together, the two of them managed to lever it up and into position.

The ladder swayed and bowed as they manhandled it, but it remained intact. For now. There was no knowing how long it might last. The top extended a few feet past the ledge the tree was growing on.

"Up you go," Eli said when it was in position.

"What? You should go! You're clearly nimbler than I am." Robin just barely managed to keep from bringing up how elves had superior dexterity and reflexes. Not only might that be inaccurate in this world but assumptions like that struck him as somewhat racist.

"Your plan, your execution."

"Great word choice." Robin looked at the cleric sourly, then he glanced at the ladder. It swayed slightly in the breeze. "Fine. But you'd best have enough divine energies to heal me if I fall."

"You can rely on me!" Eli gave a mock bow with a flourish. "Now up you pop. Chop-chop. We're on a time limit."

Rather than waste time arguing, Robin just began the climb. He went slowly, testing each step as he went. The ladder swayed and creaked disturbingly, but nothing gave way. He made his way up to the ledge and stepped off with relief; the stone beneath his feet was much more solid and reassuring.

Robin took a moment to turn and look out across the forest. The rock was tall, but not so much it was above the canopy. Still, he could see through the trees better at this height, and they were thinner in places. The tops of the mountain ranges that cradled the forest like granite arms were easily visible, but he couldn't find the keep from this vantage. Well, that was what scrying was for.

Still, it was a lovely view, and Robin indulged for a couple of minutes before he turned back to the task at hand.

The rowan tree was mature but not old. That, or growing up here had stunted it slightly; there probably wasn't a huge amount of nutrients available in the rock. Though once again, magic, so who knew.

Robin reached out. There were several branches within range, some too large to break off, but the smaller offshoots should be doable if he was careful. He'd probably have to break them, then twist around several times until the bark gave way, but he didn't need much for the charms.

The bark felt surprisingly alive beneath his fingers. Robin paused. He was in a world of magic. He was creating a charm from a magical tradition that respected and maintained harmony with the natural world. Just taking what he wanted might not be the way to go here.

Robin thought for a moment before laying his hand on the sky-rowan's trunk.

"What's the holdup?" Eli shouted from below.

"Give me a minute," Robin yelled back down. "I want to try something."

He focused back on the sky-rowan. Did it speak the same language as Neher's Oak? Couldn't hurt to try. Robin ran through a few different phrasings, thinking back to some of the books on ritual magic he'd had in his collection on Earth.

"Hear me, Rowan, sky tree, witchwood, delight of the eye, I am in great need of a gift of your wood, of several twigs to bind up with red thread into a charm to protect me from those who would do me ill and keep me bound."

Suddenly inspired, Robin flicked his free hand through the motions of **[Lesser Phantasm]**, and illusory music began to play softly as a backdrop to his words.

Rowan tree, red thread . . .

The song flowed out of his memory, and with his level gains and repeated use of the spell, Robin found it a simple thing to add harp and bodhran to bolster the music.

The leaves of the rowan rustled.

"I do not ask for much," Robin continued. "Merely enough strong twigs to form into bundles for warding charms for myself and—"

Robin felt a surge of alien emotion. It felt like someone giving him a warning? Then there was a sharp *crack*, and a medium-size branch fell from the tree. It plummeted straight down with unnatural speed and force.

Eli dove out of the way with a yelp.

"Some warning would have been nice!" the priest called up.

What was that? Magic, sentient trees, new world. This was amazing!

Robin smiled with delight and murmured profound thanks to the tree. Not sure what else to offer, he reached up and pricked his thumb on the splintered end where the branch had been. He could spare a few drops of blood.

"All right," he called to Eli. "Steady the ladder. I'm headed back down."

He was less than a quarter of the way down when a small mote of cerulean light danced into view before his eyes.

Aha! Found you! Found you!

Fuck. One of Cherry's pixies. And he was midclimb. He had the world-swimming sensation he'd come to associate with the pixie's illusions.

No, no, no. If he couldn't trust his senses, he was sure to fall!

His stomach clenched. Unacceptable. He needed to think of something, fast.

Pixies. What did he know about pixies?

"Oh good," Robin said, playing for time. "I was hoping you'd find us!"

The little ball of light stopped bobbing in front of him for a moment. Robin took that as confusion. Pixies. Pixies loved fun and pranks and games, and they were often defeated by trickery or the guiles of the person in the fairy tale. That was certainly the case in the tale of *The Witchweed and the Widow* . . . where had he heard that one?

Never mind. Not now.

You wanted to be found?

"Of course," Robin lied smoothly. "That's the whole point of the game, isn't it?"

Game? Game! I want to play!

"I can't believe Cherry didn't tell you the rules! Oh no, wait! I forgot." Robin made his eyes go wide. "I'm not supposed to tell anyone the rules. Part of playing the game is figuring out you're playing a game, and then figuring out what the rules are. I was having so much fun, I lost track of who did and did not know we were playing!"

Tell me!

Pixies were also demanding. Well, Robin could work with that. He mashed up the rules for hide-and-seek, sardines, and Mau, and let the pixie have fun goading him into revealing more than he should.

So I need to make up my own rule and try to get my friends to play without telling them the rules I've figured out, but I can make fun of them when they get one wrong even if they don't know it?

The pixie seemed delighted at the complicated shenanigans Robin had whipped up.

"Yes, and I can't believe you figured out that my secret rule is you can't tell anyone you saw me or Eli here! You're so clever." Robin was laying it on thick, but these pixies seemed to be in a hive-intelligence sort of situation—they were smarter in large groups. And here, he was facing only one.

I did? Oh! Yes. Yes, I did! Clever me!

The mote of light zipped thrice around Robin's head before darting off into the forest, muttering potential rules to itself.

Robin allowed himself to relax slightly. That had been close. And he'd had to think on his feet while those feet were perched uncomfortably on a rickety ladder that would do Tim Burton proud.

Ugh. Time to get down. Finally.

Robin shifted his weight in preparation for resuming his climb down. Unfortunately, that proved too much stress for the already straining rung he was on, and it snapped. One of Robin's hands had been reaching for the next step down, and the other lost its grip as his weight was suddenly no longer supported by his feet, so Robin fell backward, arms pinwheeling in the air. He tried to grab the ladder, but it was out of reach.

Robin plummeted toward the ground, and when he hit the forest floor, blackness swallowed him.

The first thing Robin felt when he woke up was the scratchy comfort of the sheets. Having slept in the bed in the tower for several nights now, the sensation was more comforting than annoying. How did he get back here?

"Oh good, you're awake!" Eli leaned over him. "Pretty nasty fall you took. I had to enhance my strength to carry both you and that branch that nearly killed me back here by myself."

"You can do that?" Robin asked, sitting up. He noted that this time he got to keep all his clothes on. He could faintly feel the texture of the sheets through the illusory coat he was wearing. That was an odd sensation.

"If I have the divine energies stored up, yes. Would you like some water?"

"Yes, please."

"Be right back."

The cleric rose to his feet and left the room. Robin glanced around. Ah. There was the branch of rowan wood, next to Eli's bunk and the cleric's makeshift pack.

Robin slid out of his bunk to go inspect the wood. It had been enough trouble to acquire; best make sure it would actually serve its intended purpose.

Before he could inspect it more closely, however, Eli's pack caught his eye. It was slightly open, and Robin could clearly see there were packets of paint ingredients inside. Right on top was the root the cleric had used to make his red paint. Robin recognized it because he'd paid such close attention wanting to be sure he got his *Crafting* rank from the quest.

Eli had said he was out of those ingredients.

The priest had lied.

Chapter 12

Robin's stomach churned. It had been restless since he'd woken up in the tower after falling from the ladder. He forced the sensation out of his mind with some difficulty.

A day had passed since the events with the sky-rowan. Robin had feigned feeling weaker than he actually did in order to gain some time to think and some space to act.

The first thing he did, before Eli even returned with his water, was to steal a large piece of the root used for making red paint and stow it in his storage ring with several of the smaller twigs of rowan, the ones he could snap off without making it too obvious that part of the branch was missing.

Currently, he was standing in the main room of the tower, going through the Greater and Lesser Arcana database looking for spells he could learn or more powerful ones to aim for learning in the future. At least that was what he had intended to do. At the moment, he was staring into the middle distance, thinking.

Why hadn't he been more suspicious of Eli? Why hadn't he noticed the priest's lying and evasions earlier? Well, obviously, part of it was the circumstances he'd awoken in, imprisoned with another. That was a classic move; he should have expected something there. Then there was no denying that Eli was distractingly handsome. Another cliché, but, well, sometimes things were cliché because there was an element of truth to them.

Robin shook his head. No point in self-recrimination; it was a bad habit from his old world. Maybe he should try some fresh ones in this new reality, starting with choosing proactive solutions over crippling overanalysis.

Eli had lied. Robin had been taken in. Ergo, Robin wasn't good enough at spotting lies, even if he was proving pretty talented at spinning illusions and deceptions of his own. What was the opposite of *Deception*? Probably *Insight*. Possibly *Perception*.

He pulled up the proficiency descriptions.

Insight

Insight is a measure of how well you can understand the motivations of other beings, how quickly (and how effectively) you see through attempts to deceive you, and other related uses. This proficiency can also be used to see patterns in events and aid in connecting seemingly unrelated events into a larger picture. Insight is generally conceived to govern subtle or hidden truths, as opposed to hard-to-notice but unbidden aspects of a physical environment.

Perception

Perception is a measure of your awareness. It generally covers all manner of noticing fine details about your environment. This proficiency can also have a minor effect on how likely or not you are to be surprised by an ambush or fooled by a sensory illusion. Where Insight is often considered to be focused on the interior truths of a situation, Perception is often viewed as most concerned with external details.

After reading the entries, Robin decided he needed both of them to the max. It was clear he didn't know nearly enough about what was going on here. He had some experience after his encounter with the pixie, possibly also from his successful retrieval of the sky-rowan wood. What could he afford right now?

He played with the interface a tad and bit back a curse. He didn't have enough to raise both *Insight* and *Perception* to five. He could manage a five in one and a four in the other. That's it.

Unless he used one of his banked proficiency ranks. Robin was loath to do that, though. He had no idea how common such rewards were, and using them now meant spending more experience later.

Of course, if he didn't live to see later because he'd been deceived or ambushed, it might be a moot point.

Robin went back and forth on that in his head. Part of him, the gamer part, really hated to lose that bit of efficiency. But the more practical side of him won out. He hadn't seen anything to suggest there were experience or level caps of some kind in place, and the evidence he'd gotten from the interface suggested it rewarded him as long as he kept on learning, growing, and trying new things.

Right. He would use experience and one of his banked points to bring both *Insight* and *Perception* to five. One stat at a time. He didn't want to risk a sensory overload again.

Robin willed the changes through his interface. He decided to start with *Insight*, as it was the lower of the two scores. The pop-up dialogue box appeared, asking for confirmation. Before he could confirm, however, the text blurred from *Insight* to *Perception*.

Odd. Well, it wasn't like he didn't intend to raise that proficiency as well, so Robin willed through the change.

The world sharpened slightly, like putting on a new pair of glasses for the first time. It was also a little bit like the fishbowl effect—nothing seemed to be quite where it should be.

His stomach roiled. Robin pushed the discomfort away and refocused on his interface.

He paused.

What was he doing again? His mind felt as fuzzy as his vision seemed clear. He shook his head. Vision. *Perception.* Right. *Insight.*

Robin willed the changes to *Insight*, riding the wave of discomfort that came with the change. It was somehow worse than the *Perception* shift.

Should he hold off on upping *Insight* to five? No. He had the free rank to use, and he needed every edge he could muster. Something odd was going on here.

He forced through the change. This time it was easier, for some reason.

Robin pulled up his character sheet to examine it.

Robin Parker

Heritage: Shadeling, Mature
Profession: None
Tier: 0
Progress to Tier 1: 68%

Properties

(Free Ranks Available: 1)

Physical
  -Strength: 11
  -Dexterity: 14
  -Fortitude: 11

Mental
  -Intelligence: 17
  -Cunning: 19
  -Resilience: 14
Social
  -Charisma: 15
  -Manipulation: 13
  -Poise: 15

Proficiencies

(Free Ranks Available: 2)

Physical (9/9)
  -Athletics: 1
  -Brawl: 0
  -Dodge: 4
  -Melee Combat: 2
  -Pilot: 4
  -Ranged Combat: 0
  -Sleight of Hand: 1
  -Stealth: 5
  -Survival: 1
Mental (9/9)
  -Arcane Lore: 4
  -Bureaucracy: 1
  -Concentration: 5
  -Crafting: 5
  -Healing: 0
  -Insight: 5
  -Learning: 4
  -Natural Wisdom: 3
  -Perception: 5
Social (9/9)
  -Animism: 0
  -Deception: 5
  -Empathy: 1
  -Expression: 5
  -Gossip: 0
  -Intimidation: 3
  -Persuasion: 3

-Socialize: 1
-Streetwise: 0

Peculiarities

Blessing of Rhyth
Tongue of the Fallen Tower
Mark of the Trickster
Chronicle of Infinite Visions
Shard of the Shattered Manymind

Perks

Wayfaring Stranger

It flickered as he looked at it. How could a magical interface be glitching? That was not something he had expected to need to worry about. The lettering kept shifting, as if someone were cycling the whole document through some sort of mad translation algorithm.

On the one hand, it was kind of nice, as he absorbed fragments of dozens of new languages that he could use with [**Tongue of the Fallen Tower**]. On the other hand, it was distracting as fuck, and he kept seeing unexpected words out of the corner of his eye.

Was this connected to Eli somehow? It was hard to say. But this was a world of magic, and he of all people knew it was a pretty trivial affair to mess with someone's perceptions. There were so many ways.

Wait, what was [**Shard of the Shattered Manymind**]? He didn't remember getting a notification for that peculiarity.

Robin focused his will on the tooltip function. What did the extra information there say?

Eli chose that moment to enter the room. Robin glanced over, reflexively minimizing his interface. He needed all of his wits about him right now. No distractions.

"Ready to go hunt for crimson bedstraw?" The cleric was almost annoyingly cheery.

"Yeah. Just let me shut this down." Robin powered down the interface.

Technically, he didn't need to go hunting for more of the root. He had the large one he'd swiped from Eli's pack, and that was more than enough to dye the small amount of thread needed for the charm. Mounting another expedition with Eli into the wood, however, would give him a chance to test the priest some more.

It would also give him a chance to pick up some other useful herbs and magical plants. He'd spent enough time looking through the magical database in the tower that his *Bureaucracy* had naturally risen to one without the need for any experience, and what he remembered of growing crops from the farm had combined with his exploration of the Botany and Biology section to similarly lift his *Natural Wisdom* to three.

He had chosen the spot to gather crimson bedstraw carefully. Close enough to the tower not to alarm Eli, but along a meandering path that would take him past several specimens he could stealthily nab and stow in his ring; there was plenty of room. Right now, the staff he'd kept from the fight with the ghourds was the only thing taking up an appreciable amount of space in there. Adding the herbs and plants would give him a bit more to work with.

Robin gestured, and the illusory interface vanished. He resolved, not for the first time, to figure out how to create one of these on his own someday. He was certainly coming back here when he had the chance to salvage what was left.

. . . Provided someone else didn't get here first. He shot a glance at Eli.

The priest smiled at him.

"Shall we?"

"Let's." Robin willed an illusory pair of sunglasses to form on his face. They wouldn't keep the light out, but by the same token, they were very easy to see through, even in the dim light inside the tower.

Huh. The more powerful his illusions, the more reality they carried. He would have to be careful with that. Right now, part of the advantage of his illusory powers was his ability to see through his own illusions without a problem. The demireal ones, however, didn't offer that option—or they didn't yet. There had to be a peculiarity to deal with that.

Robin mused on the possibilities a bit as he and Eli delved once more into the forest, but he had to set the train of thought aside after a few minutes. This was still Cherry's territory, and there were plenty of dangers to be on the lookout for.

As well as opportunities.

Robin pocketed several clumps of herbs as Eli scouted a bit ahead, keeping his finely tuned senses peeled for any sign of Cherry or the pixies.

They moved quietly and carefully through the wood. This meant slowly as well, but that suited Robin's purposes just fine. More time to sneak in some gathering, and more time to ask Eli any number of questions about him, his past, and his devotion to Vané. Hopefully, something would be useful.

Robin discovered that Eli was relatively young, for an elf. He had grown up on another of the floating continents and traveled here in search of new and beautiful sights with which to glorify Vané. Personally, Robin's new suspicions made him think Eli was laying it on a bit thick, but there was no way he could prove or disprove the priest's devotion.

Or even Vané's existence, come to think of it.

But he discovered other things. Eli was very fond of berries and had a tendency to eat them, even though at this time of year, they should still be merely flowers. Then again, magical wood in a magical world, so screw the order of the seasons, right?

Eli also had a wicked sense of humor. He laughed loudest and longest at the rudest jokes Robin could remember. Robin had to shush him numerous times and remind him they were very much still in enemy territory. And if anything was going to bring a cloud of curious pixies down on them, it was laughter echoing through the trees.

"—then I returned the Golden Idol to the temple the Jhonzes had stolen it from and leapt back through the World Tree Seedling before it was too late." Eli was regaling him with tales of his previous adventures.

Robin frowned. That last bit, though, that was a lie. Elvish High Magic could do many miraculous things, but it was as much spiritual as it was anything else and would never be used for so frivolous a purpose as transporting adventurers. Excavations, sure. But not something like this. The High Mages held too much control over the knowledge, and the Elvish Pantheon generally united in backing up that exclusivity.

Robin frowned. How did he know that? He didn't recall Lantha saying anything about it, and he certainly hadn't read it in the tower database.

Had he?

"Here we are," Eli said, interrupting his train of thought again.

They had reached the clearing, small red flowers dotting the grass. Crimson bedstraw. But that wasn't the only thing of note.

"Looks like we should have gone with the patch I was thinking of after all," Eli whispered.

Robin bit back a curse. The clearing was home not only to a large patch of crimson bedstraw but also to a large community of thornlings.

Chapter 13

Robin stood in the woods, sun slightly warm on his face and the bark of the tree he hid behind rough on his hands. The clearing was full of crimson bedstraw, yes, but also thornlings. They were small and ranged in size from several inches to about two feet tall. Roughly humanoid, they looked like tiny wicker men made from roses and briars and hawthorn twigs.

"Well," Eli whispered. "What's the plan?"

What *was* his plan? He already had the dye he needed. Was it worth fighting a bunch of monsters to maintain that secret? Was it worth confronting Eli about his lie?

"There are other patches of crimson bedstraw in the forest. I say we try one of those. No need for a pointless battle." Robin started backing away quietly. "Though it's odd there are so many thornlings here. I didn't notice them when I scried out the patches earlier this morning."

"Maybe they weren't active," Eli replied softly. "Or maybe Cherry sent them."

"How would she know to do that?" Robin watched the priest carefully out of the corner of his eye.

"Maybe the woods sensed our path and told her. We did take a while to get here. There would have been plenty of time for her to organize some form of response."

"All the more reason to retreat, then," Robin said, then decided to test Eli just a bit. "Maybe we should just go back to the tower and see if we can find any paint or root you might have missed."

"I didn't miss any," Eli replied. "I can promise you that."

That definitely twigged Robin's *Insight*. He knew all about lying with the truth, and the words Eli had just used smacked of it. If he hadn't already been suspicious, they might have flicked right past without Robin thinking anything of it, but now? His stomach clenched.

Robin stopped in his tracks. There was something else in the forest.

"Do you hear that?" he asked.

"What?"

"It sounds like a lot of voices, all whispering at once." Robin cocked his head to one side, trying to figure out where the sound was coming from. But he couldn't. His *Survival* was letting him down, even combined with **[Wayfaring Stranger]**.

"I don't hear anything." Eli looked suddenly very wary. "Maybe we *should* get back to the tower."

Robin felt a wave of emotion at those words. It wasn't fear, exactly. More like concern. The strange thing was it didn't feel like *his* emotion. He was angry and freaked out; he wasn't *concerned*.

He looked at Eli. The thornlings had been left behind in the clearing, and while there might be small animals all around that he couldn't see, if it wasn't his own emotion Robin was feeling, was it Eli's? How?

No. First figure out if it's a fluke or not.

"Hey, Eli," Robin began. "Have you heard the one about the errant knight and the shepherdess?" And proceeded to tell a fantasy version of one of the rudest jokes he'd ever heard.

He was rewarded with a short laugh and a wave of mixed amusement and irritation. Mostly irritation. Even Eli's laugh had sounded a bit forced.

Robin was definitely feeling Eli's emotions, somehow.

Was this a shadeling thing? There was so much magic in this world. Could it be a gift from the sky-rowan, maybe, or something he'd unconsciously absorbed from the tower's interface? One of the magical plants he had gathered this morning?

Well, no point looking a gift horse in the mouth if it could help him get to the bottom of whatever Eli was up to.

"We have no time for jokes. Let's just head back to the tower. It's not safe out here."

The priest stepped quickly through the woods, taking a more direct route back to the tower than the one Robin had followed to secretly gather herbs and plants.

Robin followed, his mind churning. Eli's feelings weren't always matching his words. It wasn't a lie detector test per se, but maybe he could use it like one. It would certainly help him figure out which questions were worth chasing some more.

As they went, Robin forced conversation between himself and the cleric. It wasn't difficult. This was hardly the first foraging trip they'd been on, chatting quietly so as not to draw the attention of the trees or Cherry's pixies.

Robin quickly amassed a few areas that didn't match up emotionally with what Eli was saying. Particularly concerning was his lack of emotion when Robin brought up Vané. He didn't get any anger off of Eli when he asked about the cleric losing access to his divinely granted abilities temporarily, and he didn't get any sense of awe or love or devotion in general when the deity was brought up.

The elf was definitely a divine caster of some form, though. Robin was certain of that. Based on the spells he'd seen Eli use and the way they had felt . . . the way they had felt . . .

Hmm. There was something there, but he couldn't quite put his finger on it.

The whispers in the forest around them suddenly sharpened. They'd followed the two of them the whole way back, but the sound kept slipping out of Robin's mind as he focused on figuring out the threat closest to him.

"What?" Eli had stopped, noticing his reaction. "What is it?"

"It's those whispers," Robin replied, looking around. "They just got more agitated or something."

"We need to get you behind the tower wards, and fast."

Eli quickened his pace again, and Robin had no choice but to follow. Wards definitely sounded good right now, and the tower was a place where he felt safe. He was confident he had a much better handle on its systems than Eli did, so if worse came to worse, Robin would be safer there than anywhere else.

"Wait." Eli froze before pointing carefully ahead. "Do you see that?"

Robin followed the cleric's finger. At first, he saw nothing, but after a moment, he caught a glimpse of a dancing mote of golden light.

Pixies!

"I do not need this right now!" Eli all but growled before muttering something else to himself.

Robin's new *Perception* might not be yet superhuman, but it was definitely sharp enough to catch a few of those words. Eli had muttered something to himself about "backstabbing dryads not staying bribed."

Now *that* was interesting.

Robin considered running off into the forest but dismissed the idea almost immediately. Cherry was still a problem, and he needed to dye the thread red before he risked that; it would be easiest to do it at the tower. And he wasn't quite ready to give up on access to those magics. He needed to scry out the best path to the Sisters Sharp's current location, for one thing.

But if the cleric had been working with the dryad before being betrayed, what was he really after? And which god, goddess, or other deity did he truly serve? Robin was becoming increasingly convinced it wasn't Vané.

"We need to hide until they pass." Eli cursed.

Robin agreed. He already had one crisis to manage; he didn't need to add fighting pixies or running into Cherry to that list.

"Over here." Eli gestured to a patch of bracken.

The bracken filled a small hollow between two trees. They crouched down, and Robin covered them with an illusion; thankfully, [**Visual Phantasm**] was both larger and longer lasting. Then, they waited.

After several agonizing minutes, the pixies drifted past them, motes of light tinkling and dancing that eventually disappeared from view.

They remained hidden for several minutes more, just to be safe.

"The last thing we need right now is a bad joke like that," Eli whispered.

Robin blinked.

Of course! It wasn't Vané Eli followed! It was Nevarre! It had to be.

Eli's love of rude jokes, the way the cleric's magic made Robin laugh and feel, the ease with which the elf always went along with Robin's trickiest plans—all of that fit with Eli worshipping the Elvish God of Mischief.

"Yeah, I can see how that might annoy Nevarre," he said, testing his theory on impulse.

The flare of alarm and amusement that roiled off Eli at those words all but cinched it. The cleric had to be an acolyte of the tricky deity.

But what did that mean? Robin had impressed Nevarre in the caves, enough to receive the [**Cutting Words**] cantrip from him. Was this whole setup to help him? An elaborate prank? Both?

A God of Mischief had to be a dangerous ally to have at the best of times. Let alone when you didn't know where you stood. Robin needed to handle this carefully and with excellent humor. Getting angry and confrontational would probably just make Nevarre laugh harder at the cosmic joke that was Robin's life right now.

"You know quite a lot about elvish culture, then," Eli was saying.

"A bit," Robin hedged. "Though it's not really homogenous, is it? That's like saying you know a lot about human culture when there are actually— huh, I don't even know *how* many—loads of different human cultures."

"True, but Nevarre isn't one of the most widely known of deities outside enclaves of my people. Even within them, he's not one who is universally revered."

"Well, that's idiotic. What's more important than a good sense of humor?" *Might as well throw in some flattery. Can't hurt.* "My people have a saying that laughter is the best medicine, and honestly, wouldn't that make Nevarre a boon and an asset to anyone?" Robin touched lightly on the idea because of the sensations he'd felt when Eli had used **[Purge Impurities]** on him.

Pride, approval, and a tiny bit of suspicion flowed from Eli. Robin thought furiously. How could he trick Eli into revealing what the deal here was?

The tower appeared through the trees. They were nearly back.

Robin relaxed the bit of his mind that was constantly on edge, watching for danger from the forest. The wards were close.

Instead, he focused on his questions again. Annoyingly, Eli was focused more on the dangers around them, even though they were close to safety, and kept dodging or evading Robin's inquiries. Worse, the cleric was clearly worried about something, and that emotion was so loud it all but drowned out the other things he was feeling—the things Robin needed to sense more clearly if he was going to figure this mess out.

Well, he had this new ability, and even with his limited control, it was helping. Maybe he could figure out how to use it more effectively.

Robin attempted to force the strange sensation that fed him information on Eli's emotions into greater clarity. Something struggled at the edges of his mind, like an animal trying to free itself from a snare. The feeling flickered, emotion coming in and out of focus like a stuttering radio, before Robin *yanked* at it with his mind, drawing it in. Then, he wasn't just feeling Eli's emotions; he was hearing the elf's thoughts!

"We need to get inside," the elf was saying. *We're too exposed right now. Cherry's ruined the whole thing, and I need to get—*

Robin didn't know how he knew this was what was happening, but he knew it was happening.

"We need to get behind the wards, now," Eli urged. "And cut off the source of those whispers before—"

Eli stopped speaking suddenly. Consternation and concern flashed across his face.

"What?" Robin snapped, expecting another trick or evasion.

"Your eyes," the cleric said. "They've turned golden."

Chapter 14

$\mathcal{R}$obin blinked. Golden eyes? He flicked out a [**Lesser Phantasm**], and a small silver mirror hung in the air in front of him. It showed him his reflection as Eli saw it. It was real enough to do that, at least.

His eyes *were* golden. The rest of him still looked as human as he normally did save for the auburn hair, which he had been keeping up in place of his usual brown. It looked good; the golden eyes, though . . . where had he seen that shade before . . .

His mind fuzzed as he struggled to remember. Robin was nothing if not determined, however, and he'd had more than enough of the mysteries plaguing him in this woodland.

He focused.

Oh. *Oh*, that was not good.

"It's the same color as the ghilded ghourd," he yelped.

"Get behind the wards," Eli urged. "Quickly!"

Robin dashed for the tower. Every third step or so, his feet struggled against him, causing him to stagger. What was going on? It was like—oh.

His mind flashed over the battle. The spraying seed. He must have swallowed one during the fight, and it had been growing within him somehow.

He staggered into the tower, the cool stone welcome against his hands as he braced himself against the entryway and then against the walls. As soon as he made it inside, the feeling of having to fight his own feet ceased.

"Get it out of me," he demanded as soon as Eli followed him inside. "How is it even still *in* me? You purged—"

"It doesn't work on parasitical entities," Eli cut in. "Not while they're alive and viable. I'd need a different spell for that."

"Need? *Need?* Does that mean you don't have one?"

A world of magic, and he was being taken over by a sentient stomach pumpkin because the closest cleric didn't have the right spell? Unbelievable!

"Not for something this advanced!" Eli snapped. "It was never supposed to get this far—"

"Wait, you *expected* this to happen?!" Robin shouted. "You backstabbing, god-bothering artistic *hack*!" he let fly with **[Cutting Words]**, and it felt *good*.

"It was just supposed to be a joke," the cleric protested, wincing.

"A joke? You? You're about as funny as a hernia!" Robin snapped.

Eli jerked back at the **[Cutting Words]**.

"If you want me to help get that thing out of you, you're going to need to stop doing that," the cleric said.

Robin struggled with that. He didn't trust Eli, but he didn't have any other option. If the cleric wanted him dead or mind controlled, he could have already done either of those things. And Nevarre had already helped him once. A joke, he could understand; it made a twisted sort of sense. Robin didn't like it, but he could deal with that *after* he got this thing out of him.

His stomach clenched again. Robin groaned and looked down. He wasn't wearing a shirt, just his illusory coat, so he could clearly see his stomach distend and shift as something *moved* underneath the skin.

That was too much.

Robin screamed. His hand started toward his stomach but jerked back as the ghourd seedling moved again. He couldn't bring himself to touch it; not any more than he already had.

"Get it out! Get it out, get it out, get it out!"

"I'll do what I can, but you have to distract it," Eli said, guiding him into the barracks and helping him onto the bed.

Robin grabbed the sheets in a death grip. It felt good to hold onto something, and it helped ground him. He focused on his breathing—slow, deep, measured. He needed to get himself under control.

Eli was digging through his pack, opening small packets of roots and herbs and discarding them as he muttered to himself. He was alarmed, actually concerned. Robin could feel that.

Oh sweet, shadowy Rhyth. The ghourd. That was why he could sense Eli's emotions. When he had fought it in the clearing, it had controlled several animals, tried to control Eli as well. It must have some kind of psychic or mental abilities.

And now it was trying to meld with his mind?

It was!

Several small events snapped into focus as he thought about it. Times he had known something or guessed something he had no way or reason to know. He'd brushed it off as coincidence and luck and half-remembered fragments from his exploration of the tower database, but it had actually been this plant!

And it must have been nudging him along, soothing his suspicions, distracting him when his train of thought got too close to discovering its secret . . .

This thing was insidious.

"What are you doing?" he called to Eli. He needed to know what the plan was.

Or did he? Did him knowing make it easier for the plant to fight back? He called out before the elf could answer.

"Or should I not ask? Can you telling me that make it easier for the plant to fight back?"

"No," the cleric replied. "It's as dug in as it's going to get. It clearly doesn't have full control, and we're not going to let it get there. You'll be fine as long as it doesn't have a chance to grow much more."

"How much is much more?"

"How long is a piece of string? There's no way to really measure these things!" The cleric was pulling roots and leaves from his pack. "I'm going to make you something to drink that will taste horrible but will hopefully help kill the ghourd."

"Hopefully? What do you mean *hopefully*?" Robin almost lost control of his breath.

He focused again.

"It's not exactly my area. I've learned the cure—well, way to deal with the thing, but I didn't expect to need to use it on a ghourd that was this mature."

Eli pulled a mortar and pestle out of one of the smaller pockets on the side of his bag. There was no way that normal physics would allow anything that big to fit in a pocket that small. Actually, now that he was looking at it again, the bag looked completely different. It wasn't a scavenged sack at all! It was a full-on proper haversack.

Well, of course a cleric of a trickster deity would have a bag that could hide itself from various inspections and sneak all sorts of smuggled goodies in pockets too small to be worth checking. Handy.

"So scrounging for stones to use as makeshift mortar and pestle was also part of the joke," Robin observed snidely before another wave of pain lanced through his stomach. "Ugh. Hurry up. The stowaway I'm packing is getting really restless."

"Fight back," Eli said. "That mental connection is a two-way street. You're going to have to fight it mind to mind anyway if you want to get rid of it, so you might as well start now."

The cleric began to grind together various roots and leaves. Robin felt his stomach clench and what felt like a tangle of moving vines slithering at the edges of his mind. Mind-to-mind combat? With a plant?

Robin gritted his teeth and did his best to ignore the uncomfortable sensations. Likely, they were an attempt to weasel into his mind even deeper. He needed to go on the offensive.

What would a plant fear?

Robin brought up his memories of fire. Logs crackling in the fireplace, bonfires at Halloween and Guy Fawkes Day, candle flames that burned too hot when you snuffed them with your fingers . . . Robin gathered each of these images, these memories of sensation, and flung them like miniature fireballs into the thickest of the shadowy vines he could feel at the edges of his mind.

It helped. He felt faint stirrings of fear and pain. The feelings were in his mind, but they weren't his. His fear didn't taste like that. Robin should know—he'd had to stomach enough of it in his old life on Earth.

Robin spared a glance at Eli. The cleric was carefully mixing the ground roots and leaves with fresh water to make some kind of paste. Whatever that was, it wasn't ready yet.

"Keep fighting," the cleric commanded without looking at him. "You need to break its mind. Break the mind, and the ghourd will shatter. Besides, it'll be much easier to get out that way than if it's still intact as well as struggling."

Robin didn't trust himself to reply, but he swore then and there that Eli was going to pay for this—and pay triple what Robin was suffering. *Prank.* Robin bit back a hiss. He'd show him a ghourd-damned prank!

That gave him an idea, actually. The thing had started as a prank, and it had fed him snippets of song from his own memory to lead him to the charm recipe, so it must have some understanding of music. Hadn't Eli said the vines consumed the minds of their victims? Or was that another piece of knowledge leaking through the connection between Robin and the thing growing in his stomach?

In any case, he could use it, so use it he would.

This is a song without an end . . .

Robin focused on the catchy tune, the upbeat lyrics, and most of all, on the inevitability of the song he was singing with all his mental might at the stupid ghourd slithering in his belly.

He looped through the song once and cycled through it again, though this time, his mind caught on one of the words. Friend? More like bell-end. Still.

A few alterations to make it fit his exact situation . . .

Some creatures started singing it

They knew not what it was . . .

Robin really put his mental back into the catchy tune, reinforcing the loop of the words, cycling the song around and around and around in his mind, projecting it at the ghourd as strongly and insidiously as he could.

Forever. Sing forever. And sing forever . . .

. . . just because . . .

Robin channeled every car journey with his younger cousins, every annoying minute, every time the song had played on the TV or on the CD of kids music someone had given him (probably as an act of revenge upon his parents). He was relentless, the song was relentless, and each reinforced the other.

The tendrils at the back of his mind were knotting about themselves in annoyance, he could feel. *Yeah, deal with that, you overripe, invading squash blossom!* Robin's tolerance for annoying songs was legendary. No way would he crack before this trumped-up pumpkin.

Wait. Could he somehow use **[Cutting Words]** to target the ghourd too? It was certainly worth a try. Words could be thought as well as spoken, they just needed to be heard, and what was telepathy if not hearing words that had been thought instead of spoken?

Before Robin could try, however, Eli was ready with the mixture.

"Here," the cleric said. "You've got two options. One, you fight it to the death—mentally—and win, and I use this stuff to help you by weakening it and then flushing the pieces out of your system. Or . . ."

Robin didn't like that pause.

"Or what?"

"I could try cutting it out of you and using the paste to kill it directly, and then heal you back up with my magic and the Grace of Nevarre."

"Why don't we try option one first?" Robin snapped, not trusting Eli's magic *or* Nevarre's grace at the moment.

"Your body, your choice. Here, you'll have to eat some of this—it's disgusting, but don't throw it up. I don't have the ingredients for more."

And the elf clearly didn't want to risk taking the time to gather more. This ghourd must be closer to taking over Robin's mind than he'd thought.

"Right." Robin grimaced. "Let's do this. I've already got the thing on the ropes. Hit me with the paste."

Eli scooped up a big glob of the stuff on the end of his spoon. Robin couldn't help noticing the rat snake had even had utensils squirreled away. Then the smell hit him, and Robin gagged. He'd mucked out stables that smelled fresher.

No help for it, though. Robin grimaced and opened his mouth. He needed this ghourd and all the crap it was leaking into his mind *out* of him before—

"Wait!" Robin exclaimed, a sudden realization hitting him. "This thing has been leaking knowledge into my mind."

"Yes, but it's doing that in order to *take over your mind*." Eli looked at him like he had sprouted another head, spoon poised less than an inch away from Robin's face. "You can't tell me you think holding off on dealing with it to get a few more facts is a good idea."

"No, but if we extract the ghourd, I might forget how to properly carve the rowan and knot the red thread. That thing came from it, not me; I'm certain of it. And without that charm, we won't be able to escape Cherry."

Chapter 15

Robin winced as his stomach clenched again. The pain wasn't too bad at the moment; the ghourd was still fighting its way free of the "Song that Never Ends." He could tell that much. How long that reprieve would last, though, he couldn't say.

With his luck, it would end sooner rather than later.

"Right. What do you need?" Eli asked, electing not to waste time arguing.

"Give me something to trim that branch with." Robin pointed to the limb of sky-rowan on the floor nearby. "And there's a small pot hidden in the little room nearest Greater and Lesser Arcana. It's full of string and dye. Hopefully, it's red enough by now."

Robin didn't mention that he had another pot hidden away, also dyeing red thread, nor that he already had plenty of rowan twigs stowed in his ring.

"You've been busy," Eli observed, pulling a dagger from his haversack and passing it to Robin.

"You weren't completely above suspicion," Robin replied.

"Oh, so you were going to test your charm out on me first?" The cleric sounded amused. "I'd say I'm flattered, but I'm not sure that's the right word."

Robin groaned and clutched his stomach.

"Less talk, more action." He waved Eli away and began trimming more rowan twigs from the branch. "I'm not sure how long I can hold it off and get this right. The knots are going to be tricky."

Eli rose and slipped quickly out of the room.

As soon as he was gone, Robin straightened. The ghourd was still occupied, and his distress had mainly served to hurry Eli out of the room so he could work.

Robin set the dagger aside, pulled the twigs he had already prepared from his ring, and retrieved a small, hollow wooden tube from beneath his bed. He pulled out a long string, dark red and wet with dye. Slowly (because slow is smooth and smooth is precise), he bundled the twigs and tied them up with an intricate knot, muttering the words to the charm under his breath. He repeated the words three times before finishing off the work and stowing the completed charm in his ring.

Nine times would have made for a stronger charm, but he could try that with the next one. Robin wanted one on hand that he knew Eli hadn't come near to.

Speaking of, Robin could hear footsteps returning. With a thought, he covered the dye stains on his fingers with illusion courtesy of his **[Mask of Disguise]** and returned to trimming twigs. Eli entered the room moments later.

"Here," he said, setting the pot down next to Robin.

"Get the string out and pat it as dry as you can while I—" Robin's sentence got cut off with a hiss as a sharp stab of pain went through his gut and what felt like razor vine started tearing at the edges of his mind.

The cleric did as he asked; there wasn't much else he could do. None of his magic could oust the ghourd as things stood.

You call that a mental attack? Robin thought furiously at the presence within him. *I've seen sad trolls lurking in comments sections that can do better than that!*

It was a test to see whether or not his **[Cutting Words]** might have an effect. They were, after all, described as psychic energy.

The feeling of vines at the edge of his mind flinched back. Yes! It had totally worked! It hadn't done a lot of damage, but he hadn't tried tailoring his insult to the ghourd specifically.

Good enough for now. Better to hold it off with weak attacks while he finished the charms, then use the sharper insults once that was safely done and he could focus his entire being on destroying the bloody thing.

Eli was patting the string dry. Robin gritted his teeth and trimmed several more twigs from the branch of sky-rowan. It took him longer than he would have liked to assemble two piles of suitable size for the charms.

Robin fired off another mental insult, driving the ghourd back, and quickly knotted two charms. He made sure to chant the words in English;

Eli didn't need to know exactly which protections he was imbuing into the wood and thread.

As soon as he finished, he thrust one of the charms at Eli, pocketing the other. He hadn't finished a moment too soon. His fingers were beginning to tremble from the exertion of fighting off the ghourd's control of his nervous system.

"Get that disgusting gunk over here." Robin jerked his chin at Eli. "I'm going to go for the kill now."

"Get some of this in you first," the cleric said. "It'll help weaken the ghourd."

The smell alone was enough to weaken Robin, but he accepted the spoon anyway and swallowed the lot down fast. If he weren't afraid to bring his hands near the spoon in case the ghourd managed to seize control and knock it away, he would have pinched his nose shut. That would have helped with the smell and the taste.

To be honest, the stuff was so vile it probably wouldn't have done all that much. It tasted like castor oil mixed with hot rubbish, and had afternotes of locker room and rotting peas.

"You had best believe I'm going to get even with you for this," he promised the cleric before closing his eyes and directing his ire inward.

Eli ignored him. He was busy rubbing more of that disgusting concoction onto Robin's stomach. Robin reminded himself once again to learn some form of cleansing or purifying spell as soon as possible before he forced his attention on the problem inside.

Robin's mind was an arena of shadows. He imagined it as a vaulted, gray space with nebulous shadows dancing all around the edges. It was a far cry from any form of mind palace, but he didn't have time to be fancy.

"All right you," he shouted. "Free ride is over. Pack up and move out, or I'll cut you to ichorous ribbons."

Robin probed the shadows with his mind, looking for the connection between him and the ghourd. The good and bad news both was that they *were* connected, so it couldn't hide from him for long.

Shadowy tendrils lashed out at him as a prickly will tried to dig into his mind and eat it. For all its formidable powers, the ghourd was still a plant, and a single one at that. It was used to being part of a collective, one aspect of a great, vegetative hive mind comprised of the thoughts and feelings of every victim the plants had consumed.

Robin grabbed onto the tentacle vines and *pulled*. This would be easier if he could see the main body of the plant, not just its edges. He didn't have to pull hard; the ghourd seemed eager to close the distance now. Perhaps it felt he was weakening.

"That's right, come meet your doom, you Great Pumpkin wannabe!" Robin shouted as the golden bulk of the ghourd's body came into view. Here in his mindscape, it appeared nearly as big as he was. "Though the closest you'll ever get to 'great' is the business end of a vegetable peeler!"

The ghourd keened in pain, and several of its tentacle vines were sliced off.

Progress.

Robin launched into battle. It was a battle of attrition. His sharp words clashed with the shadowy tendrils of the ghilded ghourd, snipping off pieces while trying to crack the main body of the plant. For its part, the ghourd burrowed its mental roots and vines deeper into his mind, and the vaults began to bleed red and gold through the shadows.

The fight was tearing into his mind. There was so much of the ghourd rooted and tangled in there, he was going to have to cut the body of it free and absorb the rest. Robin grimaced.

Well, better to eat than be eaten, in this case.

Robin stopped trying to uproot the ghourd entirely and started aiming to strike at the heart of the problem. Crack that, and the vines wouldn't have anything directing them anymore.

Robin wracked his mind thinking up insults that would hurt a ghourd.

He tried teasing out if it disliked being too bulbous or not bulbous enough. He sniped at it about color and shade. He compared its leaves to moth-eaten rags and called it aphid bait. And slowly, he made progress.

He could tell he was getting to it. The ghourd's attacks had become more frenzied, less focused. It no longer attempted to burrow into his mind, now simply tearing at any exposed surface, desperate to wound or distract him enough that it could regroup.

Robin didn't give it the chance.

"You picked the wrong guy to set up shop in," Robin shouted. "I'm going to crack you like an egg and make you wish for a pie crust coffin!"

The ghourd keened and sent all of its roots and vines at him. Robin grabbed the tendrils and yanked the ghourd closer. The rind showed strain in several places, so as Robin pulled it closer, he drilled inexorably into those spots with his will.

"It's no wonder you're having trouble keeping a grip on my mind. You're more whine than vine at this point."

Closer.

"I've heard of cowards having a yellow streak, but your color scheme is taking the idea to the extreme."

And closer.

"Honestly, they say some beings have minds like steel traps. Yours is more like a rusty wing nut: useless for its intended purpose and with a big hole in the middle."

The thing exploded in his mental face.

Phantom chunks of ghourd scattered throughout his mind, and Robin felt an answering gurgle in his gut. A wave of nausea swelled, driving the scent of Eli's ghourd-killing paste into his nostrils once more.

It was too much.

Robin flipped over on his stomach just in time to blow bright orange chunks across the room, the remains of the ghilded ghourd hitting the floor with a wet splat. It took several more heaves for Robin to get the rest of it out of his system, all the time with a blue screen flickering before his eyes.

Congratulations! You have defeated an Adolescent Ghilded Ghourd and regained control of your mind and body! Experience Awarded! Perk Awarded!

Incompatible heritage detected! Calculating . . . Adjustment created.

Perk Awarded! [Shard of the Shattered Manymind]

You have fought a complex psychic entity on its own turf and bested it! In the process, a part of the creature's hive mind has broken free and been assimilated into your own. This confers the following ability:
Eldritch Lore: You have an eclectic tangle of knowledge and memories stored in your subconscious. When faced with a new situation or prompted by a question, you have a small percentage chance to access a bit of relevant knowledge.
This ability stacks with other compatible Lore abilities.

Eventually, he stopped puking his guts up and was able to read and minimize the screens. It seemed like the ghourd really was gone.

Robin decided to check a couple more things just to be certain, but before he could, Eli interrupted.

"Here, drink this. It will help." Eli held out a cup of what smelled like herbal tea.

Robin sniffed at it suspiciously. His *Natural Wisdom* proficiency didn't

reveal any obvious poison or trap, but he wished he had a bit more knowledge to back that up.

Would you like to raise Healing with experience? Y/N?

Oh yes. Robin mentally slammed the prompt in the affirmative three
times, increasing his knowledge of the healing arts. It was long overdue,
though he still wanted to find a spell or three to supplement the knowledge
provided by the proficiency.

He sniffed at the cup again. It seemed fine, so far as he could detect.

"Thank you," he said guardedly and took the smallest of sips.

He waited a moment. Nothing happened except that his stomach
eased. Well, Eli had never poisoned him, and it didn't appear the cleric
had messed with his senses. Manipulated and tricked him, sure, but not
poisoned or hexed.

He took another sip of the tea. His stomach settled further, and he realized he was very thirsty.

Robin pulled open his character sheet. It had been behaving oddly
before, so if it looked alright now, it would go a long way to reassuring him
that things were back to normal.

Well, as normal as things around here could be, he suspected.

Robin Parker

Heritage: Shadeling, Mature
Profession: None
Tier: 0
Progress to Tier 1: 87%

Properties

Free Ranks Available: 1

Physical
   -Strength: 11
   -Dexterity: 14
   -Fortitude: 11
Mental
   -Intelligence: 17
   -Cunning: 19

   -Resilience: 14

Social
   -Charisma: 15
   -Manipulation: 13
   -Poise: 15

Proficiencies

Free Ranks Available: 2

Physical (9/9)
   -Athletics: 1
   -Brawl: 0
   -Dodge: 4
   -Melee Combat: 2
   -Pilot: 4
   -Ranged Combat: 0
   -Sleight of Hand: 1
   -Stealth: 5
   -Survival: 1

Mental (9/9)
   -Arcane Lore: 4
   -Bureaucracy: 1
   -Concentration: 5
   -Crafting: 5
   -Healing: 3
   -Insight: 5
   -Learning: 4
   -Natural Wisdom: 3
   -Perception: 5

Social (9/9)
   -Animism: 0
   -Deception: 5
   -Empathy: 1
   -Expression: 5
   -Gossip: 0
   -Intimidation: 3
   -Persuasion: 3
   -Socialize: 1
   -Streetwise: 0

Peculiarities

Blessing of Rhyth
Tongue of the Fallen Tower
Mark of the Trickster
Chronicle of Infinite Visions

Perks

Wayfaring Stranger
Shard of the Shattered Manymind

Everything seemed to be in order, even if one of his peculiarities had vanished; the one he'd never gotten the chance to investigate too closely. Instead, he had a perk with a similar name.

He had the sneaking suspicion that the peculiarity he had seen briefly had belonged to the ghourd, and killing it had removed the peculiarity. Still, the replacement perk was nice. He looked through the description again. He'd have to test that soon, but first, he had another thing he wanted to try.

Robin took some of his remaining experience and put it into *Ranged Combat*, testing again to see if anything would attempt to change his decision as it had when the ghourd had still occupied his gut.

Congratulations! Your Ranged Combat has been raised to 2 with experience!

The familiar lessening and replacing rush had never felt so good.

It was a relief. Every test he had come up with so far pointed to him being free of the ghourd's influence.

Of course, that didn't mean there weren't still problems to be dealt with. Pixies, a mad dryad, and of course, the elf-lephant in the room. Robin turned to Eli.

"You and I are going to have a nice long chat about what exactly is going on in these gorram woods."

Chapter 16

*R*obin sat on his bunk, feeling the rough sheets beneath his newly cleaned hands. Eli had used a version of **[Cleanse]** to deal with the after-effects of the ghourd extraction. Everything looked spotless and beautiful.

Of course, it could all just be a sensory trick. The cleric did worship a deity of mischief, after all. But at least Robin *felt* clean.

Eli, for his part, sat on the bunk directly across from Robin. He toyed with the charm in his hand as he sat, a little smile sitting lazily on his face.

"So," he began. "How would you like to do this?"

"You could just tell me the truth," Robin tried.

"And would you believe me?"

That was a good point. Robin didn't have access to any sort of truth-sensing spell. He'd have to rely on his innate *Perception* and *Insight* to deal with any *Deception* from the cleric. Even swearing on his god wouldn't likely do much. Nevarre was himself a trickster! There's no way he'd ever punish Eli for lying.

"How about a trade?" Robin asked slowly after thinking for several moments.

"And what do you have to offer that is worth the truth from a liar's lips?"

"We could play the question game. You ask a question and I answer truthfully, and in exchange, I ask a question and you answer truthfully."

"I still don't see what incentive I have to tell the truth," the cleric said candidly.

"I could promise to retie the thread on that charm so it actually works," Robin deadpanned.

Eli froze.

There. Robin concealed a smile. *That* was an honest reaction, and it told him a few things as well, like that Eli was definitely afraid of Cherry. The cleric couldn't replicate what Robin had done nor see through all of his deceptions, so he had some leverage here.

His mind felt unnaturally clear. Maybe it was no longer being under the influence of the ghourd; maybe it was his recent rank up in *Perception* and *Insight*; maybe it was a combination of both, but Robin felt sharper than he had in days.

"If you had the presence of mind to fake that charm while also fighting off the ghourd, I have to say you're better than I thought." Eli gave him a measuring look. "And you must have had suspicions about me prior to today." He shook his head. "I thought I was doing well, even with the complications I've had to deal with."

Robin didn't say anything. They still didn't have a deal, and he wasn't about to give up anything he didn't have to.

Eli bounced the charm thoughtfully in his hand. Robin was content to wait until the cleric spoke again.

"Very well," he eventually agreed. "We'll play your game of questions, and I agree to answer truthfully, provided you give me a charm you've tied correctly. Do we have a deal?"

Robin made a show of thinking about it. It was a petty sort of payback since he already knew he was going to take the deal. Eli was bound to mix truth and lies in his answers, and sifting through that mess of words would be annoying, but at least there would be some truth, some new information Robin didn't already have.

"Let's establish some rules first," he said finally. "Since you're the aggressor in this case, I think I should begin. Either of us can choose to answer or not as we see fit, but equal answers are owed. So if you get an answer from me, you owe me an answer in return. Either of us can choose to end the game at any time and walk away. We both agree to answer truthfully. Deal?"

"Deal."

The cleric settled back on his bunk and quirked an expectant eyebrow at Robin.

"Why did you target me?" Robin had been wondering that for a while. The Sisters Sharp had managed to escape the trap, and Robin didn't think that was a coincidence.

"I was hired to." Eli grinned. "My turn. What's your real name? As much as I like 'Red,' it's just too obvious an alias."

Robin paused. He was in a fey wood, and that was enough to give any-one pause when asked for their name. He had been asked for a real name, not a true name, so there was probably some wriggle room that he could work with.

Was there a difference between a real name and a true name in this world? Robin focused the question and cast it into his subconscious, hop-ing the answer was somewhere among the hard won passel of knowledge he'd taken from the ghilded ghourd.

No, they were different things. His instincts were telling him he'd be safe enough telling Eli his first name.

"Robin," he answered. The next question to ask was obvious. "Who hired you to target me?"

"I never saw a face, and they only referred to themselves as 'Your Patron.' As in, the patron of yourself, Robin, not my patron." Eli made a *what can you do?* sort of gesture with his hands.

Robin could tell there was more to the story, but Eli had answered the question. As Robin pondered what next to ask to get more information, Eli took his turn.

"What tipped you off?"

"I'm sorry, what?" Robin blinked.

"That I wasn't who you thought. What was your first clue? What tipped you off?"

"Oh. You left your pack open, and I saw you'd lied about having more root to use for dye."

"Damn." Eli snapped his fingers in irritation. "There's always something."

Robin made a noncommittal noise, not having extensive experience in running cons, short or long.

"What, exactly, were . . . *my patron's* instructions to you regarding me and these woods?" That should give him some idea of the mysterious fig-ure's motivations, at least, and as it wasn't something Eli should care much about, Robin might even get an honest answer out of the cleric.

"To ensure you had three encounters here before you left: one with Cherry, one with the ghilded ghourd, and one with the knowledge left behind in this tower." Eli thought for a moment. "And to make sure you escaped with your body and mind intact. More or less."

Robin resisted the urge to ask if those were the mysterious patron's exact words. With his luck, that would put him an additional question into Eli's debt, and he wasn't quite ready for that.

Cherry had prompted the quest from the system. The encounter with the ghourd had resulted in an interesting and useful perk, and the tower contained a wealth of knowledge that Robin was benefitting from. So there had been a lot of danger in exchange for some useful abilities and other gains.

He'd have to ponder what they all had in common later. It was Eli's turn to ask a question, and Robin needed his wits about him to evade any potentially dangerous ones.

"What are your feelings about me, both before and after discovering my role in the prank your patron arranged for you?" Eli's eyes sparkled, but there was a sharp edge underneath the apparent humor.

"Ah, wha—I mean, let me think that through."

Whatever Robin had been expecting as the next question, this was not it. Although, thinking on it, it did make a certain amount of sense. On one level, it was the cleric of a god of mischief yanking his chain. On a deeper level, if Robin answered honestly, it would give Eli a good indication of whether or not he was in any sort of danger from an outraged Robin.

That was an effective use of a question. Robin determined to make the answer as useless as possible while still telling the absolute truth. And he had an idea how to do just that.

"I suppose the answer to that depends on who you are asking about." Robin crossed his arms in front of his chest. "After all, I barely know *you*. The person I'm more familiar with is mostly fiction. You know, the cleric of Vané, the sculptor imprisoned by the dangerous dryad. But that's not who you are at all, really. All I know about you is that you abused my trust, endangered my life, and pretended to be someone you aren't, all for money from some mysterious patron you can't even tell me much about."

Robin quirked his head to one side. "So it's hard to answer that without more information or a clearer question, but to strictly answer you: I don't know in the case of the former, and while I'm withholding judgement on the latter for now, I'm kind of disinclined to go all in on liking you."

"Technicalities," Eli said, but frowned in thought. "Still, I suppose I'll have to accept that answer. Unsatisfying though it may be, it is fair." The cleric sighed. "Ask your next question."

Before Robin could formulate one, however, a prompt impeded his vision.

Quest Progress Update: [Freedom, Freedom, Freedom!]
Congratulations! You have successfully extracted yourself from the potential snares that lurked on your path and threatened to ensnare your heart and will! Part 3 of this quest still pending.

Reward: One random social property increased! +1 Poise. Well, that makes sense. Considering how much of an assault your personality had from that ghourd, naturally you'd end up more resistant socially! It was totally random, though, I do promise you that!

Robin blinked the notification away before Eli could notice anything out of the ordinary. And to be on the safe side, he tossed out a question of his own that was designed to set the cleric off balance.

"What was the biggest thing to go wrong with your plan to shepherd me through these experiences at the behest of that mysterious patron?" Robin resisted claiming the figure as his own. There were too many unknowns.

"Cherry's sudden—though if I'm being honest, inevitable—betrayal," Eli replied sourly. "I thought I could trust the payment I gave her to keep her to our bargain, but I guess she wanted more. Maybe when she saw you. Maybe when she realized how dangerous those women you were travelling with were. Whatever the reason, it certainly sent things off the rails early."

So the cleric had actually been a prisoner. That told him Eli definitely did fear Cherry's power and did need the charm Robin had crafted. It also meant that the cleric's discomfort had been very real. Robin didn't bother to hide his smile this time.

"That must have been terrible for you," he said with vast insincerity.

"It really was," Eli agreed.

Robin couldn't tell if the priest didn't notice Robin was delighted at his misfortune, or if Eli was just ignoring Robin's glee to deliberately undercut it.

So he waited for the next question. When it didn't come after a minute of silence, Robin quirked an eyebrow at the cleric.

"I don't think I have any more questions . . . for now, anyway. I'll keep the one you owe me in the bank for now," Eli said slowly, smiling. He grinned wider at Robin's clear consternation and extended his hand. "So I suppose all that's left is for you to retie this. As per our agreement."

Robin glared at him but took the charm and made a show of retying the string.

"There. On my honor, that is the correct knot for the warding charm we need to get past Cherry." He thrust the bundle of twigs at Eli. "Done deal."

"A pleasure doing business with you." Eli chuckled, and it vanished into a pocket or a sleeve. The cleric's hands were too fast for Robin to follow, even with his increased perception. "Here endeth the game of questions, then."

"Actually, there's one question left, but it's one we might have to answer together, I think."

"Oh?" Eli looked at him expectantly.

"Are we ready to get out of these woods?"

Chapter 17

Robin absently rubbed his finger where he'd stabbed himself with a splinter. He was standing in the room he'd come to think of as the barracks, having one last look and gathering his meager belongings before leaving. Well, at least that was what he appeared to be doing. Everything he actually valued was already stowed in his ring, not that there was much: his staff, his small collection of useful herbs and plants, a small chip of stone taken from the central room of the tower, a jug of water, some assorted useful materials, and the first charm he'd made.

In front of him was his bunk, the scavenged sack that was posing as his pack, and a sky-rowan charm. It sat where he had left it, but it wasn't the one he had left there. Last night, when he thought Robin was sleeping, Eli had quietly switched the charm Robin had repaired for him with the one in Robin's possession. It seemed the trickster priest had a small problem with trust.

Robin smiled. Eli would come to regret that particular sneaky action. Not that the swap mattered to Robin in the larger scheme of things. If—when—the time came, he had his most potent charm stowed safely in his storage ring.

The duo had taken their time making preparations. They'd scried out possible exits from the forest, tracked Cherry's movements, and gathered food and water for their respective journeys. Robin had also used the time to track down a few things he had noticed in the tower files.

Robin flicked a glance over at the magical runes lighting the room. He had managed to essentially add himself as a user to the tower systems.

He didn't have what amounted to full admin control, but he could give the tower certain limited commands. He'd use that to make sure the place stayed safe and secure until he had a chance to return.

That had not been an easy decision, but in the end, Robin had decided the tower likely wasn't going anywhere, and he'd grabbed most of the low-hanging fruit of knowledge already. If he could follow the Sisters Sharp and help them, then he could get to Noviel. Robin really wanted to see more of this world; that temptation was probably even bigger than the potential usefulness he might get from Noviel's University and Adventuring Companies.

Plus, he couldn't complete his quest until he left the enchanted wood, and Robin wanted his stacking experience modifier for that achievement. Sure, it was one use, but it would probably be more than enough to push him to the next level, all the way to Tier One.

With that in mind, Robin had done some targeted research through the tower databases, gathering experience point discounts and bumping up all of his proficiencies still at zero, as well as a couple of others he could afford to raise a bit more after that. There was no formal categorization of skills in the database, unlike spells or professions, so Robin was increasingly sure that the proficiency system was mostly invented by the interface he was using.

The broad-strokes nature of the proficiencies argued for that as well. They seemed to represent most activities he could think of, which meant this was pretty much it in terms of choices, and he wasn't going to miss out on any strange, rare, or powerful skills. He just had to raise the ones he had. Possibly find ways to upgrade them to better versions? The *Pilot* proficiency suggested that was possible.

"You ready?" Eli stuck his head into the room, interrupting Robin's train of thought.

Robin grabbed the charm and stowed it in his makeshift pack.

"Let's go."

After Robin had scried throughout the forest, he and Eli had decided the likeliest way to exit was toward the keep. That suited Robin just fine, as it was the direction he was headed. Exiting the tower, Robin fell back for just a moment and whispered a command word, his hand on the door. The place would hide itself more effectively from everyone except him and any of the original tower occupants (if any of them were somehow still alive).

Eli didn't notice. The cleric was charging forward through the trees, eager to be free of the wood and onto whatever his next escapade was. Robin followed, occasionally calling out directions to guide the headstrong priest.

He was also keeping one eye carefully peeled for Cherry and her pixies. There was no way the quest was going to let him slip free of the enchantment without another confrontation with the dryad. The world he found himself in seemed too dramatic for that. Plus, his mysterious patron seemed to want to advance Robin's power and abilities via conflict, and he wouldn't put it past the bastard to have other contingencies in place in addition to Eli to make sure that happened.

"We're here," Eli said as they entered the clearing they had been headed toward.

Robin took out a small handful of stones and began tossing them at the trees around. Most bounced off, but a few flew through the illusory forms. The feeling Robin was coming to associate with his instincts telling him something was out of place returned, albeit more muted this time.

"How many of the illusions tripping us up when we first arrived in the wood were yours?" he asked.

"None," Eli replied. "I was already a prisoner then. I admit I used a few to sort of direct you after we escaped, but none that resulted in your initial capture, I promise."

That explained the recurring feeling that something was off. Robin resolved to pay more attention to his gut in the future. Although, to be fair, he had also been under the influence of a mind-affecting ghourd at the time, so he could forgive himself for that.

"Careful," he warned. "If we're here, I'd give it better than even odds that—"

Cherry stepped out of the trees.

"—she'll be here as well," Robin finished.

"Going somewhere, little toys?" the dryad asked, her eyes already a deep fruit red.

"We're leaving," Eli declared.

"We're not toys," Robin said at the same time.

"Oh, you are both wrong." The dryad laughed, a sound like the rustling of leaves in an autumn wind.

Cherry gestured, and the trees around them creaked and stretched down their branches to try and snatch them up. Robin stepped in front of Eli and raised his rowan charm above his head.

The trees recoiled from it as if from fire. Leaves rustled uneasily and branches creaked out a question to Cherry, who snarled.

Robin tightened his grip. It was working!

"Looks like we're not the ones who are wrong," he said coolly. "We're leaving, Cherry. We're protected by rowan and red thread. Your enchantments and your minions have no sway over us. Unless you want to try your luck . . ."

Robin kindled a small ball of flame above his outstretched palm with **[Visual Phantasm]**. It was just an illusion, but it made his point. The trees drew back from him in horror, and Cherry hissed in fury.

"Tricks! Shadows and phantasms!"

"Maybe," Robin shot back. "But what if you're wrong? It's not that hard to make fire, after all. You just need a couple of dry sticks. Rub them together, and eventually, you get fire. You're made of wood, and you're definitely rubbing me the wrong way."

"I will not be bluffed!"

"You might not, but what about Neher?" Robin tried the tree. It was an obvious weak point for the dryad.

"You would not dare!" Cherry raged at him.

"Didn't we already have a long conversation about what I would and would not dare do if you pushed me?" Robin increased the size and brightness of the fireball.

"Face it, Cherry, you've lost." Eli stepped forward. Not ahead of Robin, but forward. He held his own charm tightly in hand. "Let us go. I'm sure you'll have someone else along to amuse you soon enough. The marcher lords like the luxuries they get from trading at the keep."

"Someone you won't have to stab in the back to capture and toy with," Robin added. He wanted the two of them focused on the bad blood between them.

"He was weak and foolish," Cherry called. "How could I not strike?"

"We had a deal!" Eli shouted. "Do you have any idea how much planning you ruined? How much work I had to do to improvise?"

"Bah! Such things are for the weak! The strong simply *do*," the dryad taunted Eli.

"I'll do for you, you walking pile of kindling!" The priest was clearly incensed. "I've got a bit of insurance on me, and you won't catch me by surprise again."

Robin wasn't sure how she'd managed to catch Eli by surprise the first time. It seemed out of character. But then again, the cleric did have a bit of an arrogant streak. He probably just assumed he could handle anything Cherry threw at him.

As the two bickered, Robin slowly decreased the size and brightness of the fireball so he could fade slightly into the background. There was a large boulder nearby. He edged back toward it carefully as he cast [**Lesser Phantasm**] as subtly as he could, causing said boulder to grow slightly in size on one side.

Neither Eli nor Cherry noticed. They were too busy ripping into one another with insults. In fact, they were so intent on tearing each other apart with words, they had yet to attack the other physically. Which was fine. Eli was likely to get a rude surprise if he challenged Cherry to actual battle.

When Eli had been otherwise occupied, Robin had switched out the bundle of rowan twigs for a bundle of oak ones tied with the same red thread. It looked similar enough to the rowan charm to pass cursory inspection. Of course, Eli hadn't had the time to inspect it closely when he'd been swapping his charm for the fake one on Robin's bunk.

The priest should have trusted him, not that Robin had expected him to. That was the whole point of making a fake charm and leaving it out, so exposed.

Eli continued shouting at Cherry, not realizing the charm in his hand was next to useless against her. That wasn't Robin's problem, though. His goal now was to slip away unnoticed.

He had reached the boulder. Perfect.

Robin recast [**Visual Phantasm**] and overlapped himself with the illusion of himself holding that little fireball. Then he stepped back *into* the [**Lesser Phantasm**] he'd used to extend the size of the boulder.

Robin kept up his chain casting as he edged around the boulder. Once it was between him and the other two, he carefully and quietly snuck away into the forest. Let them deal with one another. By the time they noticed he was gone, he'd have a nice lead. Hopefully enough to be out of Cherry's sphere of influence. Eli would still be stuck inside without a proper charm and would have to deal with Cherry to escape.

One good prank deserves another, right?

It seemed decent payback for Eli's part in Robin's recent "adventures" anyway. Robin had even said so in the small note he'd wrapped around the twig at the center of the fake bundle.

He reached the end of the forest before any sort of hue and cry went up. He'd maintained concentration on his [**Visual Phantasm**], but it had to have vanished by now. Even if Cherry was annoyed at his escape, she was probably still occupied dealing with Eli. And Eli was certainly busy trying to deal with Cherry.

Robin smiled.

He took one look back into the trees until he was as sure as he could be that no one was following him. There was no sign of pursuit, and no twisting unease of illusion toying with his senses. Good.

Robin turned on his heel and walked out of the forest, the sweet *ding!* of a level-up notification the music to his passing.

Chapter 18

$\mathcal{R}$obin inhaled deeply, the spring air around him sweet and tasting like freedom. The forest was a green smudge in the background, though the foothills he was steadily climbing still sported the odd clump of evergreens.

The keep was a looming presence ahead of him. Robin was using it together with the landmarks he had scried out from the tower to navigate to the last place he had found the Sisters Sharp making camp. If he was lucky, they'd still be there; if not, he could hopefully follow their tracks to wherever they were now.

Robin moved forward, making good time, the rocky hills beneath him no problem for his current form. His latest level up had brought with it the chance to finally get his hands on **[Mask of Myriad Faces]**. He was currently bounding up the hills on the legs of a satyr. The hooves were great on the terrain and worlds better than the makeshift sandals he had been wearing.

Even better, he looked exactly as he wished to thanks to his **[Mask of Disguise]**. Should anyone out here spot him, they wouldn't see the goat legs he was using. He looked as he normally did, except he'd kept the red hair and he'd given himself the illusion of some nice clothes. He was sporting a dashing pair of knee-high pirate boots and black trousers, covered with the latest version of the three-quarter, fantastical trench coat he'd been working on ever since he'd found the mask in the tunnels. It was currently black with brilliant blue accents.

As soon as he had been free of the forest, he'd received a quest notification.

Quest Complete! [Freedom, Freedom, Freedom!]
You have won your freedom thrice over, from cage, from the snares set for your heart and mind, and from the enchanted forest itself. You've defeated a triple threat, and that deserves a tripled prize!
Reward: *Lumberjack, Clothier, and Spellbreaker professions unlocked. All experience rewards relating to this quest will now be tripled, retroactively. Hold on to your butts; this is going to be a ride!*

The sensation of all that energy flowing into his body had set him all a-fizz and aflutter. He'd felt amazing! Like he could run a marathon while reading a book and belting a ballad all at once. And just as he had hoped, the experience had been enough to tip him over the edge.

Congratulations! Threshold Achieved! Level Bonuses Awarded!
Choose one Property to increase by one (1) rank!
Proficiency rank-cap raised by one (1)!
You have gained one (1) new Peculiarity slot!
Heritage advanced to Shadeling, Paragon! Professions Unlocked!

Robin had increased his *Cunning* again; it had stood him in good stead, and it was the most efficient use of points. The peculiarity had been easy, filling it with **[Mask of Myriad Faces]** immediately. And he was about to have even more options to play with!

Robin flicked through to the relevant notification.

Congratulations! Tier 1 (Conditional) achieved! Please choose a Profession!

Professions were essentially classes. Robin opened that portion of the interface and spent a lot of time going through his options. Apparently, unlocking a profession just made it available from his pool of potential "classes." He'd met the prerequisites, so to speak. There were several available, including ones that he had not gotten notifications for. He assumed those were basic options he qualified for simply due to his past experience. Scholar and Farmer were among these.

Of the others, the only ones directly dealing with magic in some form or other were Ritualist (probably from his dabbling in ceremonial magick on Earth), Spellbreaker, and Bard.

Magic in this world generally relied upon a personal store of arcane energy. All creatures had a basic capacity for it, but with the right classes (professions!), that reservoir could increase and be manipulated to produce spells and other effects.

His interface insisted on measuring this energy in thaumaturgical units or thaums, but Robin just thought of it as spell points. The energy regenerated slowly throughout the day, his pool refilling every twenty-four hours. The speed increased if he could rest in an area of compatible thaumaturgical energy, or if he selected peculiarities that aided in regenerating energy or making it more efficient to use what he had.

The advantage of the Ritualist was that he would be able to pull off major magical effects without having to rely on his personal store of arcane energies. The trade-off there was that spells took a lot longer and often required strange components to be present.

The Spellbreaker profession had been unlocked by his quest, and it was pretty clear which relevant act he'd performed to get access to it. The class focused on disruption of, resistance to, and unravelling of existing magical effects. Situationally very powerful—and attractive to someone who'd recently had to fight off a supernatural parasite.

And then there was Bard. Music, magic, performance, and living by your wits. Robin was a bit more limited in terms of the spells the interface showed him as accessible to bards, but the class made up for that to a small degree by allowing one to occasionally learn spells from *any* class. Bards were expected to possess a great deal of ancient and powerful lore, after all.

Robin pondered his options for a while, but it wasn't long until he just went with it and selected Bard. Hadn't the universe been pointing him in this direction since he'd arrived in this world? It also fit the best with his illusion skill set and his general inclinations. Plus, it would give him plenty of reasons to travel, an increased knowledge pool to draw from, and the ability to steal choice bits of magic from other classes without having to deal with multiclassing or complex builds.

Oh, this was going to be *fun*!

Profession selected! Congratulations! You have been designated a Bard (Apprentice)! Complete your introductory quest to gain access to your full profession abilities.

Robin repressed a groan. He had to complete a quest first? There was always something.

New Quest: [Seize the Spotlight!]
Congratulations on taking the first step on your journey to becoming a

bard! This is an Advanced Profession Option and requires you to complete this quest to unlock its full potential. Until this quest is complete, you will have access to between 1/3 and 2/3 of your full Bardic abilities. Your mission, should you choose to accept it (and who in their right mind wouldn't?) is to complete a performance in front of an audience of at least 99 people and gain the resounding approval of a majority. Hey, if you do well enough, maybe you'll even get your first fan! Better start thinking of your stage name!

Reward: *The title of Full Bard, the remainder of your available introductory profession options, and an increase in notoriety. Fame is linked to your performance persona, and you only benefit from it when you are recognizable.*

Well, at least that didn't sound too bad. Good thing he was headed for the keep; he should be able to find an audience there. Noviel was also an option, but Robin didn't want to wait that long to gain access to his full bardic abilities. Who knows? He might also be stuck and unable to level until he completed this quest.

At least he got *some* of his abilities. Robin went for the spells first, since he already had a solid idea of what he wanted. It looked like he would learn three cantrips with his bardic initiation, but with the quest limitation, he only had access to one.

He selected **[Legerdemain]** because it was an all-purpose cantrip which provided many small magical effects, but most importantly, could be used to *clean* himself. It wasn't as fast as the others he had seen, but it would get the job done, and the extra versatility it provided was nothing to sneeze at.

He also had the option to choose two of what should have been three Tier One–level spells. Quickly scanning through the descriptions, he narrowed it down to a short list of choices.

[Healing Note] was a no-brainer. It was a short-range, single-target healing spell. He'd been looking for an option like this; he got hurt far too often for his taste.

The other decision was trickier. **[Minor Enchanted Slumber]** provided some crowd control, but it didn't last long. **[Whispers from Beyond]** gave him an increased single-target damage option with a possible control effect. **[Dissonant Wail]** had a small amount of multitarget damage. And then there was the incredibly attractive utility of **[Invisible Servant]**.

Reluctantly, he dismissed the idea of **[Invisible Servant]**. He had a lot of utility already; he needed to expand his self-defense options. Besides, he didn't have any place to order his servant to clean, and no current shenanigans to enlist it in. He could always pick it up later if nothing better was available.

Robin shelved the debate for a moment and examined his other bardic abilities. [Bardic Lore] represented the mass of legend and story, gossip, and general knowledge floating around in his subconscious. The way the interface interpreted it, he had about a 70 percent chance of knowing useful information about any topic that fell under the description of "common knowledge." This went up through various stages of obscurity at steadily smaller percentages all the way to having a 3 percent chance of knowing useful information about an "extremely obscure" topic, the sort of thing "known only to rare experts." That was with the synergy provided by [Shard of the Shattered Manymind]. The percentage would increase as he leveled and as he raised his *Intelligence* score.

[Bardsong], on the other hand, was the knowledge and ability to imbue magical effects into his performances. His interface estimated he could use it five times a day, though at present, he was only able to manifest a single effect: [Command Attention]. He would be able to use [Bardsong] more times each day as he leveled and as he raised his *Charisma* score. At least that would be useful for his quest!

Robin paused at the top of the hill he was on. He was getting nearer the keep, nearer the area he had last seen the Sisters Sharp; he recognized the broken rock formation at the top of the next hill.

Down and up, up and down. It was a lot of hiking. Too bad he wasn't going to be able to get his hands on a magical mount until at least Tier Three. Well, Tier Two if he could steal an appropriate spell from the Paladin profession.

Until then, however, he had to make do with his own two feet—or hooves, as the case was at the moment. Robin conjured a single playing card out of thin air with [Legerdemain] and practiced sailing it at a nearby rock, refining his *Ranged Combat*. Then he set off down the hill and up the hill conjuring cards and sailing them at targets.

An idea for his performance persona began to take shape in his mind as he went; the beginnings of a theme and a few options for names. It would have to be a single-word sobriquet, of course.

Iconic.

Robin pondered as he hiked and sailed cards at stationary targets. Songs queued up in his mind, dredged out of hours of listening to the radio, to streaming music, to the albums of his friends at uni, like a mental nickelodeon. Jukebox?

He hummed to himself as he went.

. . . Ace of Hearts . . .

Robin Parker

Heritage: Shadeling, Paragon
Profession: Bard (Apprentice)
Tier: 1, Conditional (Effective Level: 3)
Progress to Tier 2: Locked
Experience: 300
Spell Points: 3
Bardsong: 5 uses

Properties

Free Ranks Available: 1

Physical
  -Strength: 11
  -Dexterity: 14
  -Fortitude: 11
Mental
  -Intelligence: 17
  -Cunning: 20
  -Resilience: 14
Social
  -Charisma: 15
  -Manipulation: 13
  -Poise: 16

Proficiencies

Free Ranks Available: 2

Physical (9/9)
  -Athletics: 1
  -Brawl: 1
  -Dodge: 4
  -Melee Combat: 2
  -Pilot: 4
  -Ranged Combat: 5

-Sleight of Hand: 1
-Stealth: 5
-Survival: 3
Mental (9/9)
-Arcane Lore: 4
-Bureaucracy: 1
-Concentration: 5
-Crafting: 5
-Healing: 3
-Insight: 5
-Learning: 4
-Natural Wisdom: 3
-Perception: 5
Social (9/9)
-Animism: 1
-Deception: 6
-Empathy: 2
-Expression: 5
-Gossip: 2
-Intimidation: 3
-Persuasion: 3
-Socialize: 2
-Streetwise: 2

Peculiarities

Blessing of Rhyth
Tongue of the Fallen Tower
Mark of the Trickster
Chronicle of Infinite Visions
Mask of Myriad Faces

Perks

Wayfaring Stranger
Shard of the Shattered Manymind

Spells

Cantrips* (*no SP cost)
-Lesser Phantasm*
-Cutting Words*
-Legerdemain*

Tier 1 (1SP each)
  -Visual Phantasm*
  -Healing Note
  -Whispers from Beyond
Tier 2 (3SP each)
  -Assume Quality (Special)

Interlude

Meanwhile, back in Wyndham Wood . . .

"Wait!" Cherry held up a hand. "Where did the delicious little morsel go?"

Eli paused midrant and glanced around him. Robin was nowhere to be seen. The priest was alone with the dryad.

What? Eli's hand reflexively tightened on the end of the charm he was gripping as if his life depended on it. The string, already strung quite tight, was no match for this added pressure and snapped. A cascade of twigs burst from Eli's hand, among them, a small flutter of something white.

The clearing froze in surprise.

Eli snatched up the slip of parchment. There was writing on it. It was a note!

One eye still on Cherry, he quickly scanned the words.

Dear Eli,

If you're reading this, then you've discovered this charm is a fake. Unlike the one
I gave you. Guess you should have trusted me! Better luck next time.
Oh, and give my love to Cherry, would you?
Yours in Pwnage,
Robin
xoxo

A strangled, desperate laugh leapt from Eli's throat. Hoist with his own petard! Part of him admired Robin's cleverness. The other part of him was busily screaming that he now had no defense against Cherry and her magics.

Fuck.

. . . and at the keep that overlooked the Borderlands . . .

Gis winced as the sound of stone crashing to the floor reverberated through the chapel. Workmen were busily redecorating since he'd assumed control of the place when Basgar had seized the keep.

"Careful, you idiots," the priest snapped.

He wasn't concerned about the shattering stone. No. The bit that had fallen was a statue of the former deity this place had been dedicated to, some weak and sniveling elvish power. He was having the chapel rededicated to Urkhan, but before he could do that, the proper ambiance needed to be in place.

His god was most exacting in his expectations.

Sssomething troublesss you.

The hissing whispers in his mind came from Gehn, the serpent that lived with and within him. A gift from His Lord and Master, Gehn was similar to a wizard's familiar, yet so much more. Sometimes, Gis's dreams burned with the divine fire that Gehn channeled to him from mighty Urkhan himself.

"Too much rebellion lurks in the hearts of the denizens of this keep. Lord Basgar was able to seize control, yes, and holds his right to rule with an iron fist, but he has not yet had time to recruit more forces. Until he does so, we are forced to rely on the services of many who lived and prospered under the former ruler of this place."

Another crash echoed throughout the chapel.

"Rebellion festers among the dissatisfied. Though they are weak, they are many, and even a lion may be felled by dogs."

Then turn them againssst one another. Let the dogsss fight amongssst themssselvesss while we grow mighty.

Gis pondered the serpent's advice as he made his way from the chapel to his personal quarters. It was a sound tactic, though he had not the requisite knowledge of the various rebellious dogs to enact it.

The priest's expression soured. He would have to enlist the aid of a specialist. There were a few around the keep, most in Basgar's camp. One of them might serve, but those who flocked to Basgar tended to lack a certain finesse. The man was an excellent iron fist, but he was a fist completely lacking in velvet glove. This plan required a fine touch or it could easily backfire on them, and their position was too tenuous as it was.

There were also many potential complications. No, while it was a wise idea, wiser still would be to consult a higher authority before taking action on the matter. And while Gis could not appeal to Urkhan directly for answers—his body could not yet withstand that level of divine energies—there were lesser divinations he could perform.

Gis's personal quarters were opulent, wealth used as an open display of power. The priest himself cared little for the aesthetics of gold or the luxurious touch of silk; he was only interested in such things for as much power and control as they could give.

He closed the door to his chamber and locked it. He could afford no interruptions. Divination was an imprecise art at the best of times, and the tools Urkhan gifted his priests for the practice were particularly dangerous to employ.

Yet employ them he would.

Gis knelt before a large chest. The scent of cedar and myrrh rose to meet his nostrils as he opened the lid. Inside were several things he would need. Salt. Blood-red candles. A sanctified dagger, and the skull of some horned humanoid engraved with runes and sigils.

Gis retrieved these and a few other things before turning the chest into an altar. In fact, it had been designed as such. The demands of conquest often called Urkhan's priests to be more mobile than their brethren of other churches.

The room grew hot, stinking of sweat and sulfur. Gis's voice droned in a harsh and guttural language while the flames of the candles danced to red and then to black as a presence entered first the room and then the skull upon the altar.

Two pinpricks of red light kindled themselves in the dark hollows of the eye sockets. A breathy, whispered laugh with an edge like a razor blade slid out of the grinning rictus.

"In the name of Urkhan, God of Tyranny and Prince of Lies, I command you speak!" Gis all but hissed the command. "Tell me—"

Beware the blade of laughter. Beware the sharpened pip. Beware the shadows.

Before the priest could ask about his planned course of action, a warning was given. Something was already in motion! Something that threatened the will of Urkhan if it had overridden the cleric's own desires in this working.

Gis's blood prickled at the whispered words from the servant of his god. Something or someone was coming to threaten their rule of the keep. That could not be allowed! He had plans for this place, and plans greater still that required his success here.

The priest banished the entity inhabiting the skull before rising and beginning to pace. Their position here was balanced on a dagger's point. It had to be secured before this outside threat arrived to tip it out of their favor.

By any means necessary.

The Keep over the Borderlands

Chapter 1

Robin padded softly into the camp, the grass soft against the pads of his feet. He had opted for stealth and used **[Mask of Myriad Faces]** to assume the form of a catkin. It didn't make him any more dexterous, really, or increase his *Stealth*, but it provided small circumstantial benefits.

It wasn't much more than a small space surrounded by boulders; an open-air hollow more than a cave. It fit in well with the rocky terrain of the plateau that housed the keep and was a nice place out of the wind. It was chillier here, farther up the mountains, than it had been down in the enchanted wood.

Searching the camp, Robin came up empty. The Sisters Sharp weren't around. There were signs they had been there, and recently, and he found a small cache of supplies that argued they planned to return, but the question was *when—*

"Don't. Move."

Robin felt the prickle of a knife at this throat. Apparently, the answer of when was *now*.

"Lantha?" he guessed.

He heard laughter in his ear, and the knife vanished from his throat. Turning, he found Lantha and Ora-Jean standing behind him. They must have hidden when they heard someone coming and he had missed the signs, even with the training he had done to increase his *Perception*.

"So you're not completely useless at trackin' then," Ora-Jean said with a grin. "I told them you'd find us if we were still here. And you managed to escape the pixies."

"The dryad was a bigger problem," Robin replied drily.

Lantha quirked an eyebrow at that. Ora-Jean opened her mouth to ask, but Lantha held up a hand.

"Wait. Fiamah and Grathilde should be back soon; no point telling the story twice," the rogue said.

Robin didn't particularly agree. After all, he needed to work on his performance skills so he could complete his bardic quest. Still, he settled in, listening to Lantha and Ora-Jean describe what had happened from their perspective.

After the pixie attack, the Sisters Sharp had realized he was missing. They'd searched for a while, but the forest had led them out, and once out, they couldn't find their way back in; the illusions just kept turning them away.

Another thing he owed Eli for—or probably Cherry. Thinking on it, it felt more like the dryad's work.

The Sisters Sharp had eventually concluded they weren't going to be able to rescue Robin and moved on toward the keep; they had vital intelligence to return to Noviel. What precisely, Lantha wouldn't allow Ora-Jean to say, but Robin didn't mind. He didn't have a dog in that hunt.

What followed was the usual tale of adventure and wandering monsters as they made their way to the keep. Robin had come face to face with a couple of hairy situations himself on the journey. Ora-Jean was good at describing the battles, though; much better than Lantha.

The woman really got into it.

Knowing Gis had seen their faces, they'd decided to split into two groups to investigate the town inside the keep's outer walls. They didn't have much they could use in the way of disguises, so they had wanted to work every angle.

Made sense. Robin approved. Not everyone could be a magical master of disguise.

"The main issue is the pass we need to get out the gate toward Noviel," Lantha said, cutting through one of Ora-Jean's many tangents. "We've tested the walls, and they're too well patrolled, not to mention warded. Basgar and Gis aren't raging incompetents, for all their other faults."

"We definitely need a pass, stolen or forged. We haven't yet found someone who'll give us a legitimate one; not for the money we've got. We're doing odd jobs and collecting bounties to amass funds to get us through the gate and outfit ourselves better for the journey back to Noviel," the scout explained.

"And the situation inside isn't making things any easier," Lantha observed sourly. "Basgar still hasn't solidified his rule, so there's a lot of chaos inside, and the petty tyrant's forces are all on high alert constantly. It makes things . . . difficult."

"So that's where we're at. Trying to find a way through the gate so we can make it back to Noviel," the barbarous scout concluded, scratching her fingers in midair at about the height a massive badger might stand, were he visible.

Fiamah and Grathilde appeared just as Ora-Jean was finishing up the tale. Grathilde took one look at him, broke into a wide grin, and held her hand out to Ora-Jean.

"He made it back," the aeromancer crowed. "Pay up!"

The scout grumbled like Robin imagined her badger would as she pulled out a couple of coins and tossed them to the aeromancer.

Fiamah simply walked over to Robin and gave him a brief hug. Robin hurriedly resumed his own form beneath the illusion of himself before the physical contact could reveal anything. That would just lead to several awkward questions.

No need to go into that now.

"It's good to see you again," the cleric said.

"Right, everyone's back. I want to hear about this dryad," Ora-Jean demanded. "How did you escape the enchanted wood?"

"Dryad?" Grathilde shot Robin a measuring look and a smirk. "I'm surprised—"

"Enough," Fiamah cut her off. "I would like to hear Robin's story."

"I've been practicing, even," Robin said with a grin. "And I've picked up a couple of new tricks to show you."

He held up his left hand. He'd nicked it on a stone climbing the hill, but as it wasn't a bad cut, he had conserved his energies. Now that he had an audience, however . . .

Robin hummed, reaching out for that resonance that his recent level up had imprinted upon his mind: the **[Healing Note]**.

The flesh knit itself back together, leaving not even the ghost of a scar behind. Robin smiled and wriggled his fingers, showing off the unbroken skin of his hand. The blood and dirt also vanished, courtesy of **[Legerdemain]**. It was a fantastic spell, honestly, and the best part was he needed only cast it once every hour and a half or so to be able to perform any of its various effects, though there were limits on the number of minor manifestations he could perform at once.

"Fantastic," Grathilde noted. "Now we won't need to rely on Fiamah to put you back together!"

"Enough," Lantha said. "I believe there was mention of a tale?"

"Of course!" Robin smiled. "Once upon a time . . ."

* * *

". . . and then I tracked my way here. The rest you know," Robin finished.

He had strategically edited bits of the tale, of course. No need to spill all his secrets, like the full extent of the tower's resources, or dwell overmuch on the more humiliating parts.

"So," he charged on. "What say I help you get through the gate so you can get back to Noviel with whatever vital intelligence you've gathered, and in exchange, you let me travel with you and get me an introduction to your adventuring company when we get to the city?"

Robin knew they weren't likely to just accept him into the party. They were a tight-knit group, and they clearly had a cohesion that came as much from working together for a higher cause as from being friends or allies.

Grathilde opened her mouth to say something, but Robin cut her off.

"Yes, I do get a cut of the loot. If I have to work for money, I won't have the time or attention for helping you with your dilemma. And that would be a shame because I can be very useful."

Grathilde closed her mouth with a snap, suspicious. Instead of saying anything, she looked to Lantha. Fiamah and Ora-Jean likewise transferred their attention to the rogue.

Lantha, for her part, merely raised an eyebrow and gestured for him to do his thing.

Fine with Robin. She wanted a show?

She'd get one.

Robin called on his [Mask of Disguise], shifting first into Fiamah, and then Lantha. He also pulled out some of the disguises he'd been practicing since he'd left the woods. He became a completely generic dude, so average in appearance as to be almost entirely forgettable. Then he assumed the guise of a guardsman in the uniform of the Keep's Watch.

The Sisters Sharp watched the show in silence. Lantha was impassive; Fiamah looked troubled; Ora-Jean and Grathilde were grinning like anything. He resumed his usual appearance.

"I can be in a lot of places and get my hands on a lot of things you might need," Robin explained. "You need to get through the gate. If we do a bit of reconnaissance, I'm sure we can find a weak spot to exploit and slip out before anyone is the wiser."

"I think we can work with that," Lantha said with a small smile. "Your skills are coming along nicely. I think we can reach an arrangement."

Grathilde groaned.

"Twenty percent isn't much less than twenty-five," Ora-Jean told her in a stage whisper. "Besides, it goes both ways. We'll get a cut of any money he makes performing."

The aeromancer perked up at the thought. Robin wasn't bothered. Either this arrangement would only last until they made it to Noviel, or he'd become a regular part of the party and could renegotiate when that happened.

It didn't take long for the Sisters Sharp to hold a whispered discussion and agree to his terms. They shook on it, and Grathilde began on the porridge while Ora-Jean used some of the flatter rocks nearby to build a nearly smokeless fire.

They took the mealtime to relax and talk, mostly. Robin still spent plenty of time practicing his **[Lesser Phantasm]**, flavoring the porridge in various ways. It had gotten nearly twice as easy to conjure various flavors around the campfire, as the cantrip now lasted nearly twenty seconds per cast. He kept it simple, calling up things like milk and honey or roasted hazelnuts, but once or twice, he dipped into savory porridges like white cheddar with red pepper and egg.

"I definitely missed that," Grathilde said as she scraped her makeshift bowl clean. "It tastes so much better, even knowing its fake."

"And it makes a change," Ora-Jean added. "It's been a bit bland, really. Not many berries to scrounge, no beehives nor animals to swipe extras from."

"Lantha won't let me spend any of our money on food in town," Grathilde complained. "It's not my fault—"

"It's a perfectly sensible measure," Fiamah cut in with the air of one who had heard this argument ad nauseam and was on the brink of going nuclear from hearing it one more time. "We need the money for equipment, supplies, and bribes. The more we save on food thanks to that spoon, the less time we have to tarry here."

"I'll head into town tomorrow and see what I can find out," Robin interjected. He could help out the Sisters Sharp and, with any luck, do a little bit of investigation into his own interests. There had to be more information about Rhyth around somewhere, so why not here? There had been a hidden shrine not far off, after all. If that fragment had survived, maybe there were more to be found. He'd scried the keep a bit, but it was too large to memorize in a few viewings, and he'd had much better things to do with his limited time in the tower.

"Give me a day or two," he continued, "and I'll figure out who can get us what we need, how much it's likely to cost, and any weaknesses they might have. Then we can come up with a plan to get it and get gone."

"Efficient," Lantha drawled. "And how do you expect to find this font of information?"

Robin grinned.

"Easy. Head to a tavern, of course!"

Chapter 2

*R*obin sneezed.

The thing about towns is that they are full of people, and when they're full of people, they're usually full of smells. In this case, Robin could smell food cooking, the scent of sawdust from a bit of construction farther down the street, animal odor from the stables on the back of the wayfarers' inn, and several other aromas he couldn't quite place.

At least it didn't reek of the worse bits of a large gathering of people in a small place. And while he had initially feared he'd be wading through streets choked with raw sewage, it looked like enough people in the settlement knew versions of [Cleanse] or [Legerdemain] to keep the place sanitary.

Robin had posed as a mountain trader, complete with a small brace of animals Ora-Jean had hunted down for him to trade. He'd been issued a day pass, warned to keep it on him at all times and to present it to any guard who asked to see it, and been sent in. It was an unexpectedly autocratic level of control from what Robin had expected to be a much more medieval sort of town. Not that pop culture had really stood him in good stead with his expectations so far.

In any case, he was inside! His first visit to a town not of Earth!

And that was wildly apparent every way he looked. There were different architectural styles, many that he could identify as having elvish elements thanks to his [Bardic Lore]. He didn't see many elves, though. Halflings, yes, the occasional dwarf, several goat- and weaselkin, lots of humans—well, humanoids.

Robin watched as a young woman with dusky skin and hair of flame walked past, careful not to edge too close to any of the occasional thatched buildings.

Robin found his way to a market square and traded his game and furs for a small bit of coin. He wasn't used to haggling as such, but he'd been along plenty of times when his dad had done so—*ah*, the life of a farmer—and his knowledge, skills, and perks helped fill in the gaps. Enough that he was sure he'd gotten at least a decent deal.

Thus provisioned, Robin revved up his *Gossip* skills and asked around about the local taverns. It was completely within his character, and key to the next phase of the plan: gathering intel. It didn't take long before he knew where he was headed next.

Soon, Robin stood outside a large building. It was whitewashed and painted in a style not unlike what he thought of now as "Earth-Tudor," and the sign hanging out front bore the painted image of a large silver bell and a huge, tusked, hairy pig: the Bell and Boar tavern.

Stepping inside, it was clear this was a popular place. It was large and open on this level, with benches carved out of each of the walls and rectangular tables lining the edges of the room. Smaller round tables were scattered throughout the middle of the space. A raised stage stood at one end, while the bar stood at the other. Robin could easily spot the door to the kitchen; it was open and blazing with light and clatter.

There was someone playing a harp and singing on the stage, but Robin ignored her for now in favor of getting a drink first. A drink said you were approachable. A drink said you were here to relax. A drink gave you something to do with your hands so things were less awkward.

The bar was polished oak, clearly lovingly cared for. A large, jovial man with muttonchops stood behind, arms crossed. Behind the man, Robin could clearly see the bill of fare. Listed drinks included ale, small beer, wine, honey mead, and birchbark tea. If Robin had wanted or needed food, it listed options like stew, bread, roasts of fowl or meat, cheese, fruit, and pudding.

Robin paused, looking at the mead. Mead was the last thing he'd drunk before waking up in this world. Was that a good sign or a bad one?

Good, he decided, and ordered one.

"Excellent choice!" The barkeep beamed at him. "You clearly have the finest of tastes, young man!"

The man's voice was the verbal equivalent of being slapped heartily on the back by an overly enthusiastic uncle. Robin managed a smile and a few words before extracting himself to find a seat.

Well over a dozen patrons were scattered throughout the tavern, although the space was so large it felt anything but crowded. In one corner, a pair of old men were clearly several pints along, even though it was only early afternoon. Across from them was a group of four individuals whose dress and manner just screamed "adventurer."

There was a curly-haired halfling woman in shining chain mail, with a tabard and shield each bearing what looked like some sort of religious sigildry. A buff man with a snide face sat across from her, wearing a combination of furs and breastplate which did not fit at all with his bizarrely bare legs and open helm sporting rampant dragon wings.

Robin decided he looked like a right pervert.

The other two occupants of the table were standing and clearly in the midst of a heated argument. The more striking of the two was a glamazonian blonde, all muscles and scars and fierce-as-fuck runway eyes. Whatever the problem was, Robin decided he was on her side. The other guy was equally tall and rangy, with a lot of gold jewelry, the fantasy equivalent of bell bottoms and a harness, and what Robin suspected were some kind of enchanted sandals. There was no reason to wear sandals like that in the mountains in spring unless they were damn well enchanted.

As he watched, the altercation hit a high point, and the woman lunged across the table, grabbing the man by the harness and hauling him across to her. Effortlessly, she spun him around until she was holding him, upside down, by the waist. She started shaking him violently until glimmering coins, sparkling gems, and even an expensive-looking book fell out of his pack and pockets.

"Oi! Not in here!" a voice echoed throughout the tavern. "If you're gonna scrap, you take it out back to the alley like the rest of the rubbish!"

A young man with dusky skin and night-dark hair started over. Robin had seen him delivering drinks and collecting empty flagons as he waited at the bar. He wasn't a tavern wench, of course. Tavern swain? Barswain? Yes. Barswain.

Before the situation could escalate any further, however, a resounding chord came from the stage. The notes rippled through the air, causing an almost visible disturbance as they passed and left stunned silence in their wake.

"I was in the middle of my set," the woman on the stage said mildly. "It's impolite to interrupt a performance."

She sat upon the stage as if it were the world's throne and she its queen. Flaming locks of auburn hair, eyes of emerald green, and a figure so generous it would make Father Christmas look like a greedy miser greeted anyone who looked at her.

If that wasn't a maxed-out *Charisma* stat, Robin didn't know what was!

Then, as if that weren't enough, she promptly ignored the patrons of the tavern and launched into another song. But what a song! She sang of clear mountain air and sunshine over snowcapped peaks. She sang of the pride of the people who made their home in this place, of the cry of the hawk and the glory of unbending stone.

She was stunning, silver tongued, and sex on harp strings; a lethal combination. Robin knew better than to try and buy her a drink, but the alter ego he was developing, his performance persona? He, Marq, certainly might.

Of course, Marq would also challenge her right here, right now, on that stage. Robin knew enough to know he'd probably lose, though. He was still getting a feel for his new bardic skill set.

Robin chose the better part of valor for now. He had a mission.

He caught the handsome barswain as he passed.

"That sort of thing happen often in here?" Robin jerked his chin toward the adventuring party, who were now all sitting quietly—if sullenly—and nursing a round of ales.

"More often than I'd like, considering I'm the one who usually has to deal with it," the lad huffed.

There was something odd about his eyes, Robin noticed. He didn't know what it was precisely, but there was a strange, fey touch to them. Not that it was creepy. Quite the opposite, really.

He managed to get only a few sentences out of the guy, Avanus, before the barswain slipped off, ostensibly back to work. Robin noticed him go directly toward a shady-looking character who slipped in the door just long enough to take a small pouch from Avanus and slip off again.

Interesting.

Robin made a mental note of that little fact and moseyed on over to talk to the two inebriated gentlemen. He had a lot of information to gather, and only so much time to do it. His pass was only good for the day, after all.

Fortunately, the two old codgers, like any old people in any small town, loved nothing more than to gossip and swap stories about everyone and everything in a hundred-mile radius. If they didn't know it, it was hardly worth knowing—or so well hidden you'd need a map and compass to find it.

For the price of a few drinks, Robin got a lot of good information out of them: about who worked which gate and when, what their personal failings were, and more. Of course, he had to sift it out of reams of chatter about this feller being the son of that lady who was from off t'other side of the mountain, or oh weren't it a scandal that he ran off with blah blah blah.

He even got plenty of gossip and speculation about Avanus. A good enough lad, the two old codgers thought, but a pity he's caught up in some shady business with . . . well, it was rebels or organized crime or those strange folk out in the wood. The two old men couldn't quite agree on which.

Whatever it was, Robin marked Avanus as someone definitely worth investigating a bit more. In fact, this tavern had quite a few interesting characters.

His eyes drifted back to the red-haired bard on the stage.

"She's a good performer, our Lena," the older of the two codgers, Liam, said with a nod. "Could do well for herself in any of the big cities to the north, and she travels a lot, aye, but she always comes back here to play for the town."

Robin couldn't tell if that was pride in a local making good, or pride in some sort of relative or descendant, but he decided it ultimately didn't matter. In places like this, that line could get very blurry.

"Not that these new fellers in charge make it easy on her, or any entertainers, these days," the other codger, Willam, grumbled. "Ye'd think they had a grudge against havin' a good time!"

Oho. A bit of unrest with the new overlords. Robin was happy to hear that. Might make for a nice diversion when the time came.

"I'm a bard myself," he said, not really paying attention to the words, his mind sorting through all the fresh information the two old men had provided.

He should have kept his mouth shut. The two old men immediately seized on that fact and began to make trouble. After all, couldn't have a stranger to town showing up the local talent! Not that they'd ever believe that possible, but best put the stranger in his place anyway, right?

The two codgers hassled him for details, egging him on more and more to "show 'em what ye've got."

Robin tried to downplay things, to defuse the situation, but in that, he failed spectacularly.

The two old men appealed to a higher authority.

"Oi! Lena!" Liam shouted. "Ye've got yerself a rival!"

Robin suddenly found himself on the receiving end of a very pointed stare from the woman on the stage.

Fuck.

Chapter 3

*T*he room around Robin was suddenly both cold and hot all at once. He was conscious of the greasy wood beneath his fingers, smoothed by the elbows of untold patrons over unknown years. It was a stark contrast to the sharp, prickling attention of everyone in the tavern.

"Well, I'm due a break," Lena said in a voice that positively dripped with derision. "Why don't you hop on up here and show us what you've got while I have a glass of something to restore my voice?"

It was a challenge, pure and simple, and between Robin's need to get closer to completing his bardic initiation quest, the two old codgers next to him egging things on, and the inescapable idea that Marq would never refuse such a challenge or such an opportunity, Robin had no choice but to stand and accept.

"I suppose I could share a song or three," Robin replied lazily, shouldering into his stage persona like a new coat. It was a bit stiff and tugged at him in directions he wasn't used to yet.

He ignored the sympathetic look Avanus shot him from near the bar. Robin—Marq—strode up to the stage and stepped lightly onto it. He executed a sharp heel turn, taking full command of the attention Lena had given him. If she thought he'd stumble in front of the unexpected scrutiny, she was going to be sadly disappointed.

In fact, as Robin looked at the redheaded bard, he knew exactly which song he was going to open with.

The song of the red-haired wanton woman called "Jolene."

Swaying gently along with the rhythm of the song as it built, Robin slipped in the gestures for [Lesser Phantasm] and hit that final "Jolene" with illusory duplicates of his own voice in a three-part harmony. The crowd perked up in spite of the unfamiliar words and music, and Robin saw Lena shoot him a startled glance out of the corner of his eye.

That's right. Not just a pretty face.

Robin gestured again, and more voices layered themselves into the song, providing rhythm and texture and backup vocals in the grand tradition of a cappella everywhere. He was just doing it all himself; nine voices joined by a single will.

His will. His magic. His performance.

Robin willed the ghostly image of a handsome man—looking remarkably similar to Avanus—to appear over his right shoulder, while a breathtakingly beautiful woman—looking remarkably like Lena—appeared over his left.

Thank you [**Chronicle of Infinite Visions**]*!* The whole thing gave the performance a nice '80s rock ballad vibe, and the images faded after just a moment. *Can't peak early, after all. Gotta keep some room to build.*

And build he did. Robin took all of the classic longing that infused that song, amped it through an increase in tempo, and twisted it slightly over the top. This crowd felt like it would respond better to camp, glam, and high energy, so he gave it to them.

Let it be all they can do to keep from crying when he sings the name Jolene!

Robin conjured illusory tears which sparkled impossibly in his eyes. He flirted outrageously with both Lena and Avanus throughout the song, eliciting first a few chuckles, then roars of approval. Flashes of scenes, ghostly and flickering, appeared and disappeared as the music ebbed and flowed until he brought the song to a beseeching, clarion end.

He reached his hand out toward Lena in supplication before letting it fall gently to his side with a final two whispered words to end the song: "Oh, Jolene."

The room was quiet for a moment. Robin let the silence ride for no more than a breath or two before he launched into his next song. He was going to fit in at least three.

Lena and Avanus exchanged a glance. Robin ignored them. There would be time for dealing with whatever that was *after* his impromptu set. Now that he had their attention, Robin dispensed with the visual illusions, keeping instead to simply duplicating and enhancing his voice with [**Lesser Phantasm**].

The next song he performed was "She's a Rebel" because who didn't love a little pop punk? And he wanted to watch Avanus's reaction. It might give him a hint as to whether or not the barswain actually had a connection to the restive elements of Bordertown.

Oh yeah. There was definitely something going on there. Avanus maintained a stoic demeanor for the most part, but when Robin locked eyes with him on the word "rebel," the barswain flinched.

Bingo.

Best not push it for now, though. Robin wanted at least a little plausible deniability so Avanus didn't run off before he could corner the lad for a conversation.

Robin finished up the song with a flourish and then immediately launched into "The Lusty Young Smith." There was enough energy in the room, it fit better with the whole medieval fantasy vibe this place had going, and it had an easy chorus that everyone could sing along with.

And in no time, he had them singing along when they weren't laughing at the cheeky innuendo of the lyrics, all the way through to the final repetition of the chorus.

Rum-bum-bum, rum-bum-bum

In-and-out, in-and-out

Ho!

He finished with a flourish, let the laughter settle just a tad, then called out over the—admittedly, rather small—crowd, "Thank you! My name is Marq, and you've been a wonderful audience!" He smiled broadly at Lena. "And I will now return the stage to the lovely Jolene—I mean Lena!"

Congratulations! For completing your first performance without causing the audience to pelt you mercilessly with rotten produce, you have earned an experience reduction of 1/3 on your next purchase of the Expression proficiency!

He exited the stage to a final smatter of laughter and headed to the bar to claim another drink. That had gone well enough; he'd certainly raised a little interest. Hopefully, he could spin that into a larger performance soon and complete that quest.

It was another honey mead. The tavern keeper seemed to approve of him, and Robin saw no reason not to keep that going. He'd need a place to perform, after all. He mentally tried to count out how many people could fit in the space. It needed to be at least ninety-nine . . .

"Not bad," Lena said as she walked past him toward the stage. "Not enough to rival my own performances, of course, but not bad."

She wasn't wrong. Robin was new to this, and even flashy illusions and cheap theatrics couldn't wholly disguise that fact. They certainly didn't hurt, though!

Robin grinned.

Might as well take another step or two along the road to superstardom. He had some spare experience points, and he had a discount voucher for an *Expression* increase, so he might as well use them.

Robin opened his character sheet and upped the relevant proficiency.

Robin Parker

Heritage: Shadeling, Paragon
Profession: Bard (Apprentice)
Tier: 1, Conditional (Effective Level: 3)
Experience: 400
Spell Points: 3
Bardsong: 5 uses

Properties

Free Ranks Available: 1

Physical
  -Strength: 11
  -Dexterity: 14
  -Fortitude: 11
Mental
  -Intelligence: 17
  -Cunning: 20
  -Resilience: 14
Social
  -Charisma: 15
  -Manipulation: 13
  -Poise: 16

Proficiencies

Free Ranks Available: 2

Physical (9/9)
  -Athletics: 1
  -Brawl: 1

-Dodge: 4
-Melee Combat: 2
-Pilot: 4
-Ranged Combat: 5
-Sleight of Hand: 2
-Stealth: 5
-Survival: 3
Mental (9/9)
-Arcane Lore: 4
-Bureaucracy: 1
-Concentration: 5
-Crafting: 5
-Healing: 3
-Insight: 5
-Learning: 4
-Natural Wisdom: 3
-Perception: 5
Social (9/9)
-Animism: 1
-Deception: 6
-Empathy: 2
-Expression: 6
-Gossip: 3
-Intimidation: 3
-Persuasion: 3
-Socialize: 2
-Streetwise: 3

Peculiarities

Blessing of Rhyth
Tongue of the Fallen Tower
Mark of the Trickster
Chronicle of Infinite Visions
Mask of Myriad Faces

Perks

Wayfaring Stranger
Shard of the Shattered Manymind

Spells

Cantrips* (*no SP cost)
  -Lesser Phantasm*
  -Cutting Words*
  -Legerdemain*
Tier 1 (1SP each)
  -Visual Phantasm*
  -Healing Note
  -Whispers from Beyond
Tier 2 (3SP each)
  -Assume Quality (Special)

He was a long way from being able to raise his *Charisma* with experience points. Robin briefly considered using his free Property rank to boost it, but decided against it for now.

Lena was performing again. The room thrummed with energy, and the patrons sang and thumped along to the music. There was a noticeable increase in the energy of her performance now. Robin grinned. She was showing him up, sure, but she was working at it, at least a little. She couldn't just coast through and humiliate him without a bit of effort.

"Nice set," a voice said from over his shoulder.

Robin turned to see Avanus grinning down at him.

"Thank you," he replied. His Marq persona probably would have been a bit more arrogant about it, but Robin hadn't figured that bit out yet. "Songs from the land I'm from. I figured—"

"I meant your bollocks," Avanus interrupted. "You've got to have a nice set of 'em if you're willing to let those old codgers talk you into challenging Lena."

"I've not had any complaints," Robin shot back. If Avanus was trying to unsettle him, he'd have to work harder than that!

The barswain laughed.

"You're interesting." Avanus grinned at him. "I could tell you came in here looking for something, but I didn't think you'd have quite so much to offer."

Was Avanus flirting with him? Robin couldn't quite tell. Best play it ambiguous in return, then. Avanus certainly had information he wanted. Possibly more.

"I suppose you're the guy to go to for a hookup, then?" Robin put on an easy smile. "I'm new to the area, and it might be that I'm looking for a few things, yeah."

Avanus's eyes, deep as a well of shadows, glimmered. Again, Robin was struck by the thought that there was something more to that gaze. Something magical was going on there, something his gut told him was fey and eldritch and strange.

"I know a few people," Avanus replied. "I can generally get people what they need, even if it's more . . . difficult to acquire. Such services come at a premium, of course."

"Of course," Robin agreed.

"Like I said, I get things that people need." Avanus shot a careful glance around to make sure they weren't being overheard. "And I have a client who wants something quite particular. I think you're the one who might be able to retrieve it, if you're game."

"I haven't told you what it is I want yet," Robin teased, playing for time as his mind worked furiously. Avanus was too much in control of this negotiation. He needed to upset the barswain's equilibrium. "And we only just met! I don't even know if you work for the more restive elements in town, the good fellas working to organize less traditional business practices, or that strange cult out in the wood."

Avanus froze. It was only for a moment, but Robin hadn't been investing in *Perception* and *Insight* for nothing. Yeah. This lad had some sort of shady connection. Good. That's exactly the sort of thing Robin was looking for.

"You've been listening to Liam and Willam." Avanus shook his head. "Old gossips, especially when they've been at the ale. Which is pretty much always."

"Say I trust that you have what I need and that your offer is a good fit, price-wise, for my situation. How would we go about having that discussion?" Robin pressed the issue now that he had control of the conversation.

"It's a bit crowded in here for talking this over," Avanus said. "We could step out through the kitchen into the back and talk there?"

Well, that was a setup if Robin had ever heard one. He kept his face unconcerned, however. After all, if you didn't take a few risks, you wouldn't score any rewards.

Besides, he definitely had tricks this barswain had never seen.

New Quest: [A Dangerous Bargain!]

You have found a lead on getting what you and the **Sisters Sharp** *need to escape the Bordertown and make your way back to Noviel! Investigate what Avanus promises and possibly find precisely what it is you need . . . if you're willing to pay the price.*

Reward(s): *A way out, obviously.*
This is an evolving quest line. Requirements and rewards will vary and shift based on the choices you make.

Well, that cinched it. He was definitely on the right track. Not that it made things any safer, mind. Quests were by definition dangerous things.

Robin nodded, tossed back the last of his honey mead, and rose to follow Avanus.

The barswain led him through the kitchen. Lena's performance here was a boon; everyone's attention was on her, not them. The room was roasting but filled with the hearty smell of baked bread and stewing meat. Robin dodged around the irascible cook, who shook a cleaver threateningly at him.

The door at the back of the blazing room was propped open. Cool air seeped in from what appeared to be a narrow alleyway. It wended so tightly between the buildings that almost none of the afternoon sun managed to make its way into that crooked path of shadows.

Avanus went on ahead; Robin made sure of that. He didn't want anyone between him and a quick exit back into the kitchen. The barswain stepped into the alley, and after a moment, Robin followed.

As soon as he was out, several shadowy figures stepped out of hiding.

Oh, yeah. Definitely an ambush.

Chapter 4

*A*drenaline bit into the sides of Robin's neck, hard. [**Cutting Words**] leapt to the tip of his tongue, but he held them for now. The shadowy figures firmly outnumbered him, and though his eyes easily pierced the darkness of the alleyway, his enhanced vision couldn't do much about the deeply cowled robes everyone save himself and Avanus were wearing.

"Cult in the woods, then," Robin drawled, fighting to keep up a blasé facade. The open door to the kitchen was a warm promise of safety at his back, but he hadn't come out here for *safe*. He'd come here to make a dangerous bargain.

"Among other things," Avanus acknowledged. "Sorry, Our Lady has been rather vocal in her appreciation of you, and we all wanted a look."

Our Lady? Someone knew of Robin? Knew he was coming and told these people about him? That was less good. He was kind of banking on anonymity shielding him a bit, particularly as Gis was in this town somewhere.

Robin had no desire to come face-to-face with that snake again. Or the serpent that lived in his eye socket.

"I think I'm going to need a few more details before we proceed with this discussion," Robin said. Part of him wanted to cross his arms and lean against the doorjamb, but the smarter part—the one that said he might need his hands free—prevailed.

"We serve the Queen of Air and Darkness," Avanus explained.

Robin prodded his [**Bardic Lore**] but came up empty. That particular bit of knowledge wasn't knocking about in his subconscious. It certainly sounded fey as frell, though. And that matched Avanus's eyes.

That sparked a connection.

Robin's mind was suddenly filled with lore on warlocks, those who made bargains with strange entities—often Lords and Ladies of the Fey, or eldritch horrors from beyond the ends of time and space—in exchange for magical or physical prowess.

"You're a warlock." Robin tested out his new theory.

"I am," Avanus replied, confirming both Robin's theory and that his **[Bardic Lore]** could indeed provide useful information when needed.

"And your queen told you about me. How much, precisely?" Robin didn't bother to conceal the irritation he felt.

"Enough to be interested. Not enough to satisfy curiosity." Avanus gestured to the hooded figures around them. "Obviously."

"Right. Well, they've all had a look-see, but if we're going to get down to business and have a chat, I'd prefer to do it one-on-one." Robin tested the waters by setting some terms.

"Fair enough." Avanus jerked his head, and the robed figures reluctantly faded back into the shadows. "Sorry. Most of us are fey blooded to some degree or another, and that leads to impulsiveness and curiosity."

Made sense. Robin was sure they were still lurking, just hidden, but cults gonna cult, and it was unlikely Avanus would keep their dealings secret from his friends anyway.

"So what do you want?" Robin asked.

"Basgar and his right-hand man are a plague on this city. We want them gone. They won't go easily, however, and all of the people or organizations who could mount a resistance are fighting among themselves. My Queen has informed me that there is something I can use to unite the quarrelling factions under one purpose and oppose the petty tyrants making our lives miserable."

"And you want me to acquire this thing, somehow."

"She implied it would be well within your capabilities, and that you would be amenable to my offer." Avanus held up his hands helplessly. "Unless she was mistaken . . ."

"Depends on what the offer is. Spit it out." There was too much dancing around for Robin's taste. He was on a clock, and if this didn't pan out, he needed to find something else.

"My Queen instructed me to give you a choice. I am to either aid you and your friends in your escape from this place, seeing you off toward the north with supplies and no pursuers at your heels, or . . ." Avanus hesitated.

"Or?" Robin prompted, his curiosity piqued.

"Or I am to act as a vessel for My Queen and give you the opportunity to ask three questions about someone called Rhyth."

Robin froze. The fact that this Queen of Air and Darkness knew so much made him uneasy. Of course, it was also an opportunity—if he could trust it. He'd have to speak face-to-face (face-to-channeled?) with a fey entity of unknown power to get his answers, and the fey weren't terribly notorious for being easy and forthcoming with those.

"Does everyone in this town know who I am and what I want?" he asked with some exasperation. The question was to stall for time, though the frustration behind it was genuine.

"I don't imagine they do, no. I think you've just stumbled into a bit of luck, meeting me so soon." Avanus smiled.

Well, whatever he had thought before, Robin now knew Avanus was going to get his deal. Both of the prizes were things Robin wanted— needed, even. Having to choose between them was just a cruel trick this queen was playing on him. Unless . . .

Unless it was an opportunity disguised as a trick. Both prizes existed, so could he figure out a way to win both of them?

"I'll agree to your deal on one condition," Robin said slowly, thinking the logic through until he was happy with his decision.

"I'm listening."

"I want the option to choose which of the offered rewards I get when I fulfill my end of the bargain. Then, not now. I'll get your MacGuffin or whatever for you, but I want time to properly think on my choices, not have the process rushed in a back alley." Robin quirked a grin. "Not that rushed in a back alley is necessarily bad, mind you. Sometimes, it's just the thing to cap off a night out."

"Your terms are acceptable." Avanus answered Robin's grin with one of his own.

"What am I stealing for you, then?" Robin asked, knowing it was going to be a nightmare to find.

"I don't know," Avanus replied. "But My Queen assures me you will know when you see it, and you will find it in the personal quarters of Gis, Priest of Urkhan."

Fan-fucking-tastic.

Lantha and the others hadn't exactly been ecstatic when Robin had told them he had a lead on solving their problems. Of course, he hadn't been fully forthcoming with all the details, either. The dark, selfish part of him kept the secret in case he couldn't figure out a way to have his cake and eat it too. If he chose to take the answers about Rhyth rather than Avanus's aid in escaping Bordertown . . . well, no reason to make it a fight if he didn't have to. What the Sisters Sharp didn't know wouldn't hurt them.

His meeting with Avanus had been two days ago. Robin had taken the time to gather more information, particularly on where Gis's personal quarters were and the priest's habits. Fortunately, the priest was distinctive, and with Basgar's recent takeover of the keep, everyone was keeping an eye on the tyrant's supporters.

Gis kept his personal quarters at the back of the main chapel in the keep proper. A great deal of work was in progress there at present. It was easy enough gossip to pick up, as quite a lot of the Bordertowners weren't happy that the chapel was being defaced and rededicated.

Robin's feelings on the matter were more complex, mainly because the steady flow of workmen in and out of that chapel meant getting into the keep and into the chapel were trivial matters, particularly for a shapeshifter like himself.

Gis's private quarters were likely to be more of an issue, but he'd cross that stream when he came to it.

Lantha and Fiamah, even Ora-Jean, would have counseled him not to barge in so recklessly, but Robin had faith in his skills. They were new, to be sure, but he felt so *powerful* now. He had magic at his fingertips, thrumming through his veins! How could he possibly fail?

The only way to find out was to try.

Which was why Robin was currently trudging under the portcullis of the keep, head down and practically staggering under a heavy load of bricklaying supplies. Or something like that. He'd grabbed something heavy from the pile and fallen in with the workers.

As long as he looked busy, no one questioned him. The keep guards loomed sourly over everyone and discouraged idle chitchat, and Robin was grateful for that as well. It meant none of his fellow workers bothered to question the "new guy."

He trusted his "forgettable average guy" disguise, and so far, it was holding up just fine.

Robin slipped under the watchful eye of a corporal of the Keep's Guard and crossed the massive flagstones of the entry yard. Considering how paranoid the guards at the outer gates had been, it was shocking that the workers were allowed entry so easily, but Robin wasn't going to look that gift horse in the mouth.

He tried very hard not to think that it instead reflected just how confident Basgar and Gis were that they had this town in the palm of their hand.

There was a moment where he almost blew it, walking into the actual chapel, but after a moment of standing stunned in the entryway, he forced himself to move along and find a place to relieve himself of his burden.

The chapel was a thing of beauty, all graceful arches and soaring stonework. It matched what his **[Bardic Lore]** had earlier identified as an elvish influence on the architecture. The windows had been boarded up, however, and the niches where one might expect to see statues were empty of all save for bits of rubble.

Robin put his wonder at seeing a whole new form of architecture aside and, no longer weighed down by a massive bag of fancy dirt, began edging his way around the room toward the back of the chapel where he knew the priest's quarters lay.

He didn't make it halfway before he was challenged.

"Where do you think you're going?" a rough voice called out after him.

Robin glanced back. The man looked like some kind of overseer, gruff and brawny with a solid bit of fat over his muscle. Thinking quickly, Robin reached for one of the excuses he had prepared in case he was stopped.

"The guard at the gate told me I had to carry this message to one of the acolytes," Robin lied, flashing a bit of parchment he'd scavenged for just this purpose. He'd even scrawled some nonsense in English on it in case anyone demanded to see the message.

For a moment, the man looked him over. Robin bit gently on the inside of his cheek and concentrated on looking a bit dopey and entirely incapable of deception. Apparently, his ruse worked, as he was waved on after a moment.

"Just be quick about it," the overseer dismissed him with a grunt. "There's more to haul in, and new guys do the grunt work."

"Yessir," Robin answered. "I'll head right back out as soon as I'm done."

The man grunted and turned away, and Robin let out a slow sigh of relief. With any luck, he'd be gone from the overseer's mind in no time. There were always a dozen things competing for the attention of anyone in charge on a large job site. Things always slipped through the cracks.

Robin slipped behind the altar and through the shadowed archway hidden behind an ornate screen. It was clearly a thing celebrating Urkhan, with none of the graceful, almost art nouveau sensibility of the original chapel. Clenched fists, gauntlets, and lightning seemed to feature prominently.

It would hide his movements nicely from the other workers.

Through the archway was a small hall. Robin followed it right to the end, where a simple yet solid oaken door barred his progress: the entry to Gis's private quarters.

Robin checked for traps, albeit his knowledge of what to look for was limited to what he'd been gifted with as part of his proficiency upgrades. He didn't find any, not that that was reassuring. Still, nothing ventured, nothing gained, and Robin was here for gains.

He reached out to open the door, praying the priest was not in residence.

Chapter 5

*T*he room smelled of oil, old blood, and bitter resentment. And beeswax candles.

Robin wrinkled his nose as he stepped carefully away from the closed door behind him. The place was so ostentatiously luxurious as to be downright tacky. True wealth was never so obvious. There was far too much gold plating and furs draped over everything.

Robin did a quick pass around the room, slipping the most profitable-looking items into the storage space in his ring. The cadaverous old priest owed him that much, at least, for tormenting him in the tunnels beneath Yvon-Rael's mountain, as Robin had come to think of the place. His petty larceny would also have the side benefit of disguising his true purpose here: the search for information.

There was a desk littered with parchment; Robin would begin there. The chest at the foot of the priest's bed also seemed promising, but Robin was a bit leery of what he might discover there.

Nobody liked finding someone else's extracurricular marital aids. Not without a lot more wine than Robin currently had flowing through his veins, anyway.

Pausing his petty theft, Robin moved over to the desk to search through the correspondence. Once again, [Tongue of the Fallen Tower] came to his rescue, as without it, there was no way he would be able to read any of the languages represented here, and there were at least three that he could see.

Shuffling through the papers made enough noise that it prompted a small chorus of squeaks from a wicker cage set next to the desk. Looking in, Robin saw several mice.

Why would Gis have—

Robin suddenly felt queasy. He knew exactly why Gis had mice.

The mental image of the priest calmly composing missives while the snake that lived in his eye socket calmly gulped down whole mice was not one Robin wished to dwell on. He put it firmly out of his mind and went back to picking through the letters on Gis's desk.

There were quite a lot; the priest seemed to be fond of written orders. Several letters seemed to be from Basgar, and Robin eagerly read through those, hoping something would leap out as being obviously what Avanus was after. Nothing did, though Robin quickly began to piece together a solid idea of Basgar's plans for the region.

They weren't good.

The tyrant had seized control of the keep with the help of Gis, some other minor clergy of Urkhan, and a company of top mercenaries hired out of the Gilded Lands. Since then, he had begun relentlessly building up his forces, recruiting heavily from the local citizenry, sometimes by force.

Ah! Here was something. Basgar and Gis were deliberately building up food stockpiles and causing shortages in Bordertown to drive the more desperate to enlist.

Robin managed to find the location of one of the warehouses from the correspondence, but there were clearly several more he couldn't ferret out just from the letters present.

It was useful, but Robin didn't feel it was quite the smoking gun Avanus needed.

He kept looking.

The next thing he found was a rather insulting letter Gis had clearly intended to send to Basgar but never did, for whatever reason. It described the priest's encounter with Robin and the Sisters Sharp in the tunnels in fairly unflattering terms.

"Here you go, little ones," Robin murmured as he fed that one to the mice.

The overall plan was starting to take shape in Robin's mind as he read through the priest's correspondence. Take out some of the nearby marcher lords before that fractious bunch could unite against the external enemy, keep the Gilded Lands happy by selling off the spoils in exchange for whatever Basgar needed to fuel his war machine, then start conquering the nearby city-states under the banner of Noviel. In relatively short order, Basgar could snip off the closest bits of all three countries and make himself a fourth kingdom, right in the center.

The Gilded Lands could be bought off. They'd still have a trading partner, and they hated mounting extended campaigns. War was expensive, and the merchants who ruled would have to pay a premium to cross the Fens and attack Basgar.

The marcher lords were fractious; it was unlikely they would unite in a force large enough to challenge the newly strengthened keep.

Noviel was the only real threat. The city-states were much more tightly knit than the marcher lordships and had much deeper pockets. Robin couldn't find anything that would protect Basgar and Gis from them except possibly arrogance.

Still, there was clearly a threat building here against Noviel and her sister city-states. Lantha would certainly want to know about this; it might even alter their plans.

Robin grimaced and started tucking away the contents of the priest's desk. He'd wanted to be more subtle, but with this evidence, he'd have to adapt. He would set the place on fire right before he left; that would cover his tracks. It wasn't subtle, but maybe he could make it look like something else, an accident or an assassination attempt gone wrong.

Robin froze, looking at the letter in his hand.

This was it! This had to be what Avanus was after. This letter was a confirmation of orders and a receipt of payment from . . . some kind of agent provocateur. Gis had brought in a specialist to stir up antipathy between the various rebel factions in Bordertown! No wonder they were at one another's throats and incapable of mounting a united front!

It was signed with a mark, not a name. In place of the signature, there was simply a small symbol, some kind of dart or small dagger with a triangular flag trailing off the handle.

Unsurprising but annoying.

Now that he knew he was going to set the place alight, Robin went ahead and broke open the locked drawers of the desk and looted the whole thing. Anything small and valuable went into storage, including a small pouch of coins, several sheets of fresh parchment paper, some nice ink, and a quill.

He'd achieved his goal, but Robin found his eyes drawn to the chest at the foot of the priest's bed.

He was already ransacking the place. Might as well take a few more minutes and loot it as well.

It was all of dark wood, and Robin noticed that several of the motifs from the screen in the chapel were also carved into this chest: the clenched fist, the lightning, and so on. He carefully checked it for traps but was unable to find any. It wasn't even locked!

If Robin was hoping for piles of gold and gemstones, however, he was disappointed. All he could see when opening the lid were vestments and various paraphernalia of worship. He swiped the expensive-looking bees-wax candles, of course, but didn't touch the priestly robes. Gis had worn them, after all. Just the thought made Robin's hands feel like greasy beetles were scuttling all over them.

Moving the robes out of the way, however, he uncovered more sinister items: a bloodstained bowl and dagger, a small book bound in dark leather, and a horned, runed skull. The whole set screamed unholy sacrament, and Robin was torn between trying to smash the things and not touching them with a ten-foot pole.

He'd have left then and there had he not realized there was a false bottom beneath the paraphernalia; the size of the chest's outside didn't match that of its insides. He was trying to figure out how best to move the unholy-looking crap on top when he heard the sound of voices approaching down the hall.

You are too late, foolish pip. Your doom is at hand!

Twin points of crimson light flared to life in the skull's eye sockets.

Robin fell back with a yelp.

Fucking demonic voices from a possessed skull! If he'd had any doubts before that Urkhan was sketchy AF, they were gone now.

He slammed the lid shut and scrambled back into a corner where he veiled his presence with a **[Visual Phantasm]** offset just slightly from the wall. That spot was lit by candlelight and a few stray beams of sunshine coming through the shuttered windows; it would be next to impossible to see anyone in there at the best of times.

Robin managed to conceal himself just in time. The door slammed open, and Gis strode in. The priest's eye patch was already off, and Gehn was undulating from his anchor at Gis's eye socket. The snake's tongue flicked out, tasting the air.

The only thing saving Robin was the planning he'd put into this escapade. The whole point was to get in and out without tipping off Gis that he or the Sisters Sharp were here. The marcher lordships were primarily beastkin, and Basgar was already making aggressive moves toward them. It made sense one might be here as a spy.

Robin flicked his fingers through the gestures of **[Lesser Phantasm]** and filled the air in the room with the scent of scared rabbit. Hopefully, it would be close enough to scared rabbitkin.

"Ssspiesss! Rabbit ssspiesss!" Gehn hissed loudly. "The ssscent of fear isss thick!"

"We passed no one," Gis snapped. "And the shutters are latched from the inside. The spy must still be here. Search them out, Gehn!"

Robin needed a distraction, and fast. Well, he'd already planned to burn the place down, right?

He used **[Mask of Myriad Faces]** to shapeshift into a rabbitkin, then cast three cantrips in quick succession, counting on his illusion and the element of surprise to buy him time.

The first was a **[Lesser Phantasm]** of a rabbit's scream, cranked to eleven. Robin timed it to cover his casting of **[Legerdemain]**. Silently, he cursed himself for not casting it when he first got into the room. The duration was long enough he could've easily maintained it, and then he wouldn't have needed the extra step.

Gis practically jumped out of his skin at the sound of the scream. Robin used the distraction to set the remaining papers on Gis's desk on fire with **[Legerdemain]**, which went up like dry hay. The snake was whipping wildly through the air, tongue flicking, seeking the source of the terrified rabbit's scream.

Robin set fire to the rug beneath the chest in two places—he wanted that skull cracked and burned by fire if he could manage it. There was no telling what the spirit in that thing could or would tell Gis, so it would be better if it were destroyed.

The third and final cantrip was a **[Lesser Phantasm]** to hide him before he dropped his **[Visual Phantasm]**. He needed the more powerful spell to act as a distraction, so even if the protection offered by the lesser was, well, lesser, he had little choice but to do it that way.

Gis was shouting for the guard. The room was in chaos.

It was now or never.

Robin used **[Visual Phantasm]** to conjure the image of a rabbitkin scrabbling out from behind the bed hangings across the room. It fooled the priest, but the snake was cannier.

Robin darted for the door, throwing it open to make his escape. Gis, facing the illusion, was caught by surprise. The snake, more suspicious by nature or equipped with better senses, was not so easily taken in. As Robin began bounding down the hall on his rabbit feet, the snake opened its mouth and shot a bolt of red-and-black energy toward him.

The bolt slammed into Robin, burning into his fur and burrowing down into the flesh beneath. This time, the rabbit's scream was real, and it burst from Robin's own throat.

The pain was intense, but it only spiked more adrenaline into Robin's veins. He ran faster, risking slower progress by serpentizing his run in an attempt to throw off the snake's aim.

It didn't work. Another bolt slammed into him, and Robin's vision flickered for a moment, but he managed to gasp out a **[Healing Note]**, and the world stabilized around him.

That snake was too talented a shot. *Fuck.* What had he been thinking?

Robin threw an illusory brick wall behind him with **[Visual Phantasm]**, completely filling the passageway. It wouldn't stop anyone from running through it, but it would break the snake's line of sight. *Can't target if you can't see.*

There were shouts and the sound of booted feet running toward him now. Robin cursed. He needed an exit, and now!

The windows? No. They were too high to climb or jump to. The doors would be guarded. It was fight his way out or—

His nose twitched.

The garderobe.

Robin groaned, both because it was cliché and because this was going to be disgusting. There wasn't any help for it, though. He didn't have time to figure out any better option.

He followed his nose and burst into the water closet. There was a board with three large holes cut into it. No partitions. Fun. He had time for a deep breath and a world of regret for the life choices that had brought him to this point before he pried up the plank and jumped down the slimy shaft, making his escape.

It was a shitty way to end the day.

Chapter 6

*T*his changes things."

Robin was sitting with his back to one of the large stones that protected their little camp outside Bordertown. Lantha was pacing back and forth while Ora-Jean, Fiamah, and Grathilde quietly argued among themselves about Robin's news.

"Does it, though?" Grathilde asked. "We still need to get back and tell"—she shot a glance at Robin—"people what we know."

"We don't want to give Basgar several more weeks to build up his strength," Ora-Jean disagreed. "We need to sabotage his efforts."

"There's no reason we can't do both," Robin interjected. "I've already made contact with a rebel faction within the town who has agreed to help us escape. We can work with them to unite the other fractious elements into an organized resistance. Then, use their first assault against Basgar's power as a distraction to help us escape. Basgar is kept too busy at home dealing with a small rebellion while we hightail it back to Noviel, and you can deliver whatever it is I'm not supposed to know about to whomever it is I don't know."

"It's a solid compromise," Fiamah conceded.

"It's ruthless," Ora-Jean said approvingly.

"It sounds fun," Grathilde added.

Lantha looked at them all.

"It could work," she finally spoke. "I don't like leaving things in the hands of someone I don't know, but there aren't many options."

"You can always get to know the someones and choose the best one to support," Robin said. "We just need an excuse that people can use to gather which won't draw any suspicion. I suggest a performance by yours truly."

Robin waved his hands through the air and used [Visual Phantasm] to have them trail rainbow sparkles.

"Fine," Lantha said after a long moment. "Set up the meeting with your friend from the tavern and get a list of the strongest elements in town that are keen to resist Basgar. We'll split the list and do some research of our own. I want to make sure these people can keep Basgar occupied long enough for us to get back to Noviel with news of the danger."

"Consider it done!" Robin grinned.

"And we keep our eyes peeled for any information that might help us get through that gate or over the wall," Lantha commanded. "I'd prefer we have some backup options in case our new 'friends' don't come through for us."

"I can focus on that," Robin offered. "I doubt I'll be much use assessing the fitness of potential insurrectionists. That's not really a skill I've had much call to develop."

"Fine," Lantha agreed. "You do that." Then she proceeded to break down her orders into individual missions for Fiamah, Grathilde, and Ora-Jean.

That suited Robin just fine; he could use some time to think. He needed to decide how to handle the forthcoming deal with Avanus and, potentially, the Queen of Air and Darkness.

He'd brushed around the subject with the others, but none save Lantha had much of an in-depth knowledge of the fey, and Robin wasn't sure he was ready to try and fish for information from someone as sharp as the elvish rogue.

So as the Sisters Sharp planned, Robin stared into the flames of their small campfire and pondered.

The streets of Bordertown were more crowded than usual. Guard patrols were up, and the place was abuzz with rumors of "Marcher rabbitkin spies." Robin suppressed a grin as he moved through the streets, a day pass and his very human appearance making him all but anonymous.

So far, it seemed his true identity remained concealed from Basgar and Gis. Definitely a good thing, considering they still hadn't found a way through that northern gate.

Speaking of . . .

Robin pulled up the latest version of the "evolving" quest, [A Dangerous Bargain!]. It had changed a bit after he had successfully escaped from

Gis's private quarters with half the priest's private correspondence (and no small amount of his personal wealth) burning a hole in his extradimensional storage space.

Quest Update: [A Dangerous Bargain!]

You have successfully acquired the information Avanus seeks in order to unite the squabbling factions of Bordertown into a single resistance! However, the warlock has presented you with a choice: escape from Bordertown, or knowledge on the Lost God Rhyth. This quest line will reward you with only one. Conclude your deal with Avanus. May your choice be a wise one.
***Reward(s):** A way out of Bordertown* **OR** *knowledge of the Lost God Rhyth.*

Robin already knew he was going to ask for the audience with the Queen of Air and Darkness. The chance of finding out more about Rhyth was too good to pass up, whereas getting out of Bordertown? There had to be ways and ways of doing that. It would be a lot more difficult without Avanus's aid, sure, but they should still be able to manage it.

He just needed to make sure Lantha and the others didn't find out he'd tossed away a sure thing in terms of completing their mission, in exchange for information only useful to himself.

Robin already had a few thoughts on how to accomplish that. He'd planted the seeds of the idea of using an outbreak as a distraction to get them through the gate, so if he stayed on Avanus's good side and helped facilitate that rebellious distraction . . . well, that should be enough to keep the Sisters Sharp off his back and happy.

The Bell and Boar smelled of apples and hops and baking bread when he stepped inside. Robin took a deep breath. There wasn't even a hint of a sour smell in here; one of the employees, at least, must have some sort of [Cleanse] variant. Probably the tavern keeper himself, judging by the gleaming state of the bar the man lorded over.

"Hello, upstart." Lena's voice was cinnamon honey. It was sweet, and it set fire to Robin's more sensitive extremities.

"Morning, glorious," Robin replied with a wink. "What brings you here at this ungodly hour?"

"I could ask you the same thing." Lena nimbly sidestepped the question.

Robin noticed, in spite of the plentiful distractions Lena's person afforded her. The woman was dangerous! He'd need to keep a rein on his head, or he'd lose track of why he was here.

Speaking of.

"I need to talk to Avanus." Robin tried to draw out the name, teasing

Lena with the memory of the rivalry he'd conjured as part of his performance of "Jolene."

Fortunately, the bard was game to play along.

"My rival?" Lena affected a stricken look. "You wound me! As if I could sully my lips to tell you of that blaggard's whereabouts"

"So you *do* know." Robin was quick to pounce on Lena's little slipup.

"Of course." Her smirk told him she'd intended him to notice. "I know everything there is to know in this town."

"And what would that particular piece of knowledge cost me?"

"Darling, you can't afford any of my prices." Lena laughed and walked away toward a table where a steaming breakfast spread had been laid out. "But the first one's free, as they say. You'll find him in the kitchen, fetching me cream for my tea."

"Thank you." Robin lingered long enough to watch Lena walk away before turning to slip into the kitchen.

He kept one eye out for the cook, Kragar. The man clearly knew his way around a cleaver, and Robin had no desire to make closer acquaintance with that particular implement.

Avanus was standing near the door to the cellar, a small jug in his hand. Presumably, that was Lena's cream. The warlock was idly chatting with Devanne, the tavern keeper's wife.

If Robin were a betting entity, he'd wager Avanus was deliberately stalling. Lena tended to be quite imperious, and there was no way that could sit well with the rebellious warlock.

"Miss Devanne," Robin greeted with a broad smile. "I don't suppose I could steal Avanus away for a moment? I have a message for him."

"Of course." The woman smiled and waved the two of them off. "I need to see to the upstairs rooms as it is. Good morning to you both."

The mistress of the house left, and Avanus and Robin stepped out into the alleyway again. This time, there were no cowled, shadowy figures crowding the place.

"I've got what you wanted," Robin informed him.

Avanus merely nodded. Of course he'd believe Robin. His Queen had told him the bard would come through, hadn't she? It was quite a lot of faith for someone who wasn't a cleric, but it did take all kinds to make a world.

Robin plucked the letter out of thin air. He'd simply willed it out of his storage ring, but the effect was nicely showy, he thought. As Avanus reached for it, however, Robin willed it back, causing it to vanish.

"I'd like to discuss payment first," he said.

"Fair enough." Avanus nodded. "Do you wish to have us secure you and your friends an exit, or do you wish for an audience with My Queen?"

"It seems to me that is oversimplifying things a bit," Robin noted. "I think I could do more to help you, maybe earn myself both rewards. Now"—he held up a hand to forestall Avanus as the warlock opened his mouth—"I'm not trying to get more than we agreed upon. I simply think I could be of great service to you and your friends while me and my friends are in town. I could even persuade them to linger a bit longer and lend our aid, if that might be of interest?"

Robin paused to gauge Avanus's response. The warlock had an excellent poker face.

Made sense, considering who his patron was.

"I'm talking experts from Noviel," he tried again, going for a bit of a hard sell. "And we've handed Gis's backside to him once already. Twice if you count the incident with the kobold rebellion I incited."

There, see? I have experience!

Sweet Rhyth, it was like applying for a job all over again. Not a skill he'd expected to be transferable to a fantasy world of dark priests and lost gods.

"I can take your offer to my friends. My other friends. Not the ones you, ah . . . met the other day," Avanus amended.

"You have a lot of friends," Robin observed.

"I'm a likeable person." Avanus smiled.

"You certainly are that." The bard grinned cheekily at him.

"And I take it from your offer that you're inclined to request the audience with My Queen." Avanus turned the conversational tables on Robin abruptly.

Tricky fey-blessed warlocks! Robin mentally scrambled to adjust. The negotiations were suddenly in a different place than he'd expected.

"I am." Might as well go with being up front. "Three questions, as offered. Provided"—he shot Avanus a look—"that my offer to your friends is given preferential treatment. I'm afraid my wishes are not the only factor I have to consider here."

Robin leaned on that truth a little, to make it bend the way he needed it to. Avanus didn't question it but merely nodded in assent.

"We will meet in the forest three days hence," Avanus indicated. "I need time to prepare for My Queen to grace me with her presence. The mental toll is not insubstantial."

At least he wouldn't be coming face-to-face with a Fairy Queen for this interview. Robin was torn between relief and disappointment at that. Perhaps if he played his cards right, it wouldn't be the last such meeting he had.

"Agreed," he said. "I'll begin working with your other friends right away." Robin retrieved the letter. "There's an agent provocateur that's sabotaging all of you, keeping tensions wound up so none of you are willing to work together to oppose Basgar."

He passed the letter to Avanus, who snatched it and read through it quickly. The warlock's face grew grave.

"My friends and I can help in trying to unmask the agent," Robin continued, sensing some of Avanus's worry and trying to address it in order to bolster his negotiating position. "I believe I mentioned we're experienced."

Robin didn't say at what. He knew better than to try to make possibly false promises to someone like Avanus. Vague, now? Vague was fine! Vague he could do.

"Agreed," Avanus said. "Help us unmask this agent provocateur so we can organize a resistance, and in exchange, we'll help you and your party make it to Noviel."

Result!

Quest Update: [A Dangerous Bargain!]

You have successfully revealed the presence of an agent provocateur to Avanus and helped the nascent Bordertown resistance!
Reward: *You have secured an audience with the Queen of Air and Darkness, who will answer three questions about the Lost God Rhyth. Choose wisely! And good luck! You know what you've gotten yourself into, right? Best watch that tongue of yours . . .*

Now he just needed to figure out which three questions to ask the Queen of Air and Darkness, finesse the truth with Lantha so she and the others didn't realize he'd cut a side deal, find and expose an agent provocateur, and not get gutted by a creepy old priest in the process!

Piece of cake.

Like a dense Christmas fruitcake that no one wanted to eat because it'd been in the tin for six or seven years and now bore more resemblance to a fancy brick than anything else but cake!

Right?

Robin Parker

Heritage: Shadeling, Paragon
Profession: Bard (Apprentice)

Tier: 1, Conditional (Effective Level: 3)
Experience: 400
Spell Points: 3
Bardsong: 5 uses

Properties

Free Ranks Available: 1

Physical
  -Strength: 11
  -Dexterity: 14
  -Fortitude: 11
Mental
  -Intelligence: 17
  -Cunning: 20
  -Resilience: 14
Social
  -Charisma: 15
  -Manipulation: 13
  -Poise: 16

Proficiencies

Free Ranks Available: 2

Physical (9/9)
  -Athletics: 1
  -Brawl: 1
  -Dodge: 4
  -Melee Combat: 2
  -Pilot: 4
  -Ranged Combat: 5
  -Sleight of Hand: 2
  -Stealth: 5
  -Survival: 3
Mental (9/9)
  -Arcane Lore: 4
  -Bureaucracy: 1
  -Concentration: 5
  -Crafting: 5
  -Healing: 3

-Insight: 5
-Learning: 4
-Natural Wisdom: 3
-Perception: 5
Social (9/9)
-Animism: 1
-Deception: 6
-Empathy: 2
-Expression: 6
-Gossip: 3
-Intimidation: 3
-Persuasion: 3
-Socialize: 2
-Streetwise: 3

Peculiarities

Blessing of Rhyth
Tongue of the Fallen Tower
Mark of the Trickster
Chronicle of Infinite Visions
Mask of Myriad Faces

Perks

Wayfaring Stranger
Shard of the Shattered Manymind

Spells

Cantrips* (*no SP cost)
-Lesser Phantasm*
-Cutting Words*
-Legerdemain*
Tier 1 (1SP each)
-Visual Phantasm*
-Healing Note
-Whispers from Beyond
Tier 2 (3SP each)
-Assume Quality (Special)

Chapter 7

I tell ya, Jakob, these double shifts are gonna kill me faster than any Marcher bunny."

Robin froze as the voice drifted through the door to the small office he was currently ransacking for information on the northern gate's shift changes. He was wearing a version of his average guy disguise, this time with a watchman-trainee uniform for extra camouflage. The outfit was easy enough to duplicate. It was basically just a navy-blue hat and coat with a brown armband for the trainee bit.

That didn't mean he wanted to get caught with his hand in the cookie jar. Though in this case, the cookies were a roster. Not at all appetizing.

He especially didn't want to get caught before he'd had a chance to swipe what he was after. He'd found the rota easily enough; that was information the people working the wall needed, and it fluctuated enough that there needed to be reliable, easy access.

What he couldn't find was any information on the actual procedures and passcodes employed at each gate. There was some kind of hidden mark that the papers needed to pass inspection, and the local forgers had yet to uncover what it was. It was just one more thing the Sisters Sharp had had to grapple with in their attempts to get home.

Robin had really been hoping to solve that problem, and he thought he might be close. There was a strange seal that didn't have any wax stuck to it in the captain's desk, and something about it twigged Robin's sixth sense. Of course, the thing was locked up tighter than a CEO's Cayman accounts.

Robin really needed more practice at lockpicking, especially under high-pressure situations like this one.

Robin relaxed slightly as the voices moved away from the door. Best get out of here, and soon. He was working on borrowed time, but he was so *close* to the seal!

Maybe there was a key hidden somewhere, like how people in his world kept spares under flowerpots and in decorative rocks.

He carefully went over the desk again. *Hang on.* Something wasn't right. Robin eyed the angles along the right-hand side. It looked like there might be a small compartment up and under . . . there!

Robin's questing fingers found a hidden niche, not even a compartment. No key, but there was a small leather satchel full of paper. *Reports!*

They seemed to be from Gis's agent provocateur, too. There were all sorts of subversive mutterings documented here—more than he could memorize—and he didn't dare steal this lot. Instead, Robin picked out a few of the names and listed activities; Lantha should be able to make good use of the information.

His eyes widened as he looked at one of the papers near the top. The captain was meeting with this mysterious agent provocateur *today*. As in *right now*. As in that was why his office was currently empty for Robin to burgle!

Robin checked the time against the details in his hand. He could just about make it to the rendezvous. However, he'd have to give up his chance to continue searching this place to do so, and there was no telling when would be the next time he'd have a chance to inspect that seal.

On the other hand, he didn't *know* that the seal was the thing that made the passes unforgeable. And he didn't know when else he'd have a chance to unmask Gis's agent.

Either way, it was a gamble.

Robin quickly stuffed everything back where he'd found it. He was going to try and catch up with the captain and the secret agent. He knew where the seal was. He didn't know where the agent was roaming.

Take the chance at the rarer target.

He straightened his fake uniform, peered out the window, and darted out of the door as soon as the coast was clear. Once free of the watch station, he slipped into an alley then broke into a run, willing his appearance to change as he went.

It wouldn't do for some puffed-up patrolman to yell at the new recruit for running. He'd draw less attention as a kid young enough to work as a runner for the merchants. That gave him an excuse as well in case anyone *did* try to stop him.

Not long left if he was going to make that meeting.

Robin put his head down and *ran*.

Robin's nose itched from the violent clash of perfume and cologne in the air. The meeting place was a brothel, all dim and shuttered light in spite of the afternoon hour, with tacky satin and brocade designed to look expensive in the seductive gloom.

Of *course* they were meeting here.

And of course Robin's first time in a brothel wasn't for the regular reason but because he was chasing a particularly nasty spy.

As secret meeting locations went, it was a good one. Plenty of discreet entrances and exits, lots of people who didn't want to ask questions of anyone lest they be asked questions in return. And a nosy madam at the door keeping track of everyone who came in and out who might possibly reek of authority.

Or at least anyone who reeked of noncorrupted authority.

Robin watched as a seedy-looking city guard greeted the woman with easy familiarity. A small amount of money changed hands.

He really needed an invisibility spell. As it was, he was just about able to make do in the dim light with judicious use of illusion and moving very carefully when attention was elsewhere. But there were a lot of rooms in this place, and no way of knowing precisely which one he was looking for.

Not without taking a risk.

Robin waited until one of the working boys walked past, alone, before slipping into the guise of the madam and, using **[Lesser Phantasm]** to duplicate her voice, asked which room the captain had ended up in.

He was counting on the man being notable enough for the working boys and girls to both take note of and gossip about.

"Top floor, little garret room, as usual. Why?" The lad wasn't sour, but he carried a bit of a resentful air about him.

Robin wondered if that was usual or if something had happened recently to annoy him.

Doesn't matter! Focus.

"Never you mind! Now off you fuck." Robin couldn't risk extended dialogue, so had to hope the command would suffice to end the interaction now that he had what he needed.

It did. Thankfully, Robin had heard several examples of the madam's colorful language as he'd been slowly sneaking into the place.

As soon as the lad was out of sight, Robin stole his appearance and made his way quickly up the stairs. No one gave him a second glance.

The top floor was mercifully empty, only a short hallway with a few doors. And only one had voices behind it.

Robin wrapped an illusion around himself and settled in, straining to catch any snippets of conversation. This could be very valuable intelligence, in addition to finally giving him a glimpse at Gis's mysterious agent provocateur.

It took a while to make out the individual voices, but Robin's investment in *Perception* paid off here as well. After a few moments, he managed to separate the sounds coming through the door into distinct voices. One was clearly the watch captain's.

The other, however . . . the other was *strange*. There was a curious affectlessness to the voice, like it had somehow been stripped of all identifying character. It was the vocal equivalent to his forgettable, average guy disguise.

That was a neat trick. He'd have to try and replicate it later with [**Lesser Phantasm**]. Robin filed the idea away for later and concentrated on picking the conversation out through the door. Unfortunately, it sounded like the bulk of the meeting had already happened.

"I don't care about your problems. The priest promised Lord Basgar results, and you are to deliver them!"

That was clearly the captain.

"The price we agreed upon doesn't cover working while some of my targets are aware they're being manipulated," the mysterious voice answered. "I'm going to require more funds or . . . other compensation."

Robin blinked. How was the agent *already* aware they were onto them? He'd only just informed Avanus of their existence. It only made sense if—*frell*. It only made sense if the agent was someone already deeply embedded in one of the groups. And of course they were! How else would they be manipulating things so effectively?

He *really* needed to find out who this person was.

"That's between you and Gis," the watch captain was saying.

This guy really didn't think much of the priest, did he? Interesting.

Robin filed that away as something they might be able to exploit later.

"Yes, well, His Eminence tasked *you* with seeing to my needs, and my needs are not being met. If my needs are not met, I cannot effectively do my job."

"Not my problem!"

"It *will* be your problem when you and your men are facing a highly motivated and organized insurrection against Lord Basgar's rule."

"Peasants," the captain sneered. "Townsfolk. What are they going to do? Threaten me with a rolling pin? Menace me with a frying pan?"

"Don't underestimate—"

Someone must have moved in the room. The conversation drifted out of his hearing, and Robin bit back a growl of frustration as he shifted about, trying to bring their words back into focus, but all he could hear were muffled sounds.

His repositioning did something else, however. His shifting weight pressed down on a loose board, and the thing creaked loudly.

The conversation through the door ceased. There were a few more muffled words, which Robin could only assume were something to the effect of "Did you hear something?"

Acting almost on instinct, Robin took several light steps back and wrapped himself in a new illusion. He was only just in time, too, as no sooner had he frozen into his new place than the door swung open and the watch captain thrust his head and neck out into the hall.

Too bad Robin wasn't an axe-wielding maniac. He could have parted the man's head from his shoulders in a trice. Such a tempting target.

But Robin was still quite a ways away from casual slaughter, if he ever reached that point. So the bard kept still, kept quiet, and watched, [**Cutting Words**] hovering on his lips just in case.

"There's no one here," the captain huffed.

"Are you quite certain?"

The owner of the mysteriously blank voice entered the hall. When Robin saw them step out the door, his heart surged briefly with hope, but it quickly crashed down and turned into disappointment. Not only was the agent provocateur's voice blanked out, their whole body was as well. They were shrouded in some kind of form-blurring illusion that bled all color and distinction from the person's form.

He should have guessed that he wasn't the only one with some illusory tricks up his sleeve. And he really should have predicted that someone playing as dangerous a game as pitting potentially violent rebels against one another would take great care that their identity never be discovered.

Still, that was an opportunity as well. Robin quickly filed away as many details of the blurring effect and the blank voice as he could. This was a disguise he might be able to use against the watch captain or even Gis in the future.

The hackles on Robin's neck rose as that featureless gaze slid over his hiding spot. Did it pause and linger on him for just a moment? He dared not even breathe. And he certainly dared not attack. There was no way he'd win in a two-on-one fight in a brothel against two opponents of unknown capabilities.

There was no way the captain didn't know his way around that sword at his hip, and no way a secret agent of any kind didn't fight all kinds of dirty.

No, Robin had better stay hidden if he could.

"Nothing," the featureless voice finally said. "The same we managed to accomplish at this meeting. We're done here, anyway. If Lords Gis and Basgar wish to continue employing my services, leave the sum I requested or its equivalent in the usual space in three days or less." The figure paused. "Or I vanish from this town, and none of you will hear from me again."

And with those words, the figure *literally* vanished.

Robin mentally cursed. Of course they'd have invisibility magic; though hopefully not in the form of a ring of great and evil power. That would be a Brandywine Bridge too far.

The captain muttered to himself before stomping off down the stairs. Robin silently renewed the **[Visual Phantasm]** he was hiding in and waited.

And stewed.

This had not turned out at all as he'd hoped. Not only was he no closer to finding out the identity of the agent provocateur, but he'd also lost his best chance at cracking the protection on the paperwork that would allow him and the Sisters Sharp passage through the northern gate.

And to cap it all off, he was standing alone in a brothel.

How was that fair?!

Chapter 8

*T*he small evergreen copse bore little resemblance to the enchanted woodland lower down the mountainside. The air was clear and cold and sharp with the scent of pine, but it was still a natural woodland, and the suggestion of faces lingered in the bark of the trees, wild and fey.

Robin was not alone here. He wouldn't feel like he was were he the only other living thing on the mountain. There was a presence all around, and it wasn't just the trees. It wasn't Avanus either, though the warlock stood next to him in one of those clichéd robes.

No, there was an intelligence threaded throughout the stones and the trees. Robin could feel it. It wasn't a feeling he'd associate with a being known as the Queen of Air and Darkness, but perhaps he was wrong. Or maybe he was right and this was some kind of ancient, sacred ground with a sentience all its own.

The last light of the evening was dying in the sky, and a touch of breeze just barely stirred the treetops around them. Avanus hadn't said when they would begin, but Robin's money was on sometime after the last of the daylight had gone. Probably when the clouds hid the stars and the wind moaned through the pines.

Wait. There were stars. He'd seen them on other nights. But he'd also seen the way this world existed, how it differed from the one he knew. So what were the stars here? Some kind of illusion? A twist in space-time allowing them to be seen even when that shouldn't be possible? The actual spirits of the dead, or just massive frakking fireflies stuck to the bottom of whatever continent-size chunk of land was orbiting over them around the same sun?

The mystery would have to wait until a later time. The last of the light had vanished a while ago, and only a green smudge of it remained.

Wait. Same problem as the stars. Where was the darkness coming from?

A chill thrilled down his spine. What if the title Queen of Air and Darkness wasn't mere fancy? What if she quite literally brought the night to this land? If so, he was likely dealing with a being of demigod-level power, if not outright deific levels of the stuff.

Robin swallowed. If he hadn't already been planning on playing things with respect and deference, he certainly would be now!

The wind moaned through the pines, and darkness glittered like black diamonds above their heads. Avanus threw his arms wide and uttered a dramatic declaration.

"'Tis time!"

His robes swirled around him, and the shadows were suddenly deeper, as if before they had been merely two-dimensional things and now they had warped into full-on three-dimensionality. Avanus's eyes became two glittering pits of ebony, visible in the darkness because they were somehow darker.

"Hello, Robin, beloved of the Memory of Rhyth."

It was Avanus's face, but not his voice. The voice that tumbled from the handsome warlock's lips was as rich and dark as wine, as alluring as a spring smile, and as cold as a moonlit arctic night.

"Your Majesty," Robin immediately genuflected. Pine needles pricked through the thin cloth of his trousers and the thinner veil of illusion that had transformed them into finery worthy of an appearance before a queen.

"Rise, Robin Far Traveler." The voice was amused. "You have aided my dear Avanus and fairly won this boon of me. Let us be about it, for it is not wise for me to linger long in this place. There are unfriendly eyes keeping watch over yon keep. Ask the first of your questions and I shall answer."

It was a good thing Robin had made a list to help him decide what to ask and practiced the wording beforehand, or he would have frozen in that moment, all thought forgotten before even this small sliver of a Fairy Queen's dark glory. But he had. He'd approached the whole thing as if he were trying to get a wish out of a recalcitrant genie.

"Your Majesty"—there was no way Robin was going to slip out of formality; not here, not now—"my first question is this: what knowledge of Rhyth do you possess that you are both willing to share candidly and would be of the most use to me with what you know of my current situation?"

That wine-rich voice laughed with Avanus's lips.

"You have had dealings with those of the Twilit Lands before, or you listen well to your grandmothers' tales. Very well. Prettily asked, so prettily I shall answer." The smile on Avanus's face was suddenly sharp. "Rhyth is lost, but neither gone nor forgotten. He can be brought back, should you manage to riddle out what happened to him and a way to open the door so he may step back into this world. I will tell you now that your feet are pointed in the correct direction, and your path will lead you to Noviel and beyond."

That was more in the nature of confirmation, but Robin had asked this as his first question to not only see what he could get but to get a sense of how the Queen of Air and Darkness would play the game. So far, it seemed she intended to play things fairly straight. Well, as straight as a being of Fairy could. There was still a lot of vagueness in her answer.

But the queen was not finished.

"I suppose I'm also willing to—quite candidly—tell you that I am one who greatly desires to see Rhyth returned to this world. Such visions of beauty and terror he wrought! The world is lessened by his absence."

Robin suddenly realized he had perhaps not been quite as clever as he had thought. The queen saw right through him. Still, if what she said was true, she had a reason to want Rhyth back, and that meant she had a reason to want to see Robin succeed.

He could take a risk here with his next question.

"What single power, ability, or spell which I can reasonably acquire will serve me best in my quest to restore Rhyth?"

"Ah, you've thought this through." Avanus's face was amused.

Robin tried not to look too long nor too closely at the warlock. In addition to fearing that the Queen of Air and Darkness might take it as disrespect if he stared too openly, Robin found the way in which Avanus's face moved in expressions that weren't his own disturbing. He hadn't known the warlock long, but it had been enough time to find the experience unsettling.

There was a long moment of silence. Robin hoped it was merely Her Majesty thinking of the best answer and not an indication that her patience had worn thin. His heart pounded and his mouth felt dry. His head swam with the effects of her presence.

Please answer soon. This is . . . a lot.

"There is a skill, a trick that those truly devoted to the primordial arts Rhyth employed would sometimes harness. I believe you might refer to it as a peculiarity. I know not what the guide behind your eyes might call it—"

Guide behind his eyes? The system? Robin perked up. This was the first indication he'd had that he wasn't just hallucinating all those messages!

"—but the faithful of Rhyth, few as they were, referred to the ability as 'The Mirror's Revenge.' The technique still exists among a rare few exceptional illusionists, and may be found in ancient texts across the land. Though I suspect your own invisible guide might be able to help you, should the need arise."

Robin longed to ask what the queen knew about his "guide"—or about him, for that matter—but he knew she wouldn't answer. Or if she did, the response wouldn't be worth trusting. The deal was questions about Rhyth, and only about Rhyth.

"What was he like?" Robin surprised himself by asking.

He'd clearly surprised the Queen of Air and Darkness as well. He could read that on Avanus's face as easily as he could read any of the mass-market fantasy paperbacks that had populated his childhood hours.

Still, the question had been asked, and there was no taking it back now. So Robin waited for the answer. When it came, he wasn't disappointed in the least.

"Rhyth was—he was unpredictable. He was a trickster, meaning he was both hilarious and deadly. Beautiful and terrible. He was older than most of the deities of this world, primordial in his origins, but you'd never know it from his face—any of his faces—or the way he acted. He was wonder and fire, both sublime and grotesque as the mood hit."

Unexpectedly, the queen laughed with Avanus's voice.

"He played the most fearsome pranks on those he thought deserved it. Why, I remember one time he dragooned me into helping him . . . well, I suppose the best way to describe it to you is short-sheeting, but for a divine dominion rather than a camp bed. I can still remember the Lady of Pain's howls of outrage!" That laugh sounded again, clear and cold as a bell on Christmas morn.

Robin listened as the Queen of Air and Darkness spooled out tale after tale of Rhyth and his exploits. Night's swift dragons raced on apace and, before he knew it, hours had passed.

He wasn't sure why he felt such a connection to Rhyth. After all, it wasn't like he was a pious person back on Earth, nor that he knew much about the deity. Sure, he'd made an offering and received a blessing, but it was hardly enough to inspire devotion.

Not that he'd call whatever he was feeling devotion, per se.

He did feel some connection, however, and it made him happy to hear about Rhyth—and to hear that the deity really stuck it good to the stuffed-shirt tyrants and other humorless deities of evil and suffering.

Besides, he was in a fantasy world now. Didn't everyone need a grand quest? And restoring a lost god of illusion to power seemed as good a task to devote himself to as any.

"Oh! And that dragon demigod he was always with. What was his name? Tlal-Aster Nightwing? Something like that. I never could keep draconian names straight. Too many ridiculous syllables, and most of them take themselves far too seriously. Always with the ludicrous titles like 'Chiefest and Mightiest and Greatest Most Calamitous Calamity of the Second Age' and the like. Tlal wasn't like that, though. Sense of humor, that one. Got along famously with Rhyth. I think you'd refer to them as 'bezzie friends' or something like that."

"Tha—" Robin almost thanked the queen before he remembered one should never thank the fey. "That is an amazing collection of stories, and I am honored to have had the privilege of hearing them."

"Good." Avanus's voice was both sharp and amused. "And now that you have your payment, this audience is at an end. Fare thee well, Robin of Rhyth. I am sure we will meet again, albeit not, perhaps, as soon as you might like."

With one last rich, echoing laugh, she was gone. The sense of her presence fled the copse, and the gentle chill of a regular mountain night once again filled the air.

Avanus collapsed to his knees, shuddering. It looked both painful and like he was in ecstasy, so Robin left him to recover his composure while he flicked through the various updates he hadn't dared check while the Queen of Air and Darkness was speaking. Robin was barely in control of his own emotions after that audience, and he desperately wanted something to distract him from the roiling well of wonder and terror the Fairy Queen had left him with.

Let's see . . . there were experience discounts for *Arcane Lore*, *Learning*, and, surprisingly, *Concentration*, as well as for *Persuasion* and *Gossip*. No doubt he'd gotten a nice chunk of experience, though likely nothing spectacular, as there'd been no trickery involved on his part.

Not this time!

Sure, he'd been garbed mostly in illusion, but that probably wasn't grounds for an experience multiplier.

Congratulations! For pleasantly surprising a Monarch of the Fair Folk, you have been awarded the perk [Mark of Fairy's Favor]!

The perk seemed to operate similarly to [Mark of the Trickster] in that it would predispose certain tribes of fairies to look on him with favor, which was no doubt a double-edged blessing of the highest order. In addition, it seemed he would be able to better perceive hidden fey creatures and possibly gain small bonuses when interacting with fairy magics.

Hopefully, that included resisting a pixie's [Sleep] spell.

His first ever quest had gotten an update as well! It was a minor one and as vague as ever, but Robin had a feeling they would stay that way for quite some time. At least until he got a lot closer to finding out what had actually happened, which would have been his third question, by the way, had his tongue not betrayed him.

Quest Update: [Gone, But Not Yet Forgotten]

Congratulations! You have taken another step along the path to unveiling one of Rhyth's mysteries! You're doing fine. Keep up the good work!
Reward(s): *Still unspecified, but you can probably imagine the depth and breadth of a deity's favor, right?*

Oh, he could imagine.

Robin laughed, feeling alive and wild and dangerous, the heady aftereffects of his audience with the Queen of Air and Darkness.

"Come on, Avanus-me-lad, shake it off!" Robin clapped his hands together in front of him and cackled like a wild thing. "We've got trouble to make!"

Chapter 9

*T*he Bell and Boar rang with voices. The tavern was crammed to the rafters with aspiring insurrectionists all pretending to be here for a good time. A good time that Robin, in his stage persona as Marq, had been loudly promising to the town for days.

He really needed to introduce flyers to this world. Or find a manager. Building fame from scratch was *hard*.

Lantha and the rest of the Sisters Sharp were circulating quietly through the crowd along with Avanus, speaking to the leaders of the various factions. Prorna, a statuesque goatkin, represented the remnants of the former power structure in the city. Guilera, a slim woman who appeared to have dark-elven heritage, represented the dissatisfied local merchants. Also in attendance were Cor'Leon, the leader of the strongest of the local organized crime elements; Sulara, a slim young woman who more or less spoke for the local rebellious youth and street kids, and Brawnhilde, a stout dwarf who represented the local militia and those elements of the town watch that were dissatisfied with Basgar's expansionist agenda. Those were the names Robin had managed to remember, at least.

Though Bordertown was not a mighty city by any stretch of the imagination, it was a *very* large town with thousands of inhabitants. Being at the center of the sole trade route connecting three countries would do that. It would probably be a city already were it not for the mountainous location constraining its growth.

Robin's job this evening was simple: he needed to keep everyone entertained and distracted. The former was to keep up the fiction should any innocent townsfolk or suspicious guards wander into the tavern. The latter was to make sure none of the unruly, suspicious elements present had enough focus to start a fight or to pay too much attention to what Lantha and the Sisters Sharp were doing in addition to sounding everyone out.

This was it. This was the point of no return. After tonight, they would be well and truly committed to this plan. The Sisters Sharp would be known by too many people, their faces too obvious.

Even so, it was a solid plan. At least Robin thought the parts he had contributed were pretty solid, and he assumed Lantha's were too. That woman practically screamed competence.

They just needed to be a bit careful. Multiple factors were in play, which complicated things, but fortunately, there was a solution to that. It just meant their plan had stages and was a bit more complex than it might be otherwise.

There was an agent provocateur at play here, so the first thing they needed to do was set a little trap. Nothing substantial would get done so long as someone was spying on these people and playing them against one another. Lantha had something in mind, but she was playing her cards close to the vest. She didn't want anyone's loose lips sinking this chance.

Robin and Grathilde were apparently the ones she was most concerned about.

They were also the ones loudest in their protests that such assessments were damaging, hurtful, and untrue.

It didn't matter, at the end of the day. Lantha had her plan, and they all had parts to play. Robin knew his, and so here he was, on stage, playing it for all he was worth.

Never mind that it galled just a bit to be providing background music rather than commanding the spotlight.

Well, it galled Marq. Robin was a lot more philosophical about things.

He wondered if this new flair for acting was something that came with being a bard, something that was a part of his new heritage as a shapeshifter, or a combination of both.

Probably both. Both is good.

Robin's eyes wandered across the crowd. First, he counted. There were definitely enough people here to make an attempt at completing his bardic initiation quest. But that would have to wait until he could really let loose later.

His gaze tracked the crowd again as his fingers pretended to wander across his lute. He wasn't really playing, instead using [Lesser Phantasm] to fill the air with music. At this point, it wasn't any harder on the hands than extensive lute playing would be anyway, and would result in far fewer calluses. Robin used what attention he had to spare to study the interactions between the different individuals present.

Brawnhilde was arguing with Prorna about something while Lantha was whispering furiously in Grathilde's ear. Either the dwarf had done something wrong or was about to be thrown into the argument in an attempt to defuse it.

Avanus was talking to Guilera, and judging by the sour look on Cor'Leon's face, the crime lordling wasn't too happy about it for some reason. Though why Cor'Leon should be so annoyed when he had a beautiful woman hanging on his arm and every word—

Wait, that was Lena!

What was she doing here? She was supposed to be traveling, not here. Not in a position to usurp the stage and undercut his performance! This could endanger his quest!

Of course, nothing worth doing was ever easy, was it?

Still, if Robin didn't know any better, he'd suspect deliberate sabotage.

Robin began to perform with a bit more skill. He shouldn't, since it might draw too much attention away from the subtle work Lantha was doing, but he couldn't help himself. There was an artistic rival in the room!

He ignored the inquisitive glance Lantha was shooting his way; she and the others could adapt. It was just a little more flourish. He was warming up the audience! Nothing wrong with that, right?

Lena ignored him. He had to assume it was on purpose.

How incredibly irritating! Just because she was stunning and talented and sang like a West End star, it didn't mean she could pretend he wasn't doing damn good work up here!

Marq was *not* just some background act!

So what if the skill he played with was not his own? So what if it was an illusion? Perception was nine-tenths of reality anyway. More, even, once he mastered "The Mirror's Revenge"!

Robin added a bit more flash and a lot more bang to the next song. This time, he actively detracted from what Lantha was doing, and the rogue shot him a glare.

He didn't care; the applause he got at the end of the number was worth it.

Unfortunately, applause wasn't all his little bit of stunting conjured up. A member of the watch stood in the door, surveying the gathering with suspicious eyes. She'd been drawn in by Robin's playing, but it was clear now that she'd found something else to be interested in.

Robin was perfectly positioned to see the woman's eyes widen at the sight of Cor'Leon. That wasn't good. She looked like she was about to charge over and interrogate him on the spot.

They couldn't have that. Fortunately, Robin had a new ability that should solve this problem nicely. Well, reroute the problem, at least.

What this place needed was a bit of classic UK punk rock, even if the song he had in mind was technically a cover. Robin ran over what he needed to do in his head, and as soon as he finished his current song, he quickly twisted through the passes of **[Lesser Phantasm]** to conjure himself some drums, electric guitar, bass, and backing vocals.

His clothing was already black leather.

The drums hit and rolled out through the tavern, a pulse-pounding percussive riff that cut conversation short and refocused attention toward the stage. Robin followed up with the guitar and vocals.

He sang of breaking rocks and the hot sun.

Eyes across the tavern focused on him, including those of the woman in the watch uniform at the door.

That's right. Eyes on me.

Robin reached out and channeled the music of the universe through his performance, aiming to **[Command Attention]** from the watchperson.

It worked. She zeroed in on him and drifted toward the stage, almost entranced by his performance. Robin amped the volume and howled into the chorus.

He fed defiance into his voice, singing of fighting the law, though the law, she won.

Maybe not the best choice of lyrics from a symbolic standpoint, but hey, he was thinking on his feet here! At least the words were English. He doubted many people would be able to understand, and only then if they had the requisite magics. In any case, it definitely took the watchperson's attention away from Cor'Leon.

Now that he had it, however, he wasn't sure what to do with it. And it wouldn't last forever. Robin thought fast as he pounded out the final measures of the song.

He hit the final chord with a flourish and immediately began talking. He had commanded attention from the crowd, and now that he had it, he had no intention of surrendering it.

"One of Bordertown's finest is among us, my friends! Let's give her a hand!" Robin put a hint of steel into that final sentence, and his manic smile communicated clear as day that he expected applause. And now.

And he got it. Stuttering and uncertain, but it was there. He could work with that. In fact, maybe he could get another potential complication out of the way at the same time.

"Lena! Get this fine upstanding member of the watch a drink, would you? Show her the quality of the patrons of the Bell and Boar!" Robin's *Charisma* reeled the other bard out of the crowd and away from Cor'Leon, who had sensibly made himself inconspicuous.

The other bard, not one to ever shy away from a spotlight, smiled and stepped forward to take the watchperson in arm.

"I would be delighted, Marq! And don't worry, I promise this won't get in the way of our duet! I did promise you, and I am nothing if not a woman of my word!"

Robin forced himself to smile and not wince at her words. So much for that idea. He'd hoped she would busy herself with keeping the woman away from what was happening in the tavern, but clearly, Lena cared more about adulation than the good of the town.

He spotted Fiamah making her way through the crowd to intercept the other two women. Good. At least he could count on the cleric to handle things properly.

Robin fell back into a more subdued mode of performance to give Lantha some more time and space to work. Soon enough, Lena would extract herself from the conversation with Fiamah and the watchperson and claim a spot on stage. When she did that, it would be much harder to maintain subtle conversation.

He had his victory, but it was not without its price. He'd successfully diverted the attention of the watch, but at the cost of completing his bardic initiation quest.

Robin forced a smile onto his face as he confronted the prospect of handling the crowd with Lena sharing his stage. It would be good exposure, good for his reputation, but there was no way he was going to be able to complete his quest. That required a performance that was incontrovertibly his own.

He looked out over the crowd at Lena laughing as if this were all completely normal.

Someone was going to pay for this.

With interest.

Chapter 10

Robin gnawed on his lower lip. It was three days later, and he was wandering through Bordertown with Lantha at his side. Ora-Jean, Grathilde, and Fiamah trailed behind them, a separate group of three to minimize attention. Only a part of his mind was on what he was supposed to be doing; most of his attention was caught up in planning his next performance.

He really needed to pass this quest! There were spells just sitting there, right out of reach, waiting for him.

Lantha, disguised as a farmer, was carrying a large basket of produce with her. As they rounded a corner, the rogue tripped and dropped it, sending root vegetables scattering across the street.

That was his cue. Robin launched into the small scene they had planned, crying out in dismay and hurrying to pick up the scattered potatoes.

The potatoes had been his idea. They rolled better than carrots or parsnips, so they would take longer to track down and pick up, giving Robin and Lantha plenty of time to covertly observe their target: a bland-looking warehouse in the southwestern corner of Bordertown.

It was one of the places Basgar was hiding food supplies skimmed from the traders and townsfolk to supply his ambitions for conquest. As Robin ostensibly scurried after the potatoes, he studied the building carefully. It was constructed of blocky stone, with high, barred windows.

It also looked exactly as it had every other time they had scouted it.

"I don't think this is it," he murmured to Lantha as he piled dusty potatoes into the basket.

"No," the rogue agreed. "I don't see any sign of increased guard presence. On to the next one, then."

The last of the potatoes gathered, Robin and Lantha continued their walk through the town. This was the third target they had assessed so far today. Two more remained on the list.

"Grathilde thinks it will be the next one," Robin said as they walked.

"Grathilde is never shy about sharing her opinions," Lantha replied. "Don't make assumptions. It just makes things harder in the long run. People often surprise you."

"It does seem like the too-obvious choice." Might as well be diplomatic about things. Robin was somewhere between Grathilde and Lantha in his thinking. He wouldn't be surprised to find that the agent provocateur was embedded with Cor'Leon's people, but he wouldn't be surprised if they weren't either.

That was the point of today's little exercise: to see if any of the seeds Lantha had planted at the secret tavern meeting had borne fruit. If they showed up to one of these locations and there was an increased guard presence, they'd know someone had talked. And because Lantha had given different targets to each and every one of the factions present, those extra guards would narrow down exactly who had blabbed. Either it took them right to the agent, or it took them to a leak that needed to be plugged before the nascent resistance took any actual steps against Basgar.

"Here we are," Lantha said as they neared the next target, a prominent blacksmith who, along with his several journeymen and apprentices, was responsible for outfitting Basgar's growing army with arms and armor.

Robin was going to go out on a limb and say this was it. There were two guards stationed prominently at the door that had not been there last week, and a few more suspiciously bulky "workmen" lounging around not doing any actual work. He shot a glance at Lantha.

She nodded in response and scratched her nose with her free hand. No potato spill here. This was definitely the place.

The two of them trudged on past, eliciting no response from the armed guards at the door, but the hackles on the back of Robin's neck rose as he felt eyes on him. Probably one of the lazy "workmen."

"Grathilde is going to be insufferable after this. You know that, don't you?" he asked once they were three streets over.

"At least no one was foolish enough to take her wager," Lantha replied. "She's even worse when she's both been right *and* won money because of it."

Robin agreed, not mentioning that the only reason he hadn't taken Grathilde's offer of a "friendly wager" was because he'd spent his small coin outfitting himself with new clothes and some other supplies, and he still didn't have a strong enough handle on the larger currency to know whether or not he was making an insane bet.

"Lucky thing," he said instead.

Robin, Lantha, and the rest of the Sisters Sharp were gathered on a rooftop, looking across the street at the seedy tenement that housed Cor'Leon's headquarters. It was part flophouse, part speakeasy, and part illegal drug and gambling den.

Hey, in small towns, you gotta work hard on a lot of hustles to make a criminal empire.

"Cor'Leon will be alone in his office right now. He will have two guards outside the door, but he's counting the week's take, and he's both greedy and paranoid about it," Lantha reviewed the plan to make sure everyone—especially Robin and Grathilde—was up to speed. "There are two guards posted on the roof, there, that we will have to take out swiftly and silently. Grathilde and Fiamah, you get us there quickly and make sure things stay silent. Ora-Jean and I will take out the guards. Robin will keep a lookout and distract any unwanted attention we may draw. Everyone got it?"

Everyone nodded.

"Good. Let's move out."

Lantha drew a heavy crossbow and two grappling bolts out of a bag at her side. Quickly and expertly, she slotted in the bolts, took aim, and shot. In short order, there were two lines strung across the gap between their building and Cor'Leon's.

Grathilde stepped up as soon as those lines were secure. Drawing a hefty coil of rope from her bag, she brought it to life with chants and gestures. The rope, animated, slithered along the lines, weaving itself back and forth to form a very rudimentary bridge.

Robin's stomach dropped. He knew what was coming next, and as much as he tried, he couldn't get excited about it.

Grathilde continued chanting, flickers of sky-blue light glinting in her eyes as she drew upon her power and the power of the high, clear air of the mountains all around them. A translucent disk tinged with only the slightest hint of blue appeared, floating in midair, perhaps a meter or so across.

"Everyone on," Grathilde ordered. "We depart in the next six seconds."

The four of them carefully sat back-to-back on the disk, legs dangling over the edge. It was floating high enough that Robin's feet were just barely unable to trail on the wood beneath him.

Meanwhile, Grathilde had cast [**Lesser Fly**] on herself. It was more levitation than anything else, hardly soaring birdlike or even like a superhero, but it would get the job done. Grathilde floated across the gap between buildings, towing the disk of force behind her. The ropes were there to give the magic something to push against so it didn't just plummet to the ground. Fortunately, it didn't need much, just the suggestion that there was a surface underneath.

Fiamah muttered to herself as they went, clutching her holy symbol of Serenya to her chest as she did. As soon as she finished her quiet chant, [**Silence**] fell all around them. Robin barely noticed, too busy using [**Visual Phantasm**] to camouflage them as wisps of cloud or fog.

The [**Silence**] was oppressive. Not only because it pressed on him, this strange lack of sensory detail, but because it deprived him of his most reliable weapon, [**Cutting Words**].

You can't assault someone with magical insults if they can't *hear the insults!*

The party made it to the other side unnoticed. With Fiamah's spell in place, even Grathilde's heavy tread went unnoticed, and Ora-Jean and Lantha made short work of the two guards, clubbing them senseless.

They bound them hand and foot, gagged them, then slipped into the building.

So far, so good.

Lantha extracted a set of keys from a downed guard and led the way inside. The top levels of the tenement were used as Cor'Leon's private quarters, this world's equivalent of a shabby penthouse in a decaying city. There was either a lot of expensive-looking trash or really cheap-and-gaudy–looking antiques, Robin couldn't quite decide which.

Fiamah's [**Silence**] expired not long after they made it inside. Lantha motioned for the rest of the party to wait in a small room that smelled of dust and disuse while she went to locate Cor'Leon. This was the worst part of the whole evening so far. The waiting wore at Robin's nerves like a power cable against a tree trunk, abrasive and electric.

When Lantha finally returned, she signaled Fiamah, and the cleric cast another [**Silence**] spell around them. They were quickly exhausting the cleric's energies, which they might regret if it came to needing healing, but Lantha was banking on the element of surprise saving them more bloodshed in the long run and being a better use of Fiamah's talents.

Then they moved out, following Lantha's lithe figure through the halls and rooms to the sturdiest door in the place. A slim line of golden light gleamed around the edges where the wood didn't quite fit perfectly into the frame.

Fiamah stopped several feet back from the door. Too close, and the [**Silence**] might overlap with Cor'Leon's location, tipping him off. Lantha pulled out a set of lock picks and went to work on the door, the edge of Fiamah's spell ensuring no noise escaped through the keyhole to warn their target.

Robin saw rather than heard the moment the latch *clicked*. He saw it in the way Lantha's body held tense for a moment and then relaxed.

The rogue gestured.

Ora-Jean braced herself to sprint through the door with Grathilde and Robin flanking it, ready to provide cover or attack with the odd spell as opportunity permitted.

Fiamah signaled that her spell was nearly spent, so Lantha threw the door open, and they charged in as silently as they could.

Cor'Leon's study was a mess. There was paper strewn everywhere, furniture askew, and a sizeable pile of money in the process of being sorted into a large carry bag. Probably one with extradimensional storage capacity.

Lantha threw a dagger; however, Cor'Leon was fast on his feet. The crime lordling spun behind his desk as soon as the party burst into the room, wasting no time in counterattacking. He pulled a slim wand from behind his back and sent unerring darts of blue-white magical energy shooting toward Lantha and Ora-Jean. The bolts slammed home with a sizzle.

Grathilde responded with a [**Minor Levinbolt**], catching the crime boss in the face. He hissed in pain and ducked back down behind his desk.

"Come out where I can hit you!" the dwarf yelled.

"I'm afraid I'm reluctant to acquiesce to your request, my dear," Cor'Leon called from behind the desk. "But to show you my abject remorse, have a gift!"

Something small and angular arced up and over Cor'Leon's makeshift barricade toward them. It slammed into the floor and released a titanic peal of thunder.

Robin clapped his hands over his ears.

Too late. They were already ringing like a school bell on the last day before summer.

"You call that a gift? If it were a horse, I'd shoot it before coming anywhere near close enough to look it in the mouth!" Robin lashed out with [**Cutting Words**].

A shout of rage answered Robin's insult, and Cor'Leon popped out of hiding long enough to fling a dagger at Robin. The man's aim was inexplicably terrible, and the knife sailed wide off its mark, clattering against the wall before hitting the floor.

Ora-Jean circled around one side while Lantha took the other. Grathilde attempted to pepper him with sparks to distract him, but Cor'Leon had donned some kind of brooch, and the thing glowed as it ate up Grathilde's cantrips.

"Give up, Cor'Leon," Lantha said with quiet intensity. "You're outnumbered and outmatched. You can't hope to beat us."

The crime lordling had the audacity to laugh in Lantha's face at that. Robin's stomach dropped. Something was wrong. This was not going according to plan.

"I don't have to win. I just have to stall you long enough for my crew to get here." Cor'Leon grinned wickedly.

Robin cursed.

The bastard wasn't wrong.

Chapter 11

Robin's heart was hammering in his chest. They needed to take Cor'Leon down—and fast—or they would be neck-deep in the crime lordling's underlings. Maybe his new spell could find a chink in the man's armor.

So Robin tried it. He hadn't really had cause to use it before now, but if not now, when?

He opened his mouth and spoke words no tongue should shape; spoke words no ear should hear. These eldritch syllables echoed with the maddening vastness beyond time, and Robin pitched them *just so*. They twisted through the air, carried by breath and dark intent, these [**Whispers from Beyond**].

And Cor'Leon . . . ignored them. Ignored them or resisted the—debatable—might of Robin's magic.

Well, most of it.

Robin could see the man's jaw clench, his eyes wince at the tearing, teasing, terrible words. But he didn't run gibbering in fear and horror, which would have been the desired effect. Instead, the damnable man retained enough presence of mind to place the desk between himself and Lantha's next attack while simultaneously casting a handful of a coarse blue powder into Ora-Jean's face.

The scout coughed and sneezed and began flailing at the air, roaring in a frothing rage.

"Ora-Jean!" Fiamah strode into the room. She was supposed to hold back—an ace in the hole, support as needed, or healing if things took a very wrong turn—but the cleric rushed in to try and deal with whatever was afflicting the scout.

Grathilde was still firing sparks at Cor'Leon. His amulet protected him, glowing brighter and brighter, but the aeromancer wasn't trying to do damage; she was trying to distract the crime boss and score Lantha an opening.

Lantha struck, her dagger coming away wet with blood. It wasn't enough to take Cor'Leon down, but it'd clearly hurt him. Robin tossed out another insult with **[Cutting Words]**, trying to keep the man off balance, and received a look of pure hatred in response.

Fiamah was trying to get close enough to Ora-Jean to lay hands on her and remove whatever affliction was plaguing the scout, but the halfling was in a berserk rage, swinging wildly at anyone and anything that came near her. Whatever that stuff was, it was clearly potent, and a very effective distraction.

"You'll never take me alive before my crew gets here," Cor'Leon taunted them. "And you'll need to do a lot better than—"

"Then we'll settle for you dead."

Lantha lunged again, forcing Cor'Leon to scramble back.

At the same time, Fiamah finally managed to get her hands on Ora-Jean, the cleansing power of the cleric's magic driving the fury from the scout's eyes.

Cor'Leon cursed.

"And who says your crew is coming?" Robin leapt in. "Foolish to think that it's hard to buy out a bunch of criminals. How do you think we got in here?"

"Lies," Cor'Leon spat at him.

Lantha used the distraction to strike at Cor'Leon again. Ora-Jean flanked, and Grathilde tossed out a covering spread of sparks, harrying and hassling. The crime boss was in very serious danger of being overwhelmed.

"If it's a lie, why aren't they here yet? You certainly made enough noise with that little toy of yours." Robin grimaced theatrically. "*My* ears are still ringing. Curious that it didn't bring anyone running."

Robin was gambling that the pressure they were putting on Cor'Leon would distract the man. He had no reason to believe the rest of the crew wasn't almost here, but if he could break Cor'Leon's spirit, they could take him down before that happened.

"Damn you." Cor'Leon's face flickered with fear, and he vanished.

"No!" Lantha lunged for the space the man had just occupied but didn't strike anything.

Robin had been waiting for something like this to happen. Ever since he'd seen the mysterious figure in the brothel vanish, he'd been thinking about ways to deal with invisibility.

"Close your eyes!" he shouted.

Robin pulled a bag of flour out of his storage space and flung it as hard as he could at the center of the room. A cloud—a wave—of white powder spread throughout the space, coating everything and everyone with a layer of fine, white dust.

Including the invisible Cor'Leon.

Like a decaying ghost, the flour clung to one side of the invisible man. And because he was now visible, he was once again easily targeted.

Lantha and Ora-Jean quickly moved back into flanking positions.

"Clever." Cor'Leon coughed. "Too clever by half. But you'll have to do better still."

The shape of the man blurred, like it had been before in the brothel. Hard to see, harder to target.

Cor'Leon managed to evade both Lantha and Ora-Jean's attacks and retreated toward the window. It was barred with thick rods of iron, but Cor'Leon didn't seem to care. With a flick of his hand, he threw something to the ground, and a bright light flashed, blinding in its intensity.

When Robin managed to blink his eyes clear, there was no sign of the man.

"Watch the floor for footprints," he shouted.

"There!" Ora-Jean pointed. "They lead to the window."

The window was still barred. Lantha rattled it.

It stayed solidly in place.

"There must be some kind of latch or hidden catch to it," she said.

"Well, find it!" Grathilde called. "We're going to have company any minute now."

Robin could hear it too; the pounding of footsteps running through the hallways. They wouldn't have time to escape. His mind flashed through his contingency plans, made some quick alterations, and he leapt into action.

"Follow my lead." He pointed to Lantha and Ora-Jean. "You two, fall to the ground when you hear the big noise. Make it convincing. I'm going to give them a little illusion show; let them see their boss for the villain he is. Fiamah, get rid of the flour!"

Robin was out of time. He quickly cast [**Visual Phantasm**], replicating the form of Cor'Leon and placing the image in front of the window, where Ora-Jean and Lantha could look like they were still threatening him. Then he started flexing his fingers through the motions for [**Lesser Phantasm**]. He needed to get the voice just right . . .

Cor'Leon's second in command, Dahn, burst into the room with a handful of others. Robin didn't give him a chance to zero in on any of the party members, launching right into the illusory performance and leaning a little on the volume to make it all but impossible to ignore.

"Fools! All of you!" the illusion of Cor'Leon roared. "You're idiots if you think Basgar hasn't got this place in the palm of his hand! Only smart play was to throw in with him!"

"Traitor!" Grathilde yelled, trying to be helpful.

Maybe it was. Dahn and the others were standing in the door, confused. Robin flexed his fingers again, keeping the narrative going.

Lantha lunged at the illusion, "narrowly missing," as Ora-Jean telegraphed some broad strokes with her axe. The scout was not the best actress.

Better wrap this up before anyone has time to start questioning things.

Robin had the illusion blur, just as Cor'Leon had, and replicated the man pulling out a stone before throwing it to the ground. [**Lesser Phantasm**] then reproduced as much of that concussive blast of a sound as it could.

It lacked the sheer force of the original, but it was loud. Robin's timing was also off. The illusory stone hit the floor well before the sound hit, but hopefully no one noticed. Everyone certainly winced when the sound went off.

Ora-Jean and Lantha were also a bit late in tumbling to the floor, but most of the attention was on Robin's illusion.

It was fine. It would be fine. No one would notice. *Just stick the ending!*

The fake Cor'Leon dissolved into mist and coiled out the window, slipping easily through the bars. Robin had no idea if that was a real spell here or not, but the man clearly had so many secrets no one should question it.

"Boss!" Dahn cried out in disbelief.

But the man didn't attack the party. He just stood there with the other men and women of Cor'Leon's crew. They looked poleaxed.

Well, betrayal was always a surprise. Unexpected that it would hit a criminal gang this hard, but maybe their loyalty had run deeper than usual?

Lantha and Ora-Jean had hopped back to their feet, and Fiamah, Grathilde, and Robin regrouped with them, keeping the desk between the party and the stunned members of Cor'Leon's crew.

"Cor'Leon was working for Gis," Lantha said, seizing control of the situation. "We came here to confront him about it and found him in the middle of clearing this place out." She pointed to the sack, money clearly spilling out of it. "We faced him, and he attacked us."

Robin was still riding high on the adrenaline from the fight, but this added tension drawing out the uncertainty was giving him a headache.

"Why should we believe you?" one of the women behind Dahn asked.

"I'm willing to cast a truth spell to prove our words," Fiamah cut in. "Unless you doubt my word as a sworn servant of Serenya?"

Robin wasn't sure how much weight that argument would carry with this group. They seemed a relatively impious lot. But instead of taking the cleric up on her offer, they merely shuffled and muttered among themselves.

"Look," Lantha began. "Cor'Leon is gone. We have no intention of messing with your business here. In fact, we'd much prefer it if you could address this in-house and get things sorted out quickly."

"What do you mean?" Dahn looked at the rogue.

"Cor'Leon—the traitor—is gone. But I assume your organization still needs a leader? And I know the resistance would still like to count on your aid as allies." Lantha looked around exaggeratedly. "Surely one of you knows enough to run this place? Has been thinking about taking over one day?"

That last sentence prompted more uneasy shuffling. Of course they'd all thought about it. But this was unexpected. And no doubt whoever took that place right now would have a massive target on their back. Especially with Cor'Leon still in the wind.

"Dahn should do it," the woman who had challenged them earlier spoke up. "He was Cor'Leon's second, sure, but we trust him. There's no way he was in on any of this."

"I don't really care," Lantha replied bluntly. "It's up to you to shake down your organization and see what other rotten fruit falls out. The source of the poison should be gone, but you still need to clean the wounds. And that is not our job."

Lantha gestured subtly. The party began moving carefully toward the exit.

No one made a move to stop them.

Dahn was staring thoughtfully at the bag of money on the floor.

"Just get your house in order fast," Lantha finished. "Now that we've cleared out the spy, we're going to hit Basgar where it hurts.

"Hard."

Chapter 12

Robin bit into a warm, freshly baked roll dotted with a small dab of butter. His eyes closed in bliss. There were very few things that could match that taste, in this or any other world.

He savored the roll like he savored the morning. This was the last bit of breathing room he'd have before things kicked into high gear in the effort against Basgar and Gis. He'd only managed to beg this much time off because he'd told Lantha he needed to "meditate on some new spells he had been studying in the hopes of mastering them before the action kicked off."

It wasn't *entirely* a lie, either. He didn't have new spells, per se, but he did have a character sheet and a sizeable mass of experience gathered up over the course of recent events. The confrontation with Cor'Leon's men after the man himself had fled had added an especially nice chunk. High-stakes trickery? Fooling the loyal supporters of a crime lordling? Apparently very lucrative in the experience department!

Robin had taken his time, burrowing down into every available tooltip and menu; there were a lot more available now that he had actually taken his first class. The peculiarities were particularly interesting, and he'd mentally flagged a couple as high priority for the next chance he got.

Sadly, "The Mirror's Revenge" would have to wait. It either required more skill or had higher prerequisites. Whatever the case, even though he had managed to find an entry for it, it was effectively grayed out for him. The Queen of Air and Darkness's words, however, reassured him that it would not remain that way forever.

Still, Robin had some priorities to see to. The first thing he did was to max out his *Expression*. The skill was key to performance, and thus to successfully completing his quest. Then he raised his *Melee Combat* skill, just in case. The next few days could get quite hairy.

Robin Parker

Heritage: Shadeling, Paragon
Profession: Bard (Apprentice)
Tier: 1, Conditional (Effective Level: 3)
Experience: 400
Spell Points: 3
Bardsong: 5 uses

Properties

Free Ranks Available: 1

Physical
  -Strength: 11
  -Dexterity: 14
  -Fortitude: 11
Mental
  -Intelligence: 17
  -Cunning: 20
  -Resilience: 14
Social
  -Charisma: 15
  -Manipulation: 13
  -Poise: 16

Proficiencies

Free Ranks Available: 2

Physical (9/9)
  -Athletics: 1
  -Brawl: 1
  -Dodge: 4
  -Melee Combat: 4
  -Pilot: 4

-Ranged Combat: 5
-Sleight of Hand: 3
-Stealth: 5
-Survival: 3
Mental (9/9)
-Arcane Lore: 4
-Bureaucracy: 1
-Concentration: 5
-Crafting: 5
-Healing: 3
-Insight: 5
-Learning: 4
-Natural Wisdom: 3
-Perception: 5
Social (9/9)
-Animism: 1
-Deception: 6
-Empathy: 3
-Expression: 6
-Gossip: 3
-Intimidation: 3
-Persuasion: 3
-Socialize: 3
-Streetwise: 4

Peculiarities

Blessing of Rhyth
Tongue of the Fallen Tower
Mark of the Trickster
Chronicle of Infinite Visions
Mask of Myriad Faces

Perks

Wayfaring Stranger
Shard of the Shattered Manymind
Mark of Fairy's Favor

Spells

Cantrips* (*no SP cost)
-Lesser Phantasm*

-Cutting Words*
-Legerdemain*
Tier 1 (1SP each)
-Visual Phantasm*
-Healing Note
-Whispers from Beyond
Tier 2 (3SP each)
-Assume Quality (Special)

Robin poked at a few more things, but he was figuring out that he was a bit stuck until he got through the performance bottleneck. He could still raise his skills, but the really interesting choices of spells or peculiarities all depended on him finishing that quest.

Well, first deal with Basgar and Gis, then clear the quest.

Then with any luck, he'd be on his way to Noviel, adventure, and hopefully more answers about Rhyth.

Lantha stuck her head through the door.

"Are you ready? I want to go over the plans once more before we meet with the others."

Robin rose. He'd already accomplished three missions for Lantha, and two more that had been of his own devising. Basgar and Gis were going to have several small problems cropping up in a few days, even if the big one the resistance was working on went pear-shaped.

"Be right there."

Robin reached out and grabbed one more roll to slather with butter. He didn't *need* to eat, but that didn't mean he wouldn't.

Delicious was still delicious.

Robin stared at the warehouse—the same one they had passed the other day while checking to see which of the faction leaders would take the bait and reveal themselves as the traitor. Now, they were back and planning to ransack the place.

Provided they could get enough guards out of the way to make it feasible.

Basgar kept his supplies in five large warehouses and one outright converted townhouse spread evenly and discreetly around the town. This was partially to present a smaller target; partially due to the petty tyrant trying to conceal from the townsfolk just how much food he had extorted, stolen, and cheated them out of.

But doing things this way also split his forces, and there was quite a distance between each supply dump. If someone were to attack one of them, it would take a while before reinforcements could be sourced from any existing location, or even from the local watch.

And Lantha fully intended to exploit that fact.

Robin and four others had been designated as "bait." They would each make an attempt at a small theft, with the idea of getting noticed and drawing off a sizeable chunk of the guards. Robin had his illusions. Some of the others had teams of people. All of them could look like a credible threat. They would allow the guards to chase them off, drop hints that they were heading to hit the next warehouse, and generally cat-and-mouse the guards from each place, running them all around in a big circle.

While they were distracted and undermanned, the actual strike force would hit, subdue the remaining people, and empty the place of supplies. There were plenty of willing townsfolk to provide ready hands, wagons, and a surprising number of extradimensional storage spaces.

As far as Robin could see, it was a nightmare of logistics, approaching impossible levels, but Lantha didn't seem concerned. There was magic, he supposed, to speed things along, and it wasn't his problem anyway.

His problem was baiting the guards and not getting caught.

Right now, he was waiting, concealed, in a small alleyway not far from his target. Lantha would be hiding with a group on the other side of the building. Grathilde, Fiamah, Ora-Jean, and Avanus were leading the other teams.

The town bell would ring soon; everyone was coordinating off of that sound.

Dong-ding, ding-dong.

The bell rang out the quarter hour. That was Robin's cue. He had fifteen minutes to get in, get the guards' attention, and lead them off on their little wild-goose chase.

Slipping in was easy. The place needed light, so there were windows. Robin had made sure to pile several boxes, barrels, and general detritus around the edge of the warehouse into a makeshift ladder for ease of access.

Smash. Grab. *Ooh, is that a packet of dried apples? Yes, please.*

Robin took a bite and was chewing away when a guard came around the corner and spotted him. He swallowed quickly.

"Run! It's the guards!"

A flurry of movement in the shadows should be plenty to convince the guard they were facing a whole gang of thieves here.

Thank you, [Visual Phantasm] and [Chronicle of Infinite Visions]! The way that casting illusions with this setup was just an act of will was fantastic. Made it really easy to hide what he was up to, which was probably the whole point.

The man shouted for backup, and Robin made sure he got a good view of an illusory young man jumping out the window with an illusory crate of food before hopping up to the window himself.

Better make this personal, just to be certain they would follow.

Before Robin got the chance, however, the guard got his own hit in first.

"I'm going to twist you into a pretzel and throw your bones to the pigeons, traitor," he sneered.

"So you're a fan of Lord Basgar, I take it," Robin replied.

"His lordship is leading us to greatness!"

Oh good. No need to feel guilty about this at all, then.

"I'd say I could see how you might think that way, but honestly, looking at you, I can't see how you manage to think at all. It must be a miracle of the gods' own making."

The [Cutting Words] landed. The man purpled, staggered, and leapt after Robin.

Fortunately, Robin was well placed to slip out the window before his pursuer could get close. A torrent of invective followed him, as well as more threats of bodily harm and exhortations for other guards to come and "teach some little rat a lesson in manners."

Ha. Good luck with that one.

Robin hopped down and sent a couple of illusory thieves with satchels and boxes of food flitting ahead of him. Had to keep the ruse up as long as possible.

His friend burst through the remains of the window, screaming.

"I'm going to kill you! I'm going to rip off your head and—"

"You don't look like the sort who can find his own head to rip off, much less anyone else's," Robin shot back over his shoulder as he took off at a moderate run.

The guard frothed at the mouth and actually slipped as he was clambering down the boxes, left entirely uncoordinated in his rage. He smacked the ground with a wet thwack.

Robin winced. Leave it to him to taunt the guard enough that he managed to kill himself before they could establish pursuit.

He rallied, though, and the man clambered to his feet.

Two other guards had made it out the window by this point, so Robin took off faster as the man he'd insulted nearly to death lumbered after him; a juggernaut amassing momentum.

The guy was a lot faster than he looked, faster than he had any right to be by the laws of physics as Robin knew them. Must be some kind of skill or spell.

He'd have to be careful. He kept forgetting that he couldn't make the same assumptions he was used to making. There were probably kittens with vorpal claws in one of these alleyways capable of literally ripping him to shreds.

So Robin ran, trying to put some distance between himself and his pursuer. It wasn't easy. The man was gaining quickly, and Robin's need to concentrate on keeping his illusions flickering in and out of sight slowed him down.

Lunkhead—as Robin had decided to call him in a split-second decision of questionable creativity levels—was getting closer. Robin needed to dip out of sight for a few moments, maybe catch his breath from a rooftop or something and direct the chase along just via his illusions.

It would certainly be safer.

He also needed to watch where he was going. Most of the streets around here were relatively empty, but one wrong turn, and he could get caught in a pedestrian nightmare. And he needed to lead these mooks by the nose, not allow himself to be herded.

Robin tried to dodge around a corner.

"Oh no, you don't!" Lunkhead roared. "[**Mark of the Hunter**]!"

Robin felt a tearing pain in his back, like a tiger was writing its name across his skin in blood and torn flesh. He stumbled then lost his footing, slamming into a wall and ricocheting off it to windmill wildly down the street.

What the cock kind of spell was this? It burned. Robin could *feel* the mark.

He'd had to help brand calves on his grandmother's farm every year. Thankfully, there were never that many, but the smell of burning hair and the sizzle as those red-hot irons hit flesh—it wasn't something you ever forgot.

Robin had even more sympathy for them now. His back felt like it was on fire.

How long was this thing going to last? And was it going to hurt like this the whole time?

"Run as much as you want, little man!" Lunkhead shouted at him. "You can't get away from me! Not with my mark in your flesh!"

Charming. Robin grimaced. *Focus.* He had to focus. He was leading them away, just as he should. Now he simply needed to not get caught.

Simple.

Then he made the mistake of looking over his shoulder and not at where he was running. Robin's foot caught on the uneven cobblestones, and his momentum was more than his balance could handle.

He tripped, tumbling ass over teakettle across the stones. The rough rock tore and abraded his skin, and it would have done quite the number on his clothes were they more reality and less illusion. He didn't stop tumbling until he rapped sharply against the stone foundations of a nearby warehouse.

Robin rolled over, groaning from the impact. He glanced behind him.

Fuck.

The guards were still bearing down on him, and fast!

Chapter 13

Robin scrambled to his feet. The stone was rough on his hands and uneven and treacherous beneath his feet. His fall had cost him too much time, and now Lunkhead and a few of his friends were closing in.

He had to even the odds a bit.

He could try running, but he wasn't in a great position to make escape that simple . . . if he could escape. He had to stay in sight long enough that they kept pursuing him!

He could use his illusions to try and draw some of them off, but he'd be risking them doubling back when they quickly lost sight of the phantasms. It wasn't like Robin could control them over large distances and without a direct line of sight.

Or he could send them on toward the next warehouse. That was the eventual plan anyway, but was it too soon? Did he dare risk the resistance job at the next spot, where they were also stealing supplies right out from under Basgar's nose?

Robin didn't have a lot of good choices.

He didn't have a lot of choices, full stop. He really needed to get his hands on an invisibility spell or a short-range travel charm.

He would have to keep playing bait, at least for a little while. Which meant he needed to either gain some ground or thin the herd. Also, he needed to get his actual self out of the direct line of fire, meaning he needed a distraction.

"Good job," he called back at the charging guards. "You came really close to catching me. But you know what they say . . ." Robin put on a wicked grin. "Close only counts in a game of horseshoes or in [Fireball] spells!"

And with that, he flicked his fingers and (the illusion of) a roaring ball of flame went coruscating toward the guards. Most of them shouted in dismay, hitting the deck or throwing themselves out of the way.

Robin took the opportunity to slam himself into the wall and cover his position with the [Lesser Phantasm] of a dilapidated crate. Then, fireball dissipating, he used [Visual Phantasm] to create an image of himself vanishing around a corner.

The guards were slowly scrambling to their feet and checking for burnt damage. They didn't have any to find, so they recovered quickly.

Just then, the city's bells rang out again. Good enough for Robin.

He could now send some of these mooks packing.

He alternated castings of [Lesser Phantasm] to reinforce his hiding space and to send shouts echoing off the walls; fragmentary voices of running thieves and other guards.

"This one said they're going to hit the southwestern warehouse next!" Robin modeled this illusory guard's voice on the woman who'd stumbled upon his last performance at the Bell and Boar. "We need to get over there and stop them before they get a chance to run off with more of our supplies!"

Robin added some general shouts of agreement and a half-heard authoritative voice shouting out orders to that effect.

Some of the guards peeled off immediately. More than Robin expected, actually. Possibly a drawback to recruiting heavily from those who uncritically accepted orders. But that was tyranny for you: big on obedience, and the punishments for noncompliance really weeded out the original thinkers.

Thank you, Basgar!

"I'll catch up," Lunkhead called. "I can still sense my mark. The little thief is still around here somewhere."

Robin was lucky it wasn't some kind of unerring arrow; Lunkhead was probably too low level for that kind of tracking magic. He kept his position and kept quiet with a watchful eye on the street around him.

Soon, it was only Lunkhead and two of his friends. Because *of course* he couldn't make this an easy one-on-one.

Fine. Wasn't like Robin was planning on fighting fair anyway.

He smiled. Maybe he could have some fun with this one and test out some of his illusion ideas. The mark still burning on his back might complicate things, but neither Lunkhead nor his pals seemed like the sharpest daggers in the belt.

Robin conjured the illusion of himself sitting atop the crate when his opponents were busy looking elsewhere.

"Well, well, well," Illusion Robin said, courtesy of [Lesser Phantasm]. "All this for little old me? And I haven't even had the chance to introduce myself!"

"It doesn't matter who you are," Lunkhead sneered. "All you're gonna be is dead!"

Well, if that wasn't a perfect entrance line, Robin didn't know what was.

"Too late," the illusion replied in a singsong voice. "Already dead! My name's John, by the way. Still is, on this side of things."

"Then I'll hit you so hard you'll feel it in the afterlife!"

Lunkhead began sprinting toward him.

Illusion Robin laughed, jaw distending and flesh peeling back from his bones until the skeleton beneath was revealed and a grinning death mask stared out at the three guards.

Lunkhead stopped his advance.

"It's a trick!" he yelled to his friends. "Just some stupid trick."

Robin twitched his fingers and started [Lesser Phantasm], chaining a horrific whispered chorus of backing music.

Have you seen the ghost of John

Long white bones with the skin all gone

Robin gave the voices a bit of atonality to really up the creepy factor, then he dipped into his reserve of spell points and sent some [Whispers from Beyond] crawling through the air to sink into the ear of the guard who looked the most creeped out.

As soon as those whispers began, he screamed. His will broke a moment later, mind quivering before the onslaught of psychic damage and fear. He immediately turned and ran.

Wouldn't it be chilly with no skin on?

The woman remaining with Lunkhead looked really spooked now. Confusion and chaos were Robin's friends, though. They bought him enough time to cast another [Whispers from Beyond] for her. She may have had a stronger will than her friend, but the ambiance and the feeling that she really should be obeying orders elsewhere combined to sap her resolve just enough to fall prey to Robin's magics. She, too, went away screaming.

"Cowards!" Lunkhead shouted after them. "It's just a trick!"

Robin had just enough juice left for one more [**Whispers from Beyond**], but he held off for now. He should be able to handle this jackanapes with [**Cutting Words**] and his wits, and if not, he still had [**Whispers from Beyond**] for a bit more magical oomph.

Besides, there was still a chance Lunkhead's friends would get over their fear and come back. Best to have a backup in case that happened.

No reason to drop the ruse, though. It was doing a fantastic job of distracting Lunkhead. The man was spitting with fury and screaming at the apparition; albeit he still wasn't quite brave enough to take a swing at it, no matter what he said.

Robin decided to push that a bit further.

John belongs in a quaint nightmare

Wobbly jaw and a hollow glare

"Stop! That! Singing!" Lunkhead was definitely unsettled.

"Ha!" Robin had to make his double lip-sync to his words. Tricky. "You wouldn't know good music if it bit you in the ass! Of course, that might just be because you can't tell your ass from your elbow!"

The [**Cutting Words**] sliced through the air and dug deep. Lunkhead had already taken several hits. His friends had abandoned him. He'd failed in his duties to Lord Basgar. Was it really any wonder that he lost it?

The man screamed in inchoate rage, gibbering and spitting at the bony apparition before him. Muscles straining, he reached down and pried up a loose cobblestone from the street. He didn't want to attack the apparition directly, but he had no problems chucking a stone at it with all his might.

Unfortunately, Robin was concealed in the center of that illusion. The rock sailed right through and slammed into his shoulder, hitting with a sickening crunch.

Robin screamed. He couldn't help it. The pain was intense. The only positive to the situation was that Robin wasn't knocked out of the middle of the illusion, but only because he had his back firmly pressed against the wall.

Lunkhead took that as a sign that the creature could be hurt, so he pulled at another cobblestone. This one was loosened only by the absence of its mate and was harder to pry up.

Robin was panting with the pain. He didn't think the shoulder was broken, but a lot of that flesh was definitely pulped. Bruised.

[**Healing Note**]? No. He needed to take that guard out first, then he could spend his last spell point on healing.

He gritted his teeth. He was going to have to sell this. Lunkhead was already pretty close to unhinged, which could be argued meant he'd taken a lot of psychic damage already. One or two more good shots should take him out.

Robin had to be quick. That next cobblestone was loosening.

Think. What did he know about Lunkhead?

The guy wasn't too bright. Hated cowards. Was *way* too into serving Lord Basgar—

Maybe there was something there. He took pride in his service, and pride was always an easy target for insults.

Call him a lapdog? No. He might like that. It implied loyalty. Value.

No. If he was going to hit this guy where it really hurt, he needed to go after how *well* he served Lord Basgar.

Robin grimaced and ran through another set of spell gestures.

The illusory skeletal Robin laughed mockingly.

"Not even stones can break these bones, but I've got words that can hurt ye!" Robin made the apparition let loose a wild cackle before going in hard with the [Cutting Words]. "They say the truth cuts like a razor, and boy, do I have a close shave for you! Because the truth is, my friend, you've failed. You've failed yourself. You've failed your lord. You really should have followed those orders earlier. By now, there will be at least five warehouses that stand empty in this city. All owned by Lord Basgar. All *formerly* stuffed to the brim with his ill-gotten supplies. You could have stopped us. But you didn't." Illusion Robin clucked his nonexistent tongue sadly. "With a record like yours? I think I'd die of shame."

Lunkhead had gone white as milk as Robin's voice cut him to the bone. When the monologue finished, the man just slumped to the ground, like a puppet whose strings had been sliced through with a razor.

Robin stared at the man for a moment, not knowing if he was dead or merely catatonic. Then he shook himself. If he wanted to stay alive, he needed to move. This world was more violent than the one he was used to.

It was also more magical. That magic was as terrible as it was wondrous was something to process when he wasn't in mortal danger.

Still, he resolved to learn that [Sleep] spell as soon as he completed his quest. Or find a way to make [Command Attention] work during combat. Or pick up some other hypnotic or enchanting ability. His lack of nonlethal options was going to become a problem. If all you had was a hammer, every problem started to look like a nail in a coffin.

Robin changed his face and his clothes, and slipped off to meet Lantha and the others at their agreed rendezvous.

* * *

Robin slipped quietly into the Sisters Sharp's camp outside of Bordertown. It was not the same one he'd tracked down when he'd first caught up to them. Ora-Jean liked to move around every so often to minimize impact on the land and to make it harder to track them in case Basgar and Gis came looking.

He rolled his shoulder. It was still stiff, painful, but he didn't think there was any serious damage. He'd used some healing magic—the last of his spell points—to improve matters.

He'd have Fiamah look at it, though, just in case.

There was a small, cheery fire in a pit-and-stone arrangement designed to minimize smoke. The Sisters Sharp were sitting around the fire, drinking and laughing quietly.

"Grab a seat," Grathilde indicated, gesturing with her bottle of beer.

"We did good work today," Lantha said. "I see you made it out alright."

"It was a bit touch and go there for a moment," Robin replied, mustering an echo of his usual cheeky grin.

"Then sit! Sit!" Ora-Jean gestured.

"Indeed," Fiamah agreed, eyeing his shoulder as if she could see through the layers of cloth and illusion to the injury beneath. "Rest and heal."

Lantha passed him a drink.

"It's time we celebrate!"

Chapter 14

*T*he feel of the bass line thrummed lightly through Robin's body as he performed on the stage of the Bell and Boar. He'd spent the past few nights practicing and translating some lyrics into the local language, with **[Tongue of the Fallen Tower]** doing a lot of the heavy lifting. Those words rolled around Robin now, enhanced by his constant use of **[Lesser Phantasm]**. Honestly, a higher-level version of the spell could not come soon enough.

He sang of champions in an achingly beautiful belt, with operatic tones and utterly Queenly power.

The whole tavern was singing along. That was one great thing about rock: it usually had a chorus people could grab on to and sing to quick. And this was one of the greatest examples Robin could think of.

He sang of keeping on fighting . . . till the end.

It fit the mood; it fit the circumstances. And could you ever truly go wrong with an overwrought, operatic rock number? No. No, you couldn't.

And it didn't hurt that Robin had such a wealth of remembered material—time tested, beloved, and entirely fresh to this world—to draw on to complete his introductory bard quest.

Sing, for we're the champions!

Robin had been performing for nearly an hour. His throat was raw, and his hands were in absolute agony from the constant spellcasting. However, he was determined to seize this chance. It wasn't every day you got a free venue, a crowd as warm and cheerful as this lot were (thanks to their recent success against Basgar's warehouses), and the added lubrication of several pints of the Bell and Boar's best drink passed about. With the deck stacked in his favor like that, he'd be hard pressed to lose.

Unless someone else upstaged him.

Robin caught sight of Lena entering the tavern.

Oh no. Not this time.

The song reached its crescendo, and Robin quickly discarded the next two songs he'd intended to play. He'd go straight for the finale, end everything on a high note before Lena had the chance to upstage him or undermine his grip on the audience.

He'd have to nail this final number. The original plan had had two more songs to build to the climax, but fuck it. He could do this!

"Thank you! Thank you, Bell and Boar! I am Marq, and I have one last song for you tonight! Are you ready?"

The crowd cheered.

"I said, *are you ready?!*"

The crowd cheered again, louder.

"Alright! Let's go! Hold on to your butts, because shiz is about to get epic!"

Robin sent a *thrum* of sound through the room, shocking most people into silence. *There.*

Into that silent sea he poured the first few notes, multiple voices in tense harmony, like a bow across violin strings.

A rhapsodic, bohemian sound. Is it life? Or is it just fantasy?

Robin conjured faint flickers of light behind him, hints of aurora matching the delicate piano notes flitting gently around the room like sparrows before the dawn.

This was not an easy transition. They had been riding high. Most of them were drunk. It took all of Robin's attention to keep the complex music going while also using ethereal patterns conjured by [Visual Phantasm] to keep everyone hooked.

He could feel his mind burning behind his eyes. Robin was certain that had he not chosen the Bard profession, he wouldn't have had a snowball's chance in Vesuvius of pulling this off. As it was, he just grabbed the wave of magic and rode it for all he was worth.

Rode it any way the wind blew. It didn't really matter.

Robin began conjuring up ghostly scenes in the space behind him, acting out snippets of scenes that resonated with the lyrics. Haunting visuals to match haunting memories and haunting words.

The crowd was shuffling, uncertain. They didn't really know what to make of this strange style of music. The upbeat stuff had been fun and easy, sure, but this? What even was this?

Robin punched the next line, one they could relate to, before he lost them.

He sang to his mother of a man he killed dead. Had to change the mention of the gun to a blade, though. Fucking fuck, were these lyrics extra.

The memory of Lunkhead flashed before his eyes and threatened to shatter his concentration. Robin shoved the specter to the back of his mind, tied it to his intent, and focused on the words. If he was going to have inconvenient memories, they could damn well serve the performance!

The performance was all!

And if the man who died in the phantom scenes behind him wore Lunkhead's face, well, who would even notice, except for Robin? He left it as a silent memorial.

The stakes right now were too high to get distracted.

Robin grabbed his messy feelings and yanked out a single strand to focus on. The one that resonated most with the lyric he was about to sing.

He didn't want to die.

There. He'd made it through. Robin shoved the memory of Lunkhead back into a dark corner of his mind and slammed a door on it.

Time to kick things into a higher gear. To take that musical bridge and cross it to whole new levels of energy, and hopefully, acclaim!

Robin poured the last of his energy reserves into this song. If he could have channeled his spell points into his performance, he would have. As it was, he was fully determined to have nothing left in the tank after he nailed that final note.

He amped up the tempo as the drums came rolling in around him. *Yes! Feel that energy!* It was coruscating throughout the room now. His audience was spellbound, and Robin took their attention and tied it firmly to him with the next set of lyrics, ones they were sure to respond to.

He sang of stoning and the bastard that spat in his eye.

The audience roared at that. People were drinking, moving to the music! Robin had them!

He tweaked the next lyric to reinforce that righteous fury against Basgar and Gis. He was building on what had happened and stoking the fires of what would come next. This resistance was only getting started!

Robin sang out a question to the audience, called them to answer if they'd dare rob someone and leave them to die.

"No!" the audience roared in response.

He had them now! Time to hit that last high-energy peak!

The song was a cry of defiance. Robin conjured flickers of men who looked suspiciously like Basgar and Gis being driven before a righteous mob. The words to the song still worked, but the meaning was tweaked a little. It became a clarion cry of resistance, and a promise to drive the petty tyrants from within these walls.

> *Can't do this to me no-way*

> *Can't do this to me no-way*

Robin relaxed fractionally. That was it. That was the high-energy peak. Now he had to navigate down to the haunting end and refrain. It wouldn't be any less tricky, but he could let himself breathe, just a touch.

He called in the energies he had stoked so high, channeling them into a refrain, forging them into a promise. It didn't make sense. It didn't have to. The song itself barely made any. It was a construct of raw emotion. That's what he was playing as much as anything.

That and the crowd. They were his instrument, and this was his true and proper debut performance.

It felt *right*.

Robin let that last note slowly die off into silence. The quiet held for a long moment, then the place erupted into applause and cheers!

"Thank you, Bell and Boar! I have been Marq! Good night!"

If Robin had had a mic, he would've dropped it. As it was, he settled for a flash of colored smoke via **[Visual Phantasm]** and a quick exit off the back of the stage and into the shadows.

He received the notification he had been waiting for moments later.

Quest Complete! [Seize the Spotlight!]

Congratulations! You have taken the first step on your journey as a bard! You have wowed an audience and begun to garner a bit of a name for yourself!

Reward(s): *The title of Full Bard; remaining introductory profession options are now available; an increase in notoriety (Fame). Remember, Fame is linked to your performance persona, and you only benefit from it when you are recognizable.*

He slumped down into a seat, an anonymous face covering his real features. He'd done it. He'd seized the spotlight. But now, someone else could take center stage for a few minutes. He needed a little time to recover!

Robin was about to dive into his interface and choose the rest of his bardic-level benefits when Lena caught his eye. He'd forgotten about her in the frenzy of his performance, but now she stood, quietly, moving slowly through the carousing rebels.

There was something predatory in the way she moved.

A slow chill traced its way down Robin's back. She hadn't tried to take the stage; not when he was performing nor now that it was vacant. Something about that wasn't right. Something about that didn't fit at all with what he knew of the other bard.

If she wasn't on that stage, it was only because she had something more important to do. But what could that be, here, in the one place where almost the entire leadership of the newly forged resistance of Bordertown was gathered to celebrate their first victory?

No. Robin told himself he was being paranoid. People here knew Lena.

But there were shapeshifters about. He knew that much. And magic could do all manner of odd things.

All he knew was she wasn't acting the way he would expect her to act.

Robin closed his interface. He could make those choices after he'd investigated what was up with Lena. If it was just his paranoia, the only thing he lost was a bit of time, and possibly some face if he embarrassed himself with the other bard.

If he was right, though, and something was going on . . .

He rose, keeping his anonymous face for now, and started treading his way through the crowd toward Lena. He passed Grathilde, pausing long enough to cast an illusion in front of her nose.

Something up. Alert Lantha. Beware.

Then he continued heading toward Lena, trusting Grathilde would take care of it. He was nearly to Lena when the door to the tavern opened.

Slammed open, in fact.

Robin froze. Striding through that door was a troop of guards led by Gis and a man he could only assume was Basgar the Blinder. The man had the supreme lack of grace to be decked head to toe in armor with a stylized eye motif repeating all over it.

The entire tavern hung suspended in time. The resistance was drunk, in the midst of a celebration. It took time for muddled brains to begin to transition to this new and incredibly dangerous reality. Robin saw Lantha begin to move out of the corner of his eye.

Before anything could happen, however, Basgar and Gis sprang into action. The guards began spreading throughout the room, weapons drawn. The tyrant leered in the firelight, a demonic smile on his face.

"Call the targets!" Basgar barked out over the stunned crowd.

"There. There, and there." Lena leapt on a nearby table and pointed out the leaders to Gis and Basgar.

"Thank you, my special agent." Gis smiled cadaverously. "Worth every clipped copper cent."

Lena was the agent provocateur?! No wonder everyone had been at each other's throats for so long! She was always in the center of everything, coming and going, and had the social skills to subtly influence just about anybody.

Wait, then what had been the deal with Cor'Leon? Alliance? Illusion? Shapeshifting?

Did it matter?

"Capture the leaders. Kill the rest," Basgar ordered.

No. Not right now it fucking didn't!

Chapter 15

Robin dodged flying splinters as a nearby patron smashed a chair over the head of a guard. The tavern was in a full-on melee. Basgar's men had blocked the windows and doors, but the rebels had mounted a stiff resistance, and Basgar and Gis were struggling to get enough men into the actual space to effectively subdue it.

Avanus had shouted something that sounded like a standing order, and people had started rushing to turn tables and chairs into a barricade across the main doors that the tyrant's forces were using to gain entry to the Bell and Boar. The rebels certainly seemed organized.

Robin crouched down next to the fireplace, taking partial cover behind the old stones. Keeping one eye on the action, he willed open his interface and quickly made the selections he'd been thinking about since he'd first discovered he'd have to wait to make all of his level choices. One of these new abilities might make all the difference.

A dagger slammed into the wall next to his ear with a *thunk*.

If he lived long enough to make use of them, that is.

Robin quickly selected **[Minor Enchanted Slumber]** for his remaining Tier One spell. An **[Invisible Servant]**, tempting as it was, was unlikely to be much use in this melee. He had two remaining cantrip slots open, and he quickly filled them with **[Minor Repair]** and **[Lesser Charm]**. He might need to talk his way past some angry guards soon, and he wanted all the boost he could get.

His progress had budged him into Tier One proper, and his completion of the quest had unlocked another peculiarity slot. Robin quickly filled it with [Initiate of the Craft], an option made available by his extensive real-world knowledge of witchcraft and pagan practices. Here, that translated to an extra Tier One spell and two more cantrips: [Familiar Bond], [Lesser Nightmare Curse], and [Lesser Witch Bolt], respectively.

Robin slammed his interface closed as a chair sailed over his head to crash against the wall. He rolled out of the way just in time and flung a [Lesser Nightmare Curse] at the nearest guard.

The man gaped as a flash of nameless, shapeless fear froze his gullet. That moment of horror would stick with him for several seconds and make it much harder to resist the next negative effect he encountered in that timeframe.

So Robin followed it up with [Cutting Words].

"Is your sword as dull as your wits or do you just not know how to use a whetstone?"

The guard purpled with rage and dropped like a stone.

"Robin!" Lantha shouted from a half-dozen paces away. "Get over here!"

He stepped into the melee. The fighting was fierce, though the rebels were holding their own—they had the defensive advantage for now. That would change as the fight dragged on and the tyrant's forces were able to replenish themselves from outside, while the defenders remained pinned down.

Robin noticed Avanus laying about himself with a broken bottle, occasionally sending bolts of purple-black energy lancing out to strike the guards. The warlock was directing a group of rebels trying to retake a section of wall near the bar which the guards had seized early on in their attack. Robin had no idea why the warlock wanted it back so badly. Maybe a hidden escape route?

He saw Prorna working with Brawnhilde and a militia group, absolutely hammering a group of guardsmen. Guilera, the merchant leader, stood at the back of the room flanked by two bodyguards, not doing battle directly, but she'd opened her pack and was passing out weapons and supplies to the other rebels. And Ora-Jean!

Sulara and a couple of her gang kids were running those supplies to the men manning the makeshift barricades, while Dahn, Cor'Leon's replacement, was shouting hair-raising threats to motivate the defenders at the barricade. It was unclear if several of the men near him were more afraid of the guards or more afraid of their leader.

Robin conjured playing cards and sailed them through the gaps in the barricade to force the attackers to flinch. He was tempted to experiment with [Lesser Witch Bolt], but the description mentioned "otherworldly fire," and he didn't want to risk setting one. The last thing they needed as part of this fight was an inferno to deal with as well.

He dodged a blade thrust through the barricade and ducked down behind the upturned table next to Lantha. The rogue was absently stabbing through the barrier whenever an attacker got careless, but her main attention was on the overall battle.

"They're doing well, aren't they?" she observed as Robin arrived.

"Who?"

"The rebels and their leaders. Well coordinated. Had a plan in case something like this happened. Avanus made sure there were additional ways out that only he knew about. He didn't even tell us. Smart."

"Is that why he's so interested in retaking the bar?"

"Yes. Though the escape tunnel runs the length of the tavern."

"That won't help if we can't chop through several feet of oak floorboards and foundation beams," Grathilde snapped from the other side of the elf, where the aeromancer was flicking sparks at the attackers.

"Ora-Jean is solving that problem as we speak." Lantha glanced across the room. "And Fiamah has her back. They'll be in position soon. Robin, we're going to need the mother of all distractions soon. Think you can cook something up?"

"Ah, of course, but what am I distracting people from? That's kind of a key bit of need-to-know knowledge. You can't trick someone into looking away from something important if you don't know *where* you want the mark to look away *from*." Robin winced as an axe blade buried itself in the table he was crouching behind.

"We've figured out a way to get everyone into the escape tunnel beneath the tavern, but it'll take time to get most of our people out, and we need Basgar and Gis distracted so they don't interfere. It'll be a fighting retreat no matter how we do it, but the bigger the head start we can manage, the better."

"Yes, I figured out that much." Robin gestured. "Just tell me what and where so I can do my thing! There's a battle happening, in case you hadn't noticed!"

"Oh? Is there?" Lantha casually stabbed a woman through the hand. The guard had gotten too close to a gap in the barrier. "Guilera has a couple of bottled holes. We're going to use them to make a temporary hole in the floor, rush our people out, then defend until the magic wears off and the floor reappears, covering our retreat. We need that point there out of sight"—she pointed—"or Basgar and Gis looking so far away they don't notice we're leaving until it's too late. Got it?"

"Got it." Robin knew he'd be one of the last—if not the last one—out, so he checked alternate escape routes before picking the best spot from which to conduct his distraction. "Give me a couple of minutes to get something set up. Your signal will be . . . I dunno, something blue."

Robin thought furiously. Obviously, he could block line of sight with an illusion, but if it was discovered too soon, it would be easy for the guards to test it repeatedly and see through it. So he needed a distraction and an illusion.

"I don't suppose you have some smoke bombs?" he asked the rogue.

"They're coming out of your cut," Lantha replied as she passed him two.

"Gotcha." Robin pocketed the incendiaries carefully.

Why he bothered to be careful, he wasn't certain. He was about to do something titanically stupid anyway.

If Lantha wanted Basgar and Gis looking away from the center of the room, the best place to focus their attention was in their own midst. Thankfully, he had a ready-made conversation piece right there: Lena.

Robin glanced through the barricade. There. That spot would do.

He invoked [**Visual Phantasm**] and began working his hands through the gestures of [**Lesser Phantasm**]. An illusion of his Marq persona appeared with a flamboyant gesture and a loud *crack*.

"Basgar! Gis! You old devils! How dare you drop by without letting us know you were coming! If you had, we would have prepared you a much warmer welcome!" Marq smiled, napalm glimmering in his eyes. "And Lena! Naughty girl! You knew and didn't tell any of us?"

Three daggers, two swords, and an axe all phased right through him, thunking into the barricade behind.

"Well, that's hardly polite," Marq sniffed.

"It's an illusion, you idiots!" Basgar snapped.

"Exactly right, Bassy old bean!" Obnoxiously posh would probably annoy the pants off the tyrant, so Robin went with that. "That one knew!" The illusion pointed at Lena. "You'd best watch her! And your pockets! She'll bleed you dry."

Now to see just how far they trusted her.

"Which we appreciate, of course." Marq smiled broadly. "Thank you ever so much for your generous donations to the cause, Lena!"

Judging by the way Basgar and Gis immediately turned to glare suspiciously at Lena, they trusted her about as far as Robin could chuck the keep.

"He's obviously lying!" she snapped.

"Careful," Marq called. "She blows a lot of smoke!"

The illusion snapped its fingers, and Robin used [Lesser Phantasm] to conjure a brief, bright blue plume of smoke around Lena.

Gis and Basgar immediately drew back and pointed their weapons at the other bard. Lena hissed in annoyance and blurred herself in defense. It was clear neither side trusted the other over there.

Robin popped the top off the first smoke bomb and rolled it through a gap in the barrier. Soon, gray-blue smoke started filling the air around the tyrant's position.

"I told you!" Lena shouted.

Robin let Marq vanish in the confusion. Instead, he used his illusions to conjure the sound of more smoke bombs hissing and a cloud of the stuff, which swiftly expanded to cut off the back of the tavern from view.

The invaders were coughing on the smoke from the real bomb and not questioning the appearance of more. If they didn't question it, they wouldn't see through the illusion.

Behind him, Robin could hear Lantha calling out quietly. He risked a glance.

There was a massive hole in the center of the floor that hadn't been there a minute ago. As he watched, Prorna jumped nimbly down, followed swiftly by Guilera, who was lowered gently down by her bodyguards.

The escape was well underway. Robin and those stationed at the barricade just needed to keep Basgar and his bullyboys busy long enough for everyone to get out, then they could withdraw themselves.

Hopefully before that hole closed magically on its own.

And now that Basgar was hidden from view from most of his troops by that very real smoke screen, it was time to sow a little more chaos. Robin twisted his hands through [Lesser Phantasm] once more, this time tuning it to match Basgar's voice and delivery.

"Fall back! Get out of the smoke! Out of the tavern! Secure the perimeter instead!"

And the thing was, tyrants instilled blind loyalty in those who survived their service. Most of Basgar's men, hearing that order, in that voice, immediately began to pull back. Those who didn't were almost immediately overwhelmed by the remaining rebels on the barrier and cut down.

The command really should have established some form of code word system. They had to know they were going up against an illusionist, right? Gis certainly should have known better.

But Gis clearly wasn't giving the orders.

"Get me an aeromancer!" Basgar roared. "Clear out this smoke!"

At least he didn't order an immediate return to attacking the barricade. Robin grinned. Arrogant, that's what he was. Assuming he controlled the whole of the battlefield.

Robin jerked his chin at the rebels left manning the barrier. The rest of the tavern was nearly empty; they might as well retreat now and slip through the hole while Basgar was waiting on his aeromancer. Robin could bring up the rear and make sure to keep the exit covered with illusions.

Any luck, and they'd all be out and the hole gone before Basgar and his men could charge forward and figure out what had happened.

Chapter 16

$\mathcal{T}$he stone behind Robin's back was cold and hard, but the fire in front of him was cheery and warm. Porridge sat in bowls, ready to be eaten. Robin and the Sisters Sharp were once again holed up in their camp outside Bordertown.

The atmosphere was all over convivial. Though Basgar and Gis had struck at the rebels during their celebration, none of the leaders had been taken, and while there'd been some casualties, Basgar and Gis had lost far more than their opponents.

"You don't think they'll shut the town down, try to impose some sort of martial law?" Grathilde was asking Lantha.

"No. They can't afford to." Lantha sounded smug. "Basgar and Gis have too tenuous a grip as it is. Not only will they be afraid they'll be sending even more people into the arms of the resistance, but they'll be afraid of insulting the merchant lords of the Gilded Lands. They need those funds to help drive their war against the marcher lords. For now."

"So they'll keep the gates open and trade flowing."

"They'll be checking everyone closely, I should expect," Fiamah added.

"They were before, anyway," Ora-Jean complained. "That's why we've dillydallied here for as long as we have." She shot a glance at Lantha. "No longer, though, I'm guessing."

"No," the rogue agreed. "We don't need to cool our heels any longer. We've set Basgar and Gis up with quite a bit of trouble to keep themselves occupied with. We should be moving on to Noviel. There are reports to make."

Robin knew better than to expect she'd mention to whom.

"So I expect we'll be needing one more diversion, just to make sure we slip through that northern gate with a minimum of trouble," he said instead.

"You expect right," Lantha replied with a smile. "Think you can manage?"

"Oh, definitely." Robin cocked his head. "Are you sure that Basgar and Gis won't just crush Avanus and his friends as soon as we're gone, though?"

"Quite certain," Lantha spoke firmly. "You saw what happened last night. Surprise attack, and they not only had a plan but a plan they didn't let us in on? And they all held their own in the fight, as well as escaped with minimal losses. No. They don't need us. Things will be well in hand here."

"I suppose you're right," Robin said, reaching for his share of the porridge.

"She usually is," Grathilde grumbled.

"So we push on to Noviel?" Ora-Jean asked in between bites of porridge and significant glances at Robin to make sure he kept using his powers to make the stuff taste delicious.

"We do," Lantha confirmed. "Basgar is currently preoccupied, and his troubles will only increase with the little problems we seeded throughout town. Now's the time to make our escape."

"We still need a diversion," Robin reminded them. "To cover our progress, sure, but also to hit Gis one last time. I think we still owe him and that little snake of his a bad turn after all they put us through beneath the mountain."

There were general murmurs of agreement.

"I could desecrate his temple?" Robin suggested, his mind going back to all the construction, the priest's quarters, and the mysteries he'd only sort of rifled through in that chest.

"Personal to Gis, but also likely to draw Urkhan's direct wrath. Probably not an effective enough target to distract the guards at the northern gate," Lantha said.

Fiamah looked torn between approval and outrage at the idea.

"We've already hit their supply stockpiles, so we can't hit those again," Ora-Jean pointed out. "And we don't really have the bodies or magic for a direct assault on the keep. Attacking their morale won't work as a diversion, so what does that leave?"

"Assassination attempt," Grathilde offered.

"Rob the treasury," Robin spoke at the same time.

"Neither of those are easy," Fiamah noted.

"Which is why we don't actually go through with it," Robin countered. "We don't need to succeed. In fact, we *want* them to get wind of things. If they're running off after the valuables in the safe, they're not watching the back door for someone leaving through it. They're afraid of what's coming in, not what's getting out."

"Robbing the treasury is probably easier," Grathilde admitted grudgingly. "We know its general location, and they'd call in a lot of guards to protect it. If we took a shot at killing Basgar . . . eh, he's too mobile, and the focus would be on concealing him or defending him. That wouldn't need as many guards."

"Exactly." Robin grinned. "Hit someone in the purse and he *feels* it. We already know Basgar is desperate for funds. Look at how he interacts with the merchants of the Gilded Lands. And we've already started messing with—"

Robin went quiet at a glance from Lantha. *Right. Don't brag about plans. There are people who can pluck words out of the air and scrying mirrors and who knows what else.*

If they wanted all of their little surprises for Basgar to actually be surprises, it was better to avoid mentioning them.

"So we have to figure out how to rob the treasury. In one of the most secure fortresses in the land." Fiamah looked profoundly skeptical. Or possibly disapproving. "This doesn't seem like a wise course of action."

"If we were actually going to try and rob it, no, it wouldn't be," Robin agreed. "But we're not. We're just going to convince them that we are, and that we have everything we need to do it."

"And I suppose you have an idea on how to accomplish that, do you?"

"Oh yes." Robin grinned. "A certain watch captain is going to get a visit from an old friend bearing the news. If you four go and spread some rumors, make some purchases . . . then yes, I think we can heighten the tension to the point where they'll be on a hair trigger. Then it's just a matter of making it look good and skipping out the gate while the guards run toward the treasury."

"What if they don't?" Grathilde asked pessimistically.

"Basgar will be forced to strip the guardhouses to a skeleton crew," Lantha answered. "He can't risk his wealth, and we've proven a credible threat already."

"Credible? We're getting downright incredible with this one!" Robin cackled.

* * *

"I will investigate these accusations you've brought me and consider taking your information to Lords Basgar and Gis *if* I can find persuasive evidence that you are actually correct this time." The watch captain was an insufferably smug jerk.

Robin was on the top floor of a brothel. Again. This time, however, he was firmly wrapped in an imitation of the disguise he'd seen Lena wear last time he'd been here. He'd just finished feeding the captain a mix of speculation and hearsay sprinkled with just enough information for the man to connect the dots between what he'd been told and the various rumors the Sisters Sharp were sowing.

The watch captain rose, and Robin mirrored the action. They were done here anyway, and his hands were getting tired from the constant [**Lesser Phantasm**] spells.

Robin waited until he was several streets away and safely hidden in an alleyway before he dropped the illusory disguise for his generic townsperson form.

He nearly jumped out of his fake skin when a voice broke the quiet around him.

"Well, that was certainly informative."

Lena appeared out of nowhere. The other bard smirked at his reaction but held up two hands, forestalling any violence.

"Now, now, no need to get feisty! I'm here under a flag of truce."

"You'll pardon my skepticism after your little display at the Bell and Boar," Robin said, senses flaring, looking for an ambush, but his curiosity kept him where he was, listening.

"Well, I sold out the ones I was paid to sell out, and you lit a fire of suspicion under Basgar and Gis that I haven't been able to fully smother, so we're a little bit even, right?" Lena smiled winningly.

"Not even close. What do you want?"

"So suspicious! No need for that! We're both professionals here. Can't I just be extending a hand in friendship? Expressing admiration for the skill of . . . well, let's just say a colleague."

"I've met some of your friends. I can see how you'd be in the market for some new ones." Robin jerked his head, indicating the watch captain. "That guy took an indecent amount of pleasure in your recent difficulties."

Lena made an indelicate noise.

"He's always been a stuffed shirt and an idiot, even when we were children."

"So you really did grow up here." Robin was a tad surprised.

"So how could I betray my home?" Lena threw back an arm dramatically. "Please. This place changes hands once or twice a generation; it's too ripe a plum. Prorna may be sweet, but her lot had their issues."

Robin didn't probe. Politics were neither here nor there. What was important was escaping with his life and sanity, followed by finding out what Lena wanted. A distant third was using this interaction to enhance the treasury theft distraction plan.

"Now, there *may* be one little thing you could do for me, if you were so inclined," Lena continued.

Here it is.

"You know who I am and who I've been working for," Lena began. "But we don't know who *you're* working for. Gis thinks it's Noviel, based on the company you keep, but his auguries say different. If you give me a name, I could trade you some very useful information in return. I collect quite a lot from my various, ah . . . *contracts*, if you're not interested in anything I might know about Lord Basgar's plans."

An information trade. Interesting. The old question game again.

Not that he had time to play.

"I know you're up to something." Lena tried a different tack. "I've been watching your friends. Arranging transport out of each of the three gates, purchasing more potions like the one I suspect your group used to escape the Bell and Boar—that was clever, by the way. Basgar nearly split Gis in half after that."

"I would have paid to see that," Robin said with a bit too much emotion.

"So you have a personal reason to dislike the priest," Lena pounced. "Interesting."

"Anyone who has met the man or the snake that lives in his skull has reason to dislike him," Robin shot back.

"Fair point." Lena shuddered. "I've never seen it myself, but one does hear things."

"No way a guy like Gis can keep it socked," Robin agreed. "He's the sort who just has to whip it out at the slightest provocation. Rude."

"So for you it's more about Gis, and for your friends it's more about Basgar, isn't it?"

Lena was far too sharp for Robin's own good.

"What can I say? I take it personally when a guy infringes on my rights and freedoms."

"So you're going to hit him where it hurts."

"I am," Robin confirmed. This line of questioning was fine. This reinforced the plan and directed attention away from his origins and motivations.

"As I told your friend back there, there's a lot of stuff going on right now. A lot of places where Basgar and Gis could get their fingers snapped at if they don't watch where they're putting those grubby mitts of theirs."

"I wouldn't get overconfident if I were you," Lena warned. "Lord Basgar has quite the suite of supporters. You and your friends have been lucky so far, but . . ."

Lena let the sentence trail off suggestively. She was trying to bait him with information again. Robin didn't have time for this, and the possible payout wasn't worth the risk.

Not right now.

"Tell you what," he said. "I'll answer one question of yours, truthfully and to the best of my capabilities, if you give me your word that you'll keep your nose out of the next matter I ask you to."

"Deal," Lena accepted. "What one thing do you want more than any other?"

"Magic," Robin replied instantly. That was easy. He'd been chasing it his whole life on Earth, and now that he was here? A place with magic in abundance?

He wanted as much as he could get his hands on.

If Lena took that to mean power, *eh*, that was her problem. Their deal had been struck, and Robin had other errands to run.

It was a lot of work faking a major heist!

Chapter 17

*Y*ou did *what?*"

Lantha's tone was disbelieving. Robin didn't know what the problem was; he'd improved upon the plan, if anything!

"I recruited a few of Dahn's folk to help with the job," he repeated.

"But there is *no* job. It's a fake job. What if they get caught?" Ora-Jean butted in. "Dahn won't thank you for going and getting a bunch of his people caught."

"They won't get caught!" Robin protested. "And for all they know, they're providing some cover, is all! I drilled them on the signals and everything! We have to make it look believable, right? We do want the guard to go rushing off to defend the treasury?"

"Yes, but—"

Robin didn't let Lantha finish.

"But nothing. These folk know what they're about. I gave them extra supplies to help them escape—out of my own pocket," he added, shaking a finger in Grathilde's face.

"Fine," Lantha said, surrendering. "Your money, your choice, but—"

"If it blows up in our faces, it's my hide as well. Yeah, yeah. I understand the risks." Robin flashed Lantha a cheeky grin. "I'd say trust me, but I know you wouldn't even trust your own mother, so I'll save my breath."

"It does let us stay closer to the gate," Fiamah observed.

"*If* Dahn's folk can be relied upon," Grathilde grumbled.

"They can be relied upon to want the money and the chance to tweak Basgar's nose," Robin said. "That's a better guarantee than you'll get from most people you can hire."

"Right. Plan," Lantha cut through the chatter. "Robin is in charge of the distraction. Grathilde coordinates the attack from the southwest; Ora-Jean the one from the southeast; Fiamah will handle the northern side. I'm keeping an eye on the gate and how many guards are posted there."

"And if they just shut the gate down during the attack, stop traffic? What then?" Grathilde asked.

"Then we go with plan B." Lantha was firm.

"I hate plan B," Grathilde muttered.

"I think it's kind of a fun idea," Robin cut in with a grin.

"You would."

"Enough! Focus. We need to coordinate from the town clock. When that bell rings, we go. Bottled holes from the sewers up into the lower levels of the keep. You'll be in charge of coordinating a team—"

"Each of whom have their own agenda," Grathilde objected.

"How else did you expect me to get them on board? Besides, more pain for Basgar and Gis if they succeed!" Robin wasn't having any of Grathilde's naysaying at this point.

"Get in, cause trouble, get the guards to chase you, then get out and go to the gate. We got it." Ora-Jean ran a whetstone along the blade of her axe.

"Right." Lantha looked at them all. "Let's go! I'll see you all at the northern gate, gods willing."

It had started out well enough. The teams snuck into the keep for their bold-as-brass daylight robbery. Honestly, it was a ludicrous plan, but the sheer audacity was certainly going to surprise them. And it was guaranteed to provoke a response.

Added benefit? It was such an insane plan that, even if it failed, people would be talking and gossiping about it for days. And then Basgar would be known as the tyrant so inept that the people he was trying to oppress were brave enough to try and rob him in broad daylight.

It was always nice to fit in these little side benefits when one could.

Robin made a mental note to rewrite the lyrics to some of the catchier songs in his memory and spread them around to mock Basgar, Gis, and Urkhan. That would have to wait, however.

Right now, things were going pear-shaped.

None of the guards were being pulled away from any of the guard posts. Those at the keep were just trying to chase down the invaders on their own. They clearly didn't feel enough of a threat, even with Robin's added recruits.

He could forge the orders, but he had no way to personally run them to each of the guardhouses. Could he just trick the northern gatehouse? No. That would make things too obvious and risk Gis or Basgar refocusing their forces exactly where he and the Sisters Sharp *didn't* want them.

He'd have to get in there, forge the orders, impersonate the right guard, and send for the reinforcements himself.

Now would be a great time to have some of Grathilde's powers, Robin reflected, looking down from his rooftop perch. *Ah, well. Nothing for it but to get the lead out.*

Robin quickly pulled out his stash of parchment and ink from the storage ring and used a combination of his proficiencies and his perks to forge some orders. They should hold up to most inspections, particularly if he did his job well enough and instilled the right level of panic in his messengers.

Now, the approach. The uniform was easy enough. Robin willed the change through his **[Mask of Disguise]**, keeping his face generic, forgettable. People would see the uniform more than the face anyway.

After a moment's thought, he tore the uniform up a bit, added some artistic scuffs, and a bit of blood. As an afterthought, he placed a touch of blood at the corner of his mouth as well.

A plan had formed in his mind. He'd need to sprint around the keep to do it, but better around the keep than to each and every gate itself. He mentally checked his map to plot his course and give him the best chance at these forged orders reaching the three gates near simultaneously.

Robin had decided to make himself look like a messenger sent for reinforcements. He'd play the part of nearly beaten to death by rebels, and impress on some likely target that they needed to take up his vital mission. With *Deception*, plenty of reason for his target not to question him, and a layer of protection in case someone decided to poke at him with divination magics, he was sure to succeed.

He found his first mark easily enough. There was enough chaos that squads had gotten broken up in the confusion, and guards had gone off chasing rebels in ones and twos. Robin found a likely young woman and played the wounded messenger for all he was worth.

He was afraid he'd overdone it, but she took the bait.

A quick dash around the outer wall and five nail-biting minutes of waiting later, he managed to pick out another target; this time, a young man. Robin gave a repeat performance with similar results.

One left.

Robin had managed to dispatch messages to both the southwestern and southeastern gatehouses. He was currently lingering near the northern side of the keep, tucked in an illusion, waiting for a likely prospect to happen by.

A group of three guardsmen rushed past. Too many. He needed a solo—*aha!*

An older woman in the uniform of a guard came into view.

There was no one else around. She seemed like the best option he was going to get, so Robin took it. He waited until she wasn't looking before stumbling out of hiding and dramatically staggering over to her.

"Ambush," he gasped. "Help!"

The woman immediately grabbed him to hold him up, hold him steady. So far, so good.

"They got my unit as well," she said. "The rebels are everywhere."

"Orders," Robin gasped. "Need . . . reinforcements from . . . the northern gate!"

"What?" The old woman looked at him suspiciously.

Oh *great. Of course* he'd find the one guard whom Basgar hadn't crushed all independent thought from. Hopefully, his *Expression* proficiency would be up to the acting requirements needed here.

Robin went with the interpretation that she just didn't understand. He pulled out the artfully crumpled orders he'd forged earlier and tried to press them into her hand.

"Take this . . . to the northern gate. I can't . . . go on."

She only went and bloody opened the thing to read it! What the cock was this? She shouldn't do that! *Ugh.* This was because his disguise didn't outrank her, wasn't it?

"Support from the northern gate," she muttered. "But Coulvis said we could handle this with the troops we had stationed nearby. Why would—"

Because things change! Robin wanted to scream at her. *No plan survives contact with the enemy and all that.*

She stood there, dithering. Robin forced himself to just hang, drooping and pathetic, from her frame. Okay, so maybe he relaxed his body into more of a deadweight than was strictly necessary for his ruse, but the woman was irritating him, and he couldn't think of a better way to get back at her.

"Quickly," he tried urging her.

Before she could respond, however, something even worse happened.

Gis appeared.

The priest strode around the corner, flanked by two guards. He was swearing and chanting, waving some kind of censer before him. The smoke curled in unnatural shapes and caused the hackles on the back of Robin's neck to rise.

"You!" Gis snapped at the woman. "What's the problem here?"

"Ambush, Your Excellency," she answered, snapping to attention.

Robin made a show of struggling to pull himself to attention as well. He didn't allow himself to succeed very well—he just couldn't bring himself to show that much deference to the cadaverous old man.

"No, that's not the problem." Gis consulted the smoke. "There's something else here."

"Orders, sir," Robin took a risk and spoke to Gis. "Need reinforcements. Too many rebels. I was taking them, but I got ambushed. I can't run. I was just passing them to her to deliver for me." He carefully didn't say *where* he wanted her to deliver them.

"Yes?" Gis's attention was still mainly on the smoke. "Well, what are you waiting for? There are orders. Carry them out. Go!"

"Yes, Your Excellency. Right away!" The woman blanched and bolted.

Robin bit back a smile. *Thank you, Gis.* Now he just had to make it out of the priest's presence without being detected and killed.

"I should . . . try to get back to the fighting." Robin decided putting on a brave face was the fastest way out of this.

"Good man." The guard next to Gis seemed to buy it, at least. "Go teach those idiots a lesson!"

Thankfully, Gis was so caught up in looking at the smoke pouring from the censer that he didn't bother to contradict the man.

Robin took the words as an order and as his opportunity to slip away.

Tendrils of the smoke flowed slowly, unnaturally, after him, but Robin was already gone. He limped off as fast as his act would allow, breaking into a run only when he was safely out of sight.

He stole away from the walls and back to a section of Bordertown where he could find easy roof access to see how well his little ruse had gone.

Robin was puffing by the time he'd climbed enough stairs to get a proper vantage point to check the progress of the plan. He squinted, heart hammering in his chest. What if the messages had gone astray? What if something had gone wrong?

Just then, he saw movement coming from the region of the southwestern gatehouse. Reinforcements! And there! From the southeast!

But the northern gate. That was the real question.

Robin stared, not seeing anything.

"Come on, come on," he muttered to himself.

Finally, after what seemed like years, his patience was rewarded with a flurry of activity.

"Yes! Result!" Robin took a moment to rejoice before hauling himself to his feet and forcing himself to run down the stairs and back through the streets, carefully avoiding those lanes that looked like they were providing thoroughfares for the reinforcements heading toward the treasury.

He had an appointment at the northern gate to keep!

Chapter 18

*T*he northernmost gate out of Bordertown was a simple affair, all clean lines and massive blocks of stone. The portcullis was a dull, gray metal that seemed to carry the weight of the mountains with it, and the chains that controlled access in and out of the keep glittered bright in the afternoon light.

It was also firmly *behind* them!

The plan had worked! Distraction, check. Forged paperwork, check. Out the gate with no one the wiser, che—hang on.

A lone figure appeared in the road in front of them.

Gis.

The priest looked hateful and haggard, and his hands were clenched tight around a scroll that crumbled to dust even as Robin watched. Without a pause, the priest drew another out of the case at his side.

"And just where do you think you're going?" Gloating was not a good color on Gis.

Then again, no color was a good color on that cadaverous old fiend.

"Home," Lantha said calmly. "Stand aside."

"I don't think so," Gis hissed.

No, wait. That was the snake. It slid out of the priest's eye socket, hissing threateningly.

Grathilde made vomiting sounds. Fiamah looked ill. Ora-Jean just pulled out her axe.

"You are going to pay for the trouble you've caused," Gis raged at them.

Yeah, no. They hadn't gotten this far only to have this wankstain pull up now and stop them. No matter how much heat he was probably packing in that scroll case.

"Fine," Robin said, stepping forward. "How much?"

"Wha-what?" Gis looked taken aback.

"You say we have to pay. I say fine. What would be equitable? Give me a figure. Hard coin. Information. Something to start negotiations off with."

Everyone just looked at him, stunned.

When in doubt, confuse them, apparently. Robin would have to remember the tactic for another time. For now, he sighed.

"Look, you don't want to see our faces any more than we want to see yours. So help us help you. Tell me what price our walking out of here might add up to. A new cart and horse? A bottle of nice, fizzy white wine? A new set of spikes for your iron maiden? What?"

"You—you will pay with your lives!"

"Seems pretty steep; not at all fair. I've got a better idea." Robin steam-rollered over the priest's protestations.

Even the snake looked bemused.

"How about I tell you what you can do, right now, to stop Basgar's temporary alliance with the merchant lords of the Gilded Lands from going up in so much smoke?"

"Robin!" Lantha snapped.

"I know what I'm doing," he snapped back, just under Gis's hearing. "Trust me."

"You're bluffing." Gis's words held a lot more conviction than his face did.

"Try me. I know you have a truth-sensing spell." Robin wiggled his fingers at the snake. "I've ssseen it in action."

The snake hissed spitefully.

He stuck out his tongue at it.

What? Like the little bastard hadn't been doing it to him all along? Rude.

"Enough!" Gis snapped.

"Not by half," Robin shot back. "Get off our backs, old man. I'm offering you a good deal. And you should know, it's time sensitive. Take too long, and it'll be far too late to salvage any goodwill you might have to the west of your borders. Goodwill you are in sore need of, for at least a little while longer, yes?"

"He ssspeaksss truth," the snake said grudgingly.

Gis's other eye widened.

"What have you done?" he demanded.

"Wouldn't you like to know?" Robin smirked. "I'll make it easy for you, though. Let us go—here, today—and I'll give you the information. No lies. No tricks. You can even come after us again later if you want. But I suspect you and Basgar will be pretty busy around here for the foreseeable future." Robin waggled his eyebrows at the priest. "Whaddaya say?"

Gis glowered at him.

"Tick tock," Robin said with a smile. "This offer won't last—can't last. There's very much an expiration date and time on this intelligence."

"I could torture it out of you," Gis threatened.

"Not before it was useless."

"Truth," the snake added.

Gis spat.

"What'll it be, Gissy? Tick tock. You can enact your revenge here, spells blazing, or you can swear upon Urkhan's might that you'll let us go today, and I'll tell you exactly where to go to stop a troubling little message from destroying your current alliance with the merchant lords."

Instead of answering directly, the priest muttered a spell. Robin guessed it was some kind of augury or request for guidance. Whatever it was, Gis was *not* happy with the answer.

"You have a deal," the priest ground out reluctantly.

"Swear it before Urkhan," Robin pressed. There were a lot of things the priest could do to get around giving his word, but breaking an oath sworn on his god was not one of them. Robin's [Bardic Lore] told him that.

"I swear before Urkhan," Gis said easily.

Robin gave him half an eye roll.

"Properly. Spell it out. Be specific. You should know better than to try that with me."

"I, Gis, swear upon Urkhan's might that if you give me the information I need to salvage Basgar's alliance with the merchant lords of the Gilded Lands, I will withdraw and take no action that could be considered harmful against you or your allies until tomorrow."

"Good enough!" Robin accepted cheerfully. "You'll want to teleport over to the home of Merchant Cal ven Diis and do your best to convince him you're not planning on drastically raising tariffs on imports and exports that pass through the keep starting with the next moon. He's *quite* upset about it, as the evidence I gave him quite handily proves you lied in the last negotiating session you had with him." Robin paused. "Well, he thinks it's the evidence Lena gave him, but never mind."

Gis gawked at him.

"That's all you need, old man. Off you fuck."

Robin made a small shooing motion with his hand.

"You will rue this day," the priest promised him darkly. "I will destroy you for this."

"But not today," Robin singsonged, a flash of defiance in his eye.

Gis extracted another scroll from the case at his side and invoked its power with a grimace. The priest had to be burning through a shocking amount of gold by using these resources. Unless Urkhan was far more generous than Robin gave the deity credit for.

Unlikely.

Robin was so caught up in his musings he didn't notice the hand headed for his head until it slapped him upside it.

"What was that?" Lantha demanded.

"Ow!" Robin rubbed his head dramatically. She hadn't hit him that hard, really. "I was getting rid of him. None of us really wanted a fight after we'd expended so many resources on that distraction."

"You gave him what he needed to preserve their alliance with the merchant lords." Lantha was not pleased.

"I helped him put out *one* fire; we started a lot more than that. I'd give a guess, but I know that you didn't tell me everything you did. Any of you." Robin jerked his chin at the Sisters Sharp. "And in a fight, there's always the chance something could go wrong. The last thing we need is to die in a stupid battle after we've already escaped. Who would carry word to Noviel if that happened?"

Lantha just grunted.

"That's her saying you're right," Ora-Jean offered. "And as close to an apology as you're ever likely to get. Don't mind her. Lantha is a perfectionist and hates to see any work go to waste."

"It's not really a waste if it saves our lives, or even saves us some serious injury," Grathilde pointed out.

They began walking as they argued. Robin didn't fully relax until the hills rose and the road turned enough to obscure the view of the keep in the background. Once it was out of sight, he felt his spine unknot.

Instead, he began to keep a lookout for a particular set of hills. He'd gotten a quest notification when he'd chosen his last peculiarity, and he wanted to complete it before they made their way down from the foothills and onto the plains. He'd just need a spare hour or two.

"I love this part of the country," Ora-Jean said. "The way the light hits the hills there and makes them all golden. There's a clarity to it you just don't see anywhere else."

"Especially in Noviel," Grathilde interjected sourly. "It has many virtues, but rustic beauty isn't one of them. And don't get me started on what a mess of architectural styles it is—"

"It's emblematic of the shared cultural heritage that formed the city," Fiamah objected. "It's really a rather beautiful testament to so many different peoples coming together and coexisting peacefully—"

"Ha!" Grathilde punctuated her interjection with a dismissive snap of her fingers. "Peaceful."

"Mostly peaceful," Fiamah amended. "And it's not like there's enough bad feeling to ever erupt into civil war or—"

"Just be aware Noviel talks a better game than it plays," Grathilde said. "And certain types get along better than others."

"What's that supposed to mean?"

"Oh, come off it! Noviel is run by a bunch of uptight traditionalists! Anyone who bucks what's expected of—"

Robin let their bickering fade off into a pleasant background susurration. He'd set foot in Noviel soon enough, and then he could form his own opinions of the place. For now, there were breathtaking hills and a certain location to be on the lookout for.

He had a familiar bond to establish before they left these mountains.

They were beautiful, these peaks, tall and sharp and shining with snow. In a very real way, they had birthed him into this world. He'd appeared deep within one of them—probably that massive frakker to the southwest—taken on a new shape, and eventually emerged from a dark tunnel into the light of a new world.

Robin committed the details of this place to memory, conjuring small illusions of the scenes he could see and several he could only remember. He had the inescapable sense that a chapter of his new life was ending, and he wanted to be sure he remembered as much as he could, though his new profession and other advantages meant he'd have a much better chance at it than in his previous life.

So yeah, a chapter was ending, but that also meant one was beginning. Robin had magic and was gaining more. Soon, he'd have a familiar and find his way to his first city in this new world, a place of knowledge and magic and likely danger and opportunity.

Party.

On to Noviel!

Epilogue

Meanwhile, deep beneath Noviel . . .

When he awoke, he didn't know who he was. He had a feeling that he should. That he'd had a name. Had had a voice. A body. That he had been . . . drinking? Whatever drinking was.

His mind was in fragments, shards, and when he put together that this consciousness that was him rested in a small, faceted jewel, he supposed that made sense.

Wait, why did he think of himself as a he? So far as he could tell, rocks— even sentient ones—didn't have a sex.

Though he supposed they could have genders; he certainly seemed to, anyway. Whether or not that was part of the fragmentary memories he had to sift through . . . well, he wasn't yet prepared to say.

He had a limited sense of the space around him. He could feel cold metal— various types and shapes—in pieces that were roughly the same size as he was, or a little larger or smaller. There were a few larger shapes as well, round and pointed and made of other, stranger things he couldn't quite identify.

Some half-forgotten part of him kept insisting that one over there was "leather," whatever that was. Gold, silver, and copper, those he could *feel,* and he was pleased once he remembered their names.

Most of the space he found himself in was lost in shadow, and his senses did not extend terribly far. It was strange, this sight, and not at all as he remembered it. Still, it was reassuring to have at least some percep-tion of his surroundings, even if his senses were behaving—to his mind, at least—strangely.

"Hello, young core."

A voice! An actual voice that produced actual sound! He felt it. He understood it. He tried to say something but failed.

Kind of hard to speak when you lacked a voice or vocal cords or any other equipment with which to do so.

"Send your thoughts to me. I will hear them." The voice sounded amused.

Hello?

"There you are. And here I am."

The shadows parted to reveal a winged woman fluttering before him. She was heart-stoppingly beautiful, with a wicked smile and rich amethyst eyes. Her wings were like the wings of a dragonfly, but tinted black and iridescent purple.

Who are you?

"You can call me Amaranthine. I'm your guide, young core."

Is Core *my name?*

"No. Core is your kind. Your name you will have to decide for yourself, if you cannot remember. I am told many in your situation do not."

My situation?

"You are a rare and precious being, my friend." Amaranthine pulled her legs up to sit in midair, wings still working. "You are the core—the center—of a living dungeon. As you grow, you'll gain wondrous powers to shape the world around you. I'm here to help you learn."

Who sent you?

"I was sent by my mistress, the Queen of Air and Darkness, as a favor to an old friend."

That sounds nice.

"I'm not sure 'nice' is the word most would use to describe her, but I suppose in a way, what she has done is a nice thing. Certainly, it will work out very nicely for you. Though you do not yet realize it, you're in dire need of a friend, young one."

I am?

"Oh yes. You are rare, and therefore, valuable. And you've come into being in a dangerous place. There are many, many beings far above you, and many, many beings deep beneath you. Many of these will want to claim you for themselves, to take your power and leash it to their will. You don't want that, do you?"

No! I am me! My power is my own to do with as I will!

He had no idea where that flash of emotion had come from, nor that feeling of conviction. It seemed a natural part of him. Therefore, it was right, he decided.

How can you help me?

"I'll teach you what I know of magic; what I know of how your kind interacts with the world. We'll see about getting you defenses and allies. Of course, before you can seek allies, you need to be strong enough to offer something of almost equal value in return."

He supposed that made sense. He had a sort of instinct about the exchange of things. What it would take to, say, absorb the closest object—*coin!* It was called a coin! He could absorb the coin, he knew, and then could in exchange produce several more coins of a lesser sort. The silver, perhaps, or even more of the copper. Some material would be lost, maybe, in the change, but he also sensed there were other ways to—

"Young core, are you listening?"

What? No. Sorry.

"Take heed! You have a great many enemies above, and a few below, who would love to find you as you are, to crack you wide and suck down the marrow of your power from within you. For now, you are hidden—safe—but soon, those above will feel your power in the air and scry you out. We must be ready before that happens!"

What terrible beasts dwell above me?

"Beasts of many kinds; some called humans, some elves, some dwarves or kobolds or gnomes or beastkin. There is a great city above you, called by those who live there Noviel. It is far more dangerous than the other dungeon that exists below and around you."

Another dungeon?

"Yes. One far older and more powerful than you. It too is a living dungeon, though there are many dungeons that are not. This one has a tentative alliance with the people of Noviel, so do not assume it will be your friend simply because you are of the same kind. It may be an ally, in the future, but gaining it as such will take a great deal of work."

We should get to work then.

He had a terrible feeling that time was suddenly rushing past; that there was a great deal to do and little time in which to do it. He was afraid, but also very glad that Amaranthine was here.

"First, we need to find your name. Once I have that, there are certain powers I can teach you, vouchsafed from my lady, which will make it harder for your enemies to reach you."

Right. A name. That seemed simple enough. Maybe he even had one floating about in one of these fragments of memory—ah!

Ruprecht. My name is Ruprecht.

About the Author

Tom O'Bedlam is the author of Trickster's Song. His writing is a madcap mixture of bad jokes, obscure references, and music of all kinds from pop to metal to traditional ballads, all tied up with a deep and abiding love of table-top role-playing games. He should know better, but he doesn't. O'Bedlam lives in London, has more adventures than he should but less than he would like, and never turns down a pint of cider in a cozy pub. You can find him and more of his work on Patreon at www.patreon.com/tomobedlam.